When America Sneezes / Jim Gray

WHEN AMERICA SNEEZES

Jim Gray

First published by Jim Gray in 2025

Book design by Lumphanan Press
www.lumphananpress.co.uk

Jim Gray has asserted his moral right
to be identified as the author of this work.

© Jim Gray 2025

jimwrites.co.uk

Aberdeen, Thorn International Golf Course, 3rd Tee

"I can't let them take it away from me." The suddenly irate former president of the USA went to slam his pitching wedge into the soft turf but stopped short. He stood upright. Drawing in a long, slow breath, he allowed the cool Scottish breeze to wash the heat from his flushed face. On regaining his composure, he joined the General, and they stood side by side, watching the waitress depart. "I'll get her name this evening," he muttered into the wind. Her tousled blonde hair, outrageously tight orange blouse and slender legs, ending in snakeskin cowboy boots, certainly now captured his undivided attention. "Oh my, George, if I were twenty years younger."

"Ha, you would still be twenty years too old." The General cracked a nervous smile. Donald's face at first darkened to a scowl, but then a grin turned to a belly laugh. George McCluskey, relieved at the acceptance of his witticism, joined in.

Donald, slapping the General harder than necessary on the back, said, "I can't let the Commie fuckers take it away from me all over again, George."

His grin gone now, a dark shadow mask crossed the politician's face. Years of battling the American legal system came flooding back to mind. It boiled his blood.

"Those bastards tried everything to bring us to heel, but we kicked their asses every time." Donald gave the General a rueful smile. He knew McCluskey considered him a friend, but to Donald, this relationship was more akin to crocodile and plover. *Yet the symbiosis would benefit if you didn't always bite their heads off*, he thought. Donald constantly fought instinct.

He looked over his windswept links course in northeast Scotland. The soft salt spray air and cut green grass aroma reminded him why the Tee was his boardroom. Yes, answers came quicker in a smoke-filled meeting or while berating someone over a phone, but this delicate plan called for some bonding, moulding and, God forbid, nuance. Compromise? He would consider letting the General win a hole or two, but that was as far as he would go with that.

Several meetings were scheduled here over the next few days. Thorn was ramping up his candidacy, firstly as the Republican nominee and then for president. This time, the pieces of the jigsaw would be in place.

Donald breathed in deeply and released it slowly through his nose. He took a sip of beer to clear the lump in his throat. "I'm going to need your help, George."

"You know that I will help you anyway I can, Mr President, but they are forcing me to retire soon, so I do not know how much help I can be." Three deep lines crossed the General's brow.

"Well, I have a role in mind for you where you could do no end of good." Thorn smiled. "How does Chief of the Joint Committee sound?" The General grinned from ear to ear.

"Sir," he said, "you know that has been my dream for many years. With you in the White House and me running the forces, we could finally get this country back on its feet."

With a quivering hand, Thorn laid his glass back on the small table. Stifling anger was not his strong suit. *McCluskey won't be working with me*, he thought, *he will be working for me*. But for now, the 47th President let it lie. He needed McCluskey like a plumber needed a plunger to get shit moving.

London, Friday 1st November 2024

"Hey, guys, check this. It's Jane and Dana from the telly."

Jane could tell the man already had too much to drink. His face was slack, and his spectacles perched precariously on the end of his nose. While it was great to be recognised sometimes, you never knew if they were a nutter.

"I am a huge fan. Are you recording just now?" He looked around for a camera crew.

"No," said Dana as she outstretched a hand to stop the teetering man encroaching further, "we are out on the town having a laugh, mate. Thanks for chatting, but we gotta go." She took Jane's arm and continued walking up the street. He jogged to keep up.

"Can we do a selfie, Jane? My folks won't believe I ever met you."

"Okay, but just a quick one. We really have to be somewhere."

The man swayed as he searched each of his pockets twice before finding the phone. Sidling up to Jane, he held it at arm's length. Jane smiled, and as he clicked, he planted a kiss on her cheek. She wiped his drool and ducked out of his embrace.

"Thanks. Your tits are even better in real life," he said, reaching to cop a feel.

Dana pulled Jane away. "Prick," she said as the pervert gave up his assault and ran to catch up with his friends, shouting to them as he went, "Hey, guys, I snogged Jane from the telly."

* * *

"That's going to be me." Jane pointed to the stretch limo cruising past slowly. They walked up Regent Street, heading for one of London's better nightclubs.

Dana looked at the car while running a comb through her long strawberry blonde hair. "We could hire a limo next time we hit the town."

"No, I'm not looking to pretend we've reached the top. I really want to make it."

"Jeez, Jane, you're the fecking face of politics on the telly."

"I know, I know, but there has to be something more than this?" Jane motioned at the busy London Street. She knew she sounded like a petulant child.

"Give it time, girl," said Dana as she returned the comb to her Gucci handbag.

Jane stopped and faced her friend. "Gravity is the only thing that comes to you and me in time. Soon there will be a perkier and prettier newsgirl standing in my place. That prick Dan will have a younger arse to slap each time he hands out an assignment."

"Dan's not all that bad," said Dana, and Jane raised her eyebrows.

"He's the chief prick amongst a team of pricks." Was that hurt in Dana's face? "Okay, he's not all that bad, but I am fed up with being used by incompetent men. I don't just want to be a female presenter, or the face to get your jollies off for guys like that." Jane pointed back down the road. "I want to be something more."

"Are you going all gender neutral on me, girl?" asked Dana.

Jane scowled. "Fuck off. You know what I mean. I want to be valued for who I am, not what I look like."

Dana nodded in agreement, and they walked in contemplative silence for a while.

"You do have great tits though." Dana laughed and ducked under the anticipated handbag swipe.

London, Saturday 2nd November 2024

Jane woke with the familiar morning desert tongue feeling and cracked leather lips. It was then she noticed there was a man on the other side of the bed. Unfortunately for Jane, this was not a unique occurrence.

"I need some water," she said to the stranger.

"Okay." He put his head back down on the pillow. "Kitchen is at the foot of the stairs." Only then did she realise she was not in her own bed.

Making to get up, she halted as the duvet fell away and cold air touched her body. All of her body. *Oh God. Not again*, she thought. Though Jane liked to party, the thirty-five-year-old woman couldn't keep up the pace that the younger model maintained.

She'd got badly out of practice during COVID. Working at the BBC, she never actually locked down the way the minions had to. Being a political correspondent, there were both official functions and illicit soirees throughout the whole emergency. Life in London had hardly changed from Jane's perspective, with one tiny omission – she didn't get drunk once. It wouldn't have looked good to be staggering about on the streets while everyone else was indoors. So, Jane kept it on the down low and, as a consequence, lost her drinking mojo.

On reaching the bottom of the carpeted stairs, she glanced along the hallway, searching for anything that resembled a kitchen. Seeing nothing like one, she then realised there was a door to her left. Tentatively pushing it open a touch; it revealed a pine laminate floor. Bingo! She poked her head around the door to check that the family and kids were not sitting down to cornflakes. The coast was thankfully clear.

While running the tap to get some chilled water, she looked

the place up and down. The kitchen units seemed expensive to her. *Curious are the things that go through your head when naked in a stranger's house*, she thought.

From behind, there came a creak. Jane turned around while gulping the water. Through the bottom of the glass, a figure stood silhouetted in the kitchen doorway. Her face reddening, Jane saw a girl, maybe late teens or early twenties, looking back at her. Her inclination was to run, but instead, she tried to play it cool.

"Hi, I'm Jane."

"Hannah," the girl replied softly.

"Sorry," Jane said. "I needed a drink and couldn't find my clothes. I didn't know there was anyone else here." Hannah was wearing a pink onesie with a teddy bear motif on the breast pocket. Thankfully, the girl finally broke the stare.

"Hold on," she said and disappeared down the corridor. Jane refilled her glass and took another long drink. The floor creaked again and announced Hannah's return. She was carrying a white towelling dressing gown with a large 'H' embroidered on it. She handed it to Jane.

"Thanks," Jane said, putting the gown on and tying it closed. "Really sorry about the whole naked stranger thing."

Hannah paused before responding. "It's…it's okay…I guess. Did Colin…er…bring you here?"

Jane pointed up. "Is Colin the dark-haired guy with the worst moustache ever, lying in bed upstairs?"

"Probably." Hannah nodded.

"Then yes," said Jane.

The quip about the moustache brought a fragment of memory from last night. She was in an exclusive London club with Dana and another couple of friends from the Beeb. None of them were due on shift today, so they decided to have a night on the tiles.

While standing at the bar, the man started talking. Had she not been tasked with getting another round in, she would have walked away. Jane hated moustaches. In her experience, the men who wore them always had something to hide, or some weird agenda to espouse. *Don't even get me started on beards*, she thought. Anyway, creepy moustache guy, or Colin, as she now knew, had actually been okay. He was asking more about Jane's friend Dana than trying to chat Jane up.

With a trayful of drinks, she took her leave and returned to the table. Unfortunately for Colin, Dana hated moustaches too, and he'd been given the cold shoulder. As far as she could recall, that was the sum of her interactions with him. So, how she ended up here, in the man's kitchen with either his sister or flatmate, she had no bloody idea.

Hannah left the room, and Jane followed her to the living room. There, on the sofa, were her clothes, but not in the condition she remembered. The very expensive designer blouse no longer had buttons, and her underwear was in pieces. She picked up the pile and headed back to the stairs.

"I'll be out of your way in two minutes," she said to Hannah.

"Are you Jane Clark?" Hannah asked. "From the news?"

Jane's heart sank. Humiliation was bad enough, but recognition too! This was not her day.

"Yeah." Jane looked forlornly up the stairs. Glad that Hannah didn't have a follow-up question, she turned away and headed back to the bedroom.

Colin stirred. He raised his head and rubbed his eyes. "Where did you find my wife's dressing gown?"

"Oh fuck," she replied.

London, Monday 4th November 2024

Lockwood opened the desk drawer and took out the ringing mobile. Not his normal phone. Only one person had this number. Her tirade began the second it reached his ear.

"Fuck sake, Lockwood, isn't there someone better than Letchford to bring her in?"

"Not my choice, boss. As soon as he heard there was a video, he jumped on it before I could do anything."

"Bollocks, he's always had a hard-on for her. I can only hope he doesn't let his dick get in the way of the task again. Only so many reporters can have accidents before people start asking questions. Is your one under control?"

"She is, boss. All loved up." Lockwood straightened the overly tight knot on his tie and smiled as he thought about the young body of his project. Bedding her wasn't an onerous task at all

"Good, we have no further need of the video maker then?"

"No, boss, he's been paid off. Should keep quiet. When is Revere coming over?" Lockwood asked

"You will know when you need to know. But the new one needs to be onside before it will happen. There must be a press blackout, or there will be hell to pay. Can you guarantee me that, Lockwood?"

He crossed the fingers of his free hand. "I will be able to answer that in the next few weeks."

"It had better be an affirmative. If I have to dig a hole for these two, you will be going in next to them."

USA, Wednesday 6th November 2024

"Mr Revere, a pleasure as always. How can I serve you today?"

"It's time, Lachlan."

"But my experts are saying…"

"It's time, son. Play your card. Don't fail our great nation now. No one had more respect for your father than I, but when his time came, son, he couldn't do it. Prove to the world that you're ready. Take control, son."

"As you wish, Mr Revere."

Fox News, Wednesday 6th November 2024

"It's approaching lunchtime here in New York, and at Fox News, we are now ready to call the election for Donald Thorn. Thorn has won a historic second term after being denied victory in 2020. Although eight states are yet to declare in this, the most controversial US presidential election in history, we at Fox believe that he has the votes already, so we are about to cross over to Thorn HQ for the victory speech."

CNN Atlanta, Wednesday 6th November 2024

"In what can only be described as a bizarre turn, Thorn supporters are pouring onto the streets of many major cities and small towns alike to celebrate after watching the pre-emptive victory speech. Although Thorn clearly won more votes than 2020, and secured one extra state, counting continues in eight states, and legal proceedings have started in at least three others, with voter fraud allegations being rife. Of course, nothing official will happen until all votes have been counted and verified by the Electoral College, but after the turmoil of 2020, the situation is already on a knife edge."

Edinburgh, Friday 15th November 2024

"You're just a fucking junkie, Deek. Fuck up one more time, and I will kick the shit out of you."

Deek, or Derek as his mother called him, was only vaguely aware of what he had done wrong. He was only vaguely aware of anything to be honest, but what he had messed up, he didn't really know.

"I need you to bring every letter back here. No matter if you think it's a 'loada shite' or not. Okay?"

"Okay," Deek replied. He remembered going to one of the regular pick-up points recently to collect mail and binning some of the stuff as he thought it was flyers and not what the guy wanted. But now he was in shit.

The drug man continued. "We send the workers the flyers so we know they are posting everything back. How do we know we are getting everything if you start sifting out what you think is not relevant?" The man poked Deek on the chest as he explained. "No mail, Deek, no drugs. You get it?"

"Sorry, boss," Deek replied, "wilna happen again."

The man went into his pocket and handed Deek a bundle. It was wrapped in the paper that told Deek where to meet on Monday.

"A word of advice. Try not to kill yourself over the weekend, you piece of shit."

With that, Deek read the note and prepared to cook the contents.

Washington DC, Sunday 17th November 2024

White House Chief of Staff Jeff Zients checked his watch. "Damn," he said. He promised Joe's family that the workaholic president would be out of the Oval Office by eight, but Jeff got lost in the multitude of reports landing on his desk and had forgotten to chase the President from the building.

Thorn supporters had taken to the streets everywhere. The government were doing everything that they could to avoid the mess turning into a bloodbath. Reports of violence and some killings were already recorded, but he knew the situation could get so much worse.

He knocked twice at the door of the Oval Office as he always did. No response. He pushed the door open and said, "Hey, you, old man, get your butt out of here and home." But Joe didn't even raise his head. Jeff came beside him and gave the President a bump on the arm, but it had no effect.

"Wake up, Sleepy Joe," Jeff said, chuckling at his use of Thorn's nickname for his opponent. The President still didn't stir.

"Oh shit," Jeff said and then yelled, "DOCTOR…SOMEONE GET THE DOCTOR IN HERE NOW!"

Transatlantic phone call, Sunday 17th November 2024

"Ah, Mr Revere, so good to hear from you. My congratulations, sir."

"Thank you, Lady Elizabeth – but as we know all too well, this is just the easy part. They will do all they can to take it away if we let them. Are things moving over there?"

"Of course, sir. We make new friends each day. When the time comes, we will be ready."

"Good news. The dominoes are falling here also. Sleepy will cause us no more trouble. The courts will eventually toe the line, and should I need them, the army are ready. Can you say the same, my lady?"

"Our flock are less rebellious, Mr Revere. They do not appreciate strength in its brute form. It's possible that they are more trusting than the free and the brave people of Atlantis, but those they do trust now work for us."

"Excellent, ma'am. I must admit, your success with the media is enviable. It rivals the Minuteman. My crop remains troublesome yet."

"I have little doubt you will bring them into line, sir."

"Thank you. It is time for me to go play my next card. To our meeting soon, ma'am."

"I look forward to it, sir."

BBC News, London, Friday 22nd November 2024

"And now to Washington, where the funeral of President Joe Bowman will take place in a couple of hours. With the current unrest in America, the funeral will be a low-key affair, and few foreign dignitaries will be in attendance. We now go over to Jane in Westminster for more." The newscaster faded from the screen and Jane stood in the lobby of Parliament.

"Thanks, Gordon. Yes, news from Westminster today is that there will be no UK politicians attending the funeral of the American president. It is believed that Britain's ambassador in Washington will be our only representative. Considering the unrest in some US cities, they have been advised that a visit would be a security risk. Jane Clark, reporting from Westminster."

Jane took her earpiece out and said, "That okay?" to Eddie the cameraman.

"Fabulous, girl," said Eddie.

Jane and Eddie were both from Edinburgh, but Eddie was younger – if Jane were honest, much younger – and boy was Eddie gay. He wore flamboyant clothes and had a flamboyant nature, but he was one of the nicest and funniest guys she knew. Eddie called her his 'Fag Hag', which would have been offensive to both if anyone else said it, but his intoxicating personality let him get away with stuff like that.

"You're a doll, Eddie," she said, looking over his lithe frame and gorgeous long hair once more. "*What a waste*," she whispered to herself. "Are you heading back to the studio?"

"Yeah," said Eddie, dropping back into his Edinburgh burr. "I better get back and show these Sassenachs how to load a video file, hen."

"I'm finished for the day," she said and visibly relaxed. "Off home to sleep."

"Bitch. Were you out partying without me again?" said Eddie.

"Not this time. I've been working late chasing a story. There's stuff going down in this building at the moment. The only reason I know something is afoot is because no one is talking to me." Her brow furrowed, and just as Eddie left, her phone rang. She picked up.

Dana's lovely Irish voice came through the speaker. "Hey there, what's been happening?"

"Same old, same old," Jane said and then asked, "How was Turkey?"

"Sea, sun, sand and shagging," said Dana. "Same as ever." She laughed loud. Dana never did anything by halves. "Have you managed to find out anything about that creep from the bar? I think he Mickey Finned you."

Jane sighed. "I haven't had time. Stuff to do. Anyway, you know me, Dana. It's not exactly my first tumble with a stranger. I can't go accusing them all of drugging me." They both laughed. "My only worry is that he took pictures, and the papers get hold of them. I'd be finished."

"Surely they'd be all over the internet by now?" said Dana. Jane looked to the heavens and preyed her friend was correct.

"Hey, did I tell you I met his wife?"

"Where are you?" Dana asked excitedly.

"In Parliament but heading home."

"I'll be there in fifteen," said Dana. "We've got a *lot* to catch up on!" she squealed with delight before ringing off.

As Jane set off for the car park, her heels clicking on the polished tile floor, she saw the Right Honourable Selwyn Letchford a few yards in front, heading the same way. The last thing she needed was to share an elevator with Selwyn 'the Letch', as he was better known, but Jane knew something was afoot in Parliament, and she was damned well going to find out what.

"Hold the lift, please," she shouted to him, and she couldn't help noticing the smile on the man's face as he held the closing doors.

"Jane, you look positively radiant today," the grey-haired Tory MP said, and a shiver ran down her spine. The creepy old bugger had at least twenty years on her, but he still thought himself appealing.

"Why thank you, sir," she said and giggled a little. She was going to have to play his game. "Heading home, sir?" she asked as the whir of the elevator jerked them into motion.

"Only in the absence of a better offer." Letchford inched closer. She ignored his crude attempt at flirting.

"Sir, are you concerned about the future of the US base in your constituency with all this uncertainty in America?"

His lecherous face morphed into a troubled frown. "Well, obviously. Are we off the record, dear?"

"Of course, sir," Jane assured the MP.

He sighed and ran his hand through thinning hair. "Half of the planes left last night, without a bloody word. There was a report of a gunshot on the base, but when the police arrived, the Yanks said it was an accident. Some of the locals have reported fist fights in the pub, and it's the Americans that are fighting for once. The PM hasn't a clue what to do about it. He hasn't a clue about anything that…" He seemed to be about to throw an insult. "We would have been better off with Boris," he added instead.

"Do you see him coming back?" Jane asked as the lift doors opened to the car park on the lower level.

"You never know," the MP whispered. He had become shy as they exited the lift. "Maybe we can talk more over supper?" His leer was plain to see. She did her best to ignore it.

"I'd *love* to," she said while trying to sound like she meant it. "But can I take a rain check? I have somewhere else to be. I'll have plenty of time one evening next week?" Bile rose in her mouth at the thought of an evening in the ageing MP's company.

"I so look forward to it," the man said with a lecherous wink.

RAF Mentford, Saturday 23rd November 2024

It was early – well, for a Saturday anyway – and Jane yawned as she parked about one hundred yards up the road. From her vantage point, the base looked quiet, but then she had no idea what a US air base was meant to look like. There were certainly no planes to be seen.

"Why in God's name did I drive all the way out here?" she asked herself. She considered waltzing up to the gate and flashing her BBC badge, but she doubted it would do much for the RAF guys guarding there.

Getting out of the car, she crossed the road and walked slowly down the pavement that would lead past the gates. As she came closer, she caught the eye of one of the guards.

He nodded her way. "Good day, madam." Not happy at being called 'madam', she sucked air through her teeth and decided that it may be best to let this one go.

"What was all the noise up here last night? I couldn't get any sleep," she said, fishing for information.

The RAF man left the barrier and headed over to her. "I wasn't on shift myself, but Barry here…" He pointed to his colleague, who was trying to hide the cigarette he smoked. "He said it was mental." Jane nodded and looked past him to the next gate. It was unmanned as far as she could see.

"Yes, it's been rowdier than usual this last week," Jane lied. "Are any of them still here?" He came a little closer. It was obvious that he really should not be discussing the situation.

"We're meant to call the Yanks each time we clock on and off. No one answered the phone today. I haven't seen a soul. It is all bloody strange."

She pushed her luck further. "Have you seen any of the fighting? My mate said they were scrapping in the pub last week?"

"I've not seen too much myself, but some of the guys said there was a Thorn rally on the base a couple of days ago. The Yank military police broke it up, but fighting went on all night. Next morning, a load of their guys walked off the base. Most headed to London by train."

"Wow!" said Jane. "I knew something was going on but didn't hear about that." The RAF man looked pleased to have been of service.

"I better get back." He pointed a thumb over his uniformed shoulder at the barricade.

Jane said. "Nice to meet you…"

"Andy," he filled in.

"Andy," she said and gave him her best smile.

She was about ten paces away, and he shouted, "Will you be in the Fox tonight?"

Her guess was that the Fox was the local, and Andy had now decided he liked what he saw. "You never know, Andy," she replied without stopping, but gave him another smile and waved. He couldn't be more than twenty. "You really have still got it," Jane chuckled to herself.

As the car wended toward the village along a narrow road lined with trees, golden leaves piled up on either side, and the low autumn sun glistened intermittently through the branches. It brought back a memory of being out in the car with Mum, Dad and Duncan as a child. Dad always wanted to go for a drive on Sundays when the leaves were falling. Even at ten years old, Jane realised her dad was just a big kid. She had him wrapped round her little finger, and Dad had spoiled her. Duncan used to get so angry at how often his little sister got everything she wanted.

When they were a few years older, Jane and Duncan actually lost touch for a while. He went off to uni, becoming a bit of a hippie, and didn't really want anything to do with a wee kid sister then. So, when Jane set off for her further education in England, she hadn't heard much from her brother in years. But it was good that they were rebuilding the relationship now. She'd even been up to Edinburgh a few times and had stayed in his Corstorphine flat after the bitch that was his ex-wife dumped him.

While slowly navigating a tight bend, Jane saw a sign for the Fox and Hound. She pulled into the car park and could smell lunch being prepared. While deciding whether to eat or not, she got out of the car and noticed four guys in cricket whites sitting at a weathered picnic table outside. Even though it was warm for November in England, and her knowledge of the game was limited, she knew they didn't usually play at this time of year.

The four heads turned and watched her cross the car park. Her high-heel leather boots were not conducive to driving, but between the boots, her skintight jeans and the extra button she'd unfastened on her blouse, it looked as if she'd shifted a few gears with the cricketers from the grins that crossed their faces.

"Food any good here?" she asked as she approached.

"It'd better be," said the one closest to her, pointing to the tall blond guy opposite. "Quentin here is the owner."

"Yeah, but I'm guessing by the attire, Quent, that you aren't doing the cooking?" Jane asked with a smile.

"No one would eat here if he did," another said, and all four laughed. Quentin may be a poor cook, but he was a real dish, as far as Jane could see.

She carried on past the guys, gave a royal wave and said, "Catch you boys later."

As she entered the bar, one of the cricketers said, "She can catch me any time," in a broad Anglian accent that made it sound as if he crunched on a carrot as he spoke. The table laughed at the 'witticism'.

Inside, the room first seemed unlit before she remembered she wore shades. Taking them off, she slipped them in her pocket. The place was empty except for an older couple in the corner. He read the paper while his partner sat next to him, stroking his arm to no effect. The sports pages were more interesting than talking to the wife, apparently.

Sauntering up to the glass-strewn bar, Jane ordered a soda and orange from the busy young barmaid who appeared to be in the middle of spring cleaning the entire stock of glasses. Jane took her drink and sat two tables away from Romeo and Juliet. She took out her phone to see if anything was happening in her world, but there were no texts or emails that needed attention. The woman in the corner looked her way.

"It's a fine day," Jane said. The woman sprang to life. She had clearly been trying to entice Hubby into conversation but seemed happy to chat with Jane instead.

"It's lovely, dear. Hasn't it been so warm for November?"

Jane agreed but steered the conversation away from the weather. "I couldn't get any sleep for all that din at the base last night." The frumpy woman abandoned her husband altogether and came over next to Jane.

"Yes, quite a kerfuffle. I believe the last of them have gone though. Should be quieter tonight. Too quiet for some. I can't see this place surviving long without the base," she said, looking around the bar.

"Indeed. Quentin will be worried, I guess," Jane said, using her new local knowledge to fit in.

"Quentin will be all right, dear. This place is a hobby for him," she said before whispering conspiratorially, "Daddy's money."

"Of course," Jane said.

The woman went further. "It was Daddy that stirred a lot of the trouble up with the article in the paper and then that Donald Thrump rally he organised."

"Thorn, dear," said the man with the paper, not even looking up from his *Daily Telegraph*.

"I'm just back from holiday," Jane said. "What rally was that?"

The woman's face beamed at the chance to impart knowledge. "Lord Letchford put an advert in the *Chronicle* congratulating

Thorn on his victory and invited locals and the Americans to a big party to celebrate. A couple hundred turned up, most from the base, but then even more arrived to protest. After quite a lot of drink had been consumed, the debating and teasing became arguing and fist fights. Me and Lester here..." She pointed to her partner. "We got out of there and went home. Word has it that it really brewed up. The police had to come from Norwich to sort it all out."

Lester, the font of all knowledge, piped up again. "He's not a lord."

"You what, love?" said the woman as she ran her fingers through her curly grey hair.

"Letchford – he's a sir, not a lord." His pearls of wisdom were divulged with his eyes never leaving the paper.

"Of course, love," the woman said, rolling her eyes.

So, the handsome cricketer outside was Letchford's son. It wasn't clear what use that information was to Jane, but it was filed away. She was snapped out of her reverie as the woman tapped her arm.

"You would have loved the party, dear. Well, at first, anyway. There was a free BBQ, complimentary drinks, and Boris even gave a speech."

"Boris Jenkins?" Jane said.

The woman nodded excitedly. "Of course, dear."

"I think Boris Karloff is dead," Lester chipped in, his face still buried in the news. The woman laughed way too hard. After a delay, Jane thought it best to join in. When they calmed down, she offered to buy them both a drink.

Through the window, she saw that the four men were still outside, so she asked the bartender what they were drinking.

"You don't 'av to buy them owt," she said in her lilting Norfolk accent. "One of them is the owner."

Jane said, "I'd like to get them a round anyway."

The girl shrugged and poured four lagers. Jane put them on a tray with her drink and headed out after a goodbye to the woman, who looked a little deflated. Juliet returned to stroking Lester's arm.

Carefully balancing the tray while walking out to the beer garden, Jane pondered how to touch base with Letchford Junior. She put the drinks at the end of their table.

"I was heading out, and the girl behind the bar asked me to take these out to you."

"You have Heather well trained," said one of the men to Quentin.

"Heather is multi-skilled," said Quentin. The four men laughed at the obvious inference.

"She is smoking hot," Jane said, immediately gaining their undivided attention.

"You what?" one of them asked.

"Heather," Jane said. "The barmaid? I wouldn't say no to that." The four of them didn't know what to do with themselves. They were all laughing and beaming like horny teenagers.

"So, you're..." one of them half asked, not wanting to say the word.

"A lesbian?" Jane said and then answered, "Not really, but I like what I like and if what I like happens to be...well, Heather, then what the hell, I say." The four went back to uncontrolled delight. "Anyway, good to meet you guys."

Quentin's mobile sat by his pint. Jane picked it up. He was about to object before she said, "I'm just giving you my number. Text me when you guys get back to cricket. I can't get enough of willow whacking leather."

Their eyes bore into her back as she walked to the car. She was glad no one had run in to give the news to Heather before she got away. Jane had no issue with that sort of thing, but Heather hadn't been her type at all. Now, Quentin… The dishy Quentin was a different story. Still, her interest hadn't been entirely sexual. Quentin may yet come in handy for more than entertainment.

She hadn't even reached the village boundary when her phone beeped. There was no doubt in her mind about who had texted her. None at all.

Westminster, Monday 25th November 2024

"They're not going to like this," said the Prime Minister to the Father of the House as they strolled into the chamber. His compatriot, Carter Davis-Jones, smiled. Suvar thought he may actually be enjoying the turmoil.

Davis-Jones said, "They really cannot expect things to carry on as normal. The markets have crashed, and the States have gone to hell in a handbasket. We'd be crazy to do anything else, Mr Prime Minister."

He's probably right, thought Suvar, *but he doesn't have to accept it with such unbidden glee.*

Prime Minister Ravi Suvar got to the despatch box and looked around the packed House. Murmurs rose to grumbles as many knew what was coming. Suvar took a sip of the tepid water and began.

"Mr Speaker, Members, Honourable Members, you are no doubt aware that the markets have been suspended owing to the turmoil in Washington. At this moment, I have no news for you as to when they may reopen. This situation, combined with the absence of a functioning government in Washington, is leading to severe disruption here in the UK. Members will be aware that the election was due in the second week of January." The volume in the House reached a fever pitch as all listening now realised what was about to take place. The Speaker rose to his feet, and the Prime Minister, interrupted, sat down.

The noise barely abated. The Leader of the Opposition was apoplectic and banged his fists on his side of the despatch box. One of the front bench SNP members had a Tory opponent by the lapels while they vigorously argued.

"Order! Order!" the Speaker tried once more. After several more minutes of turmoil, the Speaker gave up trying and shouted, "That's it. The House sitting is suspended for twenty minutes."

The Prime Minister and most of the front bench made a hasty exit from the mayhem.

BBC News, Monday 25th November 2024

"We cut into the schedule now with some breaking news. We are going live to reporter Jane Clark at Westminster."

"Thank you, Peter," said Jane in her soft Scottish accent. "We have incredible breaking news for you. The government came to Parliament today in an attempt to postpone the January election. It seems the motion was shouted down, and the House stands in recess temporarily. It is believed that they will bring the motion back as soon as order can be restored. This is Jane Clark, reporting from Westminster." The camera returned to the studio, but the host was clearly at a loss.

"Thank you, Jane," he mumbled and shuffled papers while an editor spoke in his ear. Regaining his composure, he resumed. "We now go to our Chief Political Correspondent." He turned to the man hastily occupying the chair at the right of his desk. "So, Nick, What do you think is going on here?"

"Well, Peter, this is huge news, unheard of outside war time. We do not yet know if the government seeks to postpone the election but continue with Parliament or if they will seek a longer Christmas recess. Of course, Parliament was due to shut down next week as is customary before elections. It is all up in the air at the moment," the political correspondent said.

Peter pressed his earpiece to indicate he was getting information from elsewhere. "Thank you, Nick, we can go back over to Westminster as Jane has an update."

"Yes, Peter," said Jane. "We have been told that the sitting will resume in two minutes. The Speaker has apparently expelled more than fifty members. He has warned the rest that further interruption will lead to the chamber being cleared entirely to allow the PM to speak. We can go back over live now."

Prime Minister Suvar stood in front of the despatch box again. "Mr Speaker, as I was saying, His Majesty's Government do not believe that the House can go into recess with the markets in free fall and with the political situation in the USA the way it is. Due to these factors, we feel the General Election needs to be postponed for at least six months, or until the situation calms. It is my intention to seek this approval from the House, and, if so granted, I will go to Buckingham Palace this evening and discuss the situation with the King. I will return to the House tomorrow with a concrete proposal based on these discussions."

The Prime Minister closed his notebook and took his seat. Almost every member still present stood to indicate they wanted to speak. Ignoring them all, the Speaker entered into a conflab with his deputies. While the constitutional ramifications were being considered, a Tory grandee descended the stairs, patted the Prime Minister on the back, and shook his hand as if they had won a great victory. Uproar was reignited on the opposition benches at this blatant display.

As the Tory member walked back to the stairs, a mobile phone flew from the Labour benches and struck the back of his head. He went down as if shot. Instantly, there was unbridled joy on the opposition side of the House.

The Speaker didn't see the incident but, witnessing the result, cried, "Order! Order! I am putting the House back into recess. Clear the room!"

The images and commentary went dead, and the camera returned to the studio. Peter informed the audience that there was a problem, and that the live feed from the chamber would be restored as soon as possible.

Edinburgh, Wednesday 27th November 2024

Duncan Clark sat in his flat with milk running down his chin. Unenthused, he tucked into the tasteless morning muesli. While granting his jaws a brief break from processing the soggy sawdust, he laid down the spoon and turned on the TV. It came on to the Parliament Channel. Their ratings had gone through the roof lately.

Like most people in the country, he had watched the debacle that was the cancelling of the upcoming General Election. As if the action would have not been controversial in any case, the Scottish Nationalists had been punting the next election as a de facto referendum on independence. Being refused a second referendum by the UK government, they felt that they had little choice but to hijack the national poll. Of course, the unionist parties were all claiming that it was illegitimate to use a national election in this way – but the argument was now of no consequence. Switching to BBC News, Duncan turned up the sound as he saw the Prime Minister appear.

"Bloody early for Ravi to be about," he muttered.

BBC News

The camera moved to the press room in Downing Street. The Prime Minister stood behind the podium. Reporters shouted questions, but he ignored them.

"Ladies and gentlemen. I have a short statement to make after my consultations with King Charles over the last twenty-four hours. The King has agreed on a maximum twelve-month suspension of the election and has expressed his wish that it be held sooner if at all possible. He recognised the world situation and understood that holding the vote at this time would be difficult.

"The King had one condition of the delay. I am to seek to form a government of national unity. At least three parties in Westminster must agree before this government may be formed. I will be talking with the opposition parties this morning and hope to pass the legislation through Parliament today. Sorry, but I cannot take any questions. I hope to have another press conference later today to announce the government formally and will answer your queries at that time."

Edinburgh

Duncan raised his hand to his sticky milk chin and pushed his open mouth closed. "Well, blow me over," he said. "It gets stranger and stranger." Out of force of habit, he scanned the other channels, but of course, all were covering the issue, and none had any more information. It would be a day of padding until somebody gave the hyenas of the press something better to chew on.

As the TV was turned off, he gulped down the last of his orange juice. He checked the view from the window. Thankfully it was not raining. His near neighbour, Birdy Bob, stood on the waste ground behind his flat. Duncan gave the man a wave. Many locals were unsure of the perennial birdwatcher, but Duncan thought him harmless.

After picking out the charcoal suit that his ex-wife bought, he got dressed and topped off his outfit with a boring stripey tie. Known for his silly neckwear, Duncan normally kept that idiosyncrasy for Fridays.

As he walked briskly to the car, he raised his jacket's collar. *No sign of global warming in Edinburgh*, he thought. On route, he encountered a group of university students headed in the other direction. His eye lingered on the pretty red-haired lassie who walked behind the rest a little. In her long woolly winter coat, varsity scarf and eye-catching orange tammy, she, of course, detected his gaze, as women always seemed to do.

Did she blush a little as she smiled back? he wondered.

Currently, he was not in a relationship. His wife of nine years found someone else to play with, and she left. Being on his own for over a year, he thought it may be time to get back on the metaphorical horse. However, he probably had fifteen to twenty years on the student that he now gawped at and was likely coming over a bit Jimmy Saville.

Parking in Corstorphine was not easy. It was a five-minute walk from the flat to the space he'd finally wedged the car in last night. The short trip was about the only exercise Duncan would get today.

The car radio came on too loud as the engine ignited into life. It was BBC Radio 4 and the Today programme.

"We now go over to Glasgow for the reaction from Hamza Yousal, leader of the SNP and First Minister of Scotland. Mr Yousal, how will your party deal with the request to form a Government of National Unity?" the reporter asked. Duncan listened with interest to the soft-spoken Glaswegian's reply.

"My party will not be taking part at all. As you know, Nick, we are still trying to get the decision to postpone the election overturned."

The reporter cut in, "You must realise that is a lost cause now, First Minister?"

"We will try every possible route and only accept when each has been tested. This has never happened in peacetime, certainly in the modern era. The Conservative Party cannot be allowed to cancel democracy when it suits them," Yousal replied.

"So where do you go from here?" the reporter asked.

"The Scottish government will be launching a case in the Scottish courts later today. Of course, we fully expect this to end in the Supreme Court eventually. I'll also be holding a press conference later, with the leader of the Greens and the leader of Scotland United. We will announce our official response to the government at that point."

Duncan edged out of the busy Canongate traffic and pulled into the office car park. He leant forward, turned off the radio and, mimicking a cash register, said, "Kerching!" Turmoil in government meant work, and hence money, for the company.

London, Westminster, Thursday 28th November 2024

A lot of empty green leather faced the Government, as there were less than twenty MPs on the opposition benches. It was not a choice – the Speaker removed over a hundred of them in an attempt to calm the hall. The PM was set to speak at 12pm, but there had been constant protests, and points of order were profligate.

Eventually, the Prime Minister rose to cries of "Here, here!" from the benches behind. He opened his folder and began.

"Mr Speaker, I wish to make a statement to the House on the formation of the Government of National Unity. After negotiations with the opposition parties, we have reached the target set by the King, of having at least three of the parties participate. The DUP and the Liberal Democrats will join the Conservatives in the formation of the new government. For the period that this arrangement is in place, I will serve as Prime Minister, and the leader of the Liberals will become Deputy PM. Other ministerial appointments will be announced over the next few days. Mr Speaker, I wish to commend this statement to the House. There will be a vote on the formation of the new government this afternoon once the debate has concluded." With that, the PM left the chamber to howls of derision by the few on the opposite side of the floor.

London, Friday 29th November 2024

Uneven pavements and high heels were not an ideal combination. Teetering toward the St Andrew's night function, Jane would be a guest of the Right Honourable Selwyn Letchford MP.

Oxford Street was busy as ever. The world was going to shit, but London still had to party.

The venue for this evening was the exclusive St Randolf Club. Jane wanted to talk to Letchford and was glad she had held off his invitations until this public event came about. The dirty old bugger had sent quite a few texts during the week, full of barely disguised smut. He really thought he was on to something. She had to walk the tightrope of keeping him onside and not stabbing the filthy old married perv.

Yes, she was intrigued by the message saying that he wanted to talk about a matter of 'mutual benefit', but there was a concern about just what The Letch might consider beneficial.

When nearly at the appointed venue, and still a little early, Jane retrieved her mobile phone from her bag and scrolled down her contacts list, placing a call.

"Hey, big brother."

"Hey, little sis," Duncan replied.

"Happy St Andrew's Day for tomorrow," she said. "Are you having haggis?"

"That's Burns Night, lass. You have been down there too long." Duncan chuckled.

"Of course it is," she remembered. "I've been cowking all day at the thought of having to eat that shit tonight and now I don't have to. Well, that is at least one good thing. Not sure about the rest though."

"Where are you off to tonight, sis?"

"Going fishing," she replied obtusely. "St Andrew's night hosted by Tory wankers."

Jane reprimanded herself. Obviously, Duncan could hear that, but if someone recorded her coming out with that sort of stuff, she would be fired from her beloved BBC role in a second.

"Sounds like a blast," Duncan said drily.

Jane said, hesitantly, "Dunc…"

He interrupted. "You want a favour. You only ever call me Dunc when you want a favour."

"Ah, okay, Bruce," she continued, "could you do me a wee favour?"

Jumping into the Bruce character, Duncan answered in the worst Australian accent that Jane had ever heard. "Anything for you, Shiela…just aaahsk."

"I know you have people in the office that do people searches. I need some info on someone."

"I thought the Beeb would have folk for that?"

"This isn't for the Beeb. It is just for me, Dunc."

"Oh," he said. "Names and address, please, my secretive sister."

"I only have first names but have an address."

"That should be good enough for Struan and his team." Duncan found a pen and paper on the kitchen worktop, but it wasn't needed.

She arrived at the club door. "Gotta go. I'll text you the details. Bye for now, bro."

"Watch your arse, sis," he shouted and hung up.

Jane sent the text and then smiled at the doorman. "Jane Clark for Selwyn Letchford."

On entering, she headed straight for the little girls' room and tidied herself up. She was wearing her ridiculously expensive Nensi Dojaka little black dress. The old buggers would probably have a heart attack at the sight of her, she thought. Checking the mirror, Jane knew how good she looked. In spite of moaning about her lack of anonymity, she also loved to be noticed.

The large and ornate double doors opened as she approached the ballroom. On passing through, her name was announced like she was at a debutante ball. Stopping at the edge of the tables, Jane saw Letchford stand and head her way.

"My, my," he said as he approached. "You are magnificent." His eyes slowly moved from her head to her toes. His scanning stare was as uncomfortable as if he'd used his tongue to lick her up and down.

She took a second to recompose herself. "Why, thank you, kind sir." There were a hundred other men present that she would rather be on the arm of tonight, but in her line of work, you had to kiss a lot of toads to get the story. *Metaphorically kiss*, she hoped.

An arm was offered, and he led her to the table, but not directly. The old bugger was showing her off. Clothed in what Jane guessed was a very expensive Savile Row lounge suit, the old Tory cut an acceptable figure for a man of his age. Comparisons with amphibians were perhaps unfair, but although he was clearly no Brad Pitt, it was his internal ugliness that was most off-putting to Jane. Even when being ostensibly charming and dressed to the nines, the man positively oozed sleaziness.

With the extended tour of the hall over, they arrived at the table where Jane was introduced to the collection of the good and the great, but she did her research earlier, and none of these people were of much interest. Of course, Lady Letchford, or whatever the bloody wife was called, was not present. Bad omen!

Letchford pulled out a chair for her, and she took a seat. It was lucky that the tablecloth overhung her legs – as the dress rose up, her knickers would have been on show. *Thank God I wore some*, she thought. Letchford sat and filled her champagne glass without asking.

"Thank you, sir."

"Oh, we are off the clock tonight, dear – call me Selwyn." He pulled his chair a little closer

Jane acted as the perfect dinner guest, taking interest in everyone around the table at one point or another, delighting in each course as it came, and eating almost none of it. She laughed at anything Letchford thought was funny. It was a battle to stop the old bugger filling up her glass, but he was persistent, and as Jane knew, she was weak. It really hadn't mattered when she was younger. No matter how drunk she got, she remembered every little detail the next day. It was one of the things that made her a fantastic journalist. Yet lately, her memory hadn't always been all it could be. The encounter with Colin wasn't the first time that she woke the next day with nothing retained from the evening before.

"Selwyn, we were going to have a chat about your constituency, remember?"

The MP smiled, put his hand on her upper thigh and said, "Plenty of time for that later, dear." His hand started clumsily rubbing her leg.

She lifted it back to the table. "Can we do it now, before I have too much to drink and forget, please?"

"Of course, my dear," he said. "I have the library booked so that we will have complete privacy."

They stood, and Jane followed him across the opulent, celebrity-filled room. There were some knowing nods to Letchford from colleagues as they passed. The Father of the House even winked at him and, gyrating his hips, said, "Working on good press relations again, Letchford?" The table burst into giggles and guffaws. Jane really wanted to scream at the pig but instead just smiled.

When they crossed the main corridor, she saw a door marked library. Heading that way, she noticed Letchford was on the stairs. He looked back at her perplexed expression.

"No, no, not the main library – it's still open. I have booked Albert's library on the first floor." He walked back a few steps and took her hand.

She decided it was time to break the mood that the MP was trying to set. "So, have there been any more reports of trouble at the base?"

"Not here," was all he said. They climbed the marble stairs in silence. On the ornate oak-panelled landing, the room was off to the left. He opened the door and ushered her in. "Take a seat." There was only one in the room – a Victorian-style loveseat, barely big enough for two. In front of the sofa was a leopard-skin rug, laid out beside the huge log fire that burned vigorously.

"I hope that's fake?" said Jane, pointing to the rug.

"Bagged by Albert himself," Letchford replied, "but the claws have been removed if you're worrying about scratches." He nudged her.

Jane rolled her eyes and walked over to the drinks cabinet where Letchford was now putting ice in two crystal glasses.

"We have to have a Scotch to celebrate," he said.

"Celebrate what?" she asked, dreading the answer.

The MP looked at her askance and said, "Tomorrow is St Andrew's Night!"

"Of course," she replied, exhaling the pensive breath. The room was roasting. The man loosened his tie and took the jacket off.

"You don't mind?" he said.

"No, of course not, Selwyn," she replied and silently added, *just as long as nothing more comes off.*

He cleared his throat softly and said, "Actually, will you call me sir for now, please?"

What the hell have I got myself into? Jane thought. She changed trajectory away from the loveseat and went over to the heavy curtains. Pulling the curtain aside, she took in the view. The club had a central courtyard, and colourful lights were flashing like someone was having a disco.

"What's going on over there?" she asked before immediately regretting the invitation for him to approach. He walked up behind her, put his hand on her hips and rested his head on her shoulder.

"We will have to get to know each other better before you will be allowed in there." He gave a low and dirty laugh. "That's the pond," he added. His thumbs caressed her lower back, exposed by the skimpy dress.

Maybe this dress was a bad idea, Jane thought. *Change the subject, change the subject*, her brain cried. She broke the hold and twisted past Letchford. "So, you were saying, about the base?"

"Oh yes, let's do this first," he replied. "The base is in turmoil. Most, maybe all of the Yanks have left, but we don't know whether that was official or not." Letchford looked genuinely troubled. "The base commander asked for our help and the military police were sent in. The base had been divided into opposing sides. To our knowledge, the fighting was restricted to fists." He stopped to take a drink. "Come, sit and I will tell all." The MP downed his Scotch.

Throwing caution to the wind, she tossed hers back too. She placed the empty crystal glass down and carefully lowered herself onto the seat. Sure enough, up went the dress despite her gripping the sides and pulling it down as hard as she dared. Luckily, the old lech was heading to get them refills.

On returning, he cast a long, lingering look and said, "You look…fabulous." Sirens were going off in her head. She thought it may be her last chance to leave this room with any sort of respect intact. Jane knew she made a lot of silly decisions when it came to sex, but she'd never stooped this low for a story.

"What have you got yourself into?" she said aloud, giving up trying to make the dress cover her modesty. Instead, she stood. "Selwyn," she said.

"Please call me sir," he replied in a low voice.

"Selwyn, I'm not sure what you think is going to happen here tonight, but I came out for dinner and to get an off-the-record interview. I get a strong feeling you may have other ideas."

The man looked crestfallen. He stood with his head down a while and still held both glasses. "I have been such a stupid old bugger," he said.

"Look, Selwyn, nothing's happened. Let's do the interview and we can walk out of here hand in hand so your mates downstairs think you scored," she offered.

He looked up at her with a cold expression on his face. "My dear, you don't understand. I have no problem trying to bed young reporters. Hell, you are one of the few I've yet to plough." He handed her the refilled glass. "I was a stupid bugger as I was about to give you gold before you got out of that dress." He stood about six inches away from her and gulped the whisky. Creeping forward, he moved within whispering range.

"Now, if you want a story to blow this government wide open?" The leering Tory MP took his finger and brushed a strand of hair from her face. "You have everything to gain, and nothing but those clothes to lose."

* * *

Eddie yawned and stretched his arms into the air. He began clearing up the crisp packets and Coke cans from a night in front of the telly bingeing old shows. His phone beeped. It was Jane.

Can I come round? she asked.

He quickly replied, *Of course*.

I've done something really stupid, Jane came back. Before he could reply, she added, *Answer your door*. His doorbell rang.

"Hey, Ed," Jane said. He greeted her in Scooby Doo boxer shorts and an old T-shirt. She picked a crisp crumb from his shirtfront and ate it. It was seldom anyone got to see Ed dressed like this.

"No company tonight, I'm guessing?" she asked.

"Just Joey, Chandler, Monica and Rachel," he replied.

"You were having a *Friends* marathon without me?" she had a look of mock hurt on her face.

Ed didn't answer but pointed up the hallway with his thumb. "Get your cute arse in here, babe." He stood aside to let her in. "What is it that you have done?"

"I am going to need a very large glass of wine before telling you." Jane swerved into his kitchen. She knew Ed's flat well and went straight to the drinks cupboard. Between two fingers of her free hand, she grabbed the glasses and headed through to the living room where he was finishing clearing up. She took off her coat and threw it over a chair.

"Bloody hell, Jane." Ed pointed to the dress, or lack thereof. "You look good enough to turn a poof straight," he said, laughing.

"The dress might have been the problem, my dear boy." With that, Jane relayed her evening as she uncorked the bottle.

"Oh my God, Jane, you didn't?"

She took a long gulp of her wine. "Do you know the saddest thing?" She didn't wait for an answer. "There was half a second that I thought about letting the old bastard have his way, but some reflex in me raised my knee, and I ran out of there, leaving the old goat rolling on the floor, holding his balls!"

Ed sat stunned for a couple of seconds and then burst into a fit of hysterics. She couldn't resist joining in, although she hadn't thought it funny until now. The two of them hugged and screamed with laughter. Ed was crying uncontrollably, and seeing him made her laugh more.

"Oh my God, I'm going to pee myself." She stood and ran to his toilet. "You realise I'll probably get fired," Jane shouted through from the loo seat.

"I'm not so sure," he replied. "He won't want this running around Westminster. It won't look good for him."

Jane came back into the room. "He claims to have bedded most of the media department at Parliament." She looked worried. He went to placate her, but both of their phones sounded as a message arrived. Jane picked hers up and checked.

Jedward, get your asses in here first thing, was all it said. It was from her boss Dan – Dan the Man, as he was inevitably called. Dan really was the man as far as the political reporters were concerned. Jane looked at Ed and he confirmed the same message.

Of course, Jane and Edward had been christened Jedward by their colleagues. She didn't mind too much, but it insinuated that the two of them were not the sharpest tools in the shed. Preferring to be underestimated, she could live with it.

"Do you think that this has anything to do with Letchford?"

Ed took the bottle and filled his glass once more. "Not sure why I would be coming if it was."

"Let's hope you're right," Jane said before adding, "Actually, I'm knackered. Take me to bed, you stud." They both laughed, heading through to the bedroom.

London, Saturday 30th November 2024

Jane was extremely glad she kept a change of clothes at Ed's flat. There could have been no turning up to work today in last night's party frock.

Ed stopped her texting Letchford to apologise on at least three occasions. "Babe, if you go grovelling to that guy, he will end up with a hold on you, and the bastard will abuse it."

They climbed the office stairs on their way to meet Dan. On reaching the landing, she said, "Just going to check my emails before going in," and took a right into her office. Ed followed. She sat in front of the screen and typed in her password. There weren't many emails, but the message she dreaded was there. It was one of the formal meeting appointments that MP's offices sent when you were called on official business.

The Rt Hon Selwyn Letchford MP has confirmed your meeting for 10.30am today. Meeting is in room b34. Jane pointed to the screen.

"It could be nothing to do with last night." Ed shrugged.

Just then, a loud shout of "JEDWARD!" came from the hallway. They rose and headed through to Dan's office.

"If it isn't my favourite pair of sheep shaggers," Dan said, greeting them. The BBC had suffered from many cases of inappropriate behaviour over the last few years, but it didn't look like Dan had received the several thousand emails about how to talk to fellow human beings.

He was about fifty, and absolutely not Jane's type, but he was presentable enough for a journalist, and deep down, she thought he was a decent guy. It was unfortunate that the decent guy was buried under a lot of prick.

"Well, girls," Dan continued, "I'm putting Jedward on tour. Monday morning, get your bony Scottish arses out to Heathrow. You are going to Rio, baby!" He held up a hand in anticipation of a high five. "No big 'thanks, boss'?" he said, feigning hurt.

"What's on in Rio, boss?" said Jane, dumbfounded.

"Boris," came the one-word reply. "He's doing a whirlwind speaking tour. Five days, Five countries, and you, my expendable colleagues, are going too. I've sent you both an email with all the details. Now, off you both fuck."

With the brief meeting over, Jane walked back to her flat and picked up the car. In some trepidation, she drove the short distance to Parliament. After parking in a disabled space (she was sure disabled folk didn't get out at weekends), she took the elevator up to the office level. *I have no idea how to play this*, she mused. It was all over if he took her Westminster pass and tore it up. She would probably be covering Sunday League football and sewing bees the rest of her days. Worse still, she might end up a royal correspondent.

Here it was, B34, and the blinds were closed. Was he going to start where he left off last night? She knocked.

"Come."

Hesitantly, Jane entered the utilitarian meeting room, sighing when realising no one else was present and that she was alone with the Letch again. He half smiled and pointed to the seat next to him, but she took the one at the opposite end of the table instead.

"Miss Clark." It appeared they were no longer on first-name terms.

"Sir," she said in response and saw hurt pass across his face for the briefest second.

"Miss Clark, you won't be needing your Parliamentary Pass for a while. Can I have it, please?" The MP held out his hand.

Her heart sank. "But, sir, I can't do my job without it."

He raised a hand. "No. This has nothing to do with our little… misunderstanding last night. I need your pass now." He held out his hand again. With a resigned sigh, she unfastened the pass from her jacket and forfeited it. To her surprise, he gave her an envelope in return.

"If that envelope reaches its target, *unopened*, your pass will be returned to you next week." He slipped her badge into his pocket.

She pushed the envelope back toward the MP. "Sorry, but did I suddenly become your assistant?" He sat there staring at her, and then a look of resignation seemed to cross his face.

"I can't use normal channels for this," he said, holding up the envelope. "If you had been sensible and stuck around last night, you would know what is going on, but you made your choice, and now you will bloody well do as you are told," he said with some force. He slid the envelope back over and added, "Put that in your pocket this second if you ever want to work in this building again." A hint of a smile surfaced on his time-worn features. "You are going on a trip next week." There was no hiding his delight at her stunned look. "You will be asked for this letter by a friend. He will know if you have read it. Give the letter to him, and on your return, you and I will be on the best of terms again." He gave Jane the lewd smile she had seen in the library. The MP stood and started for the door but halted. "I'm giving you a chance to mend things here. Life could have been bright for you, but now you are on probation." He shook his head. "Turn on your TV tomorrow at ten and see where cooperation can get you." With that, he strutted out.

London, Sunday 1st December 2024

Still wearing the oversized T-shirt stolen from Ed that doubled as pyjamas, Jane sat on the sofa and turned on BBC. Letchford's cryptic message had intrigued her.

She was up ridiculously early for a Sunday. She'd been packing her bags since 7am as a BBC driver was going to pick them up at lunchtime, and she wouldn't see them again until Rio.

The away days were fantastic. Being the face in front of the camera, you were treated like royalty, and everything was done for you. All she had to do was turn up.

As former prime minister Boris Jenkins had been out of the limelight for a couple of years, Jane didn't really know why they were covering the trip at all. She assumed she might end up doing a couple of interest pieces for the six o'clock news. They would probably do some file footage too.

When the football highlights programme ended, she turned the sound up.

"…and now on BBC, with Laura away for a few weeks, we bring you Sunday Politics with Dana McInteer."

Jane dropped the remote. "Nooooo, Dana, for fuck's sake," she screamed at the screen. Sure enough, there she was. One of Jane's closest friends had magically been bumped from regional politics right into the hot seat. Was this what Letchford meant? How could it not be?

"Oh shit!" she said aloud. "Dana has shagged the old goat." Dana was talking with three experts about the establishment of the Government of National Unity. She speculated on its longevity, but all Jane could think of was Dana with the Letch. "How could you, girl?" Jane asked the telly. When no answer came, she put her head in her hands and cried.

Rio Airport, Monday 2nd December 2024

The claustrophobic, bum-numbing journey stretched eleven hours. Ed slept most of the way, with his head rested on her shoulder. Jane could never sleep on planes. Yawning, eyes watering and irritable, she just wanted to get to the hotel, but Boris was doing an impromptu press conference at the airport. The gossip among the press pack on the plane was that he was getting paid half a million for each of the five talks this week. No one knew for certain, of course.

The press representatives from each paper or news outlet were clearly the company's B teams. In truth, B team was being polite to a few. It was only depressing as it showed how highly the Beeb rated her. Adding to Jane's misery, the situation with Dana still rankled. She would have never thought that Dana was the type to sleep her way up the ladder. Maybe she had this all wrong, but it didn't look good. It also bothered her that Letchford had somehow contrived this trip. He'd never seemed to be an important cog in government, and until Friday, she'd kept on his good side only because he leaked like a sieve. "What a prick," she said out loud as she stood in the queue for security.

Ed turned to her with a hurt expression. "I'm a prick?"

She shook her head. "No, sorry. Well, yes, you are a prick, but it wasn't you I was thinking about." She smiled at him. "This whole mess with Letchford and Dana has got me wound up."

On the journey over, she brought Ed up to speed on everything except the envelope – but if anyone knew how to open it without being discovered, Ed was the guy. She took him by the hand as they left customs, and they headed over to the seating area.

"Ed, one thing I didn't say earlier. Letchford gave me a letter and had me swear I wouldn't open it."

"You are working for the Letch now too?" Ed asked.

"No, but he took my pass, and I don't get it back until this is safely in someone's hands." She held up the letter.

Ed frowned. "Why didn't you tell him to bugger off and go speak to Dan? He would have got your pass back."

"I'm not sure if Dan is mixed up in this. Letchford made it plain to me that he organised this trip. He may have Dan in his pocket."

"So, what do we do?" Ed said, holding out empty palms.

She slapped the envelope into his hand. "Is there a way to read this without opening it?"

He ran his fingers over it. "You get devices that go in envelopes that will detect if the thing has been opened, or even if it has been scanned. I don't feel one in here though. Of course, we are dealing with the government here. They will have technology that I know nothing about," Ed admitted. He took an LED camera flash from his bag and set the letter on top. After first checking around to see if anyone was paying them any attention, he seemed placated they were not being watched. Ed then activated the flash, and Jane saw right through the envelope. Inside appeared to be a QR code and nothing else.

"Give me your phone," he said. Taking it from her, he switched on her QR scanner.

"Stop!" Jane said. "Use yours."

Ed handed back the phone and took his own one out. He scanned the code and switched off the flash. Giving back the letter, he looked at his phone.

"What is it?" Jane leant over to try to look at his screen.

"I can't see anything at the moment." Ed scrolled through the various screens on his device. "Oh, it has added a sudoku app to my phone."

"Sudoku?" Jane rubbed her brow. "Why be all secretive about that?" she asked Ed, knowing he had no answer.

"Weird," was all he said and then added, "We better get to the press conference."

With the press conference over, dignitaries piled into shiny black limos and headed off. Jane, Ed and the rest of the press gang hung about for forty-five minutes under a baking sun as someone looked for, and eventually found, the bus that was to take them to the hotel. It smelled like it had last been used to shift sheep. "Shows what they think of us," Ed said.

After a hot, excruciating hour sitting in Rio traffic, they finally reached the hotel. Thankfully, the man from the local Beeb office had checked them in and was waiting in the hotel lobby with key cards.

"Miss Clark," he said. "May I show you to your room?" Jane realised that the hierarchy was back in place when he handed all the other keys to Ed and left him to sort out the team. She was so tired and sweaty that she took the preferential treatment and abandoned the crew with a, "See you later, plebes." A few cries of derision came her way, but she didn't give a toss right now and walked away from the guys, her middle finger in the air.

The press pack were usually kept as far from the dignitaries as humanly possible. Across the road in another hotel if one were available. So, Jane raised an eyebrow when the guide punched the button for the top floor. That was normally where the best rooms were. She was not disappointed when the doors opened to a luxurious hallway. There was a security guard at the door, but he paid them little attention. She checked the hunk out, and as impressive as the muscles were that strained his tight silk shirt, sleep was still her top priority.

The guide showed her to a room at the end of the corridor. On entering, Jane looked round at the opulence and purred. "What a fantastic room." She smiled as she took in the luxurious scene.

After handing her the key, he turned to leave and said, "I am downstairs, room 1461. Call me if you need anything, Miss Clark." He closed the door and left before Jane realised that she didn't ask his name.

Her bag was already on a chair at the end of the bed, opened but not unpacked. She checked the door was locked, went through to the amazing bathroom and got the shower going. The room was made to look like a cave had been hewn from red sandstone with a huge bath that formed an oval pool in the rock floor. The fittings were all gold and sparkled in the warm lighting. This was not standard fare for a BBC reporter. A horrible thought crossed her mind. Was this room laid on by Letchford, assuming she had complied with his advances on Friday? *I'll take it while it lasts*, she thought.

After drying off using the thick Egyptian cotton towels, Jane took the bath robe from behind the door and then headed for bed. There was a formal dinner at nine, local time, and she really needed some sleep first.

In her sleep-deprived mind, about five seconds had elapsed when she was woken by insistent knocking at the door. "Fuck off, Ed," she shouted and turned over.

A muffled yet distinctive voice answered. "Errr…Um…It's not Ed."

"Boris fucking Jenkins," Jane said under her breath. Any thought of sleep left her, and she was up and heading to the door before her eyes had fully opened. "Sorry…er…sir. I was expecting someone else," she said on answering.

"Well, he is a lucky man," the former PM said, pointing to the gown that was now a little too open for modesty.

"Fuck." Jane tied the gown belt. "Sorry about the swearing too, Mr Jenkins."

"Don't worry about it, Miss Clark. I hear worse from the missus most days." He laughed.

"How…how may I help you?" she asked, finally gaining control of her reluctantly waking brain.

"I have a problem," he said with his palm outstretched. "Can I borrow your phone a second?" She shook her head as if it would clear the fog and allow her to understand what was happening. The place was full of phones, but here he was, knocking on a reporter's door, looking to borrow one.

"Er…okay." She went to get it from the bedside table. Upon recovering the phone, she turned to find that Jenkins had invited himself in.

He looked the place over. "Your room is nicer than mine. I will have to do something about that BBC licence fee one day." Smiling sardonically, she handed him her phone. Instead of calling anyone, he began scrolling through her open apps.

"Good, you haven't read it. Letchford said we could trust you." Jenkins passed back the phone and said, "Where is it?" Realising he meant the letter, she went to the pile of clothes thrown on the chair earlier and recovered it. She smiled as she handed it to him, and he said, "Thank you, Miss Clark. You have been helpful. I will remember this." The former prime minister turned and left the room.

Her legs now jelly, she sat on the bed. Looking at the bedside alarm, she realised that it was nearly eight. Although it felt like she was only just out of the shower, she sighed and got in there again.

International call, Monday 2nd December 2024

"Good evening, Mr Revere."

"And a good evening to you, sir. How was your trip?"

"We have just arrived, and I received your message. I will make the first donor contact tonight."

"Excellent. We need not tell you the criticality of your mission. Without the Minuteman's funding, our task would be futile."

"I understand, Mr Revere. The accounts should be in place within the week."

"And the good lady has the political situation in hand?"

"All is in motion. The tipping point will be the day after I get back home. The government will fall like the Walls of Jericho."

"Ah, if only our task here was as easy. Where you have Lady Elizabeth, I will doubtless need artillery."

"Horses for courses, Mr Revere. Guns or the girl – I wonder which is more dangerous?" The two men laughed and ended the call.

Cape Town, Tuesday 3rd December 2024

Another long flight, another sweaty bus journey, and now another boring press conference. Ed and Jane had filmed six hours of footage so far. On checking BBC News on iPlayer, Ed said they had used a fifteen-second clip.

"They could have got that from Reuters or one of the other agencies. Why the hell are we here?" Ed asked.

"Buggered if I know. Dan the Man says jump and I say how high, babe." She did a little jump to demonstrate. There were four of them on the trip. Ed, Jane, Paul the sound guy and Benjy the technician. This trip didn't come cheap. Someone at Auntie Beeb was expecting real news.

She remembered the mystery phone app from yesterday. "Did you play any sudoku yet?" She looked to Ed.

"Damnedest thing, Jane. As soon as I opened the first puzzle, the answers were all filled in. And none of them were right." He looked disappointed.

Grabbing his phone, she opened the app. Sure enough, the first grid was finished but all wrong. "Looks bugged," she said.

"Let me have a look," Benjy said. "I'm good with Samsung Galaxies."

Jane looked to Ed. He nodded, and so she passed the phone to Benjy. The man's thumbs worked at a million characters a second, but after a couple of minutes, his brow wrinkled. He went into his bag and brought out a tablet. Linking the two devices, he fiddled with the screen on the tablet.

"Nothing wrong with your phone, Edward," the technician said. "But the sudoku table is all wrong."

Jane didn't want Benjy knowing anything and so said, "No worries. Probably Ed getting a virus from all the porn he downloads." She took the phone and handed it back to Ed.

* * *

Going through the motions, the four BBC workers meticulously filmed and recorded everything at the dinner again that night. Jane was surprised to be granted a question after Boris's speech.

When the ex-PM pointed to her, she panicked but quickly blurted out, "How are you enjoying Cape Town, sir?" For once in his life, Boris answered, but it was a nothing question and a nothing answer. He looked pleased to have been referred to as 'sir'. Most of the press gang just called him Boris. They'd done that even when he was in power. Jane didn't believe in privilege, but it existed, of course. However, she respected the position of prime minister or any promoted post and would always address such appropriately. Letchford was coming close to changing that little edict, however.

They were tidying up the equipment and planning a few drinks in the bar when it was noticed that Jenkins was being whisked off somewhere. He had done the same in Rio. Probably a better bar, she thought. Maybe in Delhi she would rope Ed in, and they would follow him. *There might be news here somewhere.*

New Delhi, Thursday 5th December 2024

With the talk over, Jenkins headed for the door in the company of locals. Jane and Ed had a taxi out back already. Benjy was on the roof of the hotel and had a small drone that they mainly used for file footage. He intended to keep a track on the limo as far as possible, and he would relay info to Jane by mobile phone. They were not planning on ambushing the ex-PM. The purpose was to find where he headed after each speech.

His limo pulled away, ringed by motorbike outriders. With the traffic snarl up in this city, the cavalcade would have been going nowhere without the escort. The plan was to stay close and benefit from the road being cleared. However, Jane knew it was a long shot. She wasn't overly worried about being spotted. It was her job to report his movements after all. Anyway, she'd been treated as a valued member of the team by the Bozsquad, as the press had christened Jenkins' inner circle.

An epiphany struck. Letchford organised all this before the dinner party. He believed Jane to be sympathetic to whatever he was up to, and so far, he hadn't told anyone that Friday didn't go as planned. Of course, the sex was probably only ever Letchford's idea, but getting BBC reporters on board was the real masterplan. Jane was not naïve. The Tory Party and the BBC had a long and incestuous relationship, but seldom had the arrangement been flaunted so openly. Where her boss, Dan, sat in all this, she didn't know. That would have to be tested soon.

Their taxi pulled out into the traffic as the drone rose into the filthy Delhi air. 'Smelly Delhi', as the juvenile press pack were calling it. Half these guys had English literature degrees and that was the best they had come up with.

"Straight down the road that you are on," Benjy said, over the phone. "He's about one hundred metres ahead." The drone could go around a mile under control; they were scuppered if the car went any further, but luckily, Benjy's next message was, "They have turned right, three streets ahead of you. Oh, they have pulled up in front of a colonial-style building."

"Foreign Office," the taxi driver said, unbidden.

"Take us there, please," Jane replied.

"They won't let me drive up the street," the driver said, "but I will drop you at the end."

The end of the road was guarded. "What do we do?" asked Ed. As they watched, Jenkins and a couple of men shook hands on the stairs of the building.

"That's Modi," said Jane. "Why would Jenkins be meeting with the Indian PM in private?" She didn't expect Ed to answer. However, he proffered,

"Maybe they are friends after his time as PM."

"Could be," Jane admitted. "Wish we had followed him in Rio and Cape Town. We would know if this is a one-off or not." She decided it was time to see how far Boris's team trusted her.

"Okay, let's head back. Benjy, if you are looking down my top with that drone, I will kill you," Jane said, seeing it hovering overhead. There were howls of laughter from Benjy and Paul on the other end of the phone as it disconnected.

Jane sat sweating across from Ed and the two technicians in the hotel bar. After their pointless day's work was over, she suggested they get together for supper and a drink. It would likely be only one drink. For once, she wasn't in the mood to indulge

It was sacrilege to come to India and order pizza, but it was the safest thing on the menu. A vindaloo and then eleven hours in a plane toilet did not appeal. Just to be safe, she'd already overdosed on Imodium. Ed, on the other hand, wolfed down a veggie curry. The man had the constitution of an ox.

The guy that brought their food turned out to be Australian. He was working his way round the world. Three years in, and he had only made it to India. Jane got his life story along with her food. He was using every excuse to come back to the table. They politely declined his offer of dessert, and Jayden – she wasted no time in getting the tanned waiter's name – then said to Jane, "I'm off in an hour. Need someone to show you the town?"

Ed looked up but quickly realised the offer was not a general one.

"PHONE NUMBERS!" Benjy shouted. The interruption to Jane's waiter-baiting was annoying. "They are bloody phone numbers," Benjy repeated and said, "Give me your phone, Eddie." Benjy had been looking at the sweet menu, even though he had declined getting one. At the bottom of the menu was the hotel's address and phone number, but critically, it gave the Indian dial code. Ed handed over his phone, and Benjy opened the sudoku app.

Jane, paying more attention to Benjy now, turned back to the antipodean waiter and said, "Give us a moment, Jayden. I'll come find you later." The man left with a wide grin on his face.

"Yeah, I'm right," Benjy said. "The numbers are written vertically. The first two or three digits are the dial codes of Brazil, South Africa, India, China and Russia."

"Russia?" Ed and Jane said in unison. "Give us the phone," she ordered Benjy. The technician and soundman were not in on this mystery. The less they knew, the better. "Ed, come with me," she said and the two of them headed for the elevator.

Once they were back up in the room, Jane said, "Why would Jenkins be calling Russia? All the other numbers are where we have been already, or to where we are heading, so they might be local contacts, but then why keep this encrypted? This is bizarre."

"Shall we call one of them?" Ed asked.

"Too risky." She shook her head. "Can you Google them? If they turn out to be local escort agencies, all will be explained." She rolled her eyes.

Ed Googled the numbers on his tablet but found nothing. "They must be mobile phone numbers," he said." Some seem to have too many digits even for that though. Benjy could be wrong about this."

"Ed, copy the numbers to your tablet, somewhere no one will find them, and delete the app from your phone. This has moved from something interesting to something that might be…" She didn't want to say it.

"Dangerous?" Ed completed the sentence for her.

With a worried expression fixed on her face, she nodded. Ed did as he was told and showed her the screen.

"Good. we can talk about this more on the plane, but for now, I have an appointment with Crocodile Dundee downstairs." As she headed for the room door, Ed jumped up and stood in front of her.

"Don't, Jane."

"Don't what?" She tilted her head a little and looked at him.

"Can you not…? Can we…? Would it be okay if we watched a movie or something? We have an early start." He pointed to his wrist, even though he had no watch. There was no clue what was going on, but it was obvious that Ed wasn't up for an explanation. She sighed. For whatever reason, it seemed like he didn't want the intended romp to happen.

"Okay, Eddie boy," she said. "Order up some popcorn and see what sort of porn they have on the telly."

Asia, over the Himalayas, Friday 6th December 2024

After deciding to test her level of trust by the Bozsquad, Jane submitted an interview request to Jenkins' press secretary and asked if it could be on the plane as "It made good telly." The press secretary agreed. She was amazed to get a 6am start time.

There was little more than a snowball's chance that the interview would ever be shown. An assistant came out to the narrow corridor where Ed and Jane sat. He looked at them as if the two were lepers but then sighed and reluctantly ushered them into a small office, near the front of the 747. Well, Jane called all big planes seven-forty-sevens. She had no clue what it really was.

Boris sat behind a desk and the press secretary lurked in the background. The ex-PM was famous for opening his mouth and putting his foot in it, so Jane guessed the PS was here to try to prevent any tragedy.

"Miss Clark," Boris said, "how are you this fine day?"

While Jane took her seat, Ed set up the camera under guidance from Boris's press secretary.

"I'm good, sir. Thank you. How are you?" She stifled the need to yawn.

"Ah, well, as good as can be expected after five days in a tin can." He pointed around to show he meant the plane.

"I'm not much of a flyer either, sir."

Boris Jenkins inhaled deeply. "You, me and Icarus. We may have to do a lot more of this soon unfortunately."

He seemed to be under the impression that she knew what was

going on. For now, she decided to nod in agreement and smile. Turning to Ed. "Ready to roll?" He nodded and she asked the same of the ex-PM.

"Do your worst." He held up a thumb.

Jane did a preamble to camera, advising the people that would watch this that they were on a speaking trip and she was about to interview the man himself. Turning to the former PM, she asked all the standard questions that she already knew the answers to. Jenkins answered with concise replies, which wasn't like him at all. She went for the round-up question.

"And so finally, Mr Jenkins, would you say that you have got everything you wanted out of this trip?"

Jenkins started with the usual niceties and platitudes but then said, "The world balance is in flux. A Britain of the future will need to plough a different furrow. Of course, we all hope that America will be back to normalcy soon," he scratched an ear as he spoke, "... and I fully support Mr Suvar's attempts to bolster trade with the EU, but the BRICS are the growing trade block now. It is time for Britain to wake up to this. These economies are growing faster than any other and they have a simpler and resilient governance system. One that is resistant to the market idiosyncrasies that have long held the Western world back. The work we are doing here will begin to put Britain on top again. I hope soon to be able to implement the changes that our country desperately needs."

This was gold. Jenkins seemed to indicate that he still held aspirations to play a major role in British and world politics. He also clarified that this tour was more about building his relations with the BRICS trade group. The plane was currently heading to Beijing. That in itself was unusual for a speaking tour. It was dynamite as a trade delegation.

Westminster Green, Sunday 8th December 2024

The onset of the dark winter was further exacerbated by the overcast London sky. After the hot sun of their trip, being home felt depressing. Forlornly looking to the heavens while reaching out from under the awning, Jane let the icy cold sleet wash over her hand. Wrapped in a woolly hat and scarf, she stood under a gazebo in the park on the other side of the road from Westminster. The BBC and other networks had 'temporary' accommodation that was set up during the Brexit debates. Now, years later, they were still here as Parliament seemed to lurch from one crisis to another.

Jane was about to go to camera for the 5pm news to talk about the latest.

"Ready, Jane?" the producer asked. She confirmed she was set and removed her hat. There was a pause and then, "Five…four…three…" He counted the last two numbers with his fingers.

"Thanks, Brian," Jane said to the anchor in the studio. "Yes, here we are again, outside the Houses of Parliament as the government faces another crisis. Tory MP Sir David Sandringham has announced he is standing down. The announcement came as a shock to the media, but it also appeared to be a surprise to the government. Sir David's Christchurch constituency is the safest Tory seat in England. Even with the party's current low opinion poll rating, it is a seat they would be confident of holding. The problem they face is that, in light of the General Election being suspended, it is hard for them to justify holding a by-election.

"We at the BBC believe Sir David told the PM about his decision to stand down on Friday. It is reported that the PM sought to leave the seat unfilled, with neighbouring MPs taking on the constituency work. But a row has blown up between Tory Central Office and the local constituency chair. The chair has threatened court action if the government refuses a by-election. We are all in uncharted waters here. The country awaits the next move by either side. Jane Clark, reporting from Westminster."

"And out!" The producer gave a silent clap toward her.

She smiled and took the earpiece out. She was finished for the night. Unless this blew up, of course. *Better stay sober*, she thought.

"Drink?" Ed said, walking her way.

"Oh well, if I must." She laughed at how fickle she was when it came to alcohol. The two of them headed for town.

After walking only a few yards, Ed asked the question that neither of them knew the answer to. "What happened to the Boris interview from the plane?"

"I don't know. It got buried. I can't believe it. I thought that was dynamite, but Dan said that he might use a bit of it later. I can't decide if he is lying, or if Boris is old news."

"He's never off the telly. The press follow him like he's Bo Peep," he said holding an imaginary crook by his side.

She shook her head. "Bo Peep lost her sheep. Maybe his day has passed."

"I don't know. I smell a rat." Ed pinched his nose. For a cameraman, Ed had a reporter's beak when it came to stories worth pursuing. He'd steered Jane toward juicy leads in the past.

As if drawn by magnets, the pair crossed the pavement and swerved into Clouds Bar. It was one of London's gay bars, but also the chosen drinking hole of many MPs from across the road in Parliament. The staff were discreet. There was a 'what goes on in Clouds, stays in Clouds' air to the place, and she liked that. The staff also tended to keep the celebrity hunters away.

"Hold on," she said. He turned to watch her rummage in her bag, from which she took out a pair of glasses and put them on. It was her disguise.

"And Superman becomes Clark Kent," Ed said.

Jane took his arm. "That makes you Lois."

They entered the bar to find it busy. Many revellers went out early on Sunday and got home in time to rise, just about fit for work the next day. Jane and Ed kept working their way through the throng until they reached a corridor at the back. Donovan, the doorman at the foot of the stairs, knew them well and waved them by.

"Hey, Jedward," he said in his incredible bass voice.

"Who told you about that?" Jane said to the bouncer.

"I'm sworn to secrecy," Donovan said and laughed his earthquake laugh. She wouldn't have minded going a few rounds with the burly doorman, but Ed had more chance with him, it seemed.

"What a waste," she said to him and winked. Donovan had heard it before, many times in fact, but he smiled his brilliant white smile anyway.

Upstairs was less crowded but still busy. The music was quieter here and that suited Jane as she got older. Her raving days were long behind. She got the drinks. Ed scoped out a booth, and by the time she made her way over, he was already embroiled in conversation with a really fit guy. Places like this were torture for Jane, and she laughed at the realisation. Ed's companion was familiar, she'd maybe seen him before at a party or something. He hadn't been around a lot though. She certainly didn't think they were a thing.

"Terry!" She remembered his name before realising she said it out loud.

He looked up with the most gorgeous blue eyes and said, "Hi, Jane," before quickly returning his attention to Ed.

"Terry works in the British Museum," Ed said.

She finally placed his face. "Yes, we met at a party once before."

Jane stood and shook Terry's hand. "You promised me a tour sometime."

Terry was far more interested in talking to Ed than he was to Jane. "Maybe you both could come round one evening after close, and I'll let you have the run of the place."

"That sounds great. I'll take you up on that."

Terry nodded and turned his back on her once more. The conversation was over, she guessed.

Her attention wandered to two of the young SNP MPs standing at the bar. Suits wrinkled and ties askew, they looked rather the worse for wear. She assumed they'd been here most of the afternoon. One of them turned and saw her looking. He was staring through the darkened room and his beer goggles to see if he knew her. Her glasses probably threw him, but Jane waved, and he returned it. It looked like he'd given up on identifying her and returned his attention to his colleague, but two minutes later, Jane heard a strong West Coast Scotland accent from behind her.

"Colin said you were in." Colin was one of the two drunk MPs at the bar. "Can I buy you a drink, Jane?" said Isla Wallace, SNP MP for North Paisley and one of the youngest MPs ever to enter the House. Isla didn't like Westminster politics much, and she was due to stand down in January. She'd reluctantly agreed to stay until the end of the extended term, though.

Isla was younger than Jane and they seldom crossed paths. Anytime they did, Jane found her pleasant, but even when being nice, Isla had a voice that made you think she might be about to strangle you.

"Yeah, sure," said Jane. "G&T, please."

Isla headed for the bar but turned and pointed to the empty booth immediately behind. Jane stood and was going to tell Ed she would be back, but he and Terry were deep in conversation. She shrugged and took a seat in the empty booth.

It seemed as if Isla had fallen into conversation with a young blonde girl. Guessing her company may be less interesting, Jane was about to get up and leave when she saw the blonde pull out a mobile and move next to Isla for a selfie. Isla smiled at the girl and headed back toward the table with a tray in hand. She set it down and said, "Sorry, Jane, politics student at LSE." Isla pointed at the blonde and put on a bad London accent. "I am *such* a big fan." The Scottish MP laughed at her own impression. "You must get that a lot, too?" she asked.

"Hence the glasses," Jane said, taking them off as if to reveal her identity.

"I must try that." Isla smiled. "I heard that you were out with Boris on tour."

"Yes," said Jane. "Five days, five mega-long flights, over forty hours of footage, and so far, they have run less than a minute of the stuff. It was a blast." She rolled her eyes.

"Yeah, I'm getting out cos of shite like that," the MP said. "Other stuff, too, but Westminster is all about sitting around waiting for something to happen. I think I can do better away from here."

"Are you going to Holyrood?" Jane asked.

"I haven't decided." Isla shook her head. The two chatted about work for a while, and then Isla said, "Can I ask something personal?"

"Of course you can. I may not answer though." Jane looked down at the table and then took a sip of her drink.

"Accepted," Isla said and then, "What happened to you on St Andrew's night in the Randolf?"

Jane almost dropped her glass. "What do you mean?" she said, more to stall than anything.

"I saw you there. The SNP get a table for one night only." She shook her head and waved the hand that wasn't holding her drink. "Oh, don't get me wrong, some of our very white and very male colleagues are permitted at any time, but the local KKK chapter likes to have a few colonials around once or twice a year." She broke eye contact. "I noticed you coming running down the stairs and leaving in a rush."

What was this woman's angle? Jane didn't know. She picked up the G&T that was half finished and downed it. The tray sat between them with another six drinks on it. She pointed to it and asked, "Company?"

"No, no, just for us. Tuck in." Isla slid another over the table as a couple waltzed past, singing to the Pet Shop Boys. The female dancer, seeing Isla, made the sign of the cross as they departed, but the MP just chuckled. Isla reached over the table and took Jane's hand. "Did he…?" She left the question hanging.

Jane looked down into the fresh drink. "No, but…" She couldn't finish.

"Look, I won't do anything with what's said here tonight. I'm not going to advise you to go to the police or take matters further. Obviously, I think that you should if that happened, but you need to make that choice." The MP squeezed her hand. Jane looked up at her and saw real concern on her face.

"It wasn't like that. I was there for an interview that he promised me," Jane said and sought to change the subject. "You know the press all call him the Letch?"

"We do too," said the MP, smiling.

"Well, he came on pretty strong and he made it known that he could make life easy for me if I…" She hesitated, not sure how much to spill. "Got out of my clothes."

"The dirty old bastard," Isla said, loud enough for half the bar to hear. "Sorry." She held up a hand to Jane. "These bastards in the establishment think every lassie should drop her knickers at their will." Isla banged her drink on the table, hard. It was surprising the glass remained intact. "Did he hurt you?"

Jane looked over the top of her glass and smiled an evil smile. "I wasn't the one left in pain." After relaying all the gory details, the MP laughed until tears wet her cheeks.

In between each raucous belly laugh, she kept saying, "It isn't funny…It isn't funny," but it took ages for her to calm down. When she did finally, her face was as red as if she'd run a marathon. "That is the best thing I have heard in years." Isla took a big slurp of her drink. "I'm glad you are okay. I felt like a right bitch watching you wait for your coat and not coming over. I…haven't held people like…reporters in the highest esteem. I knew you were in distress, and I let my bias get in the way of helping. I've felt like a real cow ever since. Can you forgive me?"

Holding up their drinks, the two of them clinked glasses. "I don't think you need it, but for what it's worth, you're forgiven," said Jane.

Isla exhaled deeply, and her face went all serious. "I know we are off the record, but I don't want to compromise your position, so stop me if what I'm about to say steps on your professional toes, okay?" Jane nodded. Isla paused. She seemed to consider whether to continue or not. "You know they've got to the BBC, don't you?"

"The government?" asked Jane

"No, not exactly. I know you won't agree with me that the Beeb has been in the government's pocket for years, but some new type of press coup is underway. My sources say you were not the first senior reporter to be called to the Randolf." Jane realised she may be missing the bigger picture but liked being considered a senior reporter. The MP went on. "They have people all through your organisation now."

"Who do you mean by they?" Jane asked.

"Boris's cabal," she replied. The MP looked at her watch and said, "I've said enough for now. I am not going to try convince you of some great conspiracy as I've no idea why they are doing it, but I know they are. They're infiltrating the other outlets too. If you want to talk about it sometime, you know where to find me." The MP downed her drink, picked up another and it went the same way. "That was golden," she said, raising her knee to demonstrate what she meant. Isla headed toward her colleagues at the bar.

Jane sat for a while longer, mulling the conversation over. The idea of a coup sounded extreme, but considering all the crazy things that happened over the last few weeks, she began to think there might be a link between it all. Standing, she picked up the two remaining drinks and walked over to the bar. Isla looked round and smiled as Jane tapped her shoulder.

Christchurch, Monday 9th December 2024

Stanton Parker-Rowe wallowed in his fifteen minutes of fame. His phone rung incessantly since very early this morning. The first call being a request that he be interviewed on the Radio Four 'Today' programme. A listener all his adult life, today he was interviewed by Amol himself.

While walking to the shops an hour ago, he was accosted by almost every local – "You tell them, Stanton", "Don't let those fools in Westminster mess with you." Many other messages of support were quietly expressed or sometimes shouted on the way.

Of course, there had been a few derogatory comments. There were always the crude and uneducated – that was true even here in true-blue Christchurch. It was clear, however, that most people supported his stand against Westminster.

Here he was now, waiting in the constituency office for a call with the PM himself. How could things get any better?

Stanton always knew he would be important one day. His father represented the constituency for many years. When it came time to stand down, his father named Sir David Sandringham as his preferred candidate over his own son. Stanton was devastated, but as his father moved from politics into a multimillion-pound job on the board of the Sandringham Group, he at least placated himself that it was all about money. Of course, Stanton could have sought another constituency. A couple had even come sniffing, but after putting his hat in the ring, he'd been overlooked for Central Office parachutes. Well, no parachute was getting dropped into Christchurch this time. Stanton Parker-Rowe was in charge and no matter how high up the Tory Party you were, Stanton was doing this thing his way.

The phone at his ear clicked, and a woman said, "I have the Prime Minister for you."

Before he could reply, the line clicked again, and the unmistakeable voice said, "Stanton, may I call you Stanton?"

"Of course, Prime Minister," he replied.

"Oh, call me Ravi – we're all friends here."

Friends when you need me, Stanton thought.

"I need your help, Stanton," the PM admitted. "It doesn't look good for the Government of National Unity if we must have a by-election in Christchurch while postponing the elections. If you will accept the postponement for now, maybe we could look favourably on your candidature when the election is held?"

So, it was going to be bribery, Stanton thought. As starstruck as he was, sitting here chatting to the PM, he'd been made promises before, and he well knew, unless you had them in writing, they were not worth the paper they were not written on.

"Are you saying that I will be the Conservative Party candidate, Ravi?"

"Well, as you know, Stanton, that is not in my purview, but if I say your candidature would be favourably welcomed, you will understand that you would certainly be the frontrunner," the PM replied. Stanton heard he was being talked down to.

"Thank you, Prime Minister, but I have been a frontrunner before and seem to always find the last hurdle gets in the way." He prolonged the horse racing metaphor. "Anyway," He continued. "I have to tell you that I put my name forward in last night's selection meeting, but I was defeated by another candidate."

"There was a selection meeting?" Suvar asked.

"Yes, sir, we decided as a constituency that the role should be filled as soon as possible."

"You don't have that authority," said the PM, losing his cool.

"I assure you that I do, sir," said Stanton.

"I can prevent the by-election from being called," said the PM, his voice going up in pitch.

"For a month or so," said Stanton, "but if you could postpone indefinitely, you and I would not be having this conversation, I guess." Stanton could hear muffled curses on the other end. The PM had his hand over the mouthpiece.

"Mr Parker-Rowe, your family has long served the best interest of your country and the Conservative Party. All I ask is that you continue that tradition," the PM pleaded.

"And that is exactly what we intend to do, sir. We have the best candidate in place already. He and I will continue to do our best for Britain," Stanton said.

The PM let out a noisy breath. "Who is your candidate?" he asked.

"Boris Jenkins, sir."

London, Tuesday 10th December 2024

Meticulously completing another row of biro flowers on the desk scribble pad, Jane was killing time. On checking her watch, only an hour had elapsed, but it already felt like a lifetime. She still wasn't entirely sure what the meeting was about. Dan told her to be here and so she was. The phone vibrated in her pocket. They'd been asked to leave them outside the meeting room, but that was never going to happen. Surreptitiously, she took it out but kept it below the table. With a quick glance at the screen, she saw it was Letchford. He never gave up and had taken to sending explicit pictures now too. The man was so sure of his position that he could afford to do that to a press member, for God's sake. This one was just text, and she would read it later. With a deep sigh, the phone went back in the pocket, and she feigned interest in the talk again. Thankfully, the speaker seemed to be winding up.

"I hope that's good for you all," the girl said. "Are there any questions?"

Bob, sitting near the front, raised his hand and Jane already knew what the question would be. The girl said, "Bob, yes, Bob, is it? How can I help?"

"You can give me your phone number, sweetie," Bob said and chuckled. The girl looked deflated. Her talk fell on deaf ears and Horny Bob, as he was known to all, paid more attention than most. But for all the wrong reasons. The girl picked up her papers and walked out.

"Nice one, Bob," the gathering said in unison.

Ed added, "You realise we'll be given a lecture on respect and professionalism in the workplace because of that."

"I've done the course so often, I could give it to you now if you want?" Bob said, laughing.

"You're such a dick," said Jane as she left the meeting. She went into the little girls' room, found a cubicle and sat to read the text message.

D, my sexy news girl. Come to the flat this evening. I have a scoop for you. Wear the red dress. S X

Jane didn't own a red dress. Well, not one Letchford had ever seen anyway. She read the text multiple times before realising it was not meant for her. The Letch had got his dirty messages mixed up; this was for Dana.

Letchford's part in Dana's rapid promotion had yet to be broached. A few recent nights out got cancelled, as Jane was studiously avoiding the situation.

Do I tell him that I received it in error or not? He was going to find out when Dana didn't turn up. She knew Letchford was in deep, and it looked as if he was working to undermine his own government – but how was Dana involved? It was bad enough she had slept with him for her career, but if she was implicated in whatever was going on, then this had got a whole lot more complicated. She needed more information and there was really only one place she might get it.

Eschewing the lift, she took the stairs up to where the important people were. Here was where she would now find her friend. With Dana's promotion came a swanky new office and at least three assistants.

Knocking, she expected to hear Dana's voice in response, but a male one answered.

"Come in." Through the first door was an outer office. "How may I help you?" the male assistant asked.

"Jane Clark to see Dana McInteer, please."

"Is she expecting you?"

"She is not," Jane admitted.

He looked at her scornfully but picked up the phone and said, "Jane Clark for Miss McInteer."

The walls were paper thin, and Jane could hear the message being relayed next door. To Jane's great relief, she heard Dana scream, as only Dana could, "Jane, baby. Get your cute ass in here."

Jane smiled at the guy with the phone still to his ear. She went into the main office and decided right away to keep things professional. "Wow, this is great," she said in greeting.

Dana came running across the room and hugged her. "Where have you been, babes?"

"I was on that Boris lark and then been busy since. All this American and government stuff is keeping us flat out downstairs." This was true, but it wasn't the real reason she hadn't visited – She felt guilty for the lie.

"Yeah, tell me about it," said Dana. "When are we going to go out and get hammered? It has been too long."

Thinking fast, Jane said, "What are you up to tonight?"

"Nothing," said Dana, without a second's hesitation.

So, Letchford hadn't realised his mistake yet. "I need to show you something," Jane said.

"What is it?" her friend asked with a curious look on her face

"In private," Jane said.

"Oh no, you got another rash, babe? You know I warned you about those strange men," Dana said and laughed.

She turned to her two assistants and snapped her fingers. "Can you guys give us a moment, please?" Wordlessly, the two left the office. "You have me intrigued," said Dana. Jane tried to play the whole thing as cooly as possible.

"I got a weird text message from the Letch. Look…" She showed her screen to Dana. Jane watched the other girl's face closely.

Dana took way too long to reply, and then blurted out, "Ah,

that dirty old bugger sends me messages all the time. He has no bloody chance."

Outwardly disinterested, Jane shrugged her shoulders and deleted the text. "Yeah, he's sent me a few too. He's mixed us up in his little black book. I brought it to you in case it was a story you were working."

A look of sheer relief came over Dana's face. On the assumption there would be a conversation about this between the Letch and Dana later, Jane decided to fill her friend in with some of the detail of what had been going on.

"He tried it on with me big time at a do a few weeks ago. I almost had to fight him off."

"Been there, done that." Dana rolled her eyes.

Was that a cryptic confession? Jane let it lie. "So, where do you want to go?"

Dana's eyes narrowed.

"Tonight." Jane clarified by miming lifting a glass to her mouth.

"Oh yes, of course," Dana said. "Tell you what, babe, I will buzz you down later once I have double-checked the schedule. Okay?"

"Cool," said Jane as she turned to go. It was 100% certain that some unexpected work appointment would make Dana cancel.

Westminster, Wednesday 11th December 2024

While preparing for her piece covering the day in Parliament, Jane sat with her jacket buttoned up against the cold of the 'temporary' Westminster portacabin. The producer had just cut her time from one minute to thirty seconds and now she sat frantically, biro cap in her mouth, scoring out parts of the report. The programme was about to go live, and Jane wondered why Dana was sitting to the right of the main anchor. There was no mention on the running order.

"And now we go over to our Senior Political Correspondent, Dana McInteer, who is going to bring us some breaking news. Dana," the anchor said.

The camera turned to Dana. "Thank you, David. Yes, my sources at Westminster have broken news of another rebellion. As we heard at the weekend, the government were keen to leave the Christchurch seat vacant after the sitting MP resigned, but the local Conservative Party did not agree, and I can tell you exclusively now that they have selected Boris Jenkins as their candidate. I can also reveal that it was the government's intention simply not to issue the writ that would enable the by-election, but that a rebellion by cabinet member Selwyn Letchford has ensured that the writ will be lodged with the Speaker later today. The by-election should now go ahead by the end of January."

The camera returned to the anchor. "Thank you, Dana. Stunning news indeed."

The strapline was already scrolling, *BORIS SET TO RETURN*.

"You've been pulled, Jane," the producer shouted over.

"Jesus H Christ," she said, crumpling her notes and launching the ball of paper at his head.

It wasn't really a surprise that her daily round-up was pushed aside. Dana's news was going to fill the rest of the slots today. This was big, and the pieces of Isla Wallace's conspiracy theory were falling into place. Jane used to think of Selwyn Letchford as a simple, perverted buffoon, but more and more, the man seemed to be pulling the strings of power. She looked at the screen and realised that this situation was his doing. He had already taken control of the agenda, and it looked like Dana was his tool. *What had she got herself in to?*

Jane had now exhausted her current sources, trying to discover what was going on. She went back to Isla's flat on Sunday. There had been a few strange looks as the two of them walked out of the gay club together. Isla said, "Hold my hand and we will really get the tongues wagging." Jane declined. But Isla had little more meat to add to her conspiracy bone.

Letchford was heading up a cabal to get Boris back, and Isla believed there would be a leadership change after Suvar lost the next election. Jane didn't disagree, but none of that was really news. The over-friendly alliances with the media were also not exactly groundbreaking. If Boris was going to stand, some in the media were going to tear into him. It made electoral sense to bring others onside, however unscrupulously it was achieved.

No, she was no further forward. Maybe it was time for another visit to Letchford's constituency.

Mentford, Friday 13th December 2024

Jane and Ed drew into the Fox and Hound car park.

"He will cream himself, girl," Ed said, looking at Jane's incredibly tight purple dress. Tonight, he was meant to be her boyfriend.

After making him go back and change his flowery shirts three times, Jane was finally happy he was straight date material.

There'd been a few texts from Quentin over the weeks since her visit. He may have flirted a little, but she wasn't really sure. Most were witty quips about nothing in particular. Drunk texting him one night, she hadn't even remembered until next day, but after being horrified at seeing her explicit messages to him, she noticed that he'd been nothing but polite in return. However, he told her that he and Heather were now officially dating. Jane hadn't been sure if this news was there to ward her off or not, but sticking with her original cricket-loving story, she had asked if they could meet up when Quentin mentioned the annual Mentford Cricket Club Christmas party. *Oh, and can I take my man, Eddie?* she'd asked. The invitation was issued and accepted.

Jane had checked Letchford Senior was out of the country because, as far as Quentin knew, she worked in human resources.

She turned to Ed. "Behave yourself."

"I always behave myself," he said and laughed. Ed liked to be outrageous when in new company.

"This is work, Ed. I know I told you he's a stud, but I'm here to find out what is going on with Daddy, okay?"

"You got it, dearest," he said in his Edinburgh accent.

She smiled, and a little shiver ran through her. Nibbling his ear, she whispered, "What a waste," and the two laughed as if it was the first time. Walking across the car park, he slipped his hand down her back and onto her bum.

"You're supposed to be my boyfriend, not my stalker. Give me your hand, you prick." She looked up into his toffee-brown eyes and smiled. Part of her wished he'd ignored the request.

A mix of heat and music hit them as they walked from the overlit car park and into the darkened lounge. Both stopped to let their eyes adjust. It was busy and a seventies disco song pumped through the speakers. Jane could feel Eddie start to move with the rhythm. She gripped his hand and said, "Edinburgh Eddie tonight, remember."

He slipped into a more masculine register and said, "Roger, hen."

Quentin waved from a table in the corner, and he pointed to seats that were vacant. Jane and Ed headed over.

"Hey, Jane," Quentin said. "You have met Heather, I seem to

remember." The cricketer beamed as he introduced them. His cricket whites had been replaced by a Savile Row suit and, much to Jane's surprise, one of the exact shirts she'd forbade Ed to wear tonight.

She took Heather's hand. "Indeed. Hi, Heather, you look lovely."

"Hi," Heather almost whispered as she whipped her hand away, blushing.

Jane turned and pointed to Ed. "And this is my hubby Ed." It was hard to choose who had the more shocked face, Ed or Quentin. She'd asked Ed to behave, but she was damned if she had to.

"Married?" said Quentin. "Lovely to meet you, Ed." The guys shook hands, but there was a delay before Quentin released Ed's. "How long?" Quentin asked, directing his attention to Ed.

"Three years," said Jane while Ed simultaneously replied, "Two years."

"Don't listen to him." Jane flung her arms up in mock exasperation. "He never even remembers my birthday. However, he's not completely wrong for once – it is actually two years, eight months, five days and…four hours," she said, checking the fake Rolex she'd bought on a holiday in Turkey.

"Really, dear?" said Ed, raising an eyebrow. "It seems so much longer."

"Anyway, take a seat," said Quentin, waving a hand toward the bar. A minute later, a tray was laid on the table with a champagne bucket, a bottle of ridiculously expensive plonk and four crystal champagne flutes. "Here's to marriage," said Quentin while pouring the drinks. She took time to look the flawless adonis up and down. Quentin would look good in jeans and a tee, but tonight, in a suit and an open-neck pink shirt, her hungry eyes drank in the intoxicating image.

While their host filled them in on the background of the cricket club and pointed out important people in the lounge, Jane feigned interest and nipped Ed's knee in a prearranged sign.

"I love this song. I want to dance," Ed said and, giving Heather no option, took her by the hand and dragged her to her feet. He pirouetted and wiggled his way to the dance floor, still clutching onto the girl. She covered her eyes and giggled.

"Your husband is nice," Quentin said. "I'm a little surprised that…" He left it hanging.

"I'm married?" Jane said.

"Well, yes, I suppose. I misunderstood our little…chats," he said.

"Maybe you didn't," Jane replied and winked. "Anyway, you and Heather, you old dog. How is that going?"

"She's okay, I guess," he said, showing no enthusiasm. "My parents like her."

"Isn't your dad a lord or something?" Jane asked, trying to look disinterested. She pushed the fake glasses back up the bridge of her nose and shifted her leg under the table so that it lay on his.

"No, not a lord. Well, not yet anyway. He is an MP," Quentin replied.

"That's cool. Do you get a lot of celebs round the house?" she said, brushing an imaginary speck from his shoulder.

"None you would find interesting, I guess. Politicians mainly," he said.

"Booorriing." She faked a yawn. "Have you had that dishy prime minister over?" She licked her lips.

Quentin laughed and her heart beat a little faster with the first sight of his perfect white teeth. It was hard for her to choose the exact purpose of tonight's visit. Was she looking to pump him for information, or get pumped herself?

"Oh God no," he replied. "My father is not a fan. He blames the guy for the downfall of Boris."

"I remember Boris," she said, trying hard to remain professional. "You had him over?"

"He's hardly away from the place," Quentin said, but Jane knew he was losing interest in the subject. He kept turning to watch the dancers. It was early, and the party had not long started, but the floor was already full. Some, like Quentin, were dressed to the nines, while others wore jeans. As far as she could tell, there was no one from the base present, and if Romeo and Juliet were around, they must be secreted in one of the room's many alcoves.

"So, did you tell Heather about our little conversation?" she asked.

"I might have," he admitted and grinned.

"Can I be honest with you?" she said, leaning over to whisper in his ear conspiratorially.

"Of course," he replied, and it now seemed as if she had his full attention again.

"She's not really my type at all," she said and then slowly ran her tongue round his ear.

He purred a little. "Not really mine either, if truth be told." Jane nibbled his earlobe and brushed her leg against him.

"What about your husband?" he said.

"Oh, don't worry about Eddie. He'll notice nothing while he is dancing. He loves it so much I sometimes think he is gay." She laughed. Quentin turned and looked at Ed and Heather. They seemed to be performing some sort of Dashing White Sergeant to a Hot Chocolate song.

"He *is* on the flamboyant side," he said, smiling.

"Ed has a similar attitude to me about partners," Jane said to cover. "Our relationship is not conventional." She ran a finger over Quentin's cheek and then circled his lips. He kissed the tip of her finger but then removed her hand, and she thought he looked slightly irritated.

"Somehow, that's no surprise." There was a knowing look on his face. He broke their embrace and stood abruptly. "I will go get another bottle."

Jane deflated. Her mind was clearly swaying toward being the pumpee tonight, but, thus far, Quentin showed little interest in either plan. He headed toward the bar, then stopped at the dancing couple and spoke to Heather. She nodded and walked back to the table. Quentin patted Ed on the back and the two made their way off through the throng. Heather came back over and sat as far from Jane as she could.

"How long have you and Quentin been going out?" Jane asked.

"Only a few weeks really, but we have been…seeing each other on and off for a year or so," Heather replied.

"How long have you worked here?" Jane toyed with her fake glasses.

"Round about eighteen months. I did bar work on the base mainly, only did here a couple of weeknights when they needed cover. Now the base is closed, I'm here full time." The girl sat with her knees facing the dance floor and had she moved away another inch, she would have fallen off the seat altogether. Jane doubted Heather would have looked less comfortable in a lion's cage.

"Has the base closed altogether?" It seemed as if Heather may turn out to be a better source of information than Quentin. Letchford's son showed a distinct lack of interest in discussing his parents.

"Well, yeah, the Yanks have gone anyway," Heather replied.

Jane could hardly hear the girl as she was a whisperer. Her voice now drowned out by the Bay City Rollers, Jane wondered if Ed had driven through a time warp on their way to Mentford.

"Heather, come closer. I don't bite." She patted the seat next to her. Heather flushed and looked tense again but reluctantly shuffled over next to Jane. "That's better, I couldn't hear you over the music. So, Quentin says you get on well with his parents?" The girl shuffled away a couple of inches, deciding Jane was too close for safety.

"Yeah, I guess. I get on okay with them, but his father is a little too friendly when he thinks there is no one looking." Jane closed the newly opened gap between the two. She realised that the whole Heather attraction fib had worked and got her to this meeting with Quentin. There was no further reason to mess with the girl, but she couldn't help it.

"Can I tell you a secret?" Jane asked.

"Er…yeah," said Heather, though she didn't look sure that it was going to be something she would like.

"Quentin's father has a bit of a reputation for the girls. He is called 'the Letch' at work and it has nothing to do with his surname."

Heather giggled, displaying a pretty smile. Jane thought the girl should really smile more, but decided it best not to say that to her now. Seemingly relaxing a little, Heather shuffled closer and took out her phone.

"Look," she said to Jane, showing her the screen. It was a picture of a man's genitals, and to Jane's horror, she recognised them well. "Quentin's dad sent me the photo and then gave me this." She took a necklace out from under her blouse. Jane wasn't a jewellery expert but knew enough to recognise a very expensive piece. The sixty-odd-year-old was seducing a twenty-something girl that dated his son. Weirdly Jane was both horrified and relieved that he wasn't only trying to buy reporters. No, Letchford truly was a lech of the highest order.

"Have you told anyone about this, Heather?" Jane asked. "He is old enough to be your grandfather."

"No, I couldn't if I wanted to. He owns this place," Heather said.

Jane said, "You'd get bar work somewhere else no problem."

"No, not the bar – he owns the county. There was a situation last year where a local girl accused him of feeling her up at a party. A couple of weeks later, her father got fired and the bank foreclosed on their mortgage. They had to move to Wales," Heather said furtively while checking no one was listening. She added, "It never even made the newspaper."

Was Letchford untouchable? Jane wondered. If so, where did that leave her? Of course, she never reported her own run-in with the man. Okay. her job at the BBC afforded some protection, but it may be better to be more wary of Letchford in future.

"What are you going to do?" Jane asked the girl.

"Whatever he wants," she said in a matter-of-fact voice.

Jane didn't know what to say. Heather was shy and young, but she didn't really come across as naïve. "You could get on a train and go somewhere else tomorrow," she suggested.

"Jane," Heather said with a sudden look of wisdom or maybe inevitability on her face. "When you are twenty-five and work in bars, there are Letchfords wherever you go. I'm going to do my best to keep away from the old creep, but if it happens, it happens."

Jane realised there was no point pursuing this further. "You landed on your feet with Quentin though," she said, changing the subject. "He's a bit of all right." She dug her elbow into the other girl's ribs playfully.

"He's nice, yes," said Heather, "but he doesn't seem that interested in me. I think he likes the idea of me more than he actually likes *me*."

"What do you mean?" Jane asked.

"Well, tonight for example. We go out, he introduces me to

complete strangers and then disappears. Sometimes I get a taxi and go home, but if I stick about, he might reappear. I would dump him, but he's my boss, and I sorta need this job after the base... you know."

"Yeah," said Jane, nodding.

"Is Ed the same?" Heather asked.

"Oh, he and I often end up going our different ways," Jane said.

"What's happened to the drinks anyway?" said Heather. "They'll be talking football or cricket, no doubt," the girl added, scanning the surroundings.

"Knowing Ed, I very much doubt that," said Jane, but she also looked around and could see neither. "I'll get us a drink." From her bag, Jane retrieved her purse.

"I need to go to the loo," said Heather.

"Want me to come?" Jane asked.

Heather blushed again, for the first time in a while. She turned and said, "I'm...I'm not...Jane, I like guys."

Jane looked at Heather and laughed. "Me too, hun. I'm guessing Quentin told you what I said last time we met?"

"Well, yeah, it's all he has talked about since," said the crimson-faced young girl.

"I was pulling their legs. You are drop-dead gorgeous and you really need to smile more often, but I like my partners to have a little more...er...penis," Jane said, and the two of them laughed.

"Oh, thank God," said Heather, the ice broken. "I have been bricking it all night that you were about to make a move."

Jane said, "Well, get another couple of drinks down me and you never know." The two laughed again. Jane thought Heather's mirth was mostly out of relief. *Poor sod*, she thought as she headed for the bar.

Being served by a girl who looked a lot like Heather but was shorter and plumper, Jane realised that whoever employed the staff had a type. The girl handed over the bottle, and Jane asked, "Have you seen Quentin anywhere?"

The girl chuckled. "He's busy upstairs."

"Okay, thanks," said Jane, wondering what on earth that meant. She collected the bottle from the bar and headed back over to the table just as Heather returned.

"What goes on upstairs?" Jane asked.

Heather scowled. "Why do you ask?"

"I think your boyfriend and my hubby are up there."

"Does Ed like to game?" Heather asked and Jane nodded. "Well, Quentin has been known to take girls up there, but he also has a sixty-inch gaming system, so I'm guessing they're playing something."

"The girl behind the bar laughed when I asked where they were," Jane said with a furrowed brow.

"Was it Mandy?" Heather asked, as if Jane knew them all by name. She pointed out the plump girl. "Heather stood and walked over to talk with the barmaid. Even from here, Jane could tell that they didn't like each other. Heather headed back and the other girl was watching her go with a smirk on her face.

"That bitch," Heather said on her return.

Jane asked, "What's up?"

"Mandy has been lusting after Quentin for years. The two of us were friends, but she turned all weird when I started dating him. I bloody well asked her if it was okay before I did. She said she was cool but…" Heather tailed off, shaking her head in place of words.

"And the guys?" Jane asked.

"Mandy said they picked up a couple of goth girls in the bar and now all four are upstairs." It perplexed Jane that Heather didn't really seem bothered, while she thought it highly unlikely that Ed had disappeared upstairs for a romp with a goth. A girl goth, anyway.

Jane pointed to the ceiling. "Are we allowed up there?"

"Yes," said Heather, "but do you really want to know what is going on?"

After thinking for a while, Jane texted Ed, asking where he was. He didn't respond. "Fuck it," she said. "I'm going. You don't have to come along, but show me the way."

Heather led them past the toilets to a door marked private. She typed a code into the keypad and said, "Top of the stairs." Standing, she held the door but moved no further. Jane considered if any of what was going on up there was her business. She realised that she was checking on Quentin more than Ed, maybe. No doubt Ed would be sitting with a game controller in hand, but what was Quentin doing with two goths while his lovely girlfriend sat downstairs? It then dawned on her that he did this deliberately. He assumed she was really interested in his girlfriend, and he left the two to go about their business. It turned out that the apple didn't fall far from the tree in the Letchford family.

"Sorry, Heather. I might have caused all of this," she said, deciding not to elaborate.

"Jane," said Heather, "the reason he and I have had an on and off relationship is that he has done this before. He doesn't even bother to hide it from me."

Jane started up the stairs. The loud bass sound of gaming music came from a door at the top. Reaching it, she found herself to be nervous for some reason. There was a part of her that didn't want to know what Quentin was up to. Yet, the reporter in her had to see. She walked in. The room was dark except for the flashing lights from the huge screen. Two silhouetted figures sat in front, the cacophony of sound from the TV made them oblivious to her presence.

She walked over behind the pair, intending to scare the shit out of them. Only then did she see the other two figures on the sofa. Neither were clothed. Quentin lay flat out while the other shadowy figure was working and sweating above him. It was Ed.

Panic seized her. She had to get out of here. Backing away toward the door, one of the gaming goth girls turned her head, seeing movement. She smiled and waved to Jane.

Still shocked, Jane mouthed, "Bye," as she exited.

For the longest time, she stood, dumbstruck at the top of the stairs, considering whether to go back in there and kick the shit out of Ed. *What was he thinking?*

"Are you okay?" Heather said from below.

"I will be after a shit ton of drink," Jane said, descending. "Is there a hotel in the village?"

"No, next one over, but you would have to drive," Heather explained.

"That's the problem, girl. I would be gone already if I was sober, but my driver is upstairs shagging, and I'm needing out of here," Jane said. She decided not to say *who* Ed was coupling with, leaving Heather believing the goths were involved.

"You can stay with me," Heather said, pointing to herself.

"You got drink and Abba?" Jane asked.

"Drink, yes, I nick it from here. Abba? I am sure we can get some oldies going on Spotify," Heather said.

"Well, get your jacket. You've pulled," said Jane, and the two girls laughed as they headed out.

London, Tuesday 24th December 2024

Jane took her swimsuit, four pairs of trousers, three blouses and her running shoes back out of the case. It was destination Mum's for Christmas, and hopefully to catch up with Duncan. Also, in need of a serious head clearing, it was time to leave London.

The rattling diesel taxi coughed up outside. Pulling on her coat, she went down to the cold December Street. Ice coated the frost-cracked paving stones. Her high heels were not exactly the best at handling these conditions, but she made her precarious way to the cab.

What happened in Mentford still commanded her thoughts, but she couldn't figure why it irked so. Okay, she fancied Quentin, but that wasn't the reason they were at the cricket club. Or was it? Was she annoyed that he hadn't taken *her* up to the games room? She couldn't have done that with Heather sitting downstairs, could she? Maybe it was best to swerve her own question. "Am I the bitch here?" she enquired under her breath.

The taxi driver said, "Sorry, dear?"

"Nothing," Jane replied and then, "Drop me here. This is fine."

She navigated the mayhem that was King's Cross Station just before Christmas and was relieved to see her train was running. The unions and train companies locked horns in their three-year-old wage dispute. The filthy, spluttering, decrepit train sat on platform eight with a young boy writing *wash me please* in the caked mud coating the carriage's side. All around, lost tourists trailed wheelie luggage and got in the way of the locals that dashed about and shot disapproving looks at their mobile obstacles.

Jane stopped as she saw her boss, Dan, ahead. It looked like he and the woman that he was with were heading for the same train. Yep, they were boarding – Jane hung back, trying to remain out of sight.

"Bugger it," she cursed. The cabin she'd booked on the sleeper was in the section that Dan just boarded. Waiting until they were out of sight, she gave them another few minutes to get settled.

Then, sneaking on while checking up and down the train, she made a break for the safety of her allotted sanctuary. After locking the door behind her, the case was dumped on the table by the window. It was a family room, but she'd booked it all to herself. Being unsure if you were still doubled up in the single rooms with a random stranger, there was no way Jane would be doing that.

In desperate need of some booze, she wondered if her Clark Kent glasses would work on Dan. Finally deciding to wear them anyway, she went out to the passageway.

The chattering train made its way through the suburbs of London. She stood a while, mesmerised by the rhythm of the wheels clacking on the rails. Jane loved to be on the move. Trains and boats were better than planes, but she didn't mind them either, on shorter trips. Given the choice, driving would have been the option. As much as she enjoyed the transport, she hated airports and train stations. *Way too many people with too much time on their hands.* The train won out this time. Driving in mid-winter wasn't the cleverest of ideas.

Another train blasted past in the opposite direction and the air in the carriage seemed to disappear for half a second and then be replaced by a cool breeze.

Her mind returned to alcohol. Taking a random direction, she struck gold and, one carriage away, found the catering car with its small bar at the back. She sat at an empty table. A bit further down the carriage, there was a guy serving customers. Raising a finger for attention, Jane gave her best smile. He nodded her way before returning to his order-taking. Outside the dirt smeared window, the suburban streetlights rushed by as they thinned and then finally disappeared.

Two minutes later, the waiter sauntered up to her. In a Glasgow accent, he asked, "What can I get you?"

"I'll have a G&T. Oh, and one for my friend too, please. He'll also have a bottle of beer."

"Becks okay?" the waiter asked. She nodded. He headed off to the bar, and to Jane's dismay, Dan and the mysterious woman entered the car, taking a seat on the other side of the corridor. She opened her book and held it as high as she thought she could get away with. A few minutes later, the waiter returned with a tray and laid it on the table.

"Your friend delayed?" he asked, laying a drink out in front of each seat.

"Something like that," she mumbled in return. He asked for her cabin number and then turned to serve Dan.

Jane took a long sip of her drink behind her book. Out of the corner of her eye, she saw Dan slip something to the waiter and then whisper.

The waiter turned back sheepishly and said, "Sorry, miss, but the couple at the next table would really like your autograph."

She looked up at him and said, "Tell them to fuck off."

The poor guy looked horrified, but Dan roared with laughter. "Miss Clark, you wee goat shagger. What are you doing here?" Uninvited, he and the woman stood and took the seats opposite. Jane did her best not to look disappointed. She dog-eared her book, closed it and laid it down near the condiments.

The woman with Dan said, "Sorry, are you expecting company?" pointing to the drink in front of her. Dan took it and the one in front of him and slid them over to Jane.

"No, dear," he said. "Jane is hiding her drinking problem from the waiter." And he laughed again. Jane was about to jump to her own defence and say she was saving the guy a few trips, but realised Dan wasn't far off the mark.

"Where are you off to?" she asked Dan.

"Me and my lovely wife here…oh sorry, Jane, Samantha… Samantha, Jane," he said in introduction. "Samantha and I are off to the Lake District for Christmas."

"I have family there," Samantha added.

Jane took a swig from the bottle of beer. The waiter hadn't offered a glass. It didn't bother her when she was drinking alone, but now, in front of Samantha, it felt a bit stereotypically Scottish. The waiter returned with the couple's drinks and looked at the three glasses sat before Jane.

"Could I get a glass for the beer?" she asked. The waiter nodded and headed off.

"You'll be getting the best of attention from waiter boy," Dan said. "I told him you were the UK's biggest porn star." Dan guffawed. Samantha looked a bit embarrassed. Noticing his wife's discomfort, Dan said, "Don't worry about Jane, dear. She has thick skin." Jane had to agree with her boss. You didn't work for Dan for all these years without building up huge callouses.

"You going home?" Dan asked.

"Yeah, off to Mum's for Christmas," Jane replied.

"That'll be nice," Samantha chipped in.

Although she'd dreaded meeting them, the night went by pleasantly enough and it wasn't long before Dan and Samantha were getting up to alight. Jane stood and Samantha gave her a hug. Jane really liked the woman. She wasn't like Dan at all.

The couple headed for the open door, but Dan reversed. "Jane," he said, and the smile vanished from his face.

"Yes, boss," She anticipated a joke or insult.

"Stay on Letchford's good side. Change is coming, and being on the other side may well be…detrimental." He kissed her and said, "Have a good Christmas, dear." She stood as he walked out onto the sodium-lit platform. The door clicked closed, and the train was on the move before Jane could process his words.

"Bollocks." She sat back down. Out of the side of her eye, she saw the waiter and his infantile colleagues nudge each other and point when they thought she was not looking. It was strange they seemed less likely to approach a porn star than they would have a reporter.

She caught his eye and waved as seductively as she thought a wave could be. The beaming waiter walked over after being encouraged to do so by his mates. With her sweetest smile, she said, "Hey, stud, bring me another round, please," and winked at him.

Edinburgh, Friday 27th December 2024

Duncan drove into the office car park. Slumped in the passenger seat, Jane watched the all-too-familiar streets of Edinburgh go by.

"Here are the ghosts of my misspent youth," she said to him in her best documentarian's voice.

"Mine too, sis, mine too," he said, sighing in regret.

"You were never around." Jane looked over to her brother.

He said nothing for a while but stared into the middle distance. A car horn sounded, and a frown troubled his brow. "You were six years younger than me. At that age, it feels like a lifetime. I didn't want to have anything to do with you." She could see hurt in his eyes. "And all of a sudden you were gone. Gone on this compulsion to be someone. To be something. I never understood." He turned to Jane. "I'm sorry. Can you forgive me?"

"Forget it, Dunky. Water under the bridge. You can make it up to me by taking me out on the town and getting me pissed, but first, I want to see where my big bro works."

Duncan opened the locked doors. The solicitor's office was closed for Christmas like most of the offices on the Mile. The pubs were open though – this was Scotland. Jane got a tour which ended on the top floor and Duncan's office.

"So, this is where the magic happens?" she said.

"Well, I am not sure how much magic there is, but here is where it takes place." Duncan waved a hand round and walked over to his desk. He picked up a file and threw it down beside her.

"What's this?" she asked. He pointed to the manila folder. "That's everything we could find on your mystery couple."

Jane sat and opened the folder. Colin and Hannah Burton; he was forty, and Hannah twenty-one.

"He likes them young," she said. Neither had any convictions, no high-profile job, no media connections, and it turned out Hannah was Colin's third wife. "Nothing really here."

"Nope. It all looks pretty clean, but in my game, you realise people look clean until they're not. I'll keep running him to check. Are you going to tell me what he did?" Duncan asked.

"Duncan, my sweet brother, you didn't speak to me for half my life, and I wouldn't want to go back to that. So, let's keep it a mystery." She smiled.

A look of resignation crossed his face, and he said, "Fair enough." He took the folder back, filing it into the drawer.

"Dunc?" Jane said, chuckling. He already knew she wanted something. "Take a look at this." She handed him a piece of paper with the numbers from Letchford's letter. "I know they're phone numbers but is there any way to find out whose phone it is?"

He quickly scanned the piece of paper. "Not if whoever owns the number doesn't want to be found. There are half a dozen News of the World reporters in jail for handling stuff like this."

"I haven't done anything with it," said Jane. "Apart from the four of us that found it, you are the only other person that knows it exists."

"Have you tried Googling the numbers?" he asked.

"Yeah, nothing." She shook her head.

He looked again and raised his eyebrow in some sort of recognition. Sitting behind the desk, he wiggled the mouse, rousing his PC out of sleep mode. He typed something and then said to her, "They're not phone numbers. They've been made to look like it, but they have too many digits, even for a mobile. If you replace the dial code with the banking country prefix and then type them in, this comes up." He swivelled the screen so that she could see. The first number was a bank account in Brazil. After typing all others in, he said, "Yup, bank accounts. I can't check the Russian one, but I'd bet it is too."

"Can you get any details on them?" She leaned over his desk.

"Not without ending in jail." He clicked his browser closed and put the PC back to sleep. "Now, little missy, you are buying the first three rounds for all this free private eye work you have me doing."

He stood up and lifted Jane onto his shoulder. Duncan carried her down the stairs, screaming. Jane protested, but she loved having a big brother – even if he was a bully.

Christchurch, Thursday 13th February 2025

Dana stood outside the count, the collar of her knee-length jacket turned up against the night. On the other side of the cameras, Jane was getting a coffee from the mobile catering van. She stamped her feet and clapped her gloved hands. The producer looked over to find the source of the noise on his set. He raised a finger to his lips, and Jane mouthed, "Sorry." This was going to be a long night.

The producer counted down and cued Dana in. She was reporting for the BBC flagship ten o'clock news.

"And now, here in Christchurch, as the polls close, the eyes of the UK are upon us. The Government of National Unity didn't want this election, and they fought hard to postpone or delay, but a rebel group in the Conservative Party voted with the opposition, and so here we are. Twenty-three candidates stood, but only one name was on everyone's lips. Boris Jenkins. After accepting the inevitable defeat in Parliament, the government offered Boris the chance to stand on the National Unity ticket, but he declined and stood as the Conservative candidate instead. There are few that believe he will not win here tonight. With Tory ratings falling to 29% nationally, some are predicting that Boris has won 70% of the vote. I'll now hand you over to Richard in the newsroom for more."

Dana was counted out. Jane waved to her, but the anchor was in conversation with the producers, as the focus would be back here later in the bulletin.

Jane was here to do interviews and pieces for the BBC all-night coverage. Across the site, Ed stood talking with other cameramen and techs. The two of them had hardly spoken since *that* night in Mentford. *Sod him*, Jane thought and crushed her empty coffee cup.

What she wanted to do was scream at him and maybe give him a slap or three.

Jane, Ed and Dana used to be thick as thieves, but they hadn't socialised at all this year. Out of the three, Jane was the only one not to jump into bed with a Letchford. The most annoying thing about the whole situation was that neither of her friends had really done anything wrong, but still, it rankled.

Dana was preparing for an update piece. Sticking two fingers in her mouth, she produced an ear-shattering whistle. It was her trademark. The chatting techs looked up to see who she beckoned.

She shouted, "Ed, come do my camera for this bit." He picked up his machine and walked over.

Despite her latent anger, Jane longed to repair the cracks between them. After they finished their report, she plucked up the courage to go over. While Dana was talking to the producer, Ed turned to Jane and said, "Hey, girl. How are you doing?"

"I'm okay," she said with little enthusiasm as he laid the camera down and gave her a hug. With arms around her tightly, he lifted her feet off the ground. She kissed his neck and whispered, "Sorry."

"Sorry for what, babe?" he asked.

"For everything." With that, she broke down in tears.

He returned her to the ground and put his arm around her. After leading her over to a heated area with tables, he went off to get them a couple of coffees. She dried her eyes with a tissue and watched Ed Walk back over, stopping to beckon Dana.

"What's the matter?" Dana said.

Not really knowing how to answer. Shrugging, Jane just repeated, "Sorry."

Ed sat. "What are you apologising for?"

It was comforting that he'd reverted to his Edinburgh voice. Dabbing her eyes, she looked at him. "Sorry for dumping you in Mentford."

"Dumping me?" He hunched his shoulders. "I didn't know you did. I assumed you hooked up with someone and left. I got a lift back to London from a couple of goth girls that I met at the party."

"But you must have noticed that I have been avoiding you…" Jane turned to Dana. "Both."

Ed shook his head. "I guessed you were busy, and I knew you were back up home a while. Sorry, Jane, I honestly didn't know anything was wrong." He reached over the table and took her hand.

Dana spoke. "I sorta figured you were angry at me after seeing how you looked when you came to my new office. I'm guessing you are pissed I got promoted." She lowered her gaze.

"Not exactly," Jane admitted. "I'm not jealous you got promoted. You're fantastic and deserve to be." Jane paused, "It's the way it happened."

Dana's face flushed. Her nervous eyes moved back and forth between them. "You know?" She changed expression quickly and jumped to her own defence. "Look, I would have got here sooner or later. If this, er…greased the wheels a bit, then so be it, but that is not why it happened." Stoically, she stuck out her chin. "I love him, and I think he loves me. He said he'll leave his wife." Her resolution broke, and it was her turn to reach for a hanky. "Shit, I can't afford to blub," she sobbed. "I'm back on in a minute."

The three of them laughed and Jane remembered a thousand times before when they had laughed together.

Ed looked over at Dana and said what Jane was scared to. "You're in love with Letchford?"

She looked at him like an idiot. "Letchford? What has the Letch got to do with this?" Ed and Jane looked at Dana, baffled. "Oh my God," the Irish girl cried. "The text…you think I'm shacking up with Letchford." She screamed with laughter.

After she composed herself, she beckoned them close so that the trio had their heads together like naughty schoolkids. She whispered, "That old bugger has been trying it on for years, but he'll never get any. I'm shagging the boss, Dan." She broke out in hysterics again. Standing and mopping her eyes, Dana made her way back over to the set, shouting, "Letchford, for God's sake. LETCHFORD!"

Jane smiled for the first time in a while. She looked up to see a producer heading over.

"Jane, dear," he cried. "Dana is about to wrap up the regular news coverage. The result is in, and Boris has romped it. I want an interview with the man himself, and one from the Liberal that came second. Can you take Ed and hunt these guys down? Shout me when you are ready, and I will slot you into the broadcast. Okay, flower?"

"Will do, boss," said Jane.

Westminster, Monday 17th February 2025

The House was packed, nearly every seat taken. Members stood in doorways and in the aisles. Jenkins waited until a minister finished talking on housing and then walked in. As he was spotted from the government side, a huge cheer rose from those on the back benches. Many members waved papers in the air. The opposition benches were quiet, but a few stood, shouting aimlessly against the tumult. Fists shook, and irate arms waved, but these futile protests were drowned out in the sea of adulation.

BBC lunchtime news

"Jane Clark, reporting live from Westminster for the 12 o'clock news as Boris Jenkins returns to Parliament. The Conservative members are ecstatic, with some trying to hoist the prodigal son onto their shoulders. It is noticeable that the government front bench looks less enthusiastic, and the PM has chosen to be elsewhere. As the Speaker attempts to calm the room, Jenkins takes a seat in the top row and furthest left. Is it coincidental that he could be no further from the PM if he tried? Jane Clark, reporting from Westminster. Back to you, Clive."

"Aaaaaannd out," said the producer, waving an arm to emphasise the cut.

Visibly untensing, Jane exhaled, slumped back against a table and perched on the edge to relax. After carefully removing the microphone and earpiece, she handed them to the technician. Standing, she turned to find Selwyn Letchford eyeing her up and down. She was, of course, dressed conservatively for being on screen, but from the look in the MP's cold grey eyes, he could see right through her outfit.

"Jane, dear, magnificent as ever. Have you time to join me in the bar?" Letchford said.

"Sorry, sir," she replied, "I have another report to do."

"You haven't, Jane. I checked. Come." He put his hand around her back and guided her toward the stairs. She had little choice but to go with the man. "You look breathtaking as ever, dear. We really should get to be better friends."

"A reporter has to maintain a professional distance, Mr Letchford." She wriggled to increase the distance between them.

"Well, friendships often blossom when mutual..." He rubbed a finger over his chin. "..advancement is on the menu." He caressed her back slowly as they headed to a members' lounge. A man stood on the door but paid little attention to the couple entering. Jane's eyes took a second to adjust to the dim light. She saw only one table occupied, but Letchford released his hold and clapped his hands.

"Gentlemen, Miss Clark and I need some privacy, please." The men rose wordlessly and exited. "Take a seat, dear." The MP pointed to a table before heading off to get them a drink. He returned with a bottle and two glasses, pouring them large whiskies. The glass screeched as he slid one over the table and left it in front of her.

"Bottoms up!" he said, making her recall the Carry On films. If

Letchford had read the phone book, it would have sounded sleazy. Her drink went untouched.

"Jane, dear, perhaps we got off on the wrong foot. My intentions may have been misconstrued."

She looked him in the eye. "Oh, I am fairly sure they were really well construed, sir."

His eyes darkened a little before his gaze lowered to her chest. She really wanted to fasten the top button on her blouse but resisted.

"You are a fine reporter, and you deserve every success. We are more alike than you know. We came from the shadows. Backwaters where few rise to power." Letchford paused and looked round the room. "Other people aspire to this, Jane. You and I *need* it. We have to be here. This is what we were made for, but just as my constituents may one day decide on a better MP, your bosses will do likewise. I can't stop the hands of time, but I can slow them considerably. I can also help you reach your full potential. Not in a few years or even months. I can get you there in days, Jane."

He took a gulp of his whisky and replaced the glass on the table. Keeping his eyes fixed on it, he said, "I've made mistakes. Thankfully, there were people that had my back." He looked in her eyes. "I have your back and can make your mistakes go away. All I need in return is a little cooperation."

Jane felt a tremor run the length of her spine at his mention of mistakes.

"I'm not sure we have the same definition of cooperation, sir." She pulled her jacket closed a little. The action drew a smirk from him.

"Come on, Jane. You are like me. You don't settle for the mundane. You want this." He motioned his hand around. "Anyway, it is not as if you are a shrinking violet. Our mutual acquaintance,

Mr Burton, maintains that you are anything but." Letchford sneered.

"Burton?" Jane said, initially confused. Then a light flashed on inside her head. Colin Burton. The creepy moustache guy with the child-bride wife, for fuck's sake. Feeling herself blush, Jane went with, "I have no idea what you are talking about."

He looked at her, head tilted. "Oh Jane, I could easily provide a reminder if you wish? Shall I email the pictures to your office or your home?" Glee swam in his eyes. "The video is delectable by the way."

"Bastard." Slapping her hand against the table, she felt sick. As she'd feared, there were pictures, and of course, they'd be used to manipulate her. "So, what now?" she said, almost in a whisper.

He laid a hand on her shoulder. "Jane, this was nothing to do with me. That scumbag Burton does that sort of thing for a living. He hangs about venues where important people go and then drops a little something in their drink. Wham bam, thank you, ma'am. Then he hocks the pictures to the highest bidder. I've done you a huge favour and am now £5k out of pocket for it."

"My hero," she said cynically before taking a burning gulp of the smoky whisky. She repeated, "What happens now?"

He massaged her shoulder, and his eyes ran up and down her body. "I need your cooperation, that's all."

The limited options ran through her head. She could go to the police, but those pricks leaked like a sieve. The pictures would be in every newspaper the next morning. After suspension, she'd then be quietly released from a job she loved. Take this to Dan? That was a non-starter. Part of her knew that her boss was involved in this somehow.

Let the pictures come out and just fade into the background.

Yes, it would all blow over in a day or two, but her career would be done, and there would be no living with that.

She sighed. The Letch had her exactly where he wanted her. His eyes, locked on her, recognised her resignation, and a lurid smile lit his face.

More in desperation than in hope, she said, "I have conditions." She expected him to decline immediately, there being nothing in the way of leverage.

So, it was a surprise when he said, "Name them." He removed his hand, reached for the Islay Malt whisky bottle and recharged his glass. He wiggled the bottle in front of her face. She shook her head.

Jane sucked in a deep breath. "I will do nothing illegal. I will not lie on screen, and I need a 100%, cast-iron guarantee those pictures cannot appear anywhere."

He sat silently, looking at her. She could almost hear the cogs turn in his head. If she didn't know better, she would have sworn there was sympathy in his eyes.

To her surprise, "Accepted," he said.

She fought not to cry, but a tear welled up and ran down her cheek. Letchford leant forward and mopped it up with his finger.

"There, there, dear. I will take care of you. Burton will bother you no more."

Having expected him to press his advantage immediately, she was surprised when he stood. "Now, I will go do my side of the bargain and get rid of these pictures. You, dear, can go about your business. I will call when your…services are required." With that, Letchford headed for the door with a spring in his step.

Her head slumped to her hands. How could she now look anyone in the eye when she danced with the devil?

Edinburgh, Monday 24th February 2025

After carefully depositing his napkin-wrapped breakfast roll, Nancy turned and exited the office with an "Enjoy!" but her perfume lingered. Watching her depart, Duncan realised how used to the fragrance he had become and how well he liked it. The smell of the food took over, replacing her alluring floral mist.

Lowering the reading glasses to his nose, his daily routine resumed. The leather of the office chair creaked as the pages of the *Scotsman* newspaper were folded, unfolded and analysed. He cursed as a blob of runny egg landed on the article he was reading.

The papers reported the world constantly lurching from one catastrophe to another these days. He wondered if *Government in Crisis* was left on the typesetting machine permanently. Or pinned to the screen, more likely in this computer age.

Perusing the political machinations at Westminster, Duncan said, "Boris is causing trouble again." He rolled his eyes. "What a shock." He then moved on to world events. It appeared the war in Ukraine was not going well – unless you were a Russian.

The local news section looked void of anything interesting today, besides *Fatal car crash on isolated Highland road*. On reading the article, he was shocked to see that the driver was *thought to be Colin Burton, age 40, from London. The wife of the driver claims her husband did not come home from work on Tuesday and she had reported him missing to the local police on Thursday last week. The investigation continues.*

The name caught his eye. He went into his desk drawer and found the manila folder. Opening it, he read the name that his sister, Jane, had asked him to investigate.

"What are the chances?" he said. The newspaper showed a small and fuzzy picture of the missing man. He compared it to the file photo that the investigating team had tracked down. It was the same guy.

He immediately picked up his phone and called Jane.

"Hey, big bro, howzit hanging?" she said breezily on answering.

"Jane, is there anything you want to tell me?"

"Tell you what?" she asked, now serious.

"Do you want to tell me why I checked into Colin Burton for you last year?"

"Not particularly. What brought this on?"

"Your mystery man is lying dead in a ditch in remote Perthshire. Did you have him bumped off?" he laughed, but he quickly stopped as his sister didn't join in.

"Oh no," she said. "Duncan, I gotta go." He went to reply, but the line was dead.

London, Wednesday 5th March 2025

The toyed with breakfast cornflakes were more of a distraction than a meal. What was she going to do about Colin Burton's accident? Had it, in fact, even been an accident? Had she inadvertently called for his murder? If this were the case, then Letchford was a whole lot more dangerous than anticipated, and now she was in up to her neck.

Not sure she was ready to face the man, she inhaled deeply, then texted the MP, hoping they could meet during the day and clarify what was happening. If he released the pictures, her career was gone, and that would be bad enough, but now she may also be the chief suspect in a murder.

Jane got up, abandoning her cereal, and headed for the shower. It was likely to be another long shift at Westminster with all the ministrations that the government were doing to keep things in check.

Reluctantly exiting the soothing deluge, she walked, still wet, through to her bedroom to find a towel. As usual, she'd forgotten to replace the ones put in the wash yesterday. The flat felt warm before she showered, but now her teeth chattered a little, and goosebumps covered her skin.

Just then, her intercom buzzer went, and guessing it was the postman, she buzzed him in and began drying her hair with a small towel. There was a knock at the door. She was halfway there before remembering her state of undress. She wrapped the towel round herself and laughed at the lack of skin it covered. *Oh well*, she thought. *Give the postie a thrill.* She giggled as she opened the door but stopped laughing upon seeing who was there.

"Wow!" said Letchford. "I didn't realise you were so keen."

"Oh God," she cried, almost closing the door. Peering through the gap, she said, "What are you doing here? How did you get my address?"

"You said you needed me urgently, dear. Your knight in shining armour awaits!" As ever, Letchford sounded incredibly seedy.

"I was expecting to talk to you at work later," she said. "Again, how did you get this address?"

"That's for me to know…"

"Shit," she said. "Let me put something on."

"Don't go to any trouble on my account." He gave a low chuckle.

She headed for the bedroom. A creak made her look back over her shoulder to see the front door being pushed wide.

"Nice!" he said, leering, as she ran into the bedroom and got her dressing gown from the hook on the back of the door.

"Need any help?" came his sleazy voice from immediately

outside her bedroom. Jane tied the robe tight and opened the door. He stood six inches away from it.

"We need to talk," she said. He breathed her soapy fragrance in deeply. She pushed past and went to the breakfast bar in the open-plan kitchen.

She offered coffee, more as a reason to put distance between them than to service any need he had.

"No, thank you, dear. I'm in a rush," he said. "How may I be of assistance to you today?"

She really didn't know how to broach the subject tactfully, so dived straight in. "Sir, when I said to you that I needed to know the…video Burton took would never appear. What did that mean to you?"

"Have they turned up somewhere?" His face held genuine surprise.

"No," shaking her head, "but Burton has."

"Oh, I very much doubt that," said Letchford. "You have my assurance that he will not trouble you again. We have a deal, and I kept my side of the bargain."

"Oh God," she whispered, as A tremor ran through her.

He moved a little closer, his arms outstretched. "Jane, Jane, why so distressed? You are on my team now, and nothing bad happens to my team."

"You killed him." She clasped a hand over her mouth.

He stopped in his tracks as a strange look of uncertainty flitted across his ruddied face, but almost as soon as it arrived, the familiar, self-assured smile washed it away.

"Jane, I accepted your conditions and acted on them. The only existing copy of those pictures now resides in my files." He closed the distance between them further still. "I do so enjoy them, dear." With fear in her eyes, she reached for the coffee. The mug, held in front of her, was a small barrier. He took the cup out of her hand and laid it back down.

Seeing her distress, he said, "Everything will be all right." He stood only inches away with mint breath, almost concealing a telling whisky tang. Trying to retreat, she immediately bumped against the breakfast bar. She put her hands onto the edge to stabilise her week legs. Closing the gap once more, Letchford reached down and took hold of the belt that held her gown closed.

"We really must arrange another social evening. As much as I enjoy our work encounters, I do find them so…constraining." He tugged the belt, and her cotton robe fell open a few inches. "Thank you for inviting me over today, Jane. It's unfortunate that I must dash. I really would love to see more of you." His lurid eyes traversed her body. Time is not our friend today, dear." He slid the gown off her right shoulder and ran his fingers slowly along her clavicle.

Leaning forward, he pecked her on the cheek. "Sorry to kiss and run." He slowly walked out of the flat.

Propped up by the breakfast bar, Jane stood, barely moving for at least ten minutes. Shivers ran through her body, and a tear slid down her cheek.

* * *

Selwyn Letchford open his flip phone and dialled a number. "Dan, Letchford here. What's this I am hearing about Colin Burton?"

"He died in a car accident yesterday," Dan Lockwood replied while editing a fluff piece that would run on TV later today.

"Accident?" Letchford asked.

"You tell me. I'm not sure what you're implying, Letchford." Dan's full attention was now on the call with the pain-in-the-arse MP.

Letchford dialled it down a notch. "Sorry, Dan. The news was just a bit of a shock. I asked that you arrange for him to be kept quiet, and I thought you'd maybe misunderstood that I meant he was to be paid off."

Dan Lockwood smiled. "Letchford, I am placating myself with the thought that the man died in an unfortunate car accident, but if I were you, and inclined to think there was foul play involved, I may look closer to home before throwing accusations elsewhere." He ended the call.

Selwyn Letchford took the mobile phone from his ear and looked at it as if he'd never seen the thing before.

He chuckled. His given task was to persuade Jane to be sympathetic to the return of Boris Jenkins. His own little side project was to bed the beauty. Someone seemed to be making both tasks way too easy.

Croydon, Thursday 6th March 2025

The burning clutch smell that emanated from the lorry in front overpowered Jane as the traffic slowly snaked through Croydon's characterless urban sprawl.

On finally arriving at the crematorium, she sat in the car, biting her expensively manicured nails, a habit successfully avoided until two days ago. Had cigarettes been available, she would be smoking them now. Calling in sick today, she felt unable to face people at work, but she couldn't stay away from this, the funeral for the man she killed.

This morning, before setting off, an internal debate went back and forth on the wisdom of this trip. At the moment, maybe two or three people on the planet could link Jane Clark with Colin

Burton. Now, she may add dozens more. No matter how ill-advised this excursion was, it proved impossible to stay away.

With the incognito glasses donned, Jane, dressed head to foot in black, strolled across the car park to the building, where a crowd of about thirty people lingered. She wandered over and spoke to a man, standing apart from the crowd, drawing deeply on a cigarette.

"Hi, is this Colin's service?" Jane said, pointing to the doors.

"Yeah," he replied. "They're running late." He flicked ash that caught on the breeze, and some landed on Jane's jacket. With a look of disdain, her nibbled nails brushed it away. The smoker shrugged a wordless apology, then paid for his exertion with a ripping cough. Jane turned away.

As she considered whether Colin Burton's ash would be as easily discarded from her conscience, the ornate, wrought iron crematorium doors swung open, and a sombre man ushered the waiting mourners inside. She sat at the rear of the hall, staying as far from the others as possible.

Some identikit funeral music played softly until the minister took to the podium. He stood, head bowed to the patchwork pool of colour that streamed through the stained glass window above his head and onto the floor below the rostrum.

As the tune faded away, "Friends, family, we are here to commemorate a life cut short…"

It was all standard fare. A couple of speakers, a few hymns, and lies about how the man in the box was the nicest person who ever walked the earth.

When the ceremonial charade concluded, Jane hung back as the other mourners tearfully shuffled out. Upon her reaching the exit, a hoped-for incognito flight was foiled, as Hannah and two other people stood and shook the hands of all who attended. Jane kept her head low and mumbled banal niceties to the older couple that she assumed were Burton's parents. She tried saying nothing to Hannah, only briefly shaking her hand.

"Jane?" said Hannah, and Jane's heart sank. Hannah leaned forward and whispered, "Are you here…working?"

Jane stepped back, waving open palms. "No, no, not at all." Oh my *God, I wish a hole would open in the ground and swallow me up.*

A scowl crossed the young girl's face. "Then why are you here? How long did you two…er, know each other?"

Jane sucked in a deep breath. "Can we speak outside?"

With the line finished and their ceremonial duties over, Hannah nodded to her colleagues and then walked out into the garden behind the building. Even though every fibre of her body told her to run, Jane followed.

"I didn't expect any…I didn't know you were coming," Hannah said. "His death hasn't made the press down here."

"I'm not here as a member of the press. I came because…" Jane couldn't finish the sentence. *I came because I killed Colin*, would have been closest to the truth. A pregnant pause hung in the air. "I never met him before…that night," she said. The two stood surrounded by roses. The pungent fragrance caused Jane to sneeze.

"Bless you," Hannah said.

Jane put her gloved hand on Hannah's. "I came to say…sorry, about that night."

The girl relaxed a little and looked down at her black high-heel shoes. "How did you meet?"

"I have no idea," said Jane, looking into Hannah's eyes. There was no shock at the statement. Jane waited for Hannah to say something, but the other girl had averted her gaze and was scanning the horizon aimlessly. "You must have the wake now," said Jane. "Can we meet another time and talk?"

Hannah grew agitated again. "Talk about what?"

"About Colin," Jane replied.

Releasing a long-held breath, Hannah finally said, "Come to the house tonight. I will be home by seven." After staring long into Jane's eyes, she sighed and walked back over to the older couple.

* * *

Jane arrived at six thirty. Parked outside, she felt a little sick just looking at the façade of Burton's house. A peculiar revelation hit her after talking to Hannah at the funeral. She had begun to realise that Colin had really raped her. Until today, in Jane's mind, it'd been some sort of unfortunate incident – but the fucker had drugged her, dragged her home and raped her, before capturing it all on camera.

"He deserved to die," she said to herself forcefully, turning the key in the ignition as there was nothing more to discuss with Burton's wife. Hannah was complicit or at least knew full well what kind of man she was married to. Just as she was about to drive off, Hannah waved from the upstairs window. The newly found venom subsided, and Jane's determination wilted.

Hannah stood in her hallway and pointed toward the all-too-familiar kitchen. With some hesitancy, Jane pushed open the door and went in. The room held a table and six chairs she hadn't seen last time. As Hannah entered, Jane asked, "This new?"

"Err, yeah, arrived yesterday," she said before asking, "Coffee?"

"Black and strong," said Jane. While Hannah fiddled with a coffee maker, Jane took a seat.

"I'm…sorry for your loss, Hannah." Jane remembered that she hadn't said it earlier today.

"Thank you." The young girl brought two large, mismatched mugs of coffee to the table. She laid one in front of Jane and hugged the other to herself, her hands wrapped in the extended sleeves of her sweater. Hannah was a bit shorter than Jane. Long, curly blonde hair cascaded over her shoulders. The baggy sweater carried on below her waist, a denim skirt ended just above her knees. Thick black cotton tights and large Snoopy slippers completed a probably well-thought-out, 'just something I threw on' look. Heavily made up earlier, her face was now product free. Jane thought she was pretty in a plain, girl-next-door way.

After thinking through a hundred subtle methods to find out what Hannah knew about the whole situation, Jane jumped straight in with, "Colin drugged and…raped me."

Hannah pulled out a chair and took a seat. There was no shock on her face, but Jane was certainly surprised when she replied, "It doesn't matter now. He's dead."

Was Hannah in shock? "You're handling it well," was the best response Jane could muster at short notice.

"What's that supposed to mean?" Hannah's eyes scrunched to slits.

"Nothing, sorry. I only meant that you are bearing up. This must be a hard time for you," Jane replied, and Hannah's shoulders lowered back to a relaxed position. Jane walked into the house to confront the woman about her assault and now found herself apologising. This wasn't going to plan.

"Can I show you something?" Hannah said, pulling out her phone. Jane didn't answer, but Hanah shuffled her chair noisily over the wood floor and pulled up alongside her. Jane looked down at the screen, seeing Hannah was typing in the address of a porn site. She entered 'Trixi doll' into the search bar, which brought up 512 results. The girl sucked in a deep breath. "He did to me what happened to you, three years ago. I was out celebrating my eighteenth birthday. I come from a strict, religious family and had never drunk alcohol. My friends were having fun and drinking, but I stuck to orange juice while we all danced." Hannah's eyes went a little misty; Jane could see the girl remembering better times. "Colin came over and offered to buy us all drinks. The girls accepted, and when he returned, he sat with us. I noticed he wasn't drinking either. He claimed that he didn't.

"Me and drink don't get on," he said. He pulled out chewing gum and put a piece in his mouth before offering me one." Hannah went quiet a long while. "I woke next day in bed with Colin and two of my friends. We were, well, much the same as you were here last time we met." Hannah spread her hands to show she meant the kitchen. "Well," she continued, "Colin blackmailed all three of us into…performing, but then someone showed the videos to my dad. My parents threw me out and told me never to return. They wouldn't listen to what I had to say. Having nowhere to go and no money, I came back here." Hannah pointed to her surroundings. "Been here ever since." The girl looked down and shut off the phone.

"After a while, he stopped doing it for kicks and moved into blackmail. He got the idea from a victim who offered £250 to delete the footage. As time went on, the price got higher, and Colin started hanging about people he knew could pay more. I was largely forgotten after the wedding. He only married me as some sort of cover. He thought it gave him respectability. Occasionally, I would be required to perform with the…others…but it was all about money now. He even started bringing other guys back and blackmailing them too. Sorry, Jane, you were just another payday to him." With that, Hannah threw her phone against the wall.

"That bastard is dead, and I am nothing but glad." Hannah's stoic expression faded, and her eyes welled with tears. "But the internet lives forever. I'll never be free of him."

Jane stood, walked over behind Hannah and put her arms around the girl. Hannah sobbed a while, as Jane considered her next move.

"Hannah…I think I killed your husband." There it was. Out there. If this girl had any sense, tomorrow's news headline would be *BBC reporter charged with murder*. She already regretted the confession. Maybe she thought it would help end Hannah's suffering, but she was just glad the bastard was dead. Jane hugged Hannah tightly while the young girl sobbed uncontrollably. Tears and probably snot landed on Jane's hands, but she didn't move them.

Then Hannah whispered something that changed everything. "You didn't…I did."

Jane released the girl and retrieved two glasses, filling them with cold water. She made Hannah drink one.

"I killed the bastard," Hannah said with sodden, hateful eyes.

"What do you mean, Hannah?"

Her red-ringed eyes met Jane's. "You're going to have to turn me in. I've probably said enough."

"Please," Jane said, "I need to know what happened."

Hannah's head sank once more. "I was out visiting Carol the night he took you back to the house. She's one of the friends from the birthday party, and Colin is…Colin was still blackmailing her. He didn't release her videos as long as she kept paying him £500 a month. She's been paying for three years now. I was supposed to be staying over, but Carol was unwell at work and then tested positive for COVID. So, I turned round and came home. Carol texted me on the way back to say we would never be free of Colin until he was dead. While stopped to read the text, I remembered that Colin kept his drugs in the glove compartment of the car.

He uses a liquid for drinkers but has drugged chewing gum for other people. I never noticed the night he got me, but he switches the packets after taking one himself. So, I switched the packets back. To be honest, I thought he would take one, get drugged and then come back here and beat me senseless, but he must have taken one while driving to collect a pay-off in Scotland. He had a victim up there that he claimed was seventeenth in line to the throne." Hannah raised her eyebrows. "They were paying him £15k a month, always in cash."

Letchford paid Burton £5k. Jane now realised that was probably a monthly fee.

"Hannah, I'm not sure it happened the way you think," Jane said. Hannah's eyes brightened.

"What do you mean?" she asked.

"Well, I've…friends that weren't pleased with your husband, and to be honest with you, I really don't know if the chewing gum got him or if they did, but I'll tell you something now. Even if you're correct, he brought it on himself by drugging the chewing gum in the first place. You didn't force him to eat it. He may have picked the wrong packet in error. I need you to forget everything you've said tonight and leave this house. Once it's common knowledge he's dead, some of the people he blackmailed are going to come looking for their footage. Have you got somewhere to go?" Jane asked.

Hannah looked around the room, almost wistfully. "No."

"Pack a bag," said Jane. "You're coming with me." Burton's, not so grieving wife smiled for the first time that night. She leapt up and started for the door.

"Hannah," Jane said, pointing to the pine furniture. "Why did you buy this table?"

The girl stopped in the doorway and shook her head. "I didn't. Colin ordered it after watching the recording of you and I talking here." She pointed to a cabinet at the far end of the room. There was a camera on it. "He thought it might be exciting to use other places for filming the… action."

Jane massaged the muscles on the back of her neck and said, "Bollocks!" She now wondered if Letchford had all the footage.

Back in Jane's flat, the two of them sat on the mustard leather sofa and began bingeing *Friends* on Netflix. The young girl had never heard of the TV series, and the more Jane talked with her unexpected new flatmate, the more she realised that Hannah never enjoyed any sort of life at all. Hannah burst into loud laughter at Joey being Joey. She appeared to be transformed for now, but Jane knew the pain was yet to come.

Westminster, Friday 7th March 2025

Jane drove into the Parliament car park. Letchford stood in the visitor space that she'd been allocated. He smiled and waved her in. *Putting my head back in the lion's mouth*, she thought.

"We really can't go on meeting like this," he said in his inimitably sleazy way. "But my damsel calls, and I am obligated to ride to her rescue."

"Sir," she said as she made to step out of the car. "I have a request of a rather personal nature."

"If it is within my power, dear, it's yours." Taking her hand, he helped her to her feet.

Okay, here goes nothing, she thought. "Sir, would it be possible for me to view the…the film that Colin Burton made?"

Letchford said nothing at first, but he was a transparent thinker.

The MP was weighing up the reasons she might have made the request and if it would disadvantage him to acquiesce. His internal cogs ground to a halt, and the condescending smile took control of his features once more.

"Why, of course, dear," he replied. Although surprised once more by his concession, Jane didn't react; she knew the price was yet to be negotiated. "But I don't carry it on my person. I have to protect our little agreement, dear. Meet me tonight at eight, at the Randolf. I'll send a car for you at half seven."

It was Jane's turn to weigh the options. Did it really matter if an image of her naked in a kitchen was released? Perhaps, especially if the location was identified as belonging to a man who recently passed in unexplained circumstances. Yes, she would be finished.

This was the game; Letchford held all the cards, and she still wanted a seat at the table.

"That sounds fine, sir. See you there." She heard herself respond, even before the internal misgivings faded. BBC Jane would do all she could to keep things as they were. *Are you sure about that?* Edinburgh Jane tried to add, but her voice was drowned out.

London, Friday 7th March 2025

"You'll be okay?" Jane asked Hannah as they hugged on the street outside the flat.

"Yeah – thanks for everything," Hannah said.

"You know that you can stay as long as you like?"

Hannah nodded. "I know, but it's time to get my life started." A long black limo pulled up as they spoke. "Wow," said Hannah, "this must be a fancy bash." She scanned Jane up and down, and you look like a million dollars."

"Thank you," said Jane as they hugged again. "You come right back here anytime." She wagged a finger at the younger girl.

"I'm going to be fine," said Hannah. "Now get yourself off to your party. I'll call in the next couple of days. Maybe we can go for a coffee or something?"

"I'd like that," said Jane. She kissed the girl's cheek. Jane stood and watched as Hannah headed down the road. "Be safe, Hannah," she said softly. In a very short time, Jane found herself fond of the girl. Hannah was a curious mixture of vulnerability and stoicism. She'd seen the worst of life and very little of its upside. Jane decided she would do something to redress that balance.

After watching Hannah turn the corner and disappear from view, she crossed the pavement and stooped to enter the back seat of the black limo.

On arriving at the Randolf, she was greeted. "Good evening, Miss Clark. This way, please." Jane looked round to see a blonde girl stood by a door on her right. The girl opened it and ushered Jane through.

"Mr Letchford is waiting for you, miss," she said. They walked side by side through the opulent, luxuriously carpeted space. Fresh-cut flowers adorned every table, the panelled walls held portraits that should be available to all in the National Gallery, and a multitude of rooms led off the main corridor, each filled with people in cocktail dresses and evening suits. Mirth and laughter were all around. *More trappings of compromise*, Jane reminded herself.

As of this morning, her bank balance was a healthy £94671.26. She was well paid. *Okay, about ten bloody per cent of what Gary fucking Lineker got for watching football*, but she wasn't really complaining…much. *Anyway*, thought Jane, *compared to ordinary humans, I do all right, but I'm still willing to bet that I am the poorest person in this building tonight.*

The girl opened a door and pointed to another at the end of the corridor.

"You can change here, Miss Clark," she said and smiled. "Will you need any assistance?"

Slightly shocked, Jane asked, "Change into what?"

"A swimsuit," the girl replied. "You're meeting Mr Letchford in our pool. I'll be just through here. Call if you need anything," she said, pointing Jane through the door and closing it behind her.

Finding herself in a changing room, Jane looked about, dumbfounded. Her newly suspicious mind wondered if cameras lay behind the mirrors. A box waited for her on a small table, and she flipped open the lid. Inside, there lay a tiny purple swimsuit and a note. *You look so good in purple. S X.*

"Fuck!" Jane said.

"I didn't catch that," came from outside.

"Sorry, nothing," said Jane.

The girl pulled open the door, not even bothering to check that Jane was decent. "Do you need help changing?" she asked.

"What's your name?" Jane asked.

"Martha...Martha Mcbride."

"You are a Mcbride?" Jane said. "You don't sound Scottish or Irish."

The girl chuckled and changed to a Dundee accent. "They dinna approve o' it doon here."

They both laughed and Jane stood, holding out her hand.

"Jane Clark, Edinburgh."

"Everyone knows you," Martha said, shaking it. She had switched back to 'proper' English.

"Martha," Jane said, "I am bricking it here. I can't go out there in...this." Jane held up the purple string that passed as a swimsuit.

Martha looked at it and then at Jane. "It wouldn't cover much of...those," Martha said, pointing at Jane's full chest. The girl smiled and said, "I'll be back in a tick."

Sitting down, Jane kicked off her sandals before Martha returned, holding up a light green one-piece swimsuit. It was still skimpy, but compared to the other option, she loved it.

"It looks fantastic, Martha. Thank you," Jane said, taking it from the girl.

"My gran sent it for my Christmas present. Bit too big for me, but looks your size," Martha said, before hastily amending, "Sorry, sorry! That came out wrong. You have an awesome figure." She blushed.

"No offence taken, you skinny bitch." Jane smiled, and Martha laughed in relief.

Finally changed, Jane put her outdoor clothes in the provided basket and handed it to Martha. The swimmer stored them in a locker and said, "Find me when you are ready to leave." Martha led Jane through a door on the far end of the changing room. They exited onto a tiled surface and were immediately assailed by the music.

The girl put her lips to Jane's ear. "Follow me."

Martha walked slowly round the circular pool. Jane padded a few feet behind and took in the goings-on. She recognised many faces at each poolside table. Politicians, sports people, actors, celebs and...*oh, bloody hell*, Letchford, Quentin and Heather.

"Bollocks," she exclaimed, but it went unheard over the racket that was the music.

Now wiggling her athletic rear as if on the catwalk, Martha made a beeline for the glass cubicle where the three sat.

On a sun lounger, Letchford reclined, his hands behind his head, with eyes intently scanning the surroundings. He wore stripey trunks and a plain white shirt, unbuttoned and open. Behind the MP, the adonis, Quentin, sported a tiny pair of Speedos and sunglasses for some apparent reason in the darkened room. His lithe frame stretched out over his recliner, and Jane's feelings on their first encounter resurfaced. He was magnificent, but she could now only picture him lying under Ed.

Letchford spotted her and sat up. "Jane, dear, you made it." He smiled. "Thank you, Martha," he said to the girl. she turned and winked at Jane before leaving. "Jane, dear, you must meet my son, Quentin."

Quentin turned and looked at her for about a second, then, nonchalantly lay his head back down. "Good to meet you," he mumbled with zero enthusiasm.

Letchford pointed a thumb to the bed next to his. "This is my girl… Sorry, my son's girlfriend, Heather." Perhaps telling a story, Heather wore a tiny suit similar to the one Letchford provided for Jane.

Jane caught Heather's eye and shook her head a little, mouthing the word, "No."

Heather sat up and smiled. "I know you." Jane hoped the girl would have got the message to pretend they'd never met. Ice filled her veins before Heather qualified, "You're Jane Clark from the telly."

They shook hands. "Guilty as charged," said Jane.

"Can I get a selfie later?" Heather asked.

"Come on now, Heather, what did I tell you – no celeb bothering in the club." The girl looked suitably admonished and sat back.

Jane wondered if the ruse she'd played to ingratiate herself with Quentin would also work on the father. Were it to get her the video and keep his clammy hands off her, then it was worth a try. She said, "No bother at all. I would love to do one with a pretty girl like you." She flashed her sweetest smile to Heather. A wide-eyed Selwyn looked between the two of them.

He shook his head. "You're not wearing the suit I set aside." Disappointment flashed in his eyes.

Jane formed a sad face. "I don't look good in this, sir?"

He waved a hasty apology. "Oh, you look absolutely ravishing, dear. I didn't mean anything by it."

"My grandmother gave me this costume before she died," Jane lied. "It has great sentimental value."

"She had wonderful taste," he said condescendingly. "I would have loved to have met her." *She'd be more your age*, Jane wanted to say but smiled instead.

"Malt or champers?" Letchford asked, quickly changing the subject.

"Would it be possible to get an orange juice?" Jane said. Seeing the disappointment in his eyes, she added, "I drank rather a lot in the car on the way here." He relented and waved a finger in the air, gesturing to a waitress who took the order.

"Now, Heather, dear, can you shuffle over there and let the adults talk a while?"

Heather stood and freed the recliner next to Letchford. Jane sat on the edge of the vacant bed and looked at Quentin, who remained impassive. It was hard to detect what was going on through his dark glasses, but she thought he was scanning the room for something. The waitress returned and Jane took the chilled glass from her tray, drinking deeply from it.

"My, you were thirsty." Letchford ran a finger up and down her arm.

Sipping her juice, Jane realised she knew or knew of half the people in this room. A couple of the glass cubicles surrounding the pool had dark glass enabled and a curtain over the door. What went on inside could only be guessed at. A waitress stood between each pair of cubicles, hence the fast table service. Those patrons in the pool mainly stood and chatted. One or two swam, but a couple pressed against the pool wall looked to be getting to know each other intimately.

"Do you like it here?" Letchford asked.

"It is...extraordinary." Jane didn't feel comfortable admitting it, but she absolutely loved the place. A feeling that this was where she was meant to be permeated her thoughts. Anybody who was anyone was here.

"You'll be welcome here anytime now. Once invited, you can use the place as a second home. Even if I am not with you. You can't bring non-members though. Sorry. You would have to be a full member to do that and as of yet, we have no full female members. We are a bastion against modernisation." He laughed heartily.

"I doubt there are any non-white members either," Jane mumbled as she scanned the room.

"Come on, girl," Letchford said, pointing to her OJ, "get that muck down you and join me on the hard stuff." He reached over and tipped her glass to let the liquid flow quicker into her mouth. A little spilled on her chest – he picked up a napkin and took way too long mopping the single droplet up. The napkin roamed far wider than the spill.

Jane turned to look at Heather, who was a little way away from them. She was drinking what smelled like Tia Maria and Coke through a straw. Jane winked and said, "Hi, Heather, how did you and Kevin meet?"

Heather smiled in response. "Quentin," she said.

"Sorry," said Jane. "How did you meet?"

Heather ran through the highlights of the story that Jane already knew, all loud enough for Letchford to hear.

"He's a lucky guy. You are stunning."

"Thank you," Heather replied and smiled. They made small-talk for a while before Jane turned to Letchford.

"I'm just going to take a quick selfie with Heather. Is that okay with you, sir?" She gave him her best puppy eyes and smile. Sitting up, she leant to whisper in his ear. "She is…delectable." Letchford moved back and looked at her with eyebrows hitting the roof.

"Do you need me to come and hold the camera?" he offered nobly.

"Maybe later," Jane said and giggled. "Heather's phone is in the changing rooms. We'll go do it there." She stood and took Heather by the hand. The two girls walked slowly toward the door. Over her shoulder, Jane saw a look of pure glee on the face of the MP. Quentin, it appeared, hadn't even noticed them leave.

As they reached the changing room door, it opened, and Martha gave her a beaming smile. "Heading home already, Miss Clark?"

Jane smiled back. "No, no. Heather here needs her phone."

Martha stood aside and let the girls pass. Jane led Heather to the same changing cubicle as last time. She closed the door behind them.

"Thank you," Jane said, hugging Heather.

"What's going on?" Heather said but added, "It's great to see you."

"You too, but I wasn't expecting to bump into you here and certainly not with Quentin."

"His father told me to be ready at four this afternoon. A car picked me up, and Quentin was already inside. It brought us here again," Heather said.

"You've been here before?" Jane asked.

"Yes," said Heather, "a few times, but not with Quentin here too."

Jane hesitated before asking, "Has Daddy…taken things further than last time we spoke?" Heather's eyes lowered and Jane already knew the answer. "It's okay. You don't have to tell me."

Heather looked up. "What's going on here, Jane?"

Jane gave Heather a brief precis of the situation, missing out the blackmail and murder.

"He has something I need, and as a reporter, I have to mix with people like Letchford to get the stories that are required for work."

Heather paused and seemed to give thought to her next question. "Do you have to…sleep with them to get the stories?"

"Well, if Letchford has his way, yes, but that's where you can really help me. Go get your phone, and let's do the selfie," Jane said.

Perplexed, Heather left the cubicle a minute and returned with her phone. They took a few regular pictures, and then Jane said, "Cover your eyes."

Heather shrugged but did as instructed. Jane took the swimsuit off and said, "Keep your eyes closed, but hold up the camera." Jane manipulated the phone's angle in Heather's hand and then said, "Take a pic. But keep your bloody eyes closed, girl."

The camera snapped a couple of times, and Jane realised the futility of making Heather keep her eyes shut. She would see the pictures anyway. Still, it made her feel better. She put the suit back on, then took the phone from Heather.

"You can open your eyes now." Jane was scrolling through the pictures, and she deleted a couple that hadn't worked. "Right," she said, "one last picture."

Jane slipped the shoulder straps of her suit down, leant forward and kissed a surprised Heather. She pressed the shutter at the same time. "Thanks," she said and checked the result. "Perfect."

After returning the phone, she said, "He's going to want to see them in a minute. Look embarrassed and be reluctant to hand your phone over, but then give in. Okay? The rest, we will have to wing." They hung around and chatted for a few more minutes, to make their photoshoot seem even more convincing.

As they were leaving the dressing room, Heather said, "Oh, you have your suit on inside out."

Jane gave her a wicked smile, "I know."

Back in the cubicle, Quentin had done one of his disappearing acts while Letchford Senior had moved to the centre recliner. Jane and Heather took the ones on either side of him.

"Sorry that we took longer than anticipated, sir." Jane giggled.

Letchford had a lewd expression on his face. He looked at Heather and then back round to Jane. "Your…Your suit is on inside out," he said, and then cracked a huge smile.

"Oo, silly me." Jane looked down at her suit in mock surprise.

Letchford's mouth hung open. "Did…did…did you get the selfie?"

Jane laughed and said, "Oh yes, of course. We did a few, actually."

He turned to Heather and said, "Let me see, dear." She did a convincing blush. Could she do that to order? A useful skill, Jane thought.

"Go on, give me the phone," Letchford said to Heather, who demurred with a giggle.

"They're private," she held the phone away from the grabbing MP.

Jane stood and walked over to Heather. "Give me the phone," she said sternly. Heather stared back with shock, but Jane winked. The young girl did her best to seem reluctant but sighed before handing it over. Letchford held out a hand, but Jane shook her head and put the phone behind her back. He looked at her, an eyebrow raised.

"Have you got something for me, sir?" she said as sweetly as possible.

His face changed, and she thought he was about to give up the pursuit of the phone, but then he smiled a little. "Of course, dear. Sorry, I meant to give you this earlier." Letchford reached over to the table and picked something up. He gave Jane a memory stick. There was no way to check its contents now, but she doubted he went to the effort of bringing an empty device when he always had the option to say no.

She closed her fingers over the stick and handed him the phone. He had to get Heather to type in her pin, but once done, he sat down and enjoyed the little slideshow that chronicled the girls moving from innocent selfies to something more. The picture of Jane from the back, blowing a kiss to the photographer while naked, appeared to be his favourite, and he scrolled back and forth between it and the kiss. Jane laughed a little at how much he seemed to be enjoying them. He looked up at her lustfully, but just as he did, Martha appeared.

She said, "Miss Clark. You are needed urgently on the phone. A Dan somebody from the BBC, I think? He's been trying to get you on your mobile. It's urgent."

Jane turned to Letchford and said, "Sorry, sir. I left my phone in the changing rooms. I need to go take that call. Okay?"

Letchford was practically drooling as he looked at her and then Heather. "Of course, dear," he said finally. She walked over and stooped to kiss his cheek.

"Thank you, sir," she whispered. She repeated the action with Heather. "Will you be okay?" Jane asked quietly.

Heather put her hand on Jane's cheek and whispered, "He can't do anything more than he has done already. I will be fine."

"Thank you. I owe you."

On heading back into the changing rooms, Jane said, "You may just have saved my life, Miss Dundee," to Martha.

"Broughty Ferry, actually," Martha corrected her, "but it doesn't have the same ring to it."

* * *

Jane, now dressed, handed the box with the purple string swimsuit in it to Martha. "It's likely to be ridiculously expensive."

"Well, Granny's was probably a tenner from Markie's." Martha shrugged an apology.

"Regardless, it saved my bacon tonight. Swap?" Jane said, and Martha nodded.

Jane hugged the girl and left. Walking toward the door, there was Quentin, standing in an alcove, rather close to a tall man in what appeared to her to be a sailor's uniform.

Back in her flat, and with a shaking hand, Jane loaded the memory stick into her laptop. "I really don't want to watch this," she said aloud. The images started with Burton adjusting the camera for height and her sitting on his bed giggling. She had hoped to have been unconscious but had guessed he couldn't have thrown her over his shoulder and carried her from the club.

The images were worse than expected. To a casual observer (and didn't she hope there wouldn't ever be any,) she enthusiastically participated. Burton was clever enough that his face was never clearly seen. The pervert lived out his fantasies. She watched with disgust, but the worst was yet to come. Having sated himself, she watched as he lay next to her and the two of them cuddled and kissed like lovers. It was too much for her. Bile rose in her throat.

After five minutes of them together, the screen went black. "Shit," she said.

Letchford either didn't have the full footage or had held on to some. She guessed it was the former. Burton wasn't the sort to give away all the goodies in one parcel. Closing the laptop, Jane resolved to call Hannah tomorrow. She needed to search that house.

London, Sunday 9th March 2025

Jane stopped her Toyota outside the address Hannah gave her. It was a grimy building in Beckton. The now sprawling suburb barely existed forty years ago, so just how it managed to get in such a mess already was a mystery. Hannah came running down the stairs, waving. Jane leaned over the passenger seat and opened the door. The bubbly young girl jumped in.

"Thanks for calling. It's great to see you again."

Jane kissed her cheek and said, "You look happy."

"I am," said Hannah. "I feel…free."

"Whose flat is this?" Jane pointed up the garden path.

"Daniel's," Hannah said, and Jane looked at her with a wrinkled brow. "He's nice."

"Oh, Hannah, tell me you haven't started a new relationship already? You need space."

"It's not like that," said Hannah, looking at her feet.

"I know I must sound like your mum, but what is it like?" Jane thought Hannah seemed reluctant to answer and so said, "It's okay. It's none of my business."

She started the car and drove off. "Is it okay if we go to the house first?" she asked Hannah. "I'll buy you lunch after."

"Yeah, great actually. I need to get some clothes," Hannah said. "How was your party?"

"Eventful," Jane said and smiled.

They chatted like old friends and didn't stop talking all the way to Camden, but neither mentioned Colin. On arriving, Jane parked the car across the street and noticed the house curtains were closed.

"I can't remember if they were open or closed when we left," Hannah said, scratching her head.

"They were open," Jane said. "Somebody has been in. Did he have many visitors?"

"None…except…" Hannah was shaking her head, but Jane held up a hand to show she knew what Hannah meant.

"He was one of them," Hannah said, lowering her eyes and stubbing her shoe on the footwell carpet.

Jane looked at the girl. "Who was?"

"My new flatmate, Daniel," said Hannah.

"Oh Hannah…"

"Daniel didn't pay the blackmail money and Colin ruined his life. He sent pictures to Daniel's father and his boss." Hannah looked sad. Jane reached over and squeezed the girl's hand. In response, Hannah forced a smile. Jane returned to taking in the house and the surroundings.

"Let's go," she said, but once out of the car, they walked the full length of the street on the far side before circling back. Jane never looked at the house but checked every car for observers. "It's clear," she said, and the two made for the front door. Hannah used her key.

As soon as the door swung open, the mess was there for all to see. The place had been ransacked.

"You can't live here," said Jane. "There are a lot of people who will be wanting to see what they can find. That's why I'm here, after all. Did he have any hiding places you know about?"

Hannah thought for a while. "He was up in the loft a lot."

They headed up the stairs, but on reaching the landing, the

smashed loft door hung on buckled hinges. While Jane poked her head in to view the contents strewn over the floor, Hannah ran into a side room. Jane followed. The girl's clothes were scattered everywhere, yet they seemed undamaged. This hadn't been malicious – it was a search. Jane realised pretty quickly that they would get nothing here. Someone had done a thorough job.

"Pack your clothes, and let's get out of here," she said. Hannah rummaged through her scattered garments and stuffed as much as she could into a bin liner. They went back downstairs.

As they passed the fateful kitchen, the floor squeaked. Jane stopped. "How much did you pay for that kitchen?"

"It's great, isn't it? We got it done last year. It was an arm and a leg. Not sure how much actually. He never let me touch the money, but he once said something about spending thirty grand on me, so I guess it must have been that," Hannah replied.

Jane pushed the door open and stood on the threshold strip. It creaked again. "Thirty grand, and they didn't lay the floor correctly?" she asked.

"That started a few weeks later. I wanted to get them back, but Colin said it was normal expansion. He didn't ever want them in the house in the first place. This kitchen was a tip before."

Jane wasn't really listening. She was down on her hands and knees, wrenching the strip between the laminate and carpet. It popped up.

"Hey," Hannah said indignantly, "I'm going to have to put this place on the market soon."

Ignoring her protestations, Jane slipped her hand under the laminate. Her fingers hit something, and she pulled. Out came a long, thin box. About to open it, she stopped and changed her mind.

"Hannah," she said, "put this in the bottom of the bag. Leave the bag open so anyone watching sees the clothes." Jane took an armful of clothes too. She was pretty sure there was no one about but wanted to make their visit look as innocent as possible.

After closing the front door, Hannah protested when Jane made them repeat the process of walking both pavements before getting back in the car and driving away. Jane really wanted to get the box back to her flat and check it over, but she had promised Hannah lunch, and anyway, best not to lead any potential tail straight to her home.

They found a nice pub by the river and had Sunday brunch, but Jane was distracted the whole time. After finishing up, they got back in the car and headed home. She dropped Hannah at Beckton and then took a roundabout way back to her flat. Finally, she locked the door and closed the curtains, even though it was still daylight.

Cross-legged, she sat on the floor and opened the box. It contained a small diary with names in it. Some had addresses. She found her own listing, which simply had BBC next to it. There were a lot of what looked like usernames and passwords. A couple of bank cards and a toiletries bag completed the haul. No flash drives, unfortunately.

After unzipping the toiletry bag, she whistled. It was packed with fifty-pound notes. At a quick guess, north of twenty grand. On feeling down the side of the money, in the hope of finding a memory stick, she discovered two bank statements. There was £75K in one and £126K in the other. Business had obviously been good. No money had left either account in the period covered by the statements, but regular amounts, small and large, were deposited.

She put everything back in the bag, went to the kitchen, lifted the bin liner out from the bin, put the box in and then replaced the bin liner, making the rubbish cover the surface of the box.

London, Monday 10th March 2025

The government benches were packed as the PM stood to speak. Ravi Suvar was no one's first choice as leader of his party. He would not have been prime minister except for a series of incidents that led to his two predecessors being removed unceremoniously. One still sat behind him. He wasn't sure he would have chosen the position had he known what was on the horizon.

"Mister Speaker," he began, as convention dictated, "I wish to make a statement to Parliament on behalf of the Government of National Unity. I intend to address the current global situation." He stopped and looked around the chamber as a teacher in a classroom would, to ensure the pupil's attention.

"Let me turn first to the civil conflict in the USA. The British government acknowledges that there have been difficult circumstances surrounding the presidential election. Although Mr Thorn's campaign has contacted us, making an appeal for recognition to His Majesty's Government, the UK, along with our allies in France, Germany and all other European nations, feel unable to recognise the administration that the Republican Party has established." The PM shook his head and cleared his throat before continuing.

"Britain will, of course, remain America's staunchest ally. We, like most nations around the globe, grieve for the passing of the previous president and for the many lives that this breakdown in governance has taken." The PM stopped to take a sip of water.

"Many Britons are caught up in the situation, and we are doing everything in our power to get them home safely."

Crimea, Monday 10th March, 2025

The flight of 6 SU22s took off from their airbase on the East shore of the black sea and gained altitude as they arced Northwards over the water. Below the speeding aircraft, lights were dotted across Crimea and even Southern Ukraine, as turning them off had no negative effect on modern weapons.

Orders crackled over the radio. All this money and no one had ever got a bloody radio to work properly. Regardless, the instruction was received, and two of the bombers peeled off. Attaining their full ceiling (the Ukrainians would have nothing that could reach them here), the pilot of the first plane typed a series of map coordinates into his missile guidance system. He called "Check" into the mask and heard "check" in reply from the co-pilot. His shaking finger punched the launch control causing missile after missile to hurtle off into the dark of the Crimean night. "Let's go home," The pilot said through the intercom as the plane banked smoothly and reversed course. The second bomber repeated the procedure before following the flight leader.

While weaponry fired from the flight of the four planes slammed into targets in and around Odesa, the salvo from the second group sped across the Ukrainian night. Defensive systems around Kyiv detected the swarm heading up from the Southeast, but the missiles were too high to intercept. The system stood down as the threat passed 15km East of the city without losing height.

"It's not our turn tonight," said one of the two operators watching the screens.

A few hundred kilometres North of Kyiv, the Russian S500 and static air defence systems first burst into life, then almost immediately shut down. Operators ran from terminal to terminal, trying to restore the feed, but the missile defence network was dead. Les than 5 minutes later, the Wagner base in Southern Belarus erupted like a volcano. Blast after devastating blast ripped through the wooded area.

One minute after, several military targets in and around Minsk were also hit. The main residence of President Aleksandr Lukashenko was consumed in conflagration, and the parliament building ceased to exist.

Russia, Moscow. Monday 10th March 2025

The aide knocked softly but didn't wait for a response. Pushing open the door, he walked over to the table where the President of Russia was in conference with golden-braid bedecked generals. He stooped and spoke softly in the President's ear before turning to exit.

The General across from ViktorPutenov thought he detected the beginning of a smile on the face of his leader, but, like a wraith, as soon as it appeared, it was gone. The President looked round the table and asked,

"Is anyone hungry. Let's order some caviar and plomba. Two dishes that are best served cold."

London, Tuesday 11th March 2025

Still in his pink and white striped pyjamas, the PM had been up for an hour. The BBC news played softly on the large wall-mounted telly of the Downing Street flat, as he went through the documents required to be read before starting the day. On their way to his desk at 4am, twelve different people had read and filtered the details to ensure only the most relevant material got through. Yet still, the pile was massive. Sometimes, he understood why Boris had just shredded the lot.

In between Boris and Suvar, Liz Strauss enjoyed the briefest spell as PM but didn't even get time to unpack, so the inherited décor had gone unchanged since Cassie's redesign.

Cassie was Boris's current wife and, as everyone knew, had been the person really running the country while PM Jenkins got pissed. But now Boris was back, and his return already caused trouble for the shaky coalition of national unity.

The RT logo on the screen caught his eye. He turned the volume up. The BBC were picking up a feed directly from their Russian counterpart.

RT News, Tuesday 11th March 2025

"In a heinous war crime, the Ukrainian Nazis have launched an unprovoked attack on the peaceful people of Belarus. It is believed that hundreds of civilians have been killed as the targets were mainly residential areas. The presidential palace was also destroyed, and no word has been heard from the Belarusian leader. Russian troops that were based in the north of the country have begun moving to defend the borders of our closest ally. President Putenov will make a statement to the nation in one hour. We will keep you up to date with developments here. Stay tuned."

The Prime minister's head dropped. His hand was halfway to the phone when it rang. On the other end, an advisor began to explain the situation before the PM cut in with, "Why the fuck am I hearing all this from the fucking telly? Get COBRA together and tell the defence minister to fuck off to the back benches. I will be right down."

BBC News, Tuesday 11th March 2025

The screen showed images of devastation. People stood around crying while others searched through the rubble. A wailing woman waved a sheet of white metal above her head; it had burnt edges, but on it, a painted Ukrainian flag was clearly visible. The camera cut to file footage from the previous night's explosions recorded across Minsk. The BBC was, of course, taking this feed from Russian stations, so the newsreaders kept trying to tell the viewers to treat everything they saw with an open mind. 'Open mind' being code for complete cynicism.

The news was that the Belarusian president was missing. A view of his palace showed the building to be wrecked. Hundreds of people gathered outside in tears.

Edinburgh, Tuesday 11th March 2025

Duncan Clark wondered if the people were crying in relief rather than sadness. Lukashenko was a nutter in his opinion, and he doubted many in Belorussia would really grieve if he were truly dead.

Regardless of the fate of their leader, Duncan worried about what all this meant for the world at large. Of course, the Beeb was already hinting that this was a false flag operation, but the Ukrainians had become increasingly flaky as this war went on. It was now well-accepted that it was they who took out the huge dam in the south of the country in 2023. If they had lied about that, people now wondered how much of anything Zielinski said was true. In addition, the cost of the bloody war was obscene at a time that most ordinary folk in the UK were skint.

Duncan did all right for himself, though. His small law firm was based right over the road from the Scottish Parliament, and most of his work came out of that building, one way or another. The UK and Scottish governments were at each other's throats almost permanently. When an argument started, his bank balance swelled.

Guessing the COBRA committee would be meeting about now, Duncan thought about what it would be like to be a fly on the wall. He'd harboured aspirations to enter politics a few years ago, but that idea was on the back burner for now. There was too much money to be made cleaning up the mess of the current inhabitants.

Moscow, Tuesday 11th March 2025

A solemn Viktor Putenov stood unmoving and unspeaking behind a lectern. The long silence was uncomfortable for TV engineers who pushed and pulled levers on their desks to see if anything was muted. Unseen by the TV audience, a backup audio boom swung into position above the President. But everything was working fine. Putenov wasn't yet talking.

He had this speech planned all day. In truth, he knew what he would say for about a week now. The man didn't like to be unprepared, and the best way to remain prepared was to control the agenda. When he spoke at last, the TV producer released his pensive breath.

"My fellow countrymen, a crime was committed against the people of Belorussia last night. Their President died, along with hundreds of his countrymen and many Russian nationals. An unprovoked missile, launched from Kiev, got through our defence systems, causing the slaughter." He thumped a fist on the lectern. "The people of Russia will not sit by and let this go unpunished. Heroic soldiers of the Motherland are already moving to secure Belorussian government buildings, and until properly constituted elections can be held, Russia will secure the governance of our neighbour." His dark eyes stared directly into the camera lens.

"For this heinous crime, the Ukrainian people will learn their fate soon, but they did not act alone. The missiles used were a new type. They were able to elude the best anti-air systems. The first indication is that these missiles are British made. Should this evidence prove conclusive, the attack will be regarded as an act of war, and we will respond severely." The President left his ambiguous threat hanging.

"I will talk more on this tomorrow." From a glass, he stopped to take a sip of water. " We held the open hand of friendship to our neighbours and got treachery in return. Tomorrow, Russia's hand will not be empty."

Viktor Putenov stood with his fist held out in front. Lowering it slowly, he stalked off the platform and from the screens of millions of Russian, Ukrainian and Western televisions.

New York, Thorn Tower, Tuesday 11th March 2025

As Viktor Putenov stood silently on the stage in Russia, almost simultaneously, Donald Thorn took the podium in New York. Half of the US TV stations had stopped covering his press conferences. In their opinion, Thorn had no official capacity other than as a Republican candidate for the presidency. Many cities were also without power, so his announcements had a finite audience.

"My fellow Americans. As a result of continued instability at the hands of those that will not accept the democratic choice of the people, we are today calling for martial law to be extended to all major cities and towns. We have appointed General George McCluskey as head of the Joint Chiefs. He'll be contacting all US forces over the next couple of days. US forces on land, sea and air will take command from no other source. Should you choose to follow other orders, your actions will be deemed treason to the USA and punished accordingly." He raised a finger and pointed to the screen before resuming

"Overseas US forces will be deployed back home as soon as possible. We cannot allow the disruption of our economy to continue. Until peace has been restored in our great land, the US is temporarily withdrawing from NATO. We have advised the heads of European countries of this decision and that it is in immediate effect. Funding for all overseas missions will also cease. The USA cannot be expected to protect the world while our own cities burn at the hands of insurrectionists.

"General McCluskey will be rounding up the leaders of the terrorist coup and anyone who supports them. While this is being carried out, please stay off the streets. There is a twenty-hour curfew in place from today. It is countrywide. In peaceful areas, you will be permitted to leave your home for essential reasons only between the hours of 10am and 2pm. Anyone on the streets out of these hours may be arrested or shot. Looters will be shot on sight.

"With the obeyance of this new command structure, we can

begin to rebuild our nation, free from the forces of evil that have held America back for so long.

"May you and your family stay safe, and God bless America."

London, Tuesday 11th March 2025

"I can assure you the missiles were not fired by any British resource." General Sir Patrick Sanders spoke softly to the PM and ministers serving on the COBRA committee. "We have satellite data showing they probably originated in Crimea or Southern Ukraine."

"Can we publish this data?" the PM said eagerly.

"Unfortunately not, sir," the General replied. He added, "It is imperative that the Russians remain unaware that we can track their movements in the region."

The PM looked disgusted. "Fat lot of good that will do us if we are obliterated tomorrow. Where are we with the Americans?" he said, turning to his foreign secretary.

"Sorry, sir, we're getting nothing from Washington. They have their hands full. We've been forced to reduce the embassy to a skeleton. It is not safe there anymore."

I never signed up for this, the British PM thought to himself. Sure, he manipulated the situation to get the top job. A lot of noses got bent out of shape on the way, but most of the political pugilists had it coming. Here he was though – financial crash, energy crisis, mortgage crisis, nuclear obliteration. If there were anyone left to write the history books, he wouldn't come out of it looking good.

"Well, you have all been a great help. I will try Paris and Berlin first, but failing any inspiration there, somebody set up a call to the Russian ambassador and arrange for me to speak to Putenov."

Moscow, Tuesday 11th March 2025

Viktor Putenov spoke English well enough, but he wasn't going to concede a millimetre to the Englishman, so this conversation would be held through translators. It also gave the Russian president time to consider his reply. The English PM wittered on with the usual niceties. Even though the countries were in a de facto war, this crap still had to be done. Putenov wondered if the PM would notice that the mandatory reply would come from the Russian translator, without presidential input. He guessed some clever bastard that was listening in would pick up on this and advise Suvar later, but Putenov wasn't going to waste any breath on this second-rate politician from a third-rate country. Had Putenov really intended to obliterate the UK, it would be gone already. The President needed one thing and one thing alone from the irrelevant PM of the UK. Having him on this phone meant he was a long way to getting his goal already.

Once the wittering ceased, Putenov decided it was time to join the conversation.

"Mr Suvar, if you are calling with your declaration of war, like Mr Ribbentrop before you, you are a day late." The translation concluded, he continued. "You or your ally attacked a neutral country last night. In any reasonable mind, you have conducted an act of war against the Russian people. Can you deny this?"

The inevitable delay in translation over, the British prime minister responded.

"Sir, the British people have sought now—"

Cutting across the PM in Russian, a wiser man than the British PM would have recognised Putenov hadn't waited for the translation. The President spoke.

"The Russian people have no quarrel with the British people.

In that we are agreed." In the background, Putenov could hear the PM. "Mr President…Mr President, please…" But he continued. "The British people did not send arms to the Neo-Nazis; you alone chose to do so. You and your government have led your people to this place, and for your actions, your people will have to pay."

The British PM was huffing and puffing and talking about illegal invasions, so the President added, "Belorussia invaded no one." Putenov persisted, "Are you calling with a declaration of war, Mr Prime Minister? You are very short of allies currently and I believe such a war would be brief."

Suvar stopped talking. This was not going as planned. The words of the old Iron Maiden song '2 Minutes to Midnight' looped in his head.

Realising he had to cool this situation – he had received no succour in Paris or Berlin – the PM said, "Neither the British people nor their government have any wish to enter conflict with Russia. I am giving you my word that the UK played no part in the missile launch and we are certain the Ukrainians have no UK-made equipment capable of last night's attack. While His Majesty's government opposes the illegal invasion of Ukraine, we have done nothing to widen the conflict."

Putenov waited this time. "You have forces on my country's border with Estonia. You have trained and supplied men, some of whom have entered Russian territory. You have drones and intelligence equipment in Russian air space and in our waters. You and your allies have satellites flying over my head as we speak. Can you deny any of these things I have said?" The line fell silent. The President guessed conversations were taking place on the other end of the phone. He was not wrong.

Putenov decided the PM had delayed long enough and continued. "Mr Suvar, Russian forces will announce the capture of

Odessa later tonight. Kharkov will fall in less than a week. The Ukrainians are beaten and become increasingly irrational. Last night, they tried to bring Belorussia into the war with the aim of getting NATO involved further. If you and I can come to an agreement of no escalation between our countries, and that the UK will cease involvement in the region, I will stand down the Russian preparations against your country and maybe we can schedule diplomatic meetings for the months to come. It would be my hope that, in these meetings, we can correct the situation between our nations."

The translator concluded and the hubbub on the other end of the line was clear for all to hear.

There was a pause for over a minute before the PM responded. "Mr President, you have offered agreements that I will have to take to my cabinet. May we have an hour to discuss and respond?"

Putenov smiled even before the Russian translation concluded. "Of course, Prime Minister. We await your call, in the hope that the seeds of peace have been sown here tonight."

Edinburgh, Wednesday 12th March 2025

Breaking News scrolled across the BBC news screen. Duncan Clark, like almost everyone on the British Isles, was glued to the telly.

"In a historic agreement last night, Prime Minister Suvar and President Putenov of Russia concluded a peace deal that calms the current tensions and opens the door for a deal to end the conflict in Ukraine. While the conflict in that country will continue for now, a summit is to be organised between all interested parties in the upcoming months. Russia will conduct no major offensives, and the arms supplied to Ukraine from Western allies will cease. It is hoped a hiatus will prevail until the summit can begin. This is a fantastic victory for Mr Suvar and is likely to pay dividends in the poll ratings that have not been favourable to him lately.

"In a further announcement, Russia has today advised it will cease the oil and gas blockade on any country that agrees to the terms of the interim deal. The agreement is being called the New Minsk Accords. Overnight, market prices of oil and gas fell to their lowest in fourteen months."

Duncan changed the channel but needn't have bothered. Sky News was of course running the same story. Flicking through the news options, he was amazed to find RT had already reappeared on the Sky box.

"Wow, that was fast. Looks like we are all buddies again," he said to himself.

Something in the rapid change of friends and enemies reminded him of his favourite novel, *1984*. Clicking on the channel, he was intrigued to see how the situation played out in the eyes of the Russians.

RT News

"…seems that the New Minsk Accords have not been welcomed with open arms by all the nations of the European Union. We cross over now to our reporter in Paris." The screen changed to a view of a girl on a balcony with the Eiffel Tower in the background.

"Yes, Rachael, the governments here in Paris as well as those in Berlin and Rome have been joined by others in condemning the agreement as premature. Some in Europe go further and say the British PM has sold the Ukrainians out. Mr Macron, in the French parliament today, said that he would be contacting the British government to express the dissatisfaction of the French people. He will then fly to Berlin and meet with other heads of EU states to decide what action they will take." The camera moved back to Rachael in the RT newsroom.

"In spite of the French reaction, today, the government of Hungary advised that they would follow the UK in signing the new accords. It is expected that Slovakia and the Czech Republic will follow soon."

Edinburgh

There was a knock at the office door. Duncan muted the telly and called, "Come in."

His secretary, Nancy, entered and said, "Your post," as she laid the bundle in his top tray.

Knowing Nancy always read it first, he said, "Anything interesting?"

Waving a disdaining hand, she replied, "The usual pish. I fished out the bills and remittances and stuck them down to finance. Anything legal is in the relevant pigeonhole. There is a thank you letter from someone that you clearly did not charge enough, and an invitation to talk at some supper with Eck. Have these retards not heard of email?"

Duncan laughed and said, "I don't think that's politically correct nowadays, Nance."

"Fuckwits then," came the reply.

Duncan dragged the paper from the tray to the desktop. The letter was from a woman that had been subject to an immigration removal order at the hands of the UK government. Duncan and the team got the order removed. She wasn't a penniless boat person, and the company did all right out of the deal. He liked that she had taken the time to commit pen to paper.

He turned his attention to the invitation. 'Eck', as Nancy had called him, was the former first minister of Scotland. Duncan and Alex Samson had crossed paths many times, not least at these sorts of functions that seemed to preoccupy the law society in Edinburgh. He could probably have attended four or five a week had he the inclination. It wasn't really his thing, though, and the partners spread the load of the essential functions.

This one was different. The company had played a small part when the former first minister had fallen foul of the courts a few years ago. Samson had won the series of cases and Duncan was on that winning side. Ever since, Alex – they were now on first name terms – was a regular visitor to the office. They had a symbiotic relationship. The politician brought things to the company's attention that were worthy or could be beneficial, and Duncan gave legal advice on anything the Alba Party were proposing to put forward. A serious back-scratching operation.

He hadn't seen Alex since the last Edinburgh derby, so decided to attend. "Nancy, will you please send an acceptance for this function?"

She turned. "Jahohl, mein Führer," she said, clicking her heels and saluting. She swivelled and goose-stepped out of the office. Shit, she made him laugh so much.

London, Wednesday 12th March 2025

Jane traversed the soulless maze of look-a-like streets that was Beckton. It was a wonder anyone ever found their own house in this place. "I bet King Charles hates this," she murmured. Finally locating the correct street, she parked outside the world weary block, looked up and down the road and scowled. After sounding the horn, the building door opened, ejecting a breezy Hannah, who bounced her way down the path and into the car.

"Hey, Jane," said the girl who was way overdressed for the pub lunch that Jane had planned. Her forest green dress was tied up on the front. It came down to her knees, where a matching coloured pair of laced-up boots added a few inches to her height with their high heel. In jeans and a jumper, Jane felt like a slob.

"How are you doing?" Jane asked.

Hannah fastened her seatbelt then straightened her outfit. "I'm good. Things are just a bit weird. A solicitor has been in touch to get the estate sorted. Colin didn't have a will, so, according to the guy, things should go to me unless anyone contests it."

"Does he have a big family?"

"I don't know much about them," Hannah said. "I met a few at the wedding and his parents were at the funeral. But I haven't seen or heard from them since."

Jane handed the discovered toiletry bag to Hannah. She'd removed the papers with the websites and emails; otherwise, it was as she found it. "No one knows this exists, I believe. So, keep quiet, and this is yours, however it all turns out."

Hannah opened the bag, and her eyes widened. "Wow!"

"You deserve it. Check the bank statements. There's a lot more where that came from, and I don't know if the solicitor will know anything about that money. The bank cards are in there too, and I found the pin numbers. It's up to you, but I wouldn't touch the money in the bank for now. Wait and see what the solicitor turns up."

Hannah sat dumbfounded, so Jane asked, "Are you going to stick around London or move somewhere new?"

"I haven't thought about it. Daniel and Carol are the only two people I know, but they're both from here. So, I'll probably stick around."

"You know me now," Jane said, feigning hurt.

"I wasn't sure I would ever see you again," Hannah said.

"Why would you think that?" Now Jane really *was* hurt. "We're friends now, I hope,"

They drove around the area a while before finding the least seedy place for lunch. The unlikely pair took a seat and ordered. Just then, Jane caught someone approaching out of the corner of her eye.

"Oh hell," she said.

"What?" Hannah asked.

"A guy is heading over, probably looking for a selfie. I forgot my glasses," Jane said, turning to give him a dirty look.

"Sorry to interrupt you, girls, but I am a huge fan," he said, and Jane started to tell him they were having lunch, but she realised he wasn't talking to her. His lurid stare was fixed on Hannah.

"You're Trixi Doll, here in the flesh, if you know what I mean?" he said, laughing a dirty laugh. Hannah burst into tears before running out the door.

Getting to her feet, Jane said, "Dickhead," before running after the crying girl. When she caught up, Hannah was distraught.

"This will never go away," Hannah raged.

Jane hugged the girl and then slowly walked her back to the car. "Come on, I know a guy that knows everything about the internet."

"The last thing I want is more guys looking at it," said Hannah, thumping a clenched fist against her thigh.

"Believe me, girl, this one will have decidedly little interest in the content."

Half an hour of London traffic later, they parked outside Ed's flat and got out of the car. Jane knocked but let herself in anyway. They were halfway up the stairs before hearing the stumbling in the living room. Jane halted. The two of them stood on the stairs until Ed's head came round the door.

"Jane, what a nice surprise."

With an eyebrow raised, she looked up at him as he pulled on a T-shirt. "Surprise being the operative word, I guess."

On entering Ed's living room, Jane stopped dead, seeing Quentin Letchford sat casually on the sofa, his messy hair telling a story of its own. Guessing that the cat was well and truly out of the bag as far as her real identity went, she decided to play the situation cooly.

"Did we interrupt anything?" she said with a knowing smile.

"No, no," said Ed. "We were just chatting."

"Strange, I was just chatting to Hannah here." Jane stopped, introducing everyone. "But neither of us looks like we just got out of bed."

Ed smiled. "Okay, you cheeky bitch, what's up?"

In spite of Hannah's continuous protestations, Jane explained the situation to Ed, but then Quentin butted in. As it turned out, he was once in website design, and it was he who came up with the plan.

"I will tell you this now. You'll never stop this reappearing from time to time, but what we can do is make it less appealing and move it down the rankings. Once you're on page 158 of the internet, few people will ever find it. What I need you to do is take this pound." Quentin handed it to Hannah, and she stared at the coin in the palm of her hand. "Okay, I've bought your rights to this stuff. Now, I'll spam out demands to the sites that list it and ask them for payment for their use of the material. It'll then be tagged as premium content. Finally, I'll write an algorithm to let me know if it ever appears anywhere for free in future. The fewer people that are willing to pay, the further down the rankings it will go. In a month or two, it should be almost impossible to find. Unless someone knows what they are looking for, of course." Quentin smiled and sat down.

A wave of relief came over Hannah's face. "Thank you," she said, bending down to kiss the seated Quentin's forehead. Quentin patted the chair next to him. "Hannah, sit. I need some details from you."

While Hannah and Quentin chatted, Jane beckoned Ed to the kitchen. Closing the door, she turned to face him.

"What's going on, Ed?"

"What do you mean?" he shrugged his shoulders.

"How come the young Letchford is here?"

"I don't know what to tell you. He dropped in for coffee and…"

"Okay, I don't need the sordid details, but when did you and he become a thing?" Jane pointed to the living room.

"It's not like that. It's just…" Ed's face scrunched up. "Bollocks, Jane, I don't know what it is yet. Why are you bothered?"

She bit her thumbnail and mumbled. "I'm having…issues with Letchford Senior. He's trying to use every lever he can to get me into bed. Tell me this…" she wiggled a finger between Ed and the living room. "…isn't something similar?"

She began to wonder how deep the supposed control of the media had gone, and how many Letchfords were involved.

Ed smiled. "Okay, I might have lied earlier. I have a little history with our friend next door. He's really nice. It's my day off, so I called him. I was surprised to find he was in town, and well, you can guess the rest." His face reddened. She'd never seen Ed blush. It was a relief. Maybe Letchford the Younger was innocent in all this. She smiled.

"Sorry for poking my nose in. I was worried, that's all." Walking over, she put her arms around his neck. He kissed her cheek, and then they broke the hug, going back through to find the other two still discussing websites.

"How are you two getting on?" Jane asked.

"I have everything I need. I think I can make this go away," Quentin said. Hannah smiled, clapped her hands and then hugged him.

"Thank you, both," said Jane. "We'll leave you to it." She turned to Ed. "Behave."

"I can't promise you that," he said and slapped her backside as she headed for the door.

Edinburgh, Friday 14th March 2025

Nancy checked her Hotmail account. The regular Friday email was there. As always, the message included an advert for kids' clothing and an address of the store at the bottom. Only, there was never a store. She piled the regular mail and put the usual brown envelope on top. She read with disdain that the address was way down at the bottom of Leith Walk. It would take ages to get there.

Donning her coat, she shouted, "Have a good weekend," to the office as she walked out the door, down the steps and out onto the Royal Mile. There was a postbox a few doors up, and she deposited the office mail. She would now have to get a bus to Leith to post the remaining envelope through the door of her given address.

It was unclear to her just why her emailer wanted this stuff. It all seemed fairly innocuous. Copies of anything that came into the office by letter, excluding bills. This week, there were only three letters. The thank you note, the invitation and a rather strange offer for exotic pets. She guessed that the spam sender didn't know they had sent it to a solicitor's office, but she copied it anyway.

Nancy had been doing this for eighteen months now, ever since she received an email with pictures of her twenty-five-year-old son Jamie doing things she would rather the rest of the world never knew. After a weekend of no sleep, and having considered her options, she got on and followed the orders. She hadn't talked to Jamie, but she knew the images to be legitimate. Even though the mailer told her not to speak to anyone, she really wanted to talk to her boss, Duncan. Ultimately, Nancy thought better of it. It felt bad that she was concealing this from him, but she'd placated herself with the fact that the documents didn't seem that important anyway.

Remembering that she was meeting the girls at six, she eschewed the bus, flagging a taxi instead.

BBC News, Monday 17th March 2025

"Overnight, in Washington, there has been a stunning new development in the political upheaval. Patti Currie, until yesterday, president pro tempore of the United States Senate, has been appointed as interim president by the Democrat faction. In a statement, the Democratic Party said;"

"As fourth in line to be US president, Miss Currie is the legal choice in light of there being no elected candidate, no vice president and with the Speaker of the House having resigned."

Dana's face went dark. "The Republican Party contests this appointment, and they continue their claim that Donald Thorn was legally elected in the November 2024 election. In effect, America now has two presidents, and with their governmental system in total collapse, it is terrifying to all that this debate may yet be settled on the battlefield, rather than the ballot box."

London, Monday 17th March 2025

"I'm sorry, ambassador. The Prime Minister cannot take the call from a President Currie, you must understand. However, if Senator Currie were announced, he would of course answer," the Downing Street receptionist replied.

"Aren't you being rather pedantic?" the US ambassador said.

"Mr Ambassador, I have my orders. Now would you like to tell me who is calling, please?"

The ambassador sighed. He was aware that he was lucky still to be regarded as ambassador at all. Thorn hadn't thought to start on the embassy network yet. If he did, the Brits would probably shut him down too. The US ambassador to the UK was staunchly pinning his flag to the Democrat mast, but he couldn't expect the Brits to follow. No one knew how this was going to pan out. "I have Senator Patti Currie for the Prime Minister."

"Putting you through."

"Ravi, how are you?" Currie said in greeting.

"I am okay, Senator. Probably a whole lot better than you, I guess," the PM replied.

"Yes, things are rather crazy. A few days ago, I was planning retirement and looking forward to getting the garden in shape. Now I'm facing a civil war. I need your help, Prime Minister," the American leader said, cutting straight to the chase.

"Senator, we stand ready to assist in any legal way possible but…" He left it hanging.

"But your legal boffins are telling you to stay a million miles away?" she answered for him.

"Something like that," he admitted. "What sort of help were you looking for? We can of course provide humanitarian assistance," he offered.

"It hasn't come to that yet, thankfully," she said. "I need something a little more practical. I need intelligence."

The PM scratched his forehead. "Surely your systems are second to none?" he enquired.

"I am sure they are, Ravi. The problem I have is that my control over them is…patchy," Currie admitted.

There was a long delay before the PM replied. "How would you feel if the UK offered such assistance to Mr Thorn's faction, Senator?"

"I really would not be happy, and when this is over, I would kick your ass," she said with a sigh.

"Exactly. So, what happens if this conflict does not pan out the way you wish?" the PM said.

Not answering the query, Currie said, "Do you really want that idiot back in the White House? It would be a disaster for the entire Western world."

"He has made favourable approaches to the UK and offered a free trade deal if we recognise his government," the PM said.

"Is that some sort of threat, Mr Prime Minister?" Currie asked.

"Of course not. I am simply pointing out we have a lot to lose, however this ends up."

There was another sigh from the American. "Well, Mr Prime Minister, I am here now requesting help, and I promise you jack shit in return other than the thanks of a grateful president. Now are you going to grow a pair of balls and help solve this thing or not?" Currie went silent and waited.

London, Downing Street, Wednesday 19th March 2025

"...The request has been made by Senator Currie from the Democratic faction and she's really upped the stakes," the PM said. "I cannot see any way that we do not end up getting dragged into this conflict. On balance, it is my judgement that the Currie presidency has more legitimacy. I don't know how much longer we can stay on the fence, people."

"But we have been made an attractive offer by Thorn," said Selwyn Letchford MP.

The PM knew where 'the Letch's' sympathies lay. "Thank you, Selwyn, but I doubt he will ever be in a position to deliver on those promises. And as we know to our cost, the man is damned unreliable. Anyway, this will be discussed further in the COBRA meeting this afternoon. We can get the input of the Security Services at that time. For now, I know I do not need to remind you, but I am going to anyway. No mention of this outside these walls. See you back here at three." The PM closed his folder.

The boring default ringtone on Jane's iPhone sounded from her pocket. She really wanted a fun tone, but her boss Dan had warned all staff that it didn't look good if Lady Gaga burst into song in the middle of an interview. Lifting the phone to her ear, she answered.

"Jane, dear, I need to see you now," said Letchford before she could say anything.

There were a dozen things she would have rather said to the man, but she replied, "Where are you?"

"Oh, Jane, dear, I loved it when you used to call me sir," the MP replied. A few seconds of silence followed before she figured he was not going to answer her query.

"Where are you, *sir*?" she said through gritted teeth.

"Mmmm, much better. I am in the upstairs members' bar," he replied, and the line went dead.

Jane knew her debt would be called in one day soon, though she hadn't expected it to be a quickie in the Parliament toilets. Mentally, she checked that she wore matching underwear. Reaching into her pocket, she popped a mint in her mouth, and finding the Ariana Grande perfume bottle near the bottom, she reapplied a dab on her neck.

London was abuzz with car horns, bus engines and the chatter of the masses, but as she crossed the road and headed to her fate, she felt detached from the throng, not comforted by it as she usually was. Six million people were doing one thing, and it felt to Jane like she was doing something else.

She waved her pass to policeman Davie at the door. He knew her well and didn't even search her bag anymore. Walking through the hall to the stairs, Jane waved to Isla Wallace, who was deep in conversation with colleagues. Isla flashed her a smile and returned to the debate.

"There's no fucking way, pal," Jane heard her say to a terrified fellow SNP MP.

Wow, if she talks to friends like that... Jane thought.

Jane's heels clicked loudly on the marble stairs as she ascended. A burly man opened one of the heavy wooden doors for her before she even reached the top. She said nothing as she passed. It was a relief to see the members' bar was busy.

Letchford shouted over the din, "Here, Miss Clark." He stood alone at the bar, so she sauntered over. "We can do the interview here," Letchford said in an overly loud voice and pointed to a table for two by the wall. It looked like he wanted to let his colleagues believe this was a regular BBC interview.

He handed her an orange juice, picked up another from the bar and walked to the table. In his loud voice, he said, "How may I help our state broadcast network today, Miss Clark?" and smiled as if awaiting a question.

Relieved to be reporter rather than concubine, she played along, "How is the government handling the compromised situation in America, sir?"

His professional smile widened a little at the respectful pronoun. He leant forward. In a low voice, he whispered, "You read my mind, dear. We *are* so good together. I need this out on the one o'clock news." He handed her a copy of the Conservative Party manifesto. In his louder voice, he continued. "All you need to know is in there, Miss Clark." After gulping down the drink, he stood abruptly, then added, "I do hope that I have been of help." With a wink, he walked off.

She scratched the back of her thick, curly brunette hair and picked up the manifesto; a white piece of paper began to fall out. Tapping the protruding sheet back, she headed for the toilet on the landing.

London, BBC News at One

"…BBC News at One, read by Dana McInteer…"

"Another day of turmoil for Ravi Suvar's Government of National Unity. We go straight over to Westminster and reporter Jane Clark."

"Thank you, Dana. Yes, sources within Parliament have confirmed that the UK government is about to recognise the Patti Currie faction in the ongoing US conflict. The British government will offer security data and intelligence to the Washington-based authorities, and the official recognition of the new Democrat-led administration will be confirmed in this afternoon's COBRA meeting. This is likely to draw the UK into the conflict. I have been advised that the Queen Elizabeth Carrier Group stands off New York as we speak. It is unclear if the group's F35s will actually fly over US soil in active missions. The cause of the UK government coming off the fence at this time is as yet unknown, though some believe that the Prime Minister has no confidence in the word of Donald Thorn. How the estimated twenty thousand US military personnel that are still based in the UK will react to this news is yet to be seen. Jane Clark, reporting from Westminster."

Westminster, Wednesday 19th March 2025

Boris Jenkins had a magnetic nature. Both people and trouble were drawn to him. Standing to talk in the afternoon emergency debate, he ran his fingers through his flat blond hair. Boris's generally unruly mop lay matted on his scalp after being caught in the heavy rain shower. The swelling band of MPs that had gravitated toward Jenkins' position on the extremity of the government benches were likewise shaking locks and brushing suits to remove evidence of the spring shower.

Seemingly now content that his hair looked more like he just got out of bed, he rose to speak.

"Thank you, Mr Speaker, for granting this debate. I find myself standing before you today, suffering as Aulus Gabinius afore the Roman senate. I, too, am compelled to oppose my own party and bear the heavy weight of that chore. Today's news that our government is set to drag the British people into a conflict that will cause irreconcilable trouble in this land for many years to come, cannot be ignored or idly accepted." He stopped just long enough to look around the chamber and receive a few calls of support.

"Yes, a previous Conservative Party leader may have sat on his hands while a war brewed in Europe. *He* made the mistake of not recognising the dangers yet to come. So, members, you may think that I stand now in praise of the quick and decisive action of the current incumbent of that lofty position, but this could be no further from the truth. For Chamberlain, appeasement was inaction, and today's announced course may be less sederunt, yet it reeks of appeasement no less."

Around Jenkins were more calls of "Here, Here." He waited for these to die down before proceeding.

"I put it to you, Mr Speaker, that this decision to act is not one of moral virtue or even of strength. Our prime minister has had an arm twisted by a bully in the White House. He joins no moral crusade. Instead, he leads our men and women into the guns at Balaclava. Mr Speaker, when Chamberlain dithered, our nation was saved by Churchill. I can only pray to the heavens that we have a Winston on these benches today, to save us from ignominy."

Jenkins sat down, and the one hundred colleagues that had gravitated to his end of the benches rose to their feet as one. "Heeeeeeerrreeee, heeeeeeerreee," they bleated. Order papers were waved, and some even thrown at their own front bench.

Westminster, Wednesday 19th March 2025

"I want to go home and sleep," Ed said. Dana nodded, confirming that she agreed with his statement, using the minimum of energy.

Jane said, "Sorry, guys."

Mid yawn, Ed asked, "What are you sorry for now?" but Dana answered.

"Breaking this fecking story and forcing us to sit here, freezing our lady bollocks off and waiting for the muppets in there to stop slagging each other." She pointed to Parliament over her shoulder with a thumb.

"Oh that," he said, nodding with watering eyes.

"Guilty as charged," said Jane, holding her hands up.

"You had to break that one, girl," said Dana.

Jane wondered if Dana was recognising the gravitas of the story or if her friend knew she had been compelled. As blackmail duties went, Jane found nothing onerous in the task. Hell, she would have run with this story if any MP had broken it to her. Yet, she could see how it helped Letchford's faction. The Tories were ripping themselves apart.

BBC News, Wednesday 19th March 2025

"…Dana McInteer, live at Parliament, where tonight the government has been forced to allow a vote of no confidence. This outcome came as they failed to pass their motion to help the Currie faction in the US crisis. Boris Jenkins and eighty Conservative members voted with the opposition to bring the bill down. Selwyn Letchford, a long-time Boris supporter, then demanded they hold a vote of confidence, which was carried. The Parliament looks set to run late into the night, but as of now, we are unsure if the Speaker will call the vote today or tomorrow. We were already in uncharted waters with the suspension of the election and formation of the Government of National Unity. Who knows where this situation leaves the government now. Dana McInteer, live from Parliament."

Jane stood next to Ed, watching Dana's report. She was about to tell him of the note from Letchford but then realised they still had more than a bit of air-clearing to do. Now seemed like as good a time as any, if only to take her mind off being complicit in the resulting governmental devastation.

"Why did you stop me going with the Aussie waiter in India?" Jane asked.

Ed turned with eyebrows raised. "You really want to know?"

"I *really* want to know," Jane replied.

He looked thoughtful and then said, "Because he had blown me in the toilets earlier and then asked for money."

Jane was shocked, but then a smile crossed her lips and, losing control, she bent double with laughter.

"I thought you…" She couldn't finish but held up a hand to tell him to wait until she gained control. Standing upright again, she took several deep breaths. "Oh Ed, I thought you were jealous," she said and sighed. "You know I love being with you; that's why seeing you with Quentin at the Christmas party nearly ripped my heart out."

She let out a long breath as if a weight had fallen from her shoulders. Ed turned and stared.

"You saw me with him?" he asked quietly.

"Yes," she lowered her gaze. "At first, I was annoyed with you. I thought the reason was that you'd compromised what I was trying to do, workwise. Then I decided I was jealous that you had Quentin when I fancied him. But later that night, when a hundred things were running through my head about our relationship and…well, it turned out, there was only one thing that made them all come together. I wasn't annoyed you were shagging Quentin; I was pissed off it wasn't me on that sofa with you."

On completion of the confession, she couldn't look up from her shoes. Her eyes were half shut, anticipating the hammer blow of rejection that was surely inevitable.

"But I'm gay," Ed replied quietly.

She was fairly sure that this was how the conversation would pan out. There was never more than a glimmer of hope that he would pull her into his arms and announce his undying love. Yet now she'd doubtless made their relationship awkward. There was a chance he would walk out of her life forever, and she would do anything to prevent that.

"I know, Eddie." Sighing, she reluctantly looked up into his dark brown eyes and freed the collar of his shirt from under his jacket lapel. "I don't need anything from you that I don't already have. You are, and I hope you will remain, my closest friend, but friends should be honest with each other. I'm just glad you know, anyway." She smiled and patted his cheek.

He said, "You know I love you too, but…"

She laid a finger on his lips. "You don't have to finish that, Ed. You love me. That's enough," she said. He smiled a little and bent his head to kiss her.

Westminster, Thursday 20th March 2025

"I need your support on this, Mr Letchford." Prime Minister Ravi Suvar hated beseeching MPs, who should be utterly loyal, to support their own government.

"Sir, of course you have my full backing. I sided with the Jenkins' motion last night for one reason only. We must kill this rebellion off once and for all. If it is allowed to fester on the back benches, the rebels will stand in front of every piece of legislation you bring to the House."

Selwyn Letchford smiled amiably at his leader. Carter Davis-Jones, Father of the House, stood next to Letchford and nodded.

"Bring it out into the light, sir. Sunshine is always the best cure," he offered in his usual string of metaphors.

The PM looked back and forth between the two men. He was well aware they were supporters of Jenkins when the man had stood for the leadership a few years ago, but he also knew both to be fickle. They blew with whichever wind looked stronger.

"Okay, we will stop fighting this and let it go to a vote. You are both sure that your faction are on board?" he asked.

Letchford answered. "We have no doubt who the best leader is, sir. You can count on that."

The PM felt mollified. After a few seconds of contemplation, he nodded to his aide. They would ask the Speaker to hold the vote of no confidence and kill this rebellion stone dead.

Big Ben chimed the hour, and members streamed into the hall. The Speaker stood, motion paper in hand.

"Order! Order! The motion is that a vote of confidence in the Government of National Unity be held. Those that support, please say aye." He looked from bench to bench.

"AAAyyyyyyEEEEE," came the reply from almost all in the room.

"Those against?" the Speaker shouted.

"No!" came a few replies.

"Division," called the Speaker. "Clear the lobbies."

The hubbub rose among members on all sides. Everywhere, debate and persuasion began. Selwyn Letchford sat loyally beside his PM, a face like thunder. It was, of course, an affectation. Inside, Letchford was delighted at the way things were panning out. He had planned this, after all. He stood and tapped the PM on the shoulder.

"We have the numbers, sir. Everything will be fine."

The PM smiled up at him. Selwyn left the front bench and headed for the lobby. Some arms may need twisting to ensure the government whips failed in their duty.

Westminster, Thursday 20th March 2025

"Jane Clark, live at Westminster. The government finally gave in today and the vote goes ahead. The Conservative whips appear confident, but they can be seen among the members, rallying the loyal to the cause. The vote is complicated by the Liberal Democrats allowing their members free reign. We are being told some will go through the opposition lobby. PM Suvar said earlier that he is confident this motion will be defeated and that he can get on with governing the country at this critical time in world uncertainty. Dana, all is still to play for here."

Jane handed back to Dana in the studio. They quickly moved to the day's other news.

"That okay, Ed?" she said and smiled at the cameraman.

"Spot on as usual," he replied, thumb wiggling in the air. "Let's go get a coffee. This faff will be going on a while." He pointed to the turmoil all around.

"Sounds good," she replied before leading him toward the members' bar. Machinations would be underway. She needed to know who was talking to whom.

On reaching the bar, they were greeted by the smiling doorman. He stood aside for Jane but then gave Ed a dodgy look. "My cameraman," she explained. With some reluctance, Ed was allowed to pass.

Inside the busy bar, they found a table, and she quickly got them a couple of coffees.

"How did you get us in here?" Ed asked, somewhat incredulous.

"I'm a celebrity." Jane mock-swished her hair over her shoulder.

"Of course," said Ed, "I forgot. I thought this was members only?"

"It is, but I interviewed The Letch here a few times, and the locals got to know me," she explained.

It was difficult to know how much to tell Ed. He might beat Letchford to a pulp if he knew about the blackmail. That thought made her smile.

As they sipped their coffee in silence, with his phone to nose, Ed texted someone while she scanned the room. Conversations, both convivial and heated, were conducted at surrounding tables. On the large wall-mounted TV above the bar, The Speaker called the vote again to a now mostly empty chamber. He organised the tellers that would undertake the count and announce the result. This done, the division bell rang, and while a few members headed for the lobby, most continued the deliberations.

"I guess about twenty minutes," Jane said.

Ed quickly looked about. "Yeah, fifteen at best. We have time."

"Time for what?" she said and giggled.

"Behave, you tart," but he smiled too. "Is this going to be weird?" he asked, his pretty face now wrinkled with concern.

"Not at all," said Jane, but were she being honest, she wasn't sure.

Falling in love with a gay guy. What are you like? she asked herself silently. His concerned golden-brown eyes were locked on her, and while they were, she was the happiest captive alive, but all of a sudden, he gave a placatory shrug and returned his attention to the phone.

"Oh hell," she said, and Ed looked up again. Letchford had

walked in and spotted them. He came right over, grinning like a Cheshire cat.

The beaming MP held out a hand to Ed. "Edward, my dear boy," he said as the two men shook. "And Jane, the enchanting Miss Clark that keeps her light under a bushel," he leaned over and kissed her cheek. Uninvited, Letchford sat close to her, but his demeanour was more conspiratorial than lecherous for once. "We have the numbers," he almost sang with glee.

"The government?" Jane asked.

"Well, yes, but the new government," he grinned. "Boris is back, and you, my dear, were invaluable. Your contribution will be rewarded. He and I both hold you in high regard. You know you only need to call, should you ever need anything?" He kissed her cheek again and stood. "Must go do my duty. Lovely to see you both." Letchford headed for the door but stopped. He turned back to face her. "I mean anything."

The words were generous, but somehow, to Jane, it sounded more like a threat. She watched Letchford exit and gave a small shiver.

Ed turned to her. "What was that all about?" She didn't answer him.

"How come you two are such good buddies?" she asked.

"What do you mean?" he said with the corners of his mouth turning down.

"I wouldn't have thought he even knew your name, but he greeted you like a long-lost friend." She pointed to the door that the MP just left by.

"We've seen each other round this place. He's always been friendly enough," Ed replied while shuffling in his seat, but she narrowed her eyes and stared at him. He was withholding something. A lifetime of interviews gave her the ability to know when there was more left unsaid. *Leave it for now*, she thought.

"Yeah, he can certainly be friendly," she said, wiping her cheek. The two laughed. "Come on, drink up. We better be going."

The weather was warm for a March evening, and Jane, Ed, Dana and the rest of the BBC team sat huddled round a screen, awaiting the vote. The producer fussed about like a bee while getting nearly as many brush-offs. His attention alighted on Dana.

"Dana, dear. We will cut to you as soon as the result is announced. Give us the background, then hand it to Jane for the numbers. Jane, Ed, set up with the clock behind you in the picture." He moved his orbit to the crowd of reporters and technicians at large. "Right, everyone. This is going to have to be last second, but if the government hold on, I need Dana and her team over in the lobby. And techs, make sure we have bloody sound this time." He wagged a finger at the blushing group of sound engineers who had forgotten to bring a microphone to the last interview. "If Boris wins…Yes, Jane." He stopped, seeing his reporter with a hand up like a little kid at school.

"Boss, you don't need to prepare for the government winning. Go with your plans for Boris," she said. He looked at her for a second and then came over.

"Is that a prediction, Jane?" he asked quietly. She shook her head.

They locked eyes for a while. Upon finding the assurance he needed in her eyes, he sprang back up. "Forget everything I said. We are going with plan B. Dana, you will set up out here." The orders continued; the crew started off to their posts.

Jane and Ed returned their attention to the screen.

"Order!" the Speaker called and read the motion again. He then called the clerks to the bench. The motion being against the government, Suvar was looking for the Nays to win for once. He sat, wringing his hands like he applied sanitiser.

The clerk on the right of the four spoke. "The Ayes four hundred and twelve…

The House erupted. All knew the Ayes had won. There weren't enough members for the government to hold on. Suvar's head fell into his hands. Letchford, sitting two to his left, stood, walked to the stairwell and left the hall. "Order! Order!" the Speaker called. He had to try several times more before anything approximating quiet reigned.

A member near the back of the hall started chanting, "Boris, Boris, Boris…" Another joined, and more followed. The opposition benches emptied slowly. They filed out each door. There should have been smiles on their faces; they had won. Most realised this was no victory.

Isla Wallace walked past the Speaker's Chair, and Jane heard her voice, picked up quietly through the nearby microphone. "What the fuck have we done?"

Dana was now on the screen, bringing the news to the masses. She prepared to hand to Jane for the numbers, but the total of no votes still hadn't been called. Ed had the camera ready to roll, and Jane held her hand high to tell Dana to keep padding. What a pro, Jane thought. Dana had stood there ten minutes and discussed the only sentence announced so far.

"Finally!" Jane said as the clerk spoke. "The Nays to the left, 146." There had been quite a few abstentions, but no one cared. She lowered her hand and ran.

"I now hand you over to Jane Clark for more details," Dana announced.

Ed's camera light went on as Jane slid along the grass and into position. "Thanks, Dana, I can now bring you the official result…"

Jane and Ed sat in the café and awaited another call to action. The evening was a series of short stints to camera, giving the numbers, speculating on the repercussions, and interviewing members. Perhaps strangely, the bulk of the defeated Tories seemed jubilant, while the winning opposition MPs were apprehensive. While earlier interviewing the leader of the Labour Party, Jane had asked,

"This is the second time you have brought down a moderate Tory leader and ushered in Boris. You must like him?"

The uninspiring man blustered and offered no real answers for his actions. To a degree, she pitied him, but only for what she blamed herself. They had both been used, pawns in a game neither understood.

With her attention back in the café, Jane pressed Ed on his connection to Letchford.

"I met him at a party on Tufton Street," he said. "I was there with…a friend who knew him well. The Letch invited us over to join his table, and he bought me drinks all night, not that anyone was charging. He seemed to be hitting on me," Ed explained with noticeable reluctance.

"Would your friend have been a cricketer by chance?" Jane said.

"Maybe." Ed nodded, then gave a sardonic smile.

"When was this?" she asked.

"A couple of years ago," he replied.

"Wait!" she said. "You knew Quentin two years ago? Why didn't you say anything?"

"I didn't know it was him until we walked into the Christmas party. I hadn't seen him for ages. We drifted apart," he admitted. "He never told me he was Letchford's son, Jane. I would have said something had I known."

She relaxed a little. They all moved in the same circles. Government officials and press were often found around and about each other. *Some more in about than others*, she thought.

Ed wriggled in his seat. "We're going out together again soon." He drew his neck into his shoulders as if awaiting her attack.

"Are you two an item now?" she tried hard to keep a smile on her face. It was one of those questions where knowing the answer could hurt. So, why she'd asked, she couldn't figure.

"Not sure," said Ed. "He's hard to suss. He is very much in the closet and that is not my style, as you know," he chuckled.

"And Daddy doesn't know about Quentin?" she asked.

"No, but they are two apples from the same tree," he said. "Daddy has made more than one advance to me, and I have seen him around a few of the clubs."

"Don't take offence at this, Ed, but I am beginning to think that Letchford senior would shag a bag of potatoes if he got the chance." Ed laughed far harder than she anticipated. "It wasn't that funny," she said, slightly confused at his reaction.

"I was laughing at 'bag of potatoes.'" Ed affected a fake posh voice. "You would have said sack o' tatties a few years ago. When did we become civilised?" he asked, still chuckling away.

She joined in. "Too much of this bloody furry London water. Anyway, how have you…managed to keep Letchford off you? I'm asking for a friend."

He grinned. "It's different for me, Jane. He wants to do it discreetly, so all I do is ensure we're never alone. And of course, I would kick the shit out of The Letch if he tried something that I wasn't up for."

"I'm not sure how many more times I can knee him in the balls," she said, looking at her feet.

"Do you want me to talk to him?" said Ed.

She looked up at him. "No...no, thanks. God, this is so complicated. I need to keep him onside for now. He is...useful, but I don't see myself being able to keep him at arm's length for long." She hated that she wasn't telling Ed everything.

Just then her phone beeped. Looking at the screen, she said, "Talk of the devil." All that the message said was, *Call me.* She walked away from the table and dialled.

"Hi, dear," said Letchford. It sounded like there was a celebration going on in the background. "Are you free to accompany me to a party tomorrow evening?" he asked.

Despite his tone, she knew that it wasn't a request. "Of course, sir." She sighed.

"Wear something nice," he slurred, and she realised he was drunk. "I'll send a car for you at eight." He ended the call.

London, Friday 21st March 2025

The car drew up right on time. Jane arranged her jewellery while looking out the window. With her granny's old pearl earrings and the ankle-length white gown, she could have been a fifties film star. Checking the mirror, she smiled at the girl looking back. *If I grew a foot and lost two stone*, she appended the thought.

"I never wanted to be a stick insect anyway," she picked up the short white jacket that would be worn over her dress. After locking her front door, Jane took the last few steps carefully. Heels were not meant for rock climbing, after all.

There were two figures in the back of the car already. Unsure of who they were, she began curving her path to get a look before jumping in.

The car door opened, and Jane heard Dana's voice before noticing Dan was with her too. "Jane, you look magnificent. Rita Hayworth, eat your heart out." The Irish girl giggled. Slowly, Jane lowered herself into the vehicle. A ripped dress wouldn't be a good look.

Her two colleagues were already well through the first bottle of plonk. Dan leaned over to the drinks cabinet for another.

"This is going to be great," said Dana.

Jane still had no idea where they were going and what was planned, but she was a little relieved, if mystified, as to why her boss and friend were coming too. Dana and Dan were sitting on opposite seats. She wasn't supposed to know they were an item unless Dana had confessed to Dan. For now, Jane would wait and see what was going down.

"Here," Dan said, handing her a glass of champagne.

"Thanks, boss," she said as the chilled glass threatened to slide from her grasp. Hand shaking, she took a sip and lowered it to the small table that spanned the seat between her and Dan.

"Have you ever been to this place?" Dana asked.

"No, I haven't."

"Me neither," said Dana. "I've heard a lot about it, though. Apparently, everyone who's anyone will be there. It's the official launch."

Jane nodded and decided not to let on that she had no idea where they were headed. She looked out the tinted windows of the car. There was something magical about London's streets at night. Well, early evening before the drunks took over. The people silhouetted by the shop window lights, dressed to the nines, laughing and smiling, headed somewhere fun. *I used to be the one out there looking in*, she thought.

She wasn't about to deny preferring to be this side of the tint. Dreaming of nights like this as a child, she put on mum's dresses and made her way to the pretend ball. Yet tonight, perfect as it seemed, something in her belligerent head said that this wasn't right. Lifting the crystal champagne flute, she slowly tipped it back and forth, stopping just before it spilled.

"It's not poisonous," Dan said, looking at her with a strange intensity.

"I'm worried about the cost, boss," Jane replied.

For a while, he sat quietly and looked her over. It appeared that he knew she wasn't thinking about the price of champagne. "Has anything worthwhile in your life ever come free?" Dan took a sip from his own glass.

"Integrity."

"Stop the car," he barked. Braking heavily, the driver pulled over. Dan reached past Jane and opened the door. He sat back and said, "The streets of London are paved with integrity, Jane. You are a fantastic reporter, and the *Watford Advertiser* will be lucky to have you."

"No, Jane, don't," beseeched Dana, holding a hand out, her painted fingernails raking the air as if to claw Jane back from the edge of a precipice.

Jane sat and looked at the pavement, then the champagne, then Dan. Outside, passersby stopped to peer in, hoping to see that the limo held celebs. It made her feel like she was in a goldfish bowl. She didn't know where they headed tonight, but once they arrived and walked in the door, it was obvious there was no turning back. There would be no clever ploy to leave Letchford drooling. Having succumbed to the treasures on offer, she would be theirs.

Outside the car, an apparition of her socialist father stood, hand outstretched, ready to escort his daughter to a life free of compromise. She made to stand, while the promise of wealth, fame, and consequence did all they could to drag her back.

With a tear in her eye, Dana reached over and gripped Jane's arm. "Please don't."

Jane looked to her friend. "Sorry," she said and got out of the car.

Across the pavement, a half lit shop window displayed colourful camping equipment. It held no interest, yet the stoves, tents and backpacks commanded her attention like few things before. For she was sure she would die, if witnessing the limo drive her dreams off into the night. All that young Jane ever sought stood just ten feet behind her.

The tainted warmth of the vehicle spilled out of its still open door, crossed the pavement, and surrounding her ankles; in entropy, it fought against the chill of a noble life more ordinary.

Why was this difficult? So, Colin Burton had died. If Letchford killed him, she didn't know whether to hug the man or run from him. Either way, Burton was better off dead.

With his brow crossed in deep lines, the concerned ghost of her father stood among the camping display in the shop window. Dad loved his tent. The family were dragged round half of Scotland to spend school breaks in muddy fields. There was fraternity and egalitarianism in camping. No matter how fancy your tent, you all slept in the grass at night. Dad loved that sort of thing. Even at seven years old, Jane hated it. She didn't care that everyone shared the misery; she wanted her warm bed. She wanted more.

So, why are you turning your back on more now?

Dad was the only man who saw his daughter's success in the media as some sort of failing. He wasn't happy at Duncan either. Maybe had her brother fought for the poor, that would have been acceptable, but a solicitor's income and status stood as a slap in the face to Dad's socialist sensibilities. Working for the BBC was no better. Jane may have well turned up at home with a Tory Party membership card, as far as Dad cared. Right here, right now, for the first time in her life, Jane wondered if he was right all along.

If you're fine with murder and trampling on traditions, why the hell are you not in the back of that car right now?

Dad's apparition shook its head and slowly faded from the camp scene.

With the last vestiges of Dad gone, a firm hand gripped her shoulder. She spun around. Dan stood in front of her. It struck her that he looked older. Weary maybe.

"What is integrity?" he asked. Not sure he wanted an answer, she said nothing, so he continued. "Integrity boils down to being truthful. Do you see these people walking past?" Dan pointed to the passersby. "You *are* their truth. They toddle back and forth between work and the pub, regurgitating the things that you, Dana and I deign to tell them. They don't want to think for themselves. It's just too much work."

He released some pressure from the grip on her arm. "Jane, I'm not about to fire you if you decide to walk away now. You are way too good at your job for that. So tomorrow, I am going to tell a producer something, he is going to tell it to you, and then you are going to tell it to this lot." Dan ran his outstretched arm about him. "If you are happy with that, then walk away now. But come with me in the car tonight, Jane, and tomorrow, you won't just be telling the news. You will be making it. Getting in the limo, doesn't strip you of your integrity. It will empower you to define it." He looked deep into her soul, and seeing her ambition burning strong still, the corners of his mouth turned up. "Get in the car, and we will discuss your new office and the staff you need. Okay?"

The vehicle of her compromise deposited them on a quiet street that Jane didn't recognise. Dan took Dana in one arm, her in the other, and guided them giggling to their mysterious destination. Two bottles of champagne lay empty in the back of the car. Jane was sure she was responsible for most of the second. With his help, she managed the four granite steps that led to the innocuous door.

Inside, the décor completely contrasted the building's plain façade. Opulent chandeliers loomed over the revellers in each room they passed. Under their golden light, antique furnishings lay all around, and exquisite art adorned every wall. They reached the end of the long corridor and entered a shorter one with what looked like a hundred banners lining both walls – the Union flag and Stars and Stripes alternating. A plaque above the door they approached read, *Anglo American Society*. The doorman put out a hand to stall them, while another announced the three visitors.

Dan turned his head and whispered in her ear, "Everything you ever dreamed of is only three paces away, Jane. You need only step inside."

He dropped both arms, walked over the threshold and reached out to Dana. Without hesitation, she took his hand and walked over beside him. He then reached out to Jane. She stood unmoving, seeing Letchford right behind, beaming. It didn't take a mind reader to know the MP's intentions. He may as well have had his forehead tattooed with them.

What did it matter?

Jane had lived. She'd done worse for little or no gain. Letchford would certainly be the oldest creep that she had…Oh God, that shiver ran up her spine again, but he wouldn't be the worst thing she'd ever crawled into bed with. Hell, he wouldn't even crack the top five. The two men in front of her now were complete bastards, sure. But maybe this was the only door to the life she sought. One thing was certain in her mind. This door would never open again.

She started as an arm slid round her waist. "Good evening, dear. We don't want to be impolite, but you are holding up the entrance of the guest of honour," an American voice said.

Jane looked up into the face of the tall man and gasped. Donald Thorn looked back. Dan and Letchford stood aside. The ex and possibly next president of the USA walked through the door, Jane at his side. Everyone in the hall stood and applauded. An unseen band struck up 'The Star-Spangled Banner'. The unlikely couple began a circuit of the hall. He shook hands and greeted all that approached. A tall security man whispered in the ex-president's ear, and Thorn started changing his greeting.

"Hi, I'm President Thorn, and this is Miss Jane Clark."

Jane, shell-shocked, tried not to look like a rabbit in the headlights as a hundred cameras flashed her way. With the circuit completed, Thorn led her to the top table, pulled out a chair and ushered her to sit. He leant forward and said, "We heard you were impressive, but they really didn't do you justice." His hand ran down her back before he broke contact and sat next to her. A chairman stood and the hall fell silent.

"Lords, ladies and gentlemen. May I remind you that you are free to take pictures if the subject permits, but should any photos appear in the press tomorrow or anytime thereafter, the repercussions will be serious. Ladies and gentlemen, you will understand that the President's time with us is limited. So, may I now ask you to welcome President Donald Thorn to our distinguished society."

Loud applause broke out and some gave the American a standing ovation before he started speaking. It took a long while for the crowd to settle. Thorn held up a hand and a hush went over the room.

Jane scanned the faces in front as Thorn spoke. He was doing the usual platitudes and thanking people that she didn't know. Boris Jenkins sat directly in front of her. Jane wondered if she was in his chair. He was smiling, though, and didn't seem to mind. Several of the UK's richest people looked back at her. Most of the Jenkins rebels, of course. The leadership of the Brexit movement and a man who bore a stunning resemblance to a senior Saudi prince. *It couldn't really be him*, she thought.

Thorn was reaching the conclusion of his speech. "…and we can build this bond between our great nations so that the forces of socialism will never be able to break it. The curse of democracy has stopped the strong from rising for too long. How can the people be trusted to choose their leaders when they know nothing of the consequences of their choice? We are close, my friends. On the brink of achieving our goal in the USA. This week, you have set your great land on this path also. Yes, there will be dissent, but the supporters of freedom and liberty will drown out the dissenters. We, my friends, we are the force that will bring the people the freedom that they desire. No one cares about crosses on a paper. Barely half of the population vote at all. It is time for the strong to rise and the weak to leave the stage. Today, the forces of darkness are being drawn out and eliminated. Tomorrow, our two great nations will walk into the light."

He sat, and the hall rose again in rapture. As the cheering and chanting continued, he took her hand and stood. Pulling her to her feet, he slipped one arm around her waist and waved to the crowd with the other. Five full minutes passed. He turned and kissed her cheek. "We must run now. It was wonderful to make your acquaintance." Thorn headed for the door, the exhilarated crowd thronging around him.

Unsure what just happened, Jane filled a glass with water from the decanter on the table and then gulped it down. As she did, a woman came rushing up with a pen and napkin.

"Can I have your autograph, Miss Clark?" Jane took the napkin and started to scribble. She recognised her new fan – it was the wife of the Father of the House. She attended Parliament occasionally.

"Did you enjoy the speech, Lady Davis-Jones?" Jane said as she handed the napkin back.

"Very much," the overexcited woman said. She reminded Jane of a teenager at a boyband concert. "You were stunning."

"Thank you, but I'm not sure I did much." She waved aside the adulation, but her face flushed.

"Nonsense, Miss Clark."

"Call me Jane."

"Really?" The woman clapped her hands. "Why thank you, Jane. You were our Britannia next to America's Washington."

Several other approaches made, Jane was offered to visit a top industrialist's St Moritz chalet, the use of a lord's Scottish castle, and more party invitations than she could remember. A small part of her hated that she was bloody loving this. *A minuscule part.* She walked in here a nobody. Okay, not a nobody, but certainly not a somebody to these people. Seeing her with Thorn, they assumed the two had some connection, and now she was the darling of the rich and famous alike. They all kept coming.

A tall and incredibly handsome black man walked up to her, handed her a glass of champagne and said, "They gave you only water, I noticed. I thought you maybe needed something stronger?"

Her knees went weak as he smiled. She took the offered glass. "Thank you, Idris." Her head screamed, *It's James fucking Bond! And he's plying me with alcohol!*

She knew her face was doing a poor job of hiding the silly little

Bond fan inside. Jane had herself walking out of the water in a soaked swimsuit and falling into his arms, but the dream shattered as Letchford brushed past Mr Bond and hugged her.

"That was incredible. You were enchanting." He hugged her again, and Jane nearly screamed. 007 smiled at her, shrugged his shoulders, and walked over to talk to someone else.

"Oh please no," Jane said with disappointment, but Letchford misunderstood.

"Yes, you were, my dear. Enchanting." He dragged her over to the table where Dan and Dana sat.

"Back with the commoners now," Dan said and laughed.

Dana stood, hugged Jane and then kissed her cheek. "You all right?" she whispered. It was an innocent question, but it brought Jane tumbling back to earth.

She looked at her friend and answered without equivocation, "I've never been better in my life."

Dana smiled her amazing smile. "I'm so glad you're here. I've… been lonely."

Jane scanned the room and constantly hoped that James Bond would be at one of the tables around her. Another champagne appeared.

"We have a mutual friend," a stunning blonde woman said.

"We do?" Jane asked, turning to better face the woman. She thought that they were of similar age.

"Yes, my son's fiancée – Heather."

Jane's brow furrowed. She knew a few Heathers, but this woman's son couldn't be more than twenty.

"Sorry," said Jane. "You've lost me."

"My son Quentin. I am Lady Letchford," the woman answered.

Jane sat back in her chair and looked at the woman askance. She met Lady Catherine Letchford ten years ago, and this definitely wasn't her. She smiled, thinking: *Well, they can do wonders with plastic surgery these days.*

The other woman caught on and laughed. "Oh, I am not the original Lady Letchford, and of course Quentin is not really my son. I married Selwyn four years ago after his first wife…passed."

Jane relaxed, holding her hand out. "Nice to meet you, Lady Letchford."

The other woman took it. "Call me Elizabeth. Heather talks about you often. Where did you meet?" she asked.

Alarm bells went off in Jane's head. Did Lady Letchford know that her husband was entertaining Heather at the pool at all? This could be tricky.

"We met at some function organised by your husband, I seem to remember. They're getting married?" Jane asked, trying not to sound too disbelieving.

"Yes, it was only announced last week." She leant into Jane. "My husband isn't happy at all. I think he deems Heather a rung too low on the social ladder."

Feeling devilish, Jane said, "I understood Sir Letchford and Heather got on really well?"

"Oh, don't get me wrong. My husband dotes on the girl, but will she really be the next Lady Letchford? A barmaid? Sorry, Miss Clark. I am talking about your friend. I do apologise."

"I take no offence, Lady Letchford. Heather can fight her own battles," Jane replied, but she didn't like this woman.

Out of the corner of her eye, she could see Sir Letchford looking over, and recognising an opportunity in this situation; Jane shifted closer and whispered in his wife's ear, "So, can you give me any juicy gossip about your husband that I can reveal on the news?" She pointed to Letchford and smiled as she spoke.

Involuntarily, Elizabeth followed her finger and looked at her husband. Jane knew she wasn't going to comply, but she wanted Letchford to believe the two of them were talking about him.

Lady Letchford giggled. "Oh dear, you are funny to ask, but I'm afraid he's quite the most boring man in the country."

"Oh, that is a shame." Jane looked over at the MP as if his wife had handed her his deepest secret. "But you can't blame a reporter for trying."

"Of course not, dear," Lady Letchford replied. Her expression turned dismissive. "Lovely to meet you tonight; I am so glad you are on board. You will hear from me soon, dear." Jane looked at her, puzzled, but Lady Letchford then turned away and spoke with people on the other side of the table.

London, Saturday 22nd March 2025

"Oh God, not again," Jane whispered.

The pounding was already underway in her head when she opened her eyes and blinked a few times. Her tongue was stuck to the roof of her mouth. Peeking out from an unfamiliar duvet cover, she could see her white gown lying over the top of a chair. There was movement behind her, and she felt a finger slide down her back.

"Good morning," said Ed.

Hearing his familiar voice, a smile lit her face, and her dry lips cracked painfully. Even so, this was where she wanted to wake up every morning. It was where she was meant to be. She longed to duck under his duvet and never come out.

As she turned, their faces were close. Licking a finger, she flattened Ed's wayward quiff that stood, defying gravity. The finger then ran down his nose and along each deep line above his mouth.

"Laugh lines," she said, now rubbing the back of her hand over his morning stubble and grinning.

"What are you so happy about?" he said. "You must be hungover to shit."

"I am," she admitted, "but I don't care."

Ed frowned. "Don't, Jane," he said.

Realising what he meant, she said, "No, it's not the love thing – although, at this moment, I love you more than ever, you big poof. I didn't know where I was for a minute when I woke up. I was terrified of who I would turn around to. How did I get here?"

With noticeable relief on his face, he said, "Dana phoned and asked me to pick you up from the Ritz."

"I was at the Ritz?" A puzzled frown replaced her smile.

"Dan and Dana had a room. They said you had been at the champagne," he explained.

Jane pulled the duvet over her face. "Oh God, Ed, I don't even remember leaving."

"Don't worry, you were fine, apparently. You blacked out once you hit the night air. You were quite the smash, I hear."

She popped her head out again. "Oh, thank goodness. Last night could have ended so much worse. I need to stop drinking so much."

"Worse than being carried home fireman style and then waking up to a gay Scotsman?" Ed asked.

"You don't know the half of it, Ed," she replied.

They lay quietly a while before Jane looked down under the duvet. "Ed, why am I naked?"

"Oh, I did the dress; the rest was all you. I was made to watch as apparently this was going to *cure my gay*." He laughed. "It may well have worked had you not had to keep stopping to throw up in the sink."

Her hands went over her face, and she sank below the covers. "Kill me now."

Later, in one of their favourite greasy spoons, Jane picked up a sausage with her fingers and bit half, sucking it into her mouth.

"I am sooooo hungry," she said, mouth still full. "Shit, I just remembered I need to phone Heather today." She pointed over the table at Ed. "Did you know she and Quentin are engaged?"

Ed stopped eating and looked up. "Really?" His lips pursed as a scowl narrowed his pretty eyes.

"Apparently," she said, picking up a hash brown. "I met Mummy last night. The happy couple were engaged a week or two ago." Jane wielded the snippet of gossip like a weapon. Would it end whatever was going on between Ed and Quentin? If it did, was there a chance... *Stop it*, she thought

Lifting his coffee mug, he took a gulp. She traced the fluid as it flowed past his Adam's apple. "Quentin and Heather?"

"It didn't sound right to me either," she admitted. "You know that Daddy is banging his future daughter-in-law?" Jane slid another sausage into her mouth with her now greasy fingers.

He looked up at her and laughed. "Never let a straight guy catch you like that."

Jane regarded the sausage protruding from her mouth. She slowly pulled it in and out.

With a napkin, he wiped the runny grease from her chin. "You are such a tart." He smiled at her the way her dad did when he flew teaspoons of baby food into her mouth. They both returned to their plates.

"I have a date with Quentin next Friday," Ed said, out of the blue. "At least, I think I do."

"Where are you going?" she tried not to frown.

"The Randolf," he said.

"It's strange for a man that is about to be married to be off dating other men, don't you think?" She couldn't hide the disappointment in her tone.

"Less strange than you may believe," he replied, chomping on an egg and either ignoring, or in ignorance of how deflated she was that he didn't seem bothered by her news at all.

Sighing, she looked round the room. Everywhere, people tucked into heart attack food and chatted. The diner was usually one of her happy places. Ed and her, alone in a crowd.

He broke her reverie. "What did you mean last night by, 'everything will be different now' and 'will I still be your friend?'"

As pissed as Jane was, and for all the small amount she could recall of the previous evening's festivities, she definitely did remember the dread that this brave new world of riches, power and celebrity would also be one without Ed.

After getting back into the limo with Dan on Friday, he'd promised her a big promotion and a new role within the organisation. Jane was moving upstairs and accruing a fancy office, complete with assistants. She was to run the outside broadcasts for the politics section. Ed knew Jane's thoughts on Dana's move. How would he handle her hypocritical volte-face?

"Dan offered me a new job," she blurted. Ed's eyes left his plate and locked hers, but he said nothing. "I start on Monday." She hoped he would leap in. Unable to hold his stare, her attention dropped back to the greasy table. "I will be working up with Dana."

After a pause, he finally spoke, "Did you..."

"No." She cut him off before he uttered the words, but any relief was short-lived. "Not yet anyway." Like the eve of a thunderstorm, his disappointment hung over the table. An invisible black cloud that made raising her stare impossible. Her moist eyes locked on the table.

"You and Dan, too?" he said sardonically. "I thought he and Dana were in love?"

"Not Dan…" A large tear plopped onto the table as she whispered, "Letchford." She wanted to tell Ed everything, but she knew how he would react, and then it would all be over.

Moving to pick up a napkin, instead, he stopped and looked at her with a mask of disbelief on his face. "Letchford?" was all he said. Ed stood, and his chair screeched along the tarnished linoleum. Everyone looked up as he wrenched the café door open. Its bell rang noisily as he banged it back against the wall and walked out. The dam broke. Her tears came in floods.

"Everything all right, dear?" said the concerned waitress. Jane nodded, even though it was clear to everyone around her that it wasn't.

She flicked soaking bedraggled hair out of her eyes. It was chucking it down with cold London rain. Dressed only in a light jacket with no hood or brolly, Jane didn't care. "I don't deserve this," she said through gritted teeth. She pulled out her mobile phone and dialled.

"Hey, girl, how's the head today?" Dana asked.

Jane didn't answer the question. "Are you still with Dan?"

Hearing Jane's tone, Dana asked, "What do you need him for?"

"I am handing in my notice." Jane was relieved that passersby couldn't tell she was still crying. The frigid rain washed away her tears.

"Hold on," said Dana. Jane waited, expecting Dan to speak next, but she heard footsteps and a door closing on the other end of the line. Dana came back. "Where are you?"

"I've lost him," Jane said through a sob. The thought of living without Ed was brutal. Like a bereavement. She'd chosen to swim in the London sea of news and politics, leaving the security of Edinburgh far behind. It was only now she realised that Ed was the familiar rock her life here was built on. He *was* her home.

"Lost who?" Dana said with concern.

"I've lost Ed forever."

"What is this all about? Where are you this second?"

"I don't know…walking," Jane said.

Dana sounded angry. "Jane, look about you and give me a street name now."

Jane obeyed. She had been walking for at least an hour, but when she checked the road sign, she recognised the name.

"I'm outside Ed's place," she said. The phone went dead.

Twenty minutes later, Dana stopped her car at the kerb and soaking Jane got in. Dana said nothing but turned the heater up to full blast. Neither of them spoke as Dana drove through London's weekend traffic, but as the car pulled up outside Jane's, she made to exit.

"Thanks," she said.

"Don't fecking thank me, girl. I am not leaving you on your own like this." Jane opened the flat door as Dana took her by the shoulders and guided her through to the shower. The heat and flow were turned up before Dana pushed her under the jet.

"My clothes," Jane said in protest.

"They're ruined already," Dana scolded. "Now get cleaned up and I'll go make coffee."

Jane stood listlessly under the hot stream. She sighed and began removing her clothes, throwing each article into the bath. She could hear Dana shouting at someone in the living room, but she was too exhausted to care.

Fifteen minutes later, Jane padded into the living room in her dressing gown. She was now clean and warm, but the shower could do little for the misery that hung over her like an angry black pall. Dana poured the coffee. "Drink!" she commanded.

Jane wrapped her shaking hands around the mug. "What happened?" Dana asked. Jane gave her the highlights. "Thought so," said Dana. "Jane, I have lost half a dozen so-called friends since moving upstairs. And okay, I get it; I shagged the boss, and doors opened, but I was going to open those fecking doors one day soon anyway. If they can't handle that, then they can feck off."

"I can't lose him. He's everything." Jane's shoulders sank. The door buzzer went.

"Sit down," said Dana, going to answer. After buzzing the person in, she unlatched the flat door and took the seat opposite Jane. Ed walked in. Immediately jumping to her feet again, Dana got right in his surprised face.

"You," said Dana. "Sit." She pointed at Ed and stood over him, a face like thunder. "You stupid bastard. What the hell were you thinking?" She prodded his chest. "For all you knew, Jane could have been jumping off a tower block if I hadn't come to the rescue. So, she says one thing and goes and does another. People do that sometimes."

Ed hung his head, but Dana's wrath was not over.

"This poor girl has put up with all sorts of shit lately." she stopped prodding him and pointed to Jane. "Even you go and shag some guy she fancies." Her ire was unabated. "You know she loves you more than anyone in the world. Do you honestly believe she would ever do anything to spite you? And you…" She prodded him again, in case he misunderstood who she was referring to. "You love her too. Okay, I get it, you two may never bump uglies, but my fecking parents weren't half as much in love as you two and they pumped out thirteen kids. So, you, Edward, get over there and grovel to the woman you love in the hope she will ever speak to you again, because you do not deserve her." Dana gave him one last extra hard prod.

"Ow!" he said. The scolding over, she picked up her bag and left.

Like most rooms after Dana had exited, the place took on a weirdly deafening silence. Jane thought she could hear two women chatting a mile away, someone in Wimbledon cutting their grass, and a train horn wailing, across the city at Marble Arch station. Blood pumped in her ears, the tinnitus whistle only interrupted by the beautiful cacophony of Ed's breathing.

"I didn't leave you," Ed said quietly. Jane raised her eyes. "I would never…I wouldn't ever do that to you," he said. She didn't respond. Words got her into this; maybe silence would get her out. "I was angry, but I got to the flat and realised what I had done. I saw you walking round and round outside – I kept hoping you would knock on my door, but you didn't." He hung his head. "I should have…"

It took her a while to find the words. "I…I didn't know I was on your street until Dana asked,"

He slid off his chair and crawled over the carpet on his knees. Putting his hands round her waist, he laid his head on her lap. Automatically, she started playing with his long, beautiful hair. Although dark brown, it caught the sun through the window and made her feel she wound threads of gold.

"I do love you, and I trust you implicitly. If things are changing for you, then I want to be with you all the way. It's all for the best, right, Jane?" he asked, raising his head.

Her smile was fleeting. "I really don't know at all. I can't deny that I want what is on offer, but it all seems a bit like a Faustian pact. The problem is, I can't tell which one of them is the devil."

"Can I help?" said Ed.

"Not this time. They have me...compromised. I don't want them getting to you too," she replied.

Ed laid his head back down. "Do you think Quentin is involved?" he asked.

She scowled and rubbed a palm against her forehead. "I don't think so, but they are clever. Watch yourself there." The two sat quietly for a long time.

He sat back with hands clasped below his chin. "I'm sorry, Jane. Can you forgive me?"

Had he really done anything wrong? She didn't think so. This was a mess of her own making. Last night, the ambition driven Jane gladly crossed the Rubicon in the full knowledge that he was left on the other side. Though the thought of losing him broke her heart, corrupting him by bringing him along would be worse. She had no answer for him. Instead, she held his head to her lips and kissed his forehead.

London, Sunday 23rd March 2025

Jane woke with a start. She thought the door buzzer sounded but didn't know if it was real or in a dream. Leaning over the edge of the bed, she turned on the table lamp and noticed it was 6am. About to put her head back down, someone knocked on her front door.

"Bugger it!"

Reluctantly, she folded back the duvet and slid her legs over the side of the bed. A yawn and a stretch were required before attempting to stand. She looked around the room for some article of clothing to pull on. Last night's T-shirt lay on the floor. It crackled with static as she pulled it over her head. The knocking came again as her phone rang from the bedside table, but she was already heading for the hall.

The door unlocked, she opened it to find Selwyn Letchford standing in the hallway, with a Fortnum's bag and a bouquet of flowers.

"Good morning, dear," he said. A breeze ascended the stairs and carried his expensive aftershave cloud. It assailed her nostrils and eyes like mustard gas.

"What are you doing here at this time of the night?" she asked.

Letchford looked at the short T-shirt and worked his way down her legs greedily.

"We didn't get much time to chat on Friday, and since we will both be embroiled in governmental matters later today, I thought we could have some breakfast before the world awakes," he said, holding up his shopping.

"But I'm not even showered," she protested. "It's the middle of the night."

He pushed the door open, eased past her and said, "You jump in the shower; I'll get breakfast underway. How do you like your eggs?"

Jane wanted to say, "On my own and in about three hours," but instead, she exhaled deeply and went with, "Poached, please."

Letchford's chemical warfare trail of Clive Christian aftershave followed him to the kitchen. Trying not to breathe, she headed to her bedroom, looked for some clothes and put the shower on.

She'd just shampooed her hair when there was a knock at the bathroom door. It opened, and Letchford's leer appeared. "Your breakfast is nearly ready, dear." As best she could, she covered herself with her hands.

"I'll be there in a minute – now can you leave, please?" she asked.

"Are you sure you don't need a back rub?" the MP offered with a leer.

"No, thank you," said Jane.

He lingered longer than necessary but finally left. Fearing another visit, she quickly finished showering and dried herself. She peeked out of the bathroom to ensure her bedroom was clear, then got dressed in the most unflattering outfit possible: jogging pants, a baggy T-shirt and one of Ed's jumpers. On padding through to the living room, a luxurious breakfast was laid on the table.

He sat with cutlery in hand, waiting. "Come sit, dear. I'm starving," he said. She took the seat opposite, and he immediately slid his leg against her. "You can be mother," he said, and she set about dishing up the food. It briefly allowed her to move away from his contact, but with the portions allocated, she sat once more, and of course, his leg shot back into position. Jane sighed.

"Did you enjoy the party on Friday?" he asked, setting about a sausage.

"I found it… eventful," she replied. "It was *really* nice to meet your wife." Letchford didn't even blink at the comment.

He put on a theatrical voice, "She that must be obeyed."

"I doubt you are obeying her right now," Jane said, finding it difficult to ignore the aroma of the cooked breakfast any longer.

"Oh, you would be surprised," he said, taking a large mouthful of bacon and egg.

Deciding to ignore his cryptic comment, as she knew from experience that he seldom elaborated, she changed tack. "You said we'll be busy later. How would you know?" She relented to the food and tucked in.

He put down his cutlery, licked a run of egg yolk from his chin and checked his watch. "I can tell you in about an hour. Let's eat up, and then maybe we can find something interesting to do with the rest of the time," he said.

Jane placed the knife and fork on the side of her plate. Shuffling her seat across the wood floor, she got up from the table. He watched her closely. Over at the kitchen units, she found a vase and put some water in. Wordlessly, she returned to the living room, unwrapped the flowers he'd brought and put them in, taking a minute to arrange them. Happy at her effort, she returned to the table, stopped and sighed deeply.

She pulled the jumper over her head, slid the jogging bottoms down her legs and stepped out of them. His eyes widened as the T-shirt came off, too. Standing in front of him in underwear only, she took him by the hand and said, "Come on then."

They went through to the bedroom where she released his hand and folded down the duvet. Laying on the bed, she looked up at him. "Well?" she said. It was hard to decide if the look on his face was delight or shock.

"Wh…wh…what are you doing?" he asked.

"Exactly what you want me to do, sir," she replied. "You've been making unsubtle hints for weeks, and I assume this is what you wanted to happen at the Randolf?" She reached out an upturned palm.

"Yes, but…not like this," he said.

"Sorry," said Jane. "Tell me if I have got any of this wrong. You have a video of me, you also have access to breaking news that I want, and lastly, you can give me a career and lifestyle I have wanted all my life. All I need do is drop my pants? Well, here you go." Jane went to remove her underwear.

"Stop!" he said. She did so. He looked at her a long time. "I didn't want it to be like this," he said.

"How did you want it to be?" she spat back.

"I thought we had…something, Jane."

She rolled her eyes and fought hard not to laugh. "Sorry," she said, "you believed there was something between us? Me and you?"

Letchford sat down on the edge of the bed and hung his head like a naughty schoolboy. "I saw how you flirted with me. I thought…" He trailed off.

Jane pulled the duvet over herself. How on earth could he have concluded they had something real between them?

"Selwyn, I am nice to a lot of people and yes, maybe *too* nice sometimes, but it doesn't mean anything," she said.

"It meant something to me."

"So, in return, you blackmailed me?" she asked with her tone rising in disbelief.

He swallowed a lump in his throat. "Believe me, that had nothing to do with me." His voice lowered to a mumble. Well, the *making* of the video anyway,"

"Whether you took it or not, you used it to try and get your way with me and forced me to file reports for you." Her darkened eyes fixed him angrily.

"I haven't fed you anything you wouldn't have filed anyway," he said.

She looked long and hard at the bowed MP. She had the man wrong. Sure, he was a complete pervert, and yes, he had used the video for his own ends, but he was not the mastermind behind the media plot. His motivation resided principally in his trousers. The problem with this revelation was that it created more questions than answers. Who was pulling his strings? If the MP wasn't organising the promotion and lifestyle to get her into bed, then what was it all for? What would happen when Letchford went back and reported failure? Last but not least, and didn't Jane hate herself for this thought, but would they take it all away?

Were she ever to be able to answer these dilemmas, she needed to be on the inside. What must be done was suddenly apparent. She exhaled deeply. "I'm sorry, sir," Jane said. He looked up and smiled a little.

"Sorry that I got the wrong idea?" he asked.

Leaning over to him, she took his hand, folded back the duvet cover and said, "Maybe you didn't, sir." She laid back, pulling him on top.

* * *

Lying in his arms, he was affectionately running his fingers through her hair when his phone beeped.

"That will be it," he said. Letchford sat up and grabbed his phone. "Okay, it's on." He moved to perch on the edge of the bed.

Jane got out the other side and walked past him to the bathroom.

"Wow!" He gave a soft wolf whistle. She turned, walked over and kissed his forehead.

"Thank you, kind sir." And headed for the shower.

Under the steaming flow, she stood, allowing the hot water to wash over her sensitive skin. There came a wave of surprise at how sanguine she felt about what just happened. She'd dreaded this encounter so long now that, yes, there was some relief it was over. But other feelings were swilling around inside her too. Though he was generally a misogynist pig in everyday life, Letchford surprised her with his kindness and…*oh my God, am I really going to say this?*…expertise between the sheets. *Why am I rationalising this? He basically forced this on me.* Yet there was part of her that knew she used him too. *So, now we just jump in bed with anyone if it suits our goals?* Her Sunday-school-educated brain had a habit of asking questions that her demons couldn't answer. Or was it just that she didn't want to hear the reply? "Sod it all," she said and turned the taps off.

Unsure what today was going to bring, her best work togs went on. When she reached the living room, Letchford was sitting at the table, eating the now-cold breakfast.

"Do you want me to micro that?"

"No, come sit here, love." He patted the chair next to him. "Right, here is what's about to happen…"

BBC News

"In an unscheduled break, we will now go over to Jane Clark at Westminster."

"Thank you, Laura. I can now bring you the breaking news that Ravi Suvar has tendered his resignation. After last week's vote of no confidence, it seems he had little option. Conservative Party rules mean there will be an election to replace him, but I can tell you now, there will only be one name in the hat, and the party will push to have him waved through next week. Laura, the hot news is Boris Jenkins will be our next prime minister and, all going to plan, will be in place by Friday. Jane Clark, live at Westminster."

As the producer signalled the cut, Jane relaxed and handed the microphone to a tech. It was good that Ed wasn't on shift. There would be no facing him today. This morning felt like a betrayal. It wasn't that morals were compromised; she'd already made her peace about that. No, she'd let him down. Perhaps ironically, her prime fear was that Ed wouldn't necessarily agree. All in all, she decided it may be best to avoid him for a while.

London, Monday 24th March 2025

With this being the first time she'd been in the office since Friday, and also unclear what had happened at the party, Jane stood nervously inside the lift. She popped her head out and looked both ways. Thankfully, neither Ed nor Dan was anywhere to be seen. She released her held breath, the tension ebbed, and her shoulders sank back down. The first duty of the day was to check her pigeonhole for post. Few important items arrived by snail mail these days, but Dan would have a fit at anyone that allowed crap to build up.

There was only one piece of junk today, and she read it, strolling to her desk. Apparently, she'd been accepted into 'The Order of Boudica', whatever that was. "My, I am honoured," Jane said, scrunching the letter into a ball and throwing it in the first bin passed.

"Miss Clark, what are you doing here?" yelled Dan from the other side of the large press room. "You don't work here anymore." With her biggest fear being given voice, Jane's legs went to jelly.

As he crossed the office in his bull like fashion, she stood watching with a look of trepidation. *Was she indeed fired?* Dan put an arm around her shoulder, spun her around and guided her back to the elevator. "You have forgotten already, my new Chief of Outside Broadcast." They arrived back at the lifts, and he pushed the button.

Relief washed over her. There was a vague recollection of the made-up-sounding job title but with the later part of Friday being a blank, there was a fear that she'd possibly blown it.

"No, boss, I just wasn't sure if things would be in place yet," she lied as the lift doors opened. They got in.

"You did great work yesterday. I believe you will find a little bonus in your bank account," Dan said.

"Thanks, boss," she said, really hoping he was referring to the broadcast and not the tumble with the MP.

"Oh, don't thank me, Jane," he gave a gravel chuckle. "Our new benefactors are the ones ponying up the cash. It's lucky as no one at the Beeb has two ha'pennies to scrape together."

She scratched her head. "Benefactors, boss?"

He waggled a finger and winked. "All will be revealed in time."

Two floors up, the lift doors swished apart, and he led her to the new office. As promised, she was now right next door to Dana. "Welcome to your new domain, Your Majesty." He pushed open the office door. The outer office was much like Dana's set up, but inside sat a tall woman in glasses that Jane hadn't seen around.

"Angela here will be working for you," Dan said, pointing to the woman. Angela stood, smiled and shook Jane's hand. "You are free to pick the other two minions yourself."

Angela sat back down and returned her attention to her PC. Jane believed the woman's eye twitched at his slight, but seemingly oblivious, he continued the tour into the main area. Although much larger than her current space, the empty room was a little underwhelming. The carpet and décor had clearly seen better days.

"Sorry we didn't have time to get it all ready, but now you are free to furnish however you please. Angela has a note of the budget. Right, my dear," Dan said, patting her bum despite five hundred BBC regulations, "I must get back to the coal face. You get this place sorted and I will need someone appointed to replace you downstairs by the end of the week. Can you manage that?" he asked.

"Sure, boss," replied Jane, still bemused by the rapidity of the change.

Angela came through with a plastic chair. "I got you this for now, madam. The new phone lines will be installed by lunch.

Would we be able to have a sit-down this afternoon? I need some details from you to be able to operate efficiently."

Slightly shell-shocked, Jane nodded. "Yes. Is three okay?"

"Three o'clock it is," said Angela, returning to her desk.

Jane took a moment to scan her new habitat. *The carpet will have to go*, she decided. The rest of the place would likely spruce up after it was painted. Walking to the large window, she took in the view out over the expanse of London. Far to the right, Big Ben poked its head above the surrounding buildings, and over to the left, Canary Wharf stood incongruously modern to the Victorian industrial landscape that hemmed it in. She beamed like a child at Christmas. Regardless of the road, this was where she wanted to be.

"Angela," she called.

"Yes, madam?" Angela said, re-entering the room.

"What's the budget for decorating?"

"Twenty-five thousand."

"That's fine," said Jane, trying hard to keep herself from screaming. "Oh, Angela…"

"Yes, Miss Clark?"

"Call me Jane."

A thump sounded on the wall. "Coffee," she heard Dana shout.

"God, yes," Jane replied.

* * *

Dana stood in line for the drinks, chatting with others in the queue. Jane took in the scent of coffee mixed with cleaning products and fried food. *Just your normal BBC canteen*, she thought while slaloming her way to find seats. On locating a vacant table, she pulled out her phone. First checking for messages, she then opened her banking app.

"Bugger me," she squealed much louder than intended. The café went quiet. Beaming, Jane raised a hand in apology to all around. After a few seconds, the chatter resumed, and she looked back at the screen. The balance in her bank, which finally got above six figures only recently, now had one more zero on the end. Her hand went over her mouth.

"Clarkie!" Dana yelled.

Jane looked up to see Dana rubbernecking the room for her. Standing, Jane waved, and her friend navigated over with tray and two brimming mugs.

"How are things your first day? It's all a bit overwhelming initially," Dana said, as she took her plastic seat.

"Did you…did you get this too?" Jane asked, showing her bank balance.

Dana smiled and nodded. "As I said, overwhelming."

Jane let out a long, slow breath while counting the digits one more time. *Sure enough*, she thought, *I'm a millionaire.* Of course, there was now the kid inside her head that was jumping on the bed in delight, but another part of her felt a little unclean. Yesterday she'd let Letchford have his way, and today she was rich. The correlation was hard to deny. Dad would be calling her a cheap whore and accusing her of pimping herself to the highest bidder. Was he wrong?

Life isn't as simple as it was in your day, Dad, she argued, convinced she was right. She'd worked hard to get here. Woman tripping obstacles were constantly thrown in her way.

"Go make us a cuppa, darling."

"Come sit on your boss's knee and see if we can get you a raise."

"I know you have been here longer, but we needed a man for the promoted position." She'd walked the coals. Taken the shit and asked for more.

Bugger you, Dad, I've earned this. Jane slammed her phone on the table, startling Dana.

"Jeez, girl. What was that about?"

"Nothing. Sorry," Jane said.

Dana relaxed and said, "Do you want to go furniture shopping today?"

It dragged Jane back to reality. "I need to, but not sure how busy we will be. To be honest, Dana, I haven't a bloody clue what I'm supposed to be doing."

"Didn't Dan give you any instructions?"

"He asked me to find a replacement reporter by the end of the week, but surely I have other duties now?"

Dana reached over the table and put her hand on Jane's. "That is your duty. You take instruction from Dan alone now. In the office anyway. You and I are in a different division from the others." She pointed to the people around them in the canteen. "We work for the government *in* the BBC. You no longer work *for* the Beeb."

"So, who runs outside broadcasts?" Jane asked.

"I have no idea. Possibly the same person that runs the politics sections, but neither of us need worry about it," Dana said, emptying her third sachet of sugar into her mug.

Jane sipped her black, sugarless coffee and asked, "What did you do about hiring staff? They have already given me one. Her name is Angela."

Dana squinted a little and leant forward. "Angela doesn't really work for you." She held up a hand to qualify. "Oh, she will do anything you ask, but she works for *them*."

"Them?" Jane asked.

"Not 100% sure. My guess is that it is the same folk we work for, but I think Angela is there to keep an eye on you. My one is called Scott."

Jane looked thoughtful. "But I am free to appoint the others? What is it that they do?"

Dana shrugged her shoulders. "They get paid fifty grand a year to run about after your backside, missy." Jane grinned. "Don't," added Dana sharply.

"Don't what?"

"Don't even think of Ed. This is not a job for anyone you care about. My suggestion would be to find two nobodies that you can get along with and leave it at that."

"From inside the BBC?" Jane asked.

"Probably better, but it's up to you," Dana replied. "Now drink up, and I will take you furniture shopping. I've been to your flat – you're going to need help."

"Hey!" said Jane indignantly.

Edinburgh, Monday 24th March 2025

The office was warm even though the heating was off. Duncan took in the view of the Scottish Parliament. He almost had the crazy idea of opening a window before remembering it was spring in Edinburgh.

His phone rang and he returned to the desk. He smiled as he heard Nancy's voice for the first time today.

"Hey, boss, did you have a good weekend?" she asked.

"It was quiet, Nance. I went to the football and then had a couple of pints but not a lot else. You?"

"There were a couple of drugs parties and an orgy. So quiet one for me too," she replied in a deadpan voice. It was her stock answer, but he had never had the courage to ask if she was joking. His secretary continued. "I have Joan from the Alba Party for you."

"Cheers, Nance, put her through."

Joan, the long-serving secretary to Alex Samson, came on the line. She had the traditional, very polite, very proper and very Edinburgh voice. With Alex since his first minister days, Joan had loyally switched parties when Alex left the SNP. Alex trusted her with his life but often joked that he didn't know if she voted for him. Other than her duties, Joan never talked politics.

"Good morning, Mr Clark. I hope I find you well?" Joan said.

Duncan had long learned there was no point in being anything but direct with Joan. His previous attempts at humour were tolerated only. Today, Duncan could hear agitation in her voice.

"I'm all good, Joan, what's up?"

"Have you heard from Alex over the weekend?" she asked.

There was a knock at his office door and Nancy put her head round. Duncan held up a finger in a signal for her to hold. "No, but I didn't really expect to. I did notice he wasn't at the match on Saturday though."

Joan interjected. "He hasn't been seen or heard from since Friday. He was due at a meeting on Saturday, but when he didn't turn up, I assumed he was ill or something. I called his wife, but she hasn't seen him either. She told me that in itself is not unusual, but what is, though, is that he always calls to let her know where he is. Nothing has been heard."

Duncan thought for a moment. "Let me make some calls, Joan. I know a few of the non-political people that he knows too. I assume you have tried all the Party folk?"

"Yes, indeed," she replied.

"I'll call you back soon." He put the receiver down and went to make another call but then remembered, "Oh Nance, sorry. What is it?"

"I've got Dougie from across the road for you," she said. Duncan knew that 'across the road' meant the Scottish Parliament.

"Put him through."

She rolled her eyes. "No, you muppet, he's here in the office. I'll show him up."

Duncan laid the handset back on the phone. The calls to Alex's contacts would have to wait. Saliva filled his mouth. The parliamentary security officer often popped over to chat football and less important subjects but seldom came alone. The bag of doughnuts he was usually accompanied by were equally, if not more, welcome than the man himself.

"Mr Clark," Dougie cried in his broad Glaswegian accent. With disdain, Duncan saw no bakers' bag in his hand and tried to hide the disappointment.

"Hey, Dougie, what happened to your team on Saturday then?"

Dougie, hailing from Glasgow and working in politics, thought it best to tell the world he was a Partick Thistle fan as that offended no one. In reality, Dougie followed Celtic.

"Ah, it was a shocker, Dunc." Dougie shook his head. "All four goals were offside." Both men laughed before Dougie immediately switched to business. "I need your help, Dunc." A scowl crossed his face. "Some of my flock have gone missing."

"Wow!" said Duncan. "Joan just called and asked me to track down Alex. When did I become the missing person's bureau?"

Dougie asked, "Alex is missing too?"

"Yes," said Duncan, "he hasn't been seen since Friday. Who have you lost?"

Dougie plumped down on the seat in front of Duncan's desk. "The leadership of all four main parties have failed to turn up. I've come to you because I managed to speak to our former illustrious first minister, Nicola. I tried calling the others, but some stranger answered, telling me they were out. The weird thing is, it was the same guy that answered all calls." Dougie held his arms out wide. "It gets weirder, Dunc," he continued. "Nicola claims she has been put under house arrest! She thinks it has something to do with that case a couple of years ago where money was supposed to have gone missing, but I'm not so sure. This is bloody strange."

Duncan tried to process all this information. Nodding to Dougie, he picked up the phone to one of the senior partners. "Can you come through here now, Struan?" He smiled at the response and put the phone down. He turned to Dougie and said, "I'll talk to Struan. He knows more about private eye stuff than I do. Are you here to engage us officially?"

"I will nip over and get the paperwork done, my friend. Back in a while." Dougie jumped up and headed out.

Apparently accompanied by a herd of elephants, Dougie clattered down the stairs. "Still looking hot, Nance," he said, passing through the admin office. Things were crazy, but there was always time for an inappropriate comment or two in Dougie's world.

London, Monday 24th March 2025

"Sorry, Angela. I got held up in a meeting," Jane said as she burst through the office door, which bumped against a pile of boxes. "Oops." Jane and Dana's furniture shopping trip had included a few bars also.

Angela gave a brief disapproving look but quickly changed to a smile. "No problem, Miss Clark."

"Call me Jane."

"Of course, Jane. Some furniture arrived, and I took the liberty of having maintenance put it together."

"Cool," said Jane, immediately regretting the hippie vernacular. She didn't think Angela was the type to say 'cool', but then, in her mid-fifties, as Jane guessed Angela to be, she may well have been about when hippies were on the go.

"Can we do our catch-up now?" Angela asked.

"One second," said Jane. "I need to nip to the little girls' room." She went to leave the office, but Angela grabbed her arm. "Hey! I'll pee my pants." Jane giggled as she tried to break free.

Angela shook her head and led her into the main office. They crossed to the far wall where the woman opened a door to reveal a toilet.

"These are your private facilities," she said before leaving.

"I thought it was a stationery cupboard," Jane said, still giggling. The place was amazing. Aside from the usual facilities, there was a walk-in shower and a huge bath, big enough for two. *This may be the champers speaking, but I am so going to shag in here*, Jane thought to herself. As pleasing as the notion was, it unfortunately brought an image of Letchford to mind. *No, no, don't spoil it for me*, she said to her own brain. The temptation to jump in the bath now was great, but she settled for splashing water on her face before heading back.

"Ready?"

Her assistant pointed to the deluxe leather chair opposite. Jane flopped down and yelped as it tilted. Angela ignored the slapstick and got right down to business.

"Now, if acceptable, I will answer all your incoming calls and emails. Obviously, I will not touch anything personal. Is that okay?"

The 'if acceptable' bit was superfluous. Jane knew. "Fine," she said, twisting back and forth.

"Can I have your phones then, please?" Angela said, reaching out a hand. Jane heard the plural. Anticipating monitoring of their work mobiles, Dana and Jane cut into their furniture shopping to acquire new phones, which they intended to keep private. Neither were sure if this was really necessary, but holding something back from their new employer seemed reasonable in their albeit alcohol-induced state at the time. Jane only handed over the work phone. Angela took the device, laid it on something that looked like a charging unit, laid her own phone beside it and pressed a button. "Okay, I've cloned your phone."

Good luck with the pictures of Letchford's genitals, Jane thought, taking her work handset back.

"You only have one phone?" Angela stared at Jane in a way she found suspicious.

"Why would I need another?" Jane asked.

The other woman nodded. "Okay – if you can email me a list of family and friends, I will avoid answering those calls unless you are unavailable, and I will take a message."

"I'll send you the list by close of play," Jane replied.

"Then we're finished," said Angela, and Jane felt like she'd been dismissed.

Coffee was the answer to her lunchtime excess. The office machine raided, she picked up the cup and went through to her desk. On wiggling the mouse, her new and very expensive computer sprang to life. Jane composed the list and sent it. It was an exercise in futility as Angela would inevitably read all her mail and listen to all the calls anyway, but she really didn't care.

A sudden thought came into her head, and she logged into her bank. The large deposit had come in overnight. After noting the sender's account number, she got the paper from her bag that held the sudoku answers. Sure enough, the account number was on her list. The payment originated in China. What this all meant, she wasn't sure. Nor did she know what they expected for this money.

"I never asked for it," she said, thumping the mouse against the ridiculously expensive desk. *But had she?* She clicked out of the bank app and looked around the room. She had been well renumerated for the little asked of her so far. *Would the cost be higher in future?*

Fuck it, she would worry about that when it happened. Her wobbly hand spilled coffee down her blouse.

London, Wednesday 26th March 2025

Jane's new, self-appointed start time was 10am. Apparently, the only task for the week was to find her own replacement in the reporting team, and she already knew who was getting the job. There was a BBC London reporter on the local news. Jane could tell that she would be perfect. The girl was here for an interview this afternoon.

Unlocking her PC screen, she went onto the internal network and booked a meeting room. With this mammoth task completed; Jane remembered that there were meant to be minions for these things. She got her mobile from her bag and dialled.

"Hannah, it's Jane. You got any plans today? Cool, fancy lunch? No, I'll take you somewhere that we won't be bothered. Right, pick you up in about forty minutes." She ended the call and buzzed through to Dana.

"Hey, Jane, what's up?"

"Not a lot," said Jane. "I'm loving the new furniture that you picked out, by the way. You should consider a career in interior design."

"Are you trying to tell me something?" Dana laughed.

"I wondered if you'd sit in for my interview this afternoon? I have no idea what to say in these things."

"No problem," said Dana. "She had better not be fecking prettier than me though."

"No one is prettier than you," said Jane.

"Right answer," Dana said. "But Dan will want last look."

"I guessed as much. Okay, will see you at three. I am going out to round up minions."

The car pulled up outside Hannah's building, and Jane got out. When she knocked on the door, it was opened by a young man in jeans and little else. He was athletic with long hair, similar to Ed's. The hair was wet, and he was in the process of drying it with a small towel. It took a while before Jane remembered she had to talk.

"Oh, sorry. Is Hannah in?"

"Yeah, she is," he said in a disappointing Birmingham accent. "Come in." *You are only a nine out of ten now*, Jane decided.

Following him up the hallway, she was pleasantly surprised that the building's shitty exterior wasn't reflected inside. "Take a seat," he said and went into another room. He returned with a T-shirt on. She tried hard to hide her disappointment. "She will be out in a tick. Jane, is it?"

"Yeah," said Jane, standing. "Daniel, I guess?" They shook hands.

Hannah did her usual Tigger appearance from the same room that Daniel was dressing in. *Were they an item?*

"Ready for lunch?" Jane asked.

"Yes, indeed, I'm famished," Hannah said.

"Hey, Daniel. Do you fancy coming along?" Jane asked but

didn't let him answer. "How could you turn down lunch at the Ritz with two hot babes?"

"Okay," he said, slightly lacking the enthusiasm that Jane was looking for. She guessed she had twelve or more years on him, but a girl could always look.

This was only the third time Jane had ever lunched at the Ritz, but she tried to make them believe it was a daily occurrence. Hannah and Daniel sat and gawped at the opulent surroundings. The initial intention was to offer Hannah a job, but now Jane wished the young girl wasn't here at all. A new project presented itself.

"Any progress with Colin's estate?" Jane asked. Hannah looked a little uncomfortable, and Jane wondered if Daniel knew anything about it. "Hannah, girls' room."

The two of them excused themselves and left Daniel with a cold beer. Reaching the plush hotel toilets, Jane said, "Sorry, I shouldn't have said anything in front of Daniel."

"It's okay, he knows a bit about it," Hannah said.

The curiosity was too much for Jane. "Are you and Daniel getting busy?"

Hannah shook her head. "Hey, stop that," she said, her cheeks now crimson.

"You didn't tell me he was such a hunk," said Jane, and Hannah went another shade redder. Jane changed tack. "So, the solicitor?"

With that, Hannah visibly relaxed. "Colin's parents have lodged some sort of claim. I have no issue sharing the money – hell, I don't even know I want any of it at all. The solicitor said the case may now drag on for years, and he told me there may be nothing left by the time the thing is sorted. His parents were really nice to me at the funeral. I don't understand what's changed."

"Money. People go all weird when there is money involved." Jane circled her finger against the side of her head.

"I guess," said Hannah.

"I'll have a word with some people I know and see what they say. Do you know if they have found the money on the bank statement?"

"I'm not sure," said Hannah. "The solicitor said something about multiple accounts and that it was a complex case."

"Well, keep quiet about it for now. My friends may know something about how to deal with that, too. Leave it with me." Jane washed her hands and dried them under the blower. "Right, we better get back to your hunk now, you dark horse." Playfully, she punched Hannah's arm and watched the flush return to the young girl's cheeks.

Getting more than a grunt out of the taciturn Daniel took half an hour. Jane kept involving him in the conversation, but he wouldn't contribute much until she told Hannah she was thinking of changing her car, and he immediately piped up.

"Great, what type are you thinking about?"

"I'm not really sure," said Jane. "I know nothing about cars."

Hannah looked at him and beamed. "Daniel knows everything there is to know about them."

Jane's ears perked up. "Really? That's fascinating."

After lunch, they headed back to Beckton, and Jane pulled the Toyota up outside their flat. Hannah leaned over from the passenger seat, kissed Jane on the cheek and said, "Thanks for that. It was amazing."

"Anytime," said Jane. Daniel had already exited and, with hands in pockets, was slouching up their garden path. Jane shouted after him. "Daniel, have you got a second? I need some info on cars."

Turning to the girl, "See you soon, Hannah." Hannah was clearly a little put out at being dismissed, but she reluctantly got out of the car and went into the flat. Jane patted the passenger seat. Daniel got back in, leaving the door open. "Would you be able to do a couple of things for me, Daniel?"

He ran a thumbnail along his eyebrow. "Yeah, what is it?"

"So, I would like to go get a car today. I'm always like this. Once I think about something, I go and do it."

"Are you thinking new or used?" he asked.

"Oh, definitely new. I was considering a BMW maybe. Are they any good?"

"Awesome!" he said. "Yeah, they are ace."

"Do you want to come give it a test drive?"

"Now?" he asked. Excitement was written across his face.

"No time like the present," she said.

"This is going to be brill." He closed the car door and fastened his seat belt.

"I hope so too." Jane winked at herself in the mirror. "I really hope so."

She called Dana. "Hey, Dana. Would you be able to handle the interview on your own?"

"What's up?" she asked.

"Oh, nothing," Jane replied. "I've found a…project."

Dana sniggered and said, "Okay, I get you, girl. Enjoy."

Jane ended the call. "Daniel, are you working at the moment?"

He looked across at her. "No, I'm between jobs."

"Have you ever fancied being someone's driver?"

His eyes widened. "That would be, like, the coolest job in the world."

"I am going to need a driver to drive my new car. Interested?" she asked.

"Am I?" said Daniel, not really answering, but Jane got the keenness from his tone.

"Good, can you start on Monday?" With that, she reached over and put a hand on his knee.

"Really?" Daniel beamed.

"Yes, really." He didn't seem to notice, or mind, her hand.

"Awesome."

That was clearly his word, Jane thought. She already knew he wasn't going to last long in the job, but she would keep him around until the accent really pissed her off.

"You said you needed me to do a couple of things," he said. "What's the second?"

"We'll get to that after you pick me out a nice fast car." Jane smiled at the young man. He grinned back like a little puppy.

It was 1am and Jane needed to sleep. The taxi pulled up outside her flat, and she gave Daniel the fare as he headed down the stairs. Yawning, she padded across the lounge to get her mobile phone from the coffee table. There were seven missed calls and fifteen texts from Hannah, which were deleted without reading. Jane could guess what they said.

She headed for the bedroom and laughed at the clothing lying all around the room.

Westminster, Friday 28th March 2025

Jane parked her new Black 5-series BMW in one of the spaces allotted for the press. Dana's recent purchase sat in the next bay. Inhaling the new car smell, Jane ran her hand tenderly over the leather upholstery. There was a tiny bit of guilt that some rare bison had been slaughtered for her comfort, but it felt so good.

Black wasn't her first choice for a car, but the lilac one in the showroom looked too ostentatious. It would have attracted attention, the wrong kind. She certainly wasn't a car geek, but her eyes drank in Dana's sleek machine and realised the other girl had no such inhibitions. Jane knew enough that the colour was called British Racing Green and that you parted with a serious wad of cash for an Aston Martin. Maybe next time, she thought.

It was good being back out on the job. Her new role was exciting, but reporting was what she knew, and so the excitement was curbed by nerves. *What would be expected of her?* She walked across the car park to find Dana and Ed chatting on the corner. She took a deep breath. This would be the first time she had met Ed since, well, that crazy day.

"Hey, folks," she called, approaching the two.

They turned, and Jane was relieved to see a broad smile on Ed's face. He walked over, hugged her, sniffed her perfume, and said, "Where have you been all week?" She held on to him longer than normal. It felt good. It felt right. Nothing much lately felt right.

After sighing, she said, "Busy with the new job. Sorry, I haven't been around much." It was a lie, of course. The new job did anything but keep her busy. Still, lying is what she seemd to do more than ever these days.

"No worries," he said. "I guessed as much."

Dana leant in. "Group hug." They all laughed. Breaking the hug, Dana said, "Come on, we better get over to Downing Street for the speech."

Jane recalled what Dana had said about the absence of responsibility in her new role, and everything she had predicted was correct so far. However, this was an outside broadcast by the politics team, and Jane was terrified they would get there and find a gang waiting for instruction. This was meant to be her gig.

A wave of relief came over her as they arrived in the usual scene of producers and techs running around in organised chaos. Someone had things in motion, and she was off the hook. Had they even been told she was their boss now? Frankly, she didn't care. Jane loved the promotion and trappings of it but was happy to be a reporter again. Turn up, speak, shut up, as the guy who first introduced her to the role advised. He probably meant it as a sexist jibe, but regardless, it served her well over the years. Ed walked off and joined the bustle of techs and cameramen. Seeing them arrive, the producer beckoned Dana and her to him.

"Dana, dear. Over in front of the lectern, please. We need to see it over your shoulder. Jane, down by the gates. You will comment with the entire scene, press and all, in view."

The two hurried to their places.

In a grey suit, two sizes larger than needed, Boris Jenkins stood behind the closed door. He laughed and joked with the aides and advisors as Cassie fussed over him. She ran her fingers through his hair to invigorate the turmoil. Happy at the disaster, she moved to his tie. Pulling the knot too tight, she pushed it an inch off centre. "There you go, dear. Go get them," she said and patted his bum as he walked out of the door.

"...and here he comes now. The country's fourth leader change since the public were able to vote. Although, this is the man last returned by democratic selection. In these troubled times, will Boris rise to the challenge and lead Britain forward? Dana McInteer, reporting from Westminster."

There was a feed of the speech through Jane's earpiece, which was lucky as the crowd behind the gate was noisily split between Union-flag-waving supporters and those vehemently against the prodigal son's return. Passions were high in both camps, and a couple of fistfights broke out. The bobbies hauled the worst offenders away.

"He's winding up. Ready, Jane," said the producer in her ear.

Trepidation broiled within her. Letchford was correct that none of the tasks she'd been assigned thus far were outside the purview of her previous role. But now she'd been asked, if asked was the correct word, to insert a line in her report.

"Coming to you now, Jane," said the ethereal voice in her ear.

"Thank you, Dana. Yes, a momentous day in a procession of momentous days for the country. You can see the car that will take the new PM to meet the King at Buckingham Palace pass behind me now." Jane stood aside to let the viewers see the Jaguar exit through the gates and turn into Whitehall. "All being well, the PM will return in an hour or so and begin the job of governing the country." Jane surprised the producer and cameraman by walking a few feet until she was in front of the ranked Boris supporters. "From the brink of nuclear war a few weeks ago, there is now a huge optimism in the country that a corner has been turned. With our darkest day over, is this the Arthurian legend that we know so well, being played out in front of us now? These patriots…" Jane stepped aside to show the massed supporters behind her. "These patriots certainly believe so. Jane Clark. Live in Downing Street."

She handed the technician the broadcast equipment.

"What was that?" the producer asked. Jane looked him in the eye but said nothing.

"I asked for a piece covering the trip to Buckingham Palace, not a party political broadcast," he said, spraying her face with spittle.

"Give me your phone," she said to the man, holding out her hand.

"Why would I give you my phone?" he asked.

"Give me your fucking phone now."

He stepped back a little and took his phone out.

Snatching it from him, she called Dan's number. As it rang, she said, "What's your name?"

"Brian," he said with a perplexed look on his face.

The call was answered. "Dan, Jane here. Brian, the producer, has a problem with the report…Yeah…He is here now…I will put him on."

Jane handed the phone back to Brian and he put it to his ear. She walked off, looking for Dana and Ed – a drink or three was required. A noise made her look over her shoulder to see the producer had thrown his headphones and clipboard to the ground. His beetroot face was shrouded in anger. She turned back to resume the search.

"Wanker," she said.

Edinburgh, Friday 28th March 2025

"What's that all about?" *That wasn't Jane*, Duncan thought as he watched his sister broadcast from Downing Street. Okay, it clearly was Jane, but something was different. He waited until it finished and dialled her number.

"Hey, bro," she answered.

"Hi, Jane, wow!" Duncan removed the phone from his ear as a shriek of feedback came through the line. Slowly, he put it back to his ear. "What was that?" he said.

"Probably all this broadcast stuff around me. I am in Downing Street."

"Yeah, I saw you, sis. Everything okay?"

Jane heard the concern in his voice. So, he had seen through her reporter's face from four hundred miles away. *Play it cool*.

"Yes, everything's great, bro. Did you see that crap they had me spin?" She crossed her fingers.

Duncan relaxed. This was her job, and he knew the BBC were biased to shit. "Yeah, sis. You had me worried there a sec. Thought we would have to take away your Scottish passport." They both laughed.

"Sorry, Dunc. I've got important reporter shit to do now and no time for lowly colonials. Gotta go. Love you." Jane giggled and hung up.

Duncan's shoulders relaxed, and his forehead wrinkles dissipated. Jane was the same pompous bitch that she had ever been, but yes, he loved his little sister to bits. There was a lingering regret that it hadn't always been that way, but regrets were pointless in his mind.

The sound of folk music from outside distracted him, and so he walked to the office window. The music and general hubbub reminded him that there was an independence march that was due to go down the Royal Mile and past his Canongate office today. He raised the blinds and watched the thousands of flag-waving nationalists passing.

The guitarist over the road struck up one of Duncan's favourite songs, 'Caledonia,' and on looking over, he realised it was Dougie MacLean himself. He tapped his fingers along with the song and watched a while. Interested in the turnout, he strained his neck for a view of Holyrood Park and saw it filled already. Yet, still, more marchers headed down the Royal Mile. There hadn't been a march this big for years.

* * *

Duncan made another call. "Billy. Yes, Duncan Clark here. Were you at the game last Saturday?...Yes, they're not playing well at all...No worries, I'll tell you what it is...Have you seen or heard from Alex this past week?...No, you and me both, Bill...Yeah, I will let you know if he turns up...Good stuff, let's catch up soon... See you, Bill."

He replaced the receiver. That was everyone that he could think of, and no one had any clues about the missing politician. The handset lifted once more, he called Joan for the umpteenth time this week.

"Have you heard anything at all, Joan?"

"Nothing, Mr Clark. I am now extremely concerned. He hasn't been seen or heard from in a week. How did you get on?"

"I drew a blank," he admitted. "Listen, Joan, I've had Dougie over from parliamentary security. Seems Alex is not the only one missing. We're going to look into it, and I'll get back to you if there is any news," he said.

"Would this have anything to do with those horrible allegations from a few years ago?" Joan asked.

"I don't think so. If Alex had fallen foul of the police, I would have been his first call."

He wound up the conversation as Nancy strolled into his office and began sorting his outgoing mail.

"Hey, Nance," he said. "Are you going out with the girls tonight?" As she turned, he saw a concerned expression change to a smile.

"No, boss, think I am going to have a quiet one. What about you?"

"Ah, Nance, my life consists of a series of quiet ones."

Today she was dressed from head to toe in pink. His eye travelled the curve of her hips, accented by the figure-hugging skirt. He thought the blouse was unbuttoned a little further than maybe it needed to be. *What are you doing?* he asked himself. He saw Nancy a hundred times a day, but why was he now looking at her this way?

"Are you okay?" She eyed him with her head tilted slightly.

Duncan mentally gave himself a shake. "Sorry, Nance. This whole thing with Alex and Dougie has me flummoxed."

"Do you need me to stick around and help?" she offered.

"No, we will be…actually, Nance, yes. That would be great, but only if I am not keeping you from anything. You seem to be dressed for some fancy occasion."

"Dressed? This old get-up? Not at all. I pulled on whatever came to hand this morning." She tugged the blouse.

"I don't believe that for a minute. You're always so well turned out," He said, while reminding himself about nibs and company ink.

"Well, thanks for noticing," she beamed. "I really thought you were going to end that sentence with *for an older woman.* I was about to have to stab you with this letter opener." He glanced at the serrated edge as she waved the implement. "I'll take the post down, and then I have a wee errand to run. Is that okay? I'll be back in around twenty minutes."

"Sounds good," he said.

Now he had to find something for Nancy to do.

As she walked by the throngs of flag-waving independence supporters, Nancy hugged the post to her chest. They were spilling out of the park after their rally. She was on her regular Friday errand to drop the incoming mail off at some random address. It wasn't that arduous today as the place was just down the Canongate from the office. A warm breeze blew a strand of her blonde hair into her eyes. She freed one hand from the pack of letters and brushed it back into place.

As a passing man smiled at her, she realised there was a wide grin fixed on her face. Had Duncan been ogling her earlier? She hadn't seen him looking before. *Why today?* Maybe he liked pink. *Do you want Duncan looking?* Sure, it was always good to be noticed, but what if they went on a date, and then he found out about the mail?

The internal tribulations halted on realising she'd reached today's given location. She scanned the surroundings. The street was thronging although the traffic was absent due to the march. No one was paying her much attention, though. *Was that what the Duncan thing was about? Attention?* "Stop it," she whispered and went to post the mail.

"Bugger it." The postbox was sticking, and the envelope wouldn't go through. She could always open it and feed the letters through one at a time, but she wanted out of here before someone asked why she was posting letters through the door of a closed shop.

"Hey, missus, I'll take that fae you?"

Nancy turned. Behind her stood a small guy in a green parka. He looked like he may have slept rough.

"Fuck off, pal," she said.

"Hey, nae need for that," he said indignantly. "I was jist aboot to open up to collect that stuff, so you might as well jist gie it to me."

"You're the one that asks for this?" she said, holding the envelope out.

"I jist pick it up." He held out his hand. As he did so, the parka sleeve rose up, and Nancy saw the all-too-familiar track lines. She recalled the first time she saw them on her son Jamie. This could well have been Jamie were it not for the extortionate rehab she'd sent her errant son to. This poor bastard was probably being manipulated by the same people who pulled her strings. She smiled kindly at the junkie and handed him the envelope.

"Thanks," she said, making to leave. A distance up the road from the shop, Nancy stopped and watched the junkie open the door, retrieve other parcels, lock up and leave. He headed down the hill. From her bag, she pulled out a light rain jacket and put it on. Against her better instincts, she decided to follow him.

An hour later, Nancy and her prey were on the city's north side in an area she would've rather avoided. The junkie's journey came to a stop on waste ground just off the main road. He hadn't moved for ten minutes other than to pick his nose, and she was seriously considering leaving when movement caught her eye. A car turned into the street and halted about a hundred yards from the junkie. He seemed oblivious to it, and she was about to discount the black Mercedes from her vigil when it started up again and approached. It was close enough now for her to see the registration number, so she risked taking a picture while praying the phone flash didn't go off. The car pulled up, and the junkie headed to the window that slid down. The envelope was thrown on the passenger seat, and a bag handed out. Nancy turned and left, keeping the derelict building between her and the scene. Once back at the main road, she stood at a bus stop and looked around to ensure the junkie or car hadn't followed. Deciding to call a taxi; she ignored the bus that pulled up and opened its door for her. She went straight home.

Duncan's shoulders sank a little as he checked his watch. It was nearly seven and Nancy hadn't appeared. He was here by himself now. Everyone else in the company was out having a life. "What the hell are you doing?" he said aloud.

Sure, he got some work done, although he was no further forward with the investigation into missing politicians. The realisation dawned that he was sitting here now, hoping Nancy would walk back in.

"Go home, you prick," he said in his best Nancy voice.

London, Friday 28th March 2025

Clouds Bar was busy, even up in the VIP lounge where Jane sat watching Dana eat Dan's face. The two sat across from her in one of the discreet booths. Ed headed off earlier to meet Quentin, and now she was the gooseberry.

Her phone vibrated. Holding it up to the lovebirds, she informed them she would take the call. After making her way through the throng, out of the noisy hall into the main stairwell, she answered.

"Hey," came Hannah's voice. Had she known who was calling, Jane wouldn't have picked up. She'd avoided Hannah since her little interlude with Daniel.

"How're things?" she asked, trying to sound breezy. The sniffling on the other end of the call told her Hannah was still upset.

"I'm okay, I guess," Hannah said. *Did the young girl have it in her to be confrontational? I wouldn't have touched him if she'd said they were an item*, Jane tried to convince herself, but somewhere in her head, she knew it wasn't true. She'd wanted Daniel, so she had Daniel. The only real regret was offering him the job. He wasn't that great in bed. Oh, he looked great, but he didn't know what he was doing. *Unlike Letchford*, she thought and immediately wished that thought hadn't spawned.

What the hell, Jane decided to grasp the nettle. "Are you mad at me, Hannah?"

"No," she said. "Why would I be?"

The answer was vexing. "Daniel and I left you to get the car." *That's a new metaphor*, Jane thought.

"Sorry, Jane – I just got all jealous. I thought you and Daniel were…doing something more than car hunting. I confronted him when he got home, but he told me about the late-night garage and that you got a good deal for buying after midnight. He's upset with me now and says I'm too clingy. I've been trying to get you on the phone to see if you would talk to him for me?"

Oh, you poor girl, thought Jane – *but way to go, Mr Daniel. Thinking on your feet there.*

"You really like him, do you?" Jane asked but already knew the answer. Were she being honest, she'd always known, and in spite of that fact, had gone ahead and bedded him anyway.

"Yes," the girl whispered after a delay.

Jane let out a long, slow breath. "I really wish you told me when I asked," she said, desperately wanting to blame Hannah for the situation.

"Why?"

"Well, I wouldn't have kept him out all night." *How many of the sins was she going to break in a day?*

"Of course," said Hannah, perking up a little. Hannah really needed a lesson about the world. Jane owed it to her now.

"Hannah, do you own a little black dress?"

"Yes?" she said with a rising inflection that made it more of a question than an answer.

"Okay, wipe your eyes and clean yourself up. A car will pick you up in half an hour."

Jane ended the call before Hannah could decline. Then calling the BBC limo service that was normally reserved for moving celebs about, she sent a car to collect Hannah.

"Dana, can you get Dan out of your tonsils a second?" Dan and Dana looked up. "I'm expecting a visitor. Remember that story I told you earlier?"

"The young hunk?" Dana asked.

"That's the one. It never happened, okay?"

"Why?" Dana asked.

"We have company on the way, and it's his girlfriend," Jane said, smiling.

Dana giggled, but Dan looked at her with what appeared to be some new respect. "I told them you were right for this job," he said.

"Can we go to the pond when Hannah arrives?" Jane noted that Dan had just admitted he was intrinsic to whatever plot was playing out. For the moment, she decided to overlook his slip.

He turned to Dana, who nodded. "Yeah, that could be fun," he said. "It's a mixer night."

Jane still couldn't tell if Dana knew what was going on, or if she was being used too. That would have to be resolved another day, as a couple of the SNP MPs and a Labour guy stood chatting near the bar, and she needed to talk to them. "I'll be back in a mo," she said, heading over.

As she approached, one of the MPs made a sign of the cross, saying, "Watch out, guys, state broadcaster approaching. Get the garlic out."

She laughed like it was the first time anyone had made the jibe. "Hey, guys, do you know if Isla is in tonight?"

They looked at each other. "We haven't seen Isla in a few days now. She missed the meeting yesterday – it's not like her," the cross bearer said.

"Bloody weird," the other MP added.

"Have you tried calling her?" Jane asked.

"Yes, Stephen has been round to her flat too. She's done a bunk."

Upon deciding they had no further useful information, Jane left the MPs and dodged the dancing throng on her way back to the table while pondering Isla's fate. Yes, the woman was pretty fed up with Westminster. Had she just jacked it all in, or was her disappearance linked to her conspiratorial ideas?

"More questions," Jane said, avoiding the flailing arms of an exuberantly boogieing MP.

* * *

"What's a mixer night?" Dana asked as the limo pulled up in front of the Randolf and spilled the four of them out onto the pavement.

Dan laughed his low, rumbling laugh. "You'll see."

Jane was grateful to discover that the skimpy swimsuits were not mandatory tonight. Instead, people all around were in their best party togs. Martha wasn't on shift, but an equally stunning waitress showed them to a cubicle. Jane sat next to Hannah, who looked fabulous in her dress, even if she wore too much makeup for Jane's taste.

"Come with me," she said, leading Hannah to the changing rooms. Having hit the Champagne hard on the drive over, the girl teetered precariously on her heels and couldn't stop giggling. "Hannah," said Jane. "I must tell you something. Daniel is a lying prick." She set about wiping off the excess cosmetics. "It doesn't matter how I know, but just believe me, most of them are. Don't waste your time on him. This place is a sort of 'anything goes' club. Have some fun, get him out of your head. Find someone exciting and enjoy yourself."

Hannah's face smiled, but another emotion flickered deep within the girl's bleary eyes. As soon as Jane noticed it, it was gone.

"Okay Dokey," Hannah said cheerily.

With her brow furrowed, Jane reapplied Hannah's makeup more sparingly, and once she was happy at the result, the two of them ambled out to the pool again. When back at the table, Jane picked up her brandy alexander. Her ulterior motive for coming here was that Ed said he was meeting Quentin, so she scanned the room intently while sipping the creamy concoction through a straw. They were nowhere to be seen.

Over the other side of the pool, the elder Letchford sat with some of his Tory colleagues and waved to her. She smiled and returned the gesture. As usual, most of the faces present tonight were familiar from one field or another, but sadly, no James Bond.

To loud whoops from some patrons, a heavily oiled man wearing only a loincloth walked out onto the platform at the end of the pool. He raised a large tusk-shaped horn and blew into it. People around the room put their hands over their ears, but a great cacophony of giggling ensued as he finished.

Dan shouted over the noise, "You girls are required to move to the next cubicle. It's mixer night."

Hannah giggled, but Jane saw a look of thunder cross Dana's face.

"I don't go, surely." She stood with her lower lip protruding, staring up into Dan's eyes.

"I don't make the rules," said Dan, but Jane wondered if that was true. "It's just a bit of fun. Off you pop," he said, looking right to see who would be joining him. Jane took the sulking Dana by the hand. The two of them and Hannah headed to the next cubicle.

Before long, they were on their third cubicle, and as Jane and Hannah chatted away with their amiable hosts, the truculent Dana refused to join in. Instead, she constantly stared back at where Dan sat, accompanied by two women. They were just chatting and laughing, and to Jane, it really didn't look like the Irish girl had anything to worry about.

Of course, Jane was surreptitiously also looking for Ed, but there had been no sign. Hannah chatted away to a guy in his early thirties. She really seemed to be enjoying the night, but Jane had told her to stop drinking. The horn sounded again, and she realised that Letchford's gang were next.

As soon as they entered his cubicle, Letchford was on Jane like a rash. He guided them to his friends. Pointing to the girls, he said, "These, gentlemen, are the BBC's finest news team and…" He lowered his voice. "…recent converts to the cause." The three men shook their hands and kissed cheeks. "Who is this beauty, now?" Letchford asked upon seeing Hannah. She blushed.

Jane said, "Hannah is my new assistant. She starts on Monday."

With eyes wide, Hannah swivelled, but before she could say anything, Letchford cut back in. "Well, I will have even more reason to visit now." He took the girl's hand and kissed it. If Jane didn't know better, she would swear Hannah was loving the dirty old pervert's attention. It was then that the jealousy set in.

I am so fucked up, she thought.

Fruitlessly, she scanned the room for Ed once more, but her roving eye stopped its search on Dan's cubicle. He had familiar visitors, Lady Letchford and the PM's wife, Cassie Jenkins. From here, their conversation didn't seem cordial. He appeared to be getting berated, and she really wanted to know what was being discussed so vehemently.

How could she get over there without Selwyn noticing what she was doing? Currently, he seemed preoccupied with Hannah, but Jane knew he could lose interest and come looking for her anytime. She had an idea. Leaning close to Hannah's ear, she said, "He likes to be called sir." Jane doubted his attention would stray far now.

Once satisfied no one was paying her particular attention, Jane headed round the pool. On reaching the cubicle before Dan's, she swerved around the back instead of going poolside and made her way behind where the three still sat, deep in discussion.

"…you and my bloody husband are worrying more about your dicks than the job in hand, Lockwood. Now, are they under control or not?" It was Lady Letchford talking.

"I told you, they are sorted," said Dan. "We have them under constant surveillance. All their family, too. Neither has put a foot out of line."

"Okay," she said, "but pretty soon, I need loyalty to the cause and not to your dick, understood? Bring them inside next week or get rid of them, do you hear? The change is happening soon, and we need the press to be onside, or God knows we will be in the same mess here as our American cousins."

"Yes, ma'am," Dan said sheepishly.

Jane backed away. There was little doubt who they were talking about. She watched from a distance, and the conversation in the cubicle seemed to be more amiable now.

Jane wasn't sure if her sense of shock came from Lady Letchford cooly discussing her husband's dalliance, or instead from the 'get rid of them' comment. It sounded a bit terminal, but she placated herself that it more likely meant their firing from the BBC, rather than Dana and her turning up in a shallow grave. Whatever the intention, it freaked Jane. She headed back to the girls and tried to look calm.

At least it was now known who pulled Dan and Letchford's strings. Jane had followed this story for months with the full intention of writing it up as soon as that riddle was solved. But now she was the story, and it sounded like she and Dana were soon to be purposed for something more than bed partners. That suited Jane, but she wasn't sure how Dana was going to take it. She'd fallen hard for Dan. *Would she ever write this one? Where was it all heading? What a bastard*, she thought.

The glamourous night was over, and driver aside, only Jane and Hannah were left in the limo as it cruised slowly through darkened London streets. It made more sense to drop off Jane first, but she insisted the driver take Hannah home and then double back to drop her off. Of course, she had to pry Hannah from the limpet in order to get her away. Letchford appeared quite taken with the young girl. Knowing what she knew now, Jane realised that the MP was the weak link in the grand government conspiracy. As she guessed before, he had an entirely different agenda.

"I liked your friends. Thanks for tonight." Hannah's smile changed to a yawn. "I haven't been out like that since my eighteenth." Jane felt some guilt at dangling Hannah in front of the sharks, but the girl was going to have to learn about life sometime.

"I meant what I said about the job tonight, Hannah. You okay to start on Monday? There will be many more parties like tonight if you do."

"Really? That would be great." The young girl smiled.

"Hannah, Daniel is going to be my driver. Will that cause any problems? If it does, I will get rid of him."

"No, it will be okay. I'm over him," Hannah said, but Jane wasn't sure. They pulled up outside the house.

With the night now taking its toll, Jane yawned and said, "Okay, see you Monday."

Hannah pecked her cheek and left. Jane made the car wait until Hannah was safely in the house.

Halfway home, the car turned into the dockland area that fringed the Thames. It wasn't a place you wanted to be in at nighttime unless, of course, you had business of a nefarious nature. They slowly cruised past darkened warehouses. Few souls were to be seen.

"Where are you going?" she asked. The driver said nothing but pulled up in a dark cul-de-sac housing tatty garages with randomly painted doors. She thought to run, but the rear doors clicked as the locks engaged.

He turned to face her, then held up a badge. "DI Lawson, Miss Clark. You have nothing to worry about."

Jane looked at the badge and said, "I could pump that out of Photoshop in five minutes."

"Well, now you have admitted forgery, you do have something to worry about," he said, smiling. "Miss Clark, I believe you may have unwittingly become involved in a criminal conspiracy, and I need to know if you can help me?"

She narrowed her eyes and scanned DI Lawson. He looked like a copper, but then, that was easy to achieve. This could, of course, be a test of Jane's loyalty to whatever the hell Lady Letchford and Dan were discussing tonight. Jane was a decent judge of character, but she was far better at knowing what side her bread was buttered on.

"Sorry, DI Lawson, I have no idea what you're talking about."

"Well, Miss Clark, I will be honest with you and tell you I have little idea either, but I know your phone is bugged, your friend Dana's phone is too, and you have been frequenting establishments and mingling with people that hold far-right sympathies."

"Detective, I work in politics for the state broadcaster. In my time, I have consumed champagne and whiskies with communists, fascists and everything in between. Who but the bugger would know if my phone were bugged, sir?" She deliberately gave the man a sweet smile.

He appeared to lose interest in her fast. "You are not going to cooperate, are you?"

"Cooperate with what?"

The man sighed. He reached over, and Jane heard the rear doors unlock. "You are free to go." She looked through the tinted glass at the wasteland that surrounded the garages.

"You're not throwing me out here," she said.

"I will gladly drive you home if we can have an amiable chat," he said.

She first looked at him and then out of the windows again. "Bastard," she said, getting out of the car.

It took three hours to traverse the desolate dockyard wasteland and reach her street. No taxis passed by, and no Uber would accept the job from the area. Her £1200 Louboutin heels were ruined, and she also had to fend off two amorous approaches on the way home. Ironically, a taxi finally did draw up just as she turned into her own street. The driver told her she shouldn't be walking the streets alone at night. He would probably never know why she answered in such colourful language.

On finally locking London outside and slumping down on the sofa, Jane pulled the ruined leather from her aching feet. Angrily, she threw one of the shoes across the room.

The police intervention, whether legitimate or not, raised the stakes in this arrangement. She wasn't ever going to tell the copper the full story, but then she didn't really have a clue what was going on anyway. So, there was no way that she could help him, even if she had the inclination.

Should she tell Dan or Letchford about the intrusion? If it were a test, then yes, definitely. But if the man really was police, letting them know may mean her being sidelined. She didn't want to lose her new status, that was true, but there was also still a reporter inside her, and the inquisitive news hound really wanted to see what was playing out here.

Was Lawson on to something? Could these shenanigans really be a far-right conspiracy? It seemed unlikely. Anyway, conspiracies almost always turned out to be crap. People loved to see the connections between events where none existed. There was hardly a day that one side or the other weren't accused of criminal conspiracy. It was a shame that politics in Britain had followed the USA down this road. Political debate was being replaced by mud throwing. You defeated your opponent in the courts before they ever got to the ballot box. And of course, even if you didn't win the case, there were millions out there that would hold the 'no smoke without fire' theory. A lot of the mud would stick.

She missed the politics of the pre-Brexit world. Things were simpler then.

London, Saturday 29th March 2025

Half an hour ago, Jane stood in the shower and fussed over the greater issue. This…whatever the fuck was going on had crossed her line. Not her morals line – she well knew that one needed a serious repainting. The fuzzy old thing was hard to detect these days. No, it was the fairness line, and she also acknowledged the 'seriously pissing me off' line was being bumped against too. It was time for her to stop being a spectator. Time to be proactive.

The police intervention, if that's what it was, allowed her to bring some of these unknowns into the light. Maybe then a few wrongs could begin to be righted.

She wasn't on shift today, but her heels clacked down the steps as she headed to work anyway. Dan would be there. He always was. Filled with intent, this new Jane needed answers.

* * *

"Hey, boss, we need to chat."

"Of course, my wee haggis. Come along in and park your butt." Dan pointed to the deliberately rickety chair opposite. She cast it aside and got a decent one from his meeting table.

"Boss, I got a visit from the police last night." She let that one hang in the air and watched for Dan's reaction. A couple of lines appeared, but he didn't freak out. *One-nil to 'it was a test'*, she thought.

"What were the boys in blue after?" he asked calmly.

She went straight to the point. "Well, boss, apparently, I am part of some far-right attempted coup, and an offer was made if I turned king's witness and dobbed you all in."

"An offer?" he asked, his right eyebrow raised. This reaction aside, his face said they may as well have been discussing the weather.

"We didn't get to specifics before the prick chucked me out of the car in the docklands, but I guess me not joining you and Letchford in jail was part of the deal." Matching his demeanour, she smiled sweetly. Dan started drumming his fingers on the desk. She jumped back in. "I told him to piss off. I know nothing anyway, as you well know, but I didn't come here about him, boss."

Now he was interested. "Then why are you here, Jane?"

"I need you to come clean with me," she said, pointing over the table. "Boss, I know I'm being manipulated. You and Letchford have something going on, and you need my compliance." Jane held up a hand. She wasn't finished. "I have been well rewarded, and thus far, my conditions of agreement have not been breached. No lying, nothing illegal. I'm fandabidozi about the whole shebang, boss. No issues."

He swung forward and leaned on the desk with his elbows. "There is a but coming…"

She let out a long, slow breath. "But… Dana has fallen for you big time, boss. If you are stringing her along, well…just don't."

He stood and walked to the window. There was no way to tell what was going on in his head. He would make a good poker player.

Everything was being risked by her coming here today, but she had a switch, and once it turned on, no force in the world was going to stop her from doing whatever she decided was the right thing to do. Jane had been compromised but went in with her eyes open. Dana maybe didn't have that luxury.

"Are you threatening me, Jane?" Dan turned; his face now contorted.

Butterflies fluttered in her stomach, but there was no going back. "Not with the police, boss. It is more likely to be some sort of heavy implement on the back of your head when you least expect it. They'll likely discover your body battered and beaten in a bathtub somewhere.

He sat back in the chair and rubbed his eyes. "I don't respond well to threats," he mumbled. She said nothing, but held his gaze with a polite smile fixed on her face. Inhaling, he made a tiny shake of the head. "I've grown fond of Dana. I wouldn't see her hurt. But she's a big girl, Jane. She can fight her own battles."

"I know, boss. I didn't say it was me holding the murder weapon now, did I." Jane stood, placed both hands on his desk and leaned over him. "I didn't come to threaten you, boss. I came to warn you." She smiled at him sweetly once more. "See you Monday."

And with that, she walked out.

While checking her lippy in the elevator mirror, Jane tried hard to calm the broiling inside. Dan was not so different from Letchford and she now knew he was certainly not the ringleader. Like The Letch, Dan had been chosen because he was weak and vulnerable. The girl in the mirror smiled. Lady Letchford, or whoever ran this operation, would show their hand soon; There was no doubt. She and Dana had value to someone higher up the tree than their current dirty old suitors.

The male Letchford was probably more of a millstone than the step on the ladder that she believed at first. However, she'd keep him onside for now. She was once useful to him; he may prove to be useful to her one day soon.

Edinburgh, Monday 31st March 2025

I don't like Mondays. Nancy sang the song in her head as she unlocked the office door and headed up the stairs to her workplace. Mondays were seldom a problem, really, but today might be different. There was a lot of soul-searching over the weekend. She couldn't keep lying to her boss. The decision having been made, she called her cousin and lined up some bar work.

Her time here in the solicitor's office was over. She loved this job, and with the possibility of saving it, going to the police was considered, then had been considered some more, but was ultimately discounted. There was still Jamie to think of. After years of drug abuse, he was finally getting his life back to something close to normal, up in Dunfermline. Of course, that was part of the problem. The blackmailer would have nothing over Nancy had Jamie still been off the rails. Jamie was doing fine, but she knew it would take only a breeze to push him back to the wreck of a life he led before. He had a wife and kid now. Nancy was doing it all for them.

Things would be tight for a while, money-wise. Bar work could never replace the salary she enjoyed here, but Duncan couldn't leave her in place once she came clean with him about stealing the mail. Her dearest hope was that the company wouldn't take legal action against her.

Duncan's business partner, Struan, was a different matter though. Struan acted like an absent-minded professor most of the time, but when he got his claws into something he considered unfair, he was ruthless. Maybe Duncan would just let Nancy go and be done with it.

The coffee machine was loaded and on, the post sorted and distributed, and now Nancy took a seat opposite Duncan's desk. She'd gone with a silver-grey business suit today and buttoned the blouse all the way up. She managed a wee smile as she realised she often unfastened an extra one before coming into this office. "What a tart," she said under her breath.

"Art?" said Duncan, walking in and laying down the briefcase that held nothing but his sandwich. Nancy looked a little startled.

"Hey, boss," she said.

"Good morning, Nancy, what happened to you on Friday?"

"That's why I'm here, boss. Something came up."

"Ah, don't worry about it. Do you want a coffee?" he asked.

"I'll get it," she said, getting up.

"No, no," he said, "park your bum. I'll nip down." He headed for the door but stopped. "What were you saying about art when I arrived?"

"Oh, that you need to get some," she replied.

He looked around the walls at the array of diplomas, certificates and signed Hearts shirts. "You might be right. Back in a mo."

* * *

He climbed the stairs with two mugs. Was this going to be about Friday? Had Nancy detected a change and maybe saw him checking her out? Duncan seldom saw her until mid-morning, once she was happy that everything in the downstairs office was shipshape. As far as he could remember, she'd never been sitting waiting for him like this.

Over the weekend, he resolved to walk in here today and ask her out for a drink. The plan crumbled the second he scaled the stairs. *What a wuss*, he thought.

Once back in the office, he laid one coffee before her and then put his on the desk. She stood, tut-tutting. Lifting his mug, she put it on one of the leather drinks mats she had ordered with the company logo on. Taking a paper hanky out of her pocket, she wiped the water ring from the desk.

"Do you live in a midden?" she asked, sitting back down.

He held up his hands in apology. "Sorry, boss," he said and added, "To what do I owe the privilege of the early morning visit?"

"I want to hand in my notice," she said dryly.

Horrified, Duncan started a mental review of his actions on Friday. Nancy walked out early, and was nowresigning on the followingMonday morning. Had he said more than he thought? He really didn't think so. Not at all sure he wanted to know the answer, he asked anyway. "What is this all about, Nancy?" She didn't reply straight away. He asked, "Have I done something? Should I call Struan in here as a witness?"

She jumped to life. "No, no need for that. I would rather Struan didn't hear about this."

"Then what is it?"

Twenty seconds or so passed in silence. "I've been stealing stuff." Nancy looked at her shoes.

Duncan's eyes widened. "Stealing what? You have a paperclip habit?" he said and laughed, but he stopped when she didn't join in. Nancy was usually up for banter. This wasn't like her.

She sighed and then blurted out the whole story in one long unpunctuated sentence.

"Stop, stop, Nance. You're being blackmailed?"

She told him about the emails and gave him a potted history of Jamie.

"Why would anyone bother with our post?" he asked, but the question was rhetorical. "Hell, I would have emailed them the stuff if I had known. Saved you running all round town."

"The reason I didn't return to work on Friday is that I met the guy that collects the stolen mail, and I followed him. I have this." She held out her phone with a picture of a Mercedes. "This is the guy that the junkie gave the mail to."

He took the phone from her and noted down the reg number. Handing it back, he said, "Can you send me that pic, please?"

"Of course," she said. There was a tear in her eye. "But you can't go to the police or anything. Promise me you won't."

"It will be all right, Nance," he said. "We'll keep this in house."

"You can't know how this will all pan out. If the pictures of Jamie get out, he will freak and I don't know what will happen after that," she said.

He sat pondering this bizarre situation. Someone stealing their mail made no sense. Okay, they did government work, but most of it ended up in the newspapers. Anyone interested could have read it there.

"Nancy," he finally said. "Do you like working here?"

Her expression queried his sanity. "I love it here." Tears flowed freely down her cheeks and dappled her grey jacket.

His urge was to walk round the desk and hug her. Maybe this was not the time. He also wanted to say, "I love you being here." But again…

"I'm not accepting your resignation. For now, this stays between you and me. Nothing changes. You keep delivering the mail, but give me a copy of everything, too." He stood and made his way round to where she sat. "Have you got another hanky?" She went into her pocket and handed him a fresh one. Duncan unfolded it and used it to mop her cheeks and wipe her eyes. "Nancy?" he said.

Her reddened eyes landed on him expectantly. "Yes?"

"Nothing." He went back and sat down. This wasn't the time. "Get back to work, young lady," he said with false sternness. Sighing, he watched her depart.

* * *

Struan ran the number plate for Duncan and didn't ask any questions. The registration was unlisted, which was unusual. Criminals would clone plates in case the police ran them through a computer. Had any copper taken interest in this car, a scan would show the number didn't exist, leading to the driver being pulled over. A fake plate might as well be replaced with a big sign saying, *Bad Guy*.

Duncan Googled 'Unlisted car registrations' and, after sifting through various aliens and Illuminati theories, was left with a couple of results that said the secret services carried them. A police computer would run the number and advise the officer to back off, but there would be no DVLA listing.

He didn't know how much weight to put on this. Surely, MI5 would have someone in the Post Office to read mail before it ever got here. They wouldn't need an elaborate blackmail scam. This was all utterly bizarre to him.

"Okay," he said aloud. There was regular work to be done, and intriguing though it was, this mystery would have to wait for another time. He reached into the top tray for his first case, and on pulling the file, one of Nancy's tissues fell on his desk. He reached for it and scrunched it up; he was halfway to binning it when he spied something. He opened it up again and saw writing.

Boss, sorry to add to your woes, but I'm pretty sure the phones and computers are bugged. Please don't discuss anything about the case on the phone or by email.

His head went into his hands.

Edinburgh, Tuesday 1st April 2025

Today, a much happier looking Nancy stood at the door of Duncan's office, a spotty youth in biker's leathers by her side. "Motorbike courier for you. He won't give me the parcel. Jobsworth!" she said while shaking her head.

"Okay, Nance. I thought this was maybe some sort of April fool's joke," Duncan said.

"If it is, it's nowt to do with me."

The lad walked into the office and laid a small parcel on Duncan's desk. "I need you to sign this, please." He handed over a greasy paper, stuck to a clipboard.

"There you go, my friend," said Duncan, scribbling. "Can you show your boyfriend out, please, Nance?"

The courier looked at Nancy sheepishly while she gave him a once-over. "I could do worse," she said and added, "Actually, I have done worse and married the pig." Still chuckling away at the witticism, she led him out.

Getting through the parcel's packaging was a challenge. If this was a joke, someone spent a lot of time on it. He had to battle with three layers of stuff that would strangle dolphins to liberate a mobile phone box. Once the device was prized from the grasp of it's plastic container, he conducted a cursory check before switching on. It beeped, seemingly ready for use. After Clicking on a few of the Apps, he opened the contacts and found only one number listed. It wasn't one he recognised. *Well*, he thought, *this is some elaborate scam*, but he clicked the number and put the phone to his ear.

Jane answered. "Duncan, say nothing. Leave your office and call me back in two minutes on this number. Use the phone I sent." She hung up. It didn't sound like an April fool, but what were his choices? He did as he was told.

"Hey, sis. Is this an April fool?"

"Yeah, bro, I paid five hundred quid for a phone to be delivered to you to tell you that your shoelaces are undone."

Instinctively, he looked down and immediately felt like an idiot.

"You looked, didn't you?" Jane said.

"Of course not," he lied.

"Brother, I have some bad news for you. Your phones are bugged; mine are too. It was likely the cause of the feedback we experienced when you called last week. They are almost certainly reading your emails as well."

"I know," he said, "but how do you?"

"Well, it's all a bit complicated, and I am not exactly sure who is doing it, but a local bobby told me that my entire family were being watched. They have me mixed up in some strange conspiracy."

Duncan concurred. "Nancy discovered the bugs a few days ago, Jane. But we didn't know that you were linked."

"Duncan, work on the assumption that your office is bugged. Don't go acting weird, though. Call me from time to time at the usual number, and we can chat, but if you have to discuss anything related to this, leave the office and use the new phone. Don't use it for any other calls. They don't know it exists, and we want it to stay that way."

"Who is bugging us? What is it all about, Jane?" He really didn't want to ask the next question but curiosity got the better of him. "Has this anything to do with the death of that Burton guy?"

"I don't know yet, but…" Jane tailed off for a few seconds. "I think I'm getting close to the people that may be involved."

"Don't do anything stupid," he said.

"Sorry, Duncan, stupid is way behind on this one. Anyway, I gotta go as I don't want anyone seeing me using this phone. I'll head up the road soon, and we can talk more. I Promise."

"Jane…"

"What?"

"I…I…stay safe."

"I love you too, bro." She disconnected.

A tear welled up in his eye, which he fought back. He sniffled, wiped his eyes, went back to the office and booked a flight to London.

London, Wednesday 2nd April 2025

There's no better aroma than coffee and toast, Jane decided, while laying out the mugs and side plates, and waiting for Letchford to finish in the shower. Hot news never came over the phone lines these days. It arrived around 6am with flowers and groceries.

For a dirty old pervert, he had an eye for a bouquet. Today's arrangement was a stunning purple collection. She sorted them in the vase in the middle of the breakfast table as Letchford padded into the room in one of her towel robes.

Pointing to the flowers, he said, "Those are not merely a token of my affection, dear. They symbolise the news you will be breaking later."

"Yes, sir?" Jane said. The subservience still wound him up, but after their extensive sex session this morning, she doubted he would be dragging her back off to bed any time soon. Regardless, the leer wrote itself over his wrinkled face anyway. He kissed her head and sat opposite.

"I'm resigning from the Conservative Party." His conversational tone belied the headline grabbing nature of the pronouncement

She gasped, her eyes wide. "Really? What is this about?"

"Well," he continued as if discussing how he preferred his toast, "You don't need all the details now, but four colleagues and I are forming the People's Democratic Alliance. I believe Dana may have similar news about another breakaway going out at seven."

From a bag lying at his feet, he pulled out a purple rosette, waving it under her nose as if it were hard to see. His eyes now carried that twinkle. The one that said he had information that he knew she wanted, and they were both well aware she would do anything to have. This was the nuance that entered their relationship since she relented and fulfilled his sexual desires. She'd been naive to believe that Letchford had a one-track mind. Of course, he wanted her, he lusted after her, yes, but that wasn't enough for him. He needed to control her,. No, he didn't want a submissive. When she'd finally given in to his persistence, stripped off and told him to get on with it, it was against everything he desired. He'd almost walked away. In his position, he had the choice of a hundred-bed partners who would gladly do whatever he asked, but this wasn't enough. Letchford had to win. Sex and politics were as one to the depraved MP. Like the electorate, his thrill came from persuading people who had a choice, to choose him. Of course, he would bend the rules to lessen that choice. All things being fair, no one was ever sending him to Westminster or taking him to bed, but today, right here, right now, he had her. The sad thing about Jane's epiphany was that she did indeed have a choice. He wasn't even threatening the video anymore. No, he just dangled carrots, and she stripped off for him. He'd won. She'd lost. Game over.

"What is this all about?" she asked. "I thought you were a supporter of Jenkins?"

"Well, dear, to comply with our agreement that you won't have to lie on air, I am telling you now, *on* the record, that Boris and I have diverged on democratic issues, and I can no longer serve in the same party. I will not be resigning my seat, by the way." His face broke into a childish grin.

From his expression, it was obvious that he was lying, but she took the unsubtle hint and asked no more questions. The story would be reported along with the attribution.

"Okay, sir, I will call it in as I head to work later. Probably best not to quote you at this time of the morning. It may raise suspicion." Jane giggled.

"Well, that being the case, dear, we will have to find something else to do for an hour or so," he said, slipping her dressing gown off. The battle was over, and Selwyn collected his spoils. A part of Jane knew she had to let him keep winning battles, were she ever to win the war. The part beginning to enjoy losing was pushed hastily back into the dark corners of her mind.

* * *

Jane stepped out of the shower for the third time today, and it wasn't much past eight. *Some sort of a record*, she thought, but then remembered the night in Wigan with a rugby team. *Ah, but that was really one long shower*, she decided.

Letchford was gone, so she didn't bother dressing as she padded through to turn on the news. On the screen, Dana wore a pale orange outfit, which wasn't like her at all. Jane turned the sound up.

"…a breakaway group has formed the Party for Parliamentary Democracy. Father of the House, Carter Davis-Jones, has left the Conservative Party and established the PPD to fight for the House to be more involved in democracy. Davis-Jones believes that several governments have increasingly sidelined Parliament, and he aims to redress this." A PPD rosette image appeared behind Dana. It was bright orange. "Is Boris Jenkins losing the support of his back benches already? He will certainly hope not. In other news…"

She turned the TV off and cleared the table. They'd decided to leave her bit of news until ten to let the first revelation sink in. Once the dishes were done, it was time for her to get dressed. Whether Dana's choice of matching colour outfit was an accident or not, Jane chose a lilac suit anyway. *Better not make it too obvious*.

* * *

With her own news bomb now detonated, Jane strolled back out of the studio. Her phone rang constantly, but it was all the other networks calling to get more details, and she had none, so she didn't answer. Letchford and Davis-Jones were now the hottest ticket in town and would spend the rest of the day touring studios. On realising she had no more work to do, Jane went up to her office to pester the new assistants. That would fill in an hour or so, and then maybe Dana would be up for lunch.

"Hey, minions," Jane said, walking in. Hannah and Daniel smiled. They saw fun little yellow things when Jane called them that. Angela didn't look so happy, but Jane didn't give a shit about her.

"That was brilliant," Hannah said, pointing to Jane's recorded image on the screen.

"Why thank you, young lady," Jane replied. "Fancy coffee?" she asked.

Daniel jumped to his feet and said, "I'll get it."

"No," said Jane. "Let's go out for coffee. Want to come, Angela?"

Shaking her head, "I better stay here," she said.

"Okay, but Daniel will miss you. I think he has a little crush," Jane said mischievously and then had to judge whose face looked more surprised. Angela hadn't shown much in the way of emotion yet. The woman wore flat, plain shoes with no heel. Jane already had a crick from looking up at her, so she appreciated the gesture.

Angela's angular face wasn't unpleasant, just austere. The worst part of her was the total lack of emotion on her features, but now Jane saw the woman blush. *Got you*, she thought.

Jane and Hannah got in the back of the Beemer. Daniel sat in the front, wearing the driver's cap Jane had bought him. Daniel and Hannah seemed to have repaired their relationship, but any heat had clearly dissipated.

"The Dorchester, please, driver," Jane called in her best posh voice.

Hannah clapped her hands at the suggestion. Twenty minutes later, they pulled up outside the hotel. "We will only be an hour, Jeeves," Jane said as she and Hannah exited. Jane looked back to see if Daniel was disappointed at the non-invitation, but grinning from ear to ear, he sped off, so she guessed he would probably rather be driving anyway.

The concierge held the door open. "Good morning, Miss Clark."

She could only guess that he'd recognised her from TV. They breezed past him with a smile.

"I have a table booked for morning coffee," Jane said to the receptionist and was taken aback when the man replied, "Yes, Miss Clark, your guests are already seated."

"Guests?" said Hannah. Jane shrugged.

They were led to the dining room and found Lady Elizabeth Letchford sitting with Cassie Jenkins. Elizabeth waved them over. The woman was resplendent in blue from head to foot. Cassie Jenkins looked like she had nipped out from Woodstock in her paisley-pattern smock. Behind Lady Letchford, a mountain of a black man stood in white trousers and a painted-on T-shirt.

Oh my, Jane thought, licking her lips.

"Miss Clark, my dear, lovely to see you again. Sit, please." Lady Letchford pulled the seat next to her out a bit. "Hannah, dear, I see why my husband has talked of little else since meeting you. You are gorgeous. Jane asked me to book your massage. Dalton here will take you upstairs." She pointed at the man behind her.

"Massage?" squeaked Hannah.

"I will wait for you here," Jane said. Hannah walked round the table like a lamb for the slaughter. Dalton took her tiny hand in his and led her out of the room.

"You know Cassie Jenkins, of course?" Lady Letchford pointed over the table. Jane nodded to the woman. Lady Letchford raised a finger, and waiters appeared with trays of coffee, tea, sandwiches and cakes. "I believe you had a visit from the police, dear," Letchford said.

"Oh, it was nothing, my lady, I…"

"Do call me Elizabeth, dear."

Jane nodded. "Thank you, Elizabeth. It really was nothing."

"Well, Detective Inspector Lawson will not be bothering you again, I can assure you." Jane conjured up images of Lawson lying in a Perthshire ditch. "You have been impressive since you joined us, Miss Clark. The President was quite taken with you. He sent me this to present to you." Lady Letchford put a square box and a certificate in front of her.

Jane opened it and a hexagonal gold medal with a black ribbon lay inside. It was a Presidential Medal of Freedom. She covered her mouth with her hand, not sure what might fall out if she didn't.

"You join Elvis in having one of those. Elvis and me, of course." The lady laughed a little.

"Oh my God," said Jane finally. "I only met him for ten minutes."

"The President is such a decisive man, Miss Clark."

"Sorry, please call me Jane."

"Jane, of course. He really was quite enchanted by you and so impressed by our women folk in general. He insisted we have our own little Daughters of the Revolution. Not being a nation prone to revolutions, instead, we went with the Order of Boudica. You, my dear, will be one of the founding members." Elizabeth beamed at her.

Jane's head swam. This felt like the time she drank half a bottle of champagne through a straw. Her brain was no longer connected to her tongue, or legs either, as she seriously considered fleeing. "I...I..." Jane gave up.

"I know, dear. Rather overwhelming, isn't it," Elizabeth said. Jane picked up her coffee and even managed to get some of it in her mouth. Also selecting a chocolate cake, she bit into it. Chewing seemed mundane, and she needed that right now. Lady Letchford wiped the spillage and crumbs from Jane's mouth. The action pushed Jane back through time to a moment she sat in a highchair, little fat legs dangling over the edge, her face clarted with chocolate and a bright green plastic bib on her chest, full of detritus. Mum licked a paper napkin and wiped Jane's mouth. She was a mess, but Mum was grinning like this was the best day of her life. Baby Jane reached her tiny hands out to try and touch the smile as if it were beautifully infectious. The light from the window that picture-framed her mum diminished, and a shadow crossed the scene.

Dad stood behind Mum and looked at Jane disapprovingly. Jane knew he was seeing her today and not the baby with food on her face. He wasn't angry as such – no, it was much, much worse. Dad was disappointed. He shook his head, folded his arms, turned and walked away. The floorboard in their Edinburgh flat squeaked the way it used to when Dad came home from work. Strangely, the board never squeaked for Mum or Duncan. Baby Jane used to jump on it, believing that, if she could make it squeak, he would walk in the door. But now it sounded as he walked out. Walked out like the day he left to go to hospital for a minor operation. The board never squeaked again.

Jane's podgy hand reached out after her dad, but he closed the door behind him, never looking back.

She was back in the Dorchester. Then came the tears. Lady Letchford wiped her face while Cassie Jenkins was mouthing soothing things, but Jane couldn't hear the words. The rushing wind drowned them both out as she flew through her turbulent compromised life. Her tainted past zoomed up, slapped her in the face and blew away like rainy-day leaves. It wasn't Jane's fault she had been able to wind her mother round her little finger.

You should have been there! Dunky should have been there.

"I am what you made me," Jane said to Dad's apparition but

then realised she had spoken out loud. With her tears cascading, she looked up to see the two women sitting, slightly taken aback.

Lady Letchford smiled and said, "Why, that is gracious of you, dear," as she kissed Jane's tear-streaked cheek.

"Sorry, I must go clean up," said Jane, heading for the restroom.

Her hands were soon in water, splashing her face, and of course, her mobile rang. Quickly drying them on real towels, (there were no blowers or paper crap here,) she answered.

"Hey, Jane," her brother said.

"Oh Duncan."

"Anything the matter, sis?" He must have heard a change in her voice.

"No, bro. Fandabidozi. What can I do for thee?" Jane realised she was on her regular phone and hoped he remembered not to say anything.

"I'm going to be in London for business Friday. Will you have time for a catch-up?"

Jane brightened immediately. She really wanted to hug him there and then.

"Of course. Can you stay for the weekend? I have holidays available, and, barring political disasters, I will be all yours, bro."

Duncan laughed. "When was the last time this country went three days without a disaster, sis?"

"True, but please stay." She realised she put too much emphasis on the please.

"I can never refuse my little sis," he said. "See you around three, if that's okay?"

"I'll pick you up from Heathrow," she said.

"No need. I'm coming into London City. I can walk over to your place."

"Okay, brilliant. I'm really looking forward to it. See you Friday."

The call ended. She looked at herself in the mirror. The panda eyes were still there, but she couldn't give a monkey's. "My big bro is coming to town," Jane told the girl in the mirror.

Hannah was back at the table when Jane walked in, and Lady Letchford fussed over her.

"Hey, Hannah, you lucky sod. How was it?"

Hannah giggled and blushed. "Not telling."

Jane feigned hurt and said, "No worries – I am so getting you drunk later, and you can spill all."

Cassie and Elizabeth laughed at Hannah's discomfort. Jane turned to the two women. "Sorry, girls, but we have to get back to the office. Elizabeth, will you email me details of that meeting you mentioned? I will be sure to be there."

Jane shook Cassie's hand, but Lady Letchford stood and gave her a hug.

"See you next week, dear," she said. Elizabeth sounded so much like her husband it was scary.

Jane sat in the back of the car with the medal on her knee.

"What's that?" Hannah asked.

"Nothing," Jane replied, throwing it on the floor.

London, Thursday 3rd April 2025

Daniel picked Jane up as normal, if something could be normal after only four days. He'd dropped Hannah earlier, and then came back for 'Little Miss Late' as Jane now called herself. As far as she knew, her job was now to arrive, have coffee, have lunch, read an email and then go to the pub or go home. *So this is how the other half live*, she thought. Of course, if a little mischief could be had in between all this work, then even better. The two of them walked in and Jane immediately saw that Angela was dressed a bit smarter and had makeup on. Her grey hair seemed to have been dyed too.

"Morning, Angela – you smell lovely today. What is that?"

Angela blushed a little. "Chanel," she said.

"Hannah, put some Chanel on my list, please. It's certainly alluring." Jane giggled as she noticed Hannah really was writing it down.

Jane headed through to her own office and closed the door. Maybe she'd move Hannah in here with her and see what transpired with Daniel and Angela. As fun as it was to mess about with the appointed secretary like this, she really wanted Angela distracted from the job of keeping an eye on her. It must've been Angela who arranged yesterday's meeting with Lady Letchford. Maybe if the old bat had a toyboy, she would be a little less diligent.

Upon looking at her emails, one was from Lady Letchford about the inaugural meeting of 'The Order of Boudica'. It was next Friday at the Randolf. She decided to attend – more out of curiosity than any wish to be a member of something that sounded so pretentious.

She closed the email and noticed that there was also one from the lesser Letchford.

Sorry that I haven't had more time to spend with you. Things have been hectic as you must realise. A heads-up on what is about to happen…

Jane read and then re-read the email.

"Bloody hell," she said. In her head, the male Letchford kept swinging back and forth between criminal mastermind and a dirty old man. Today he was Moriarty again, although he almost certainly acted at someone else's behest.

Jane yelled, "Hannah, get your arse in here now." Hannah came running. Jane heard Angela saying, "Perfectly good intercom."

"Hannah, can you talk to the news editor and get me some time on telly before lunch, please?"

"You got it," Hannah said and left. Jane was pleased and a little surprised that Hannah was actually good at her job.

"Daniel, coffee!" Jane shouted, more to annoy Angela than anything else.

BBC News

"My sources advise that after irrevocable differences of opinion, the three parties that formed the Government of National Unity have split. The coalition, being one of the King's conditions of granting the delay in the election, will no longer be in effect, and we may be faced with a General Election sooner than we thought. Boris Jenkins has yet to comment on the situation, but after his party's splits this week, his future must now be in question."

A technician was unwiring Jane when Ed appeared in the studio. She hurriedly pulled the last wires free and threw them at the disgruntled man. "Eddie boy, where the hell have you been all week?" Running over, she jumped into his embrace.

"Er, I've been busy."

"Really? I haven't seen you around. What have you been up to?" She gave him a big wet kiss on the nose.

"Yuck." Ed was smiling while wiping his face with the sleeve of his very loud sweater. "Not really work stuff. Can we go talk somewhere?"

"Sure, one sec," Jane said, turning to the waiting Hannah. "I'm nipping out with Ed a while. You head back upstairs, okay?"

Hannah smiled and left, giving Ed a wave on the way. "She seems a lot happier now," he said as they exited the studio

"Yeah." Jane nodded. "And you won't believe this, but she is really good at the job."

The two walked in silence a while, which for Ed and Jane was unusual. She knew he had something important to tell her. She reached over and took his hand. They left the building and crossed the road to a Caffè Nero.

"So, what's up?" She already had a feeling she wouldn't like the answer.

Ed took his time putting cream in the coffee. "I'm going away, Jane." He didn't look at her.

Watching him load his coffee with sugar was usually one of her favourite parts of the day. It was an addiction both he and Dana shared. Today, he had brown sugar. It was his favourite. Well, except for cubes, but who the hell had those these days? She knew more about this man than anyone on the planet.

If I never ask, will it stop him going? "Away where?"

"Not sure yet, maybe Switzerland."

"For a holiday?" She reached over and stayed his frantic stirring hand.

"Sort of, maybe longer," he said.

"Ed, is there any chance you tell me what is happening without me having to get a baseball bat?"

As if searching for something, his brown eyes circled the room before landing back on her warily. "Quentin and I have spent a lot of time together since Friday, and we'd like to spend a lot more with each other. His parents' desire is that he will marry and settle down, but they want that to be with a woman. Quentin doesn't."

He forfeited the teaspoon to Jane but then began stirring his coffee with his finger.

"So, the two of you are going to elope?" she asked with too much indignation on show.

He let his head fall to the side a bit and grimaced. "You might put it that way."

"Eddie, you must give this a lot of thought. You have a great career ahead of you here. In a couple of years' time, you will be a floor manager or a producer. Oh, you can't throw that all away." Clenching her fist, she softly banged the table.

"I already have." He sucked coffee from his finger.

She pulled his hand away from his mouth. "What do you mean? What have you done, Eddie?"

"I handed in my notice to Dan an hour ago." He wouldn't look at her now.

"I can talk to Dan, get him to let you stay." She heard herself pleading. Panic swelled inside her. With everything else going on, the thought of losing Ed was unbearable.

He lowered his head. When he looked up, there was moisture in the corner of his eye. "If I asked you to leave this all behind and run away with me, would you do it?" he asked.

"Not a chance," she said through gritted teeth. He didn't react but kept staring. Jane's shoulders sank. "In a heartbeat." In those three words, Jane knew she just lost Ed.

"I love him," he said softly. The two looked at each other for a long time, both in tears now.

Exhaling deeply, it was she who broke the silence. "I have cried more this week than in the last ten years."

Ed smiled and then had to stop a loosed tear from splashing in his coffee. "You cry at almost every movie we watch."

More to stem her own tears than the nausea that rose within,

Jane pinched the top of her nose and sat with her head down for a moment. She mumbled, "Will we ever watch a movie again?"

His voice held only determination. "I made you a promise. I will never really leave you. Okay, I will be gone more now, but there are flights. We will have movie weekends. You can come over to the castle."

"You have a castle?" Jane wiped her reddening eyes and sniffled.

He nodded. "Well, it is his mother's, but we have the use of it."

She tilted her head, forcing a smile. "You really love him?" Ed nodded once more. "Then never let him go, Edward." Jane heard herself say the words. She both meant them and didn't.

"Edward?" he said with some incredulity. It made them laugh when it was probably the last thing they felt like doing right now.

Two old friends, born in the same city, a quarter of a mile apart, but who only met on his first day at work and had seldom been apart since, sat recalling the movies, the wine, the headaches and the heartaches. They were two, but not a couple; they loved, but were not in love; forever bound, they would never be one. The last of the friction ebbed from between them. Locking eyes, they each wore yesterday's smiles. But then a shadow came between them, and Ed's smile faded... "Jane," he said in a low whisper.

"Yes?"

"You should get out of London too. Come to Switzerland."

"Come and live with the happy couple in the castle?" she asked.

He held up a hand. "No, maybe not the castle, but get out of London. Things are about to change. You see what is happening in America."

She shook her head. "That will never happen here, Ed. We're not like Americans with their guns."

"We're not all that different. Quentin believes there is some grand plot underway. He was leaving anyway, even before we hooked up. Please think about it." Ed laid his hand on hers.

"Even if he is correct, and I admit, there is a lot of strange shit going down right now, you must know better than anyone – I have to be here," Jane said. There were other reasons that she wouldn't be allowed to leave, but it wasn't the time to broach these with Ed right now.

* * *

About an hour passed, and everything that had to be said, had been. With the coffee cups drained, the two walked back to the office hand in hand.

"So, you will be the next Lady Letchford?" Jane giggled.

He squeezed her fingers and blushed. "One step at a time," he said. "Quentin's mother is cool with it all, but Daddy isn't happy."

"Well, talking about our mutual problem, Daddy – there is something you may be able to help me with before you go." Ed knew Jane's devious face well. "Remember Terry and his offer to visit the British Museum?"

London, Friday 4th April 2025

She was already awake when the buzzer went. Letchford hadn't been round for a few days, so this visit was overdue. "Good morning, dear – sorry I've been neglecting you." As usual, Letchford entered before being asked. The food parcel and, thankfully for Jane's plan, bouquet of flowers were in hand.

"I understand, sir. You are a busy man. Those flowers are lovely. I need to shower. Can you put them in the vase on the table, please?"

Jane headed to the bathroom. She'd use the Fortnum and Mason bodywash today. Letchford seemed to like it, and she needed him distracted.

Once finished showering, she returned to the living room to discover he'd cooked breakfast and arranged the flowers. He'd done a surprisingly good job.

"A man of many talents." She pointed to the flowers. "Let me hang your coat up for you." Taking the expensive suit jacket out into the hall, she reached in his right pocket and retrieved his keys. Quietly, she opened the front door. "Hey, Ed," she whispered, handing out the bunch. "That one, please." She held up the key to be copied. Ed set off down the stairs. Jane left the door ajar and padded back through.

"Is that a new vase? It looks valuable." Letchford was turning it and giving it a good look.

"It is new, but I got it from Home Bargains for a fiver. Your talents don't extend to antiques then?" She laughed. He smiled and put the vase back.

After clearing the plates, Letchford sat back down. "Let's get the boring bit out of the way. Our illustrious prime minister will announce a new coalition later today, and so will be able to continue in power. I think that you will be unsurprised to learn that my party and Davis-Jones's party will be those joining the coalition. We sorted our differences with the Conservatives." Letchford smiled.

"You clever man," said Jane.

"Oh, that is not the clever bit, and I have to confess, my devious wife came up with the good part. The document the King issued allowed an extension for a maximum of twelve months from the forming of the coalition. However, my better half changed the draft that was voted through Parliament to say twelve months from the forming of '*a*' coalition. So, we will now have a further year in power before going to the people." He beamed.

"And as long as you keep forming coalitions, you need never have an election again?" Jane asked, feeling bile rise in her throat. Isla Wallace was on the right track, after all.

"Oh, we won't have to bother with that, dear. New rules are being drafted as we speak. The election process in future will be different. Much less…challenging." He'd clearly finished with politics as he undid his tie and started unbuttoning his shirt.

Her reporter's head was buzzing with his news, but she had to get a grip for now. It was time to rebalance their relationship. "That sounds amazing, sir. You and your wife are so clever," she managed to say, though it pained her to do so.

"To the bedroom, dear?" he said.

* * *

Letchford lay next to her, enjoying his post-exertion snooze. She slipped out the bed and tiptoed through to the hallway. The door was now closed, but his keys, along with the copy, now lay on the hall table. She put the bunch back in his pocket and hid the replica. Quietly, she made her way back to bed.

The happy MP whistled as he descended the stairs. Jane watched him go and then closed the door. She headed back to the dining table and carefully removed the flowers. From the kitchen drawer, she put a pair of white cotton gloves on and emptied the water from the vase. Drying the inside, she put it in a bag. The first part of her plan had gone well. Thanks to Ed and Terry, who they'd visited yesterday evening.

"Terry. I need to borrow a priceless artefact," Jane blurted out, when Terry was making eyes at Ed.

"What, are you mental?" was the British Museum curator's eloquent reply.

"Come on, Terry. I know you have replicas of a lot of the valuable items. I need one of an artefact that is valuable but not currently on show. Can you help?" Jane went to give him her seductive smile but remembered she had no superpowers in this company.

"What is this all about?" Terry looked between Ed and her.

"Well, Terry…"

London City Airport

Duncan walked through the scowling security at London City and headed for the exit. The small airport was a throng of people going places in organised chaos. Much like any transport hub on a Friday, he assumed. Travellers all around jumped from screen to screen like wide-eyed rabbits, searching for truth on a medium that seldom delivered. A good analogy for Britain today, he thought, but he wouldn't be expressing such to his wee sister.

Escaping the madness of arrivals, he was barely ten steps in London when Jane hit him like a runaway train. His bag abandoned, he hugged his little sister tightly. Was that a tear on her face? She was clearly glad to see him, and the feeling was reciprocated.

"Dunky, don't ever let me go," she sobbed.

"What's up, sis?"

She didn't answer. Finally, she released him and stepped back, wiping her eyes. "Sorry, I'm just really glad you're here."

He picked up his bag. "As am I, sis. You didn't have to come meet me though."

She smiled at him. "I wanted to."

"Then I'm happy you did." He took his sister's hand as they made for the street.

They walked in a comfortable silence, taking turns at looking over and smiling at the other. It was Jane that broke the truce.

"Ed's gone."

It bothered him that his sister was in love with a man who could never love her back, but now wasn't the time for that. He stopped and hugged her again. "Where has he gone?"

The question alone caused a twinge on Jane's face. "He's in love. The two of them are off to Europe."

"I'm really sorry, Jane. I know how much you care for him."

"I love him, Duncan. Always have, probably always will," she admitted.

He bit his tongue. That they had the conversation before made resurrecting the subject of her choice in men pointless, and anyway, it would result in an analysis of his own record of success in love, which would never end well. Besides, he didn't want to hurt his sister worse than Ed's departure had already done.

"Is there anyone else in your life at the moment?"

Duncan was surprised when the answer came in hysterics. The laughter sounded a little more asylum than comedy club.

Calming, Jane said, "I had a brief relationship by text with a cute guy, but he's currently eloping to Switzerland with the man I love."

He looked at his sister, his mouth open. "You fell for another gay man?" He immediately regretted the question, but thankfully, she didn't seem to take offence.

"In my defence, my homophobic big brother, I didn't know he was gay at the time." She smiled her cheeky smile that he missed so much. He planted a kiss on her nose. "Duncan," she said. "There is another reason I met you here." Jane motioned at their surroundings. "My flat may be bugged too."

He listened as she brought him up to speed with everything that had happened. He didn't know she omitted the seedier details but would have been glad she did.

"So, the police reached out to you?" he asked.

"Well, if it was the police. Duncan, I'm not sure if you heard the latest as you were on the plane, but this new coalition cuts the other parties out of government, and the way they have framed it, democracy is basically suspended now."

He stopped and watched the Thames flow below the bridge they crossed. Things always changed, and things stayed the same, he thought. Upstream, a revolution was taking place, but in the rest of the country, people were fretting about plane departures and the price of milk. It was a sad indictment of life today that were a dictatorship to form and get flights to leave on time, most people would be fine with it. Not for the first time, he wondered if they were right, and it was him that was wrong. Duncan wasted his life fretting about things he would never change. Maybe he should take Jane out and get drunk. Just forget democracy. After all, even in a dictatorship, they would still need solicitors and reporters. He and Jane would be fine.

She squeezed his hand. "Have you gone somewhere?"

"Why are we bothering, Jane? Why does it matter who sits up there in Westminster? Sure, the poor folk will probably end up getting shat on, but we'll be okay. I will likely make a mint losing cases to the new administration. You'll get lots of overtime reporting..."

He was about to say propaganda but thought better of it.

"They have already got me," she said and looked up at him, before filling in some of the gaps from earlier.

"They paid you a million?" he said, looking at her incredulously.

"So far. There's a lot more on the way if I let them pull my strings. You were right; what does it matter? For years you have said that I am the mouthpiece for the Tory establishment. That being the case, brother, why shouldn't I get paid for it? And I know this is the weakest excuse of all, but it also happens to be true. If I say no, someone else will replace me tomorrow." She broke his gaze.

He stood and looked at his little sister in disbelief. Yes, he had ribbed her for years about her job at the BBC, but not for a second did he ever believe her to be…this. The anger faded quickly as he looked at her, but the emotion was replaced by abject disappointment.

He didn't let Jane know, but he bored all his friends with tales of his amazing little sister. She could do no wrong in his eyes. Well, until now.

He picked up his hand luggage and threw it over the balustrade. It sailed in the wind a while and then plummeted into the water. On landing, the case broke open and his life spilled out over the surface of the Thames.

Even on its best day, London had a faint whiff of all the shit the English poured into their city's artery. Standing next to his sister now, hearing her tale, the whole place stank like an open sewer.

Turning, he made to walk away.

A shocked Jane grabbed his hand. "Please, Duncan, don't go." But she couldn't stop him.

* * *

Jane sank to her knees in the middle of the busy pavement and watched the only other man she loved walk right out of her life.

How could I have lost them both in one day? she sobbed, but her bloody conscience knew the answer. *You've sold your soul.*

A plan was made. She would stay right here forever. Kneeling on the cold, cracked concrete, she'd pray for restitution. One day soon, Duncan would have to cross this bridge again, surely. She would be here, waiting for him to reach out, lift her to her feet and say that everything was going to be all right.

* * *

Her phone bounced high after hitting the top of the TV, and a bright line ripped down the screen like lightning before the mobile landed among the spaghetti wires. Duncan wasn't picking up. The rent split Dana's face as she explained the political changes. How the new system would save them the bother of elections. Online referenda would replace them, and the public only needed to participate if it was an item of interest. Guest speaker after guest speaker welcomed the new system. A few low-profile opposition MPs complained, but the top leadership of all non-government parties seemed to be avoiding comment.

Friday evening was a good time for a revolution, Jane thought. By Monday, it would all be over, and few would have noticed.

She went to the window and watched the people heading to the same parties that had been planned when this country was a democracy. The suits were still sharp, heels still high and skirts still way too short for a London spring evening. Duncan was correct. No one cared.

Turning to see the damaged TV, she stumbled over and pushed the set off its stand. Amongst the desolation, the phone was found. By the time her search ended, Jane no longer remembered why she needed it. She flopped down on the sofa as if diving into a pool. The idea to cry sounded good, but then she couldn't remember why – so she just slept instead.

Westminster, Monday 7th April 2025

"I'm here with Defence Minister, Ben Welsh. Minister, can you explain this new democratic system for those that are sceptical, please?"

"Of course, Jane," the minister said. "With the old system, voters only got one chance every five years to express their views on the government of the day. Since the changes made by Prime Minister Jenkins, Brits will have their say weekly. This week, we will have a series of votes on defence and national security. For example, today I have proposed that the UK leave the European Court of Human Rights. This will be Vote 1 online. Eligible voters can choose to free the UK from these constraints by voting Yes or continue to pander to terrorists and vote No. After the votes have been counted tomorrow, the decision will be ratified by your MPs in Parliament, and it will then pass into law. From start to finish, your decision will be made law in less than one week. Not the five years you had to wait previously. Tomorrow, Vote 2 will be the choice to free my hands to deal with terrorists quickly and not be dragged through the courts by lefty lawyers, while their clients go on killing Brits. I also hope to have this on the statute book before the week is out. This is a fantastic and exciting new system. I am sure you will all agree?" The minister smiled to the camera.

"Well, that all sounds fair and, of course, we in the BBC will be holding the government to account on these votes. As Dana explained earlier, the first two have passed through our truth-checker panel, so the choice is now yours, viewers. Jane Clark, reporting live from Westminster."

"Thanks, minister," Jane said, unhooking herself from the communications gear.

"My pleasure, Jane. Will I see you at the ceremony on Friday?"

"Of course, sir."

Jane wandered out into the warm sunlight and exhaled. There was no doubt this new job was lucrative, but it wasn't fun anymore. Her lines were scripted, more or less, and there would be no probing questions to ministers. She also noticed the opposition MPs were giving her a wide berth. In fact, it was very hard to find anyone in the true opposition ranks. A few Labour MPs were milling about, but she had seen most of them at the Randolf Club. It was fairly certain their bank balances had been boosted like hers, and they were now opposition in name only. There had been less than a hundred on their benches today. Were the rest just staying away?

The worst thing of all was that Ed was not here. It was the first working day without him. It wasn't good at all. The two of them would be in a coffee house or, better still, heading for the pub by now. The bleakness of the situation became apparent when she seriously thought of calling Selwyn Letchford.

She switched her phone off.

Edinburgh, Monday 7th April 2025

The last of the day's paperwork was cleared and it was time for Duncan to go home. A horrible, hollow feeling in his stomach lingered. It wasn't hunger. The way he left things with Jane made him feel queasy. Yes, he was angry at her and had this been the first time they had fallen out, he would be entirely justified. But this wasn't the first time, was it? They once went nearly ten years without a word between them. There was no way he wanted that to happen again, but his bloody Scottish Presbyterian logic just wouldn't let him pick the phone up. Duncan was right, so Duncan had to suffer.

"We should have stayed Catholics," he mumbled as he tidied away the work. The phone rang and he remembered that Nance had left for the evening. "What is it?" he asked after lifting the handset.

"Oh! Can I speak to Duncan Clark, please?" A hesitant man's voice.

"Speaking," Duncan said, hearing a piece of paper rustling on the other end of the line.

"You don't know me. I work at a…Well, we have a mutual friend. James Kirk. He wants to meet you at the place that the two of you go fishing. Bring friends."

The phone line went dead. Duncan scowled and replaced the handset. "What the hell was that all about?" he muttered. Shrugging his shoulders, he picked up his empty briefcase and left.

Stuck in traffic on Lothian Road, Duncan had a thought and pressed a button on the steering wheel. "Call Joan," he said, really hoping the stupid thing would get it right for once – his mate John was getting fed up with the random calls.

Luckily, he heard Joan's polite voice answer. "Good evening, Mr Clark. Any news for me?"

"Maybe. I'm not sure, Joan. I need to ask you something. When Alex travels, he uses a fake name sometimes. What names does he use regularly?"

"Oh my," Joan said. "He has debit cards in several names. William Wallace, Robert Bruce, James T Kirk and Donald Ford. Why do you ask?"

"Thanks, Joan. It might be nothing. Leave it with me. Okay?"

"If you say so, Mr Clark. Goodbye." She was gone and Duncan knew where Alex Samson was. His next call was to Struan, to tell him that he'd be out of the office for a few days. He then called Nancy.

"Nance, I need a wife. You up for it?"

"My, that is a bit sudden. I don't even get a meal and a shag first?"

"Well, Nance, it's a pretend wife I need – so if you are up for a pretend shag, we're golden."

"Still the best offer I've had in ages, boss. What do you need?"

"Pack a bag, Mrs Clark. Two nights worth should be enough. I will pick you up at seven."

Westminster, Monday 7th April 2025

Luckily for Jane, Selwyn Letchford's office was in the Palace of Westminster. Had he been in the buildings along the street, she would have found it difficult to access. She walked through the ground floor, now the sole domain of cleaners and a few conscientious office staff. The door was locked, but she knocked, just in case. After a nervous minute of looking back and forth, constantly expecting someone to query why she was here so late, Jane let herself in with the replica key.

Had she entered blindfolded, she would still have known this was his office from the fog of aftershave that hung in the air. She scanned the scene. Under the window, there were some built-in cupboards that were of no use, short of storing junk.

"Perfect." She opened one, removed a box of welly boots and hid the vase in the back. Unless someone went looking, they would never see it. She restored the wellies, left and locked up.

She walked out of the Palace of Westminster wringing her hands. Should pictures of her encounter with Colin Burton ever surface, Letchford would have to explain why he had a priceless vase missing from the British Museum. Of course, he didn't have the real vase – it was now secreted in the museum. Terry would switch the replica after Letchford's fingerprints were confirmed.

Perthshire, Tuesday 8th April 2025

Duncan pulled the car into the Pitlochry Hydro Hotel car park. "Ready, Mrs Clark?"

During the trip north, he brought Nancy up to speed. They also stopped and got her a new phone after deciding that her regular one was likely bugged. Stepping out of the car, Duncan breathed in the cool, clear Highland air. He got the cases out of the boot and headed for the hotel reception.

In spite of the markets crashing, democracy being suspended, and civil war in America, life went on as normal in the tourist village.

They arranged with reception to deposit the bags for now, since they wouldn't get into their room for hours yet. The two of them changed in the hotel toilets. They were now a regular hill-walking couple – boots, cagouls and all.

"Here you go, Mrs Clark." Duncan pulled a tammy over Nancy's head. He put a matching one on his.

"We look like the kind of couple I normally throw bricks at," said Nancy.

"Just the look I was going for." He smoothed the woolly hat on her head.

They fought their way through the flocks of tourists that hoovered up the Nessie dolls and shortbread tins. The trinket-laden travellers were all either heading for, or coming from, Inverness. Pitlochry was a great 'fly cup' stop. Duncan had seen Edinburgh less busy than this wee place.

The two of them crossed the bridge beside the dam and started up the wooded road. He took Nancy's hand as they approached the Finab Castle Hotel. Only having gone fishing once in his life, if drinking beer beside a river constituted fishing, the Finab Hotel had to be the location alluded to by his secret caller. Duncan, Alex and several other Edinburgh businessmen spent a cold, wet and liver-melting weekend here a few years ago.

There were two men at the end of the road. He whispered to Nancy, "Pretend we haven't seen them and that we are heading to the hotel for brunch, okay?" She nodded.

"Sorry, sir. The hotel is currently closed for renovation," one of the men said.

"Oh, that's not good. My wife and I booked a meal here. We did it online a few weeks ago," Duncan pointed to the hotel.

"Again, my apologies. Unforeseen maintenance. Now, I need you to leave. This is a hard hat zone."

Duncan noted that neither man wore one, but he didn't see the point in drawing any more attention than they had already. He turned to Nancy. "We will eat in the town, dear."

They headed back down the road until they were out of sight of the men and then cut off into the trees.

"This is exciting," said Nancy. "Do you think that this has anything to do with our little office problem?" she asked.

"I'm not sure, Nance. I wouldn't be surprised if it is though."

They reached the riverside and headed back through the Norwegian pines, toward the hotel. About a quarter of a mile from the grounds, Duncan ducked down, and Nancy followed. He pointed silently and made a walking gesture with his fingers. Up ahead, a couple were strolling on the manicured hotel lawn. One was almost certainly a guard, but the other was a smaller woman. Duncan motioned for Nancy to stay here while he belly crawled closer. After a few minutes of getting soaked in the long, coarse grass, he raised his head once more.

"That's Isla Wallace," he whispered to himself.

After making a slow, soggy reverse crawl to where Nancy sat, picking dandelion clocks and blowing the seeds, they left the woods and headed to town. Stopping on the way back at a climbing store on the busy high street, Duncan bought a hugely overpriced pair of binoculars.

Further up the street, they found a small café and had a quick lunch to kill some time. Thankfully, they were granted room access upon returning to their hotel. Duncan ran up the stairs and was delighted to discover they had a view over the water to the Finab Hotel. Nancy came into the room and looked around. He was already scoping out the scene over the river.

"Boss?" she said.

"Nancy, call me Duncan. We're meant to be married. Not sure which freaky couples you know, but my friends don't call each other boss."

"Duncan, there is only one bed."

Still looking through the glasses, he smiled, but she only had a view of his rear.

"Yes, what side do you sleep on?"

She inhaled. "You're joking, right?"

"Well, Mrs Clark, we are married after all." He tried to keep a straight face. "We can't go breaking cover." She shrugged and laid her bag at the end of the bed.

"Wish I thought to bring pyjamas," he said, not able to hold in a snigger.

"You are taking this ruse a bit far, aren't you?" she said.

"Check the door to your left, Nance."

She walked over and opened what she thought was a toilet and found an interconnecting room.

"I booked a suite," he laughed. "I had you going though." If he hadn't maintained his vigil, he would have seen her looking a little deflated.

With just half an hour's watching, he'd already spotted Samson, and there was the First Minister, leader of the Labour Party in Scotland and, surprisingly, the leader of the Scottish Tories.

"He and Boris didn't see eye to eye," Nancy reminded him.

There were several other MSPs and a few other unknown faces in residence. Each one seemed to be allowed out for a guarded walk, but always one at a time. Duncan guessed they were otherwise locked in their rooms. "What to do with this, though?" he pondered.

He did have contacts, lots of contacts, but who should he trust? Well, he didn't know, but there was one way to find out. Composing a long text message Using the phone they just bought for Nancy, he then spammed it to everyone in the media and police that he knew.

"Now let's see who turns up," he said.

* * *

Quietly, Duncan lay in the grass a few hundred yards south of the Finab Hotel. The first vehicle to pull up at the end of the drive was a grey Mondeo. A tall, broad man exited. In his trademark double denim, Duncan recognised Tom Hartley from the Herald Newsgroup. He couldn't hear what was being said, but Tom didn't seem to be taking no for an answer. One of the security men pushed the journalist.

"Oooo, big mistake," Duncan whispered.

Just then, a police car drew up near the conflab. Two uniformed officers got out and the second security guard walked over to talk with them. Duncan saw his chance and ran. He looked to see if either guard was paying him any attention and witnessed the journalist landing a punch on the one holding him back. Like a puppet with strings cut, the man went down. The jubilant journalist headed up the driveway, fist held high in the air as if he'd scored a goal in the cup final. They arrived at the main entrance together. Tom Hartley had a smile on his face.

"Good afternoon, Mr Clark." Tom held out a spade sized hand which Duncan shook. Duncan then tried the hotel door. It was locked. He gave it a shoulder, but it wouldn't budge.

Stand back," Tom shouted from behind.

Tom held a large stone flowerpot teetering over his head. He stumbled forward and launched it through the glass door. Duncan kicked the remaining shards away and entered.

Having heard the noise, a burly man came out from behind the reception desk and ran growling toward the pair. The journalist pushed past Duncan and stood tall in front of the oncoming assailant. Just as the guard came into range, Tom took a quick step forward and headbutted him in the face. Blood erupted, hammer horror style, from where the man's nose had been a second before. Feeling a little left out of the action, Duncan swung a foot and gave the falling guard a kick,

A shout of "Magic" came from the top of the stairs, where the diminutive Isla Wallace ran down toward them. She shook Duncan's hand vigorously and introduced herself unnecessarily. "Tom," she said, nodding to the journalist. Looking down at the man on the floor, she launched her boot into his genitals. The poor man screamed.

"Right," she said, suddenly in charge. "Let's get the rest of these wankers."

Isla picked up a coat stand as two further men burst from a side room. The first interloper's head cracked open as the thick wooden weapon crashed down. The second grabbed her, trying to wrench the pole from her grasp. His struggle ended as the journalist launched a fish tank, complete with fish, which shattered on the unfortunate guard's head. The two bleeding men joined their colleague on the ground, writhing for air with several goldfish and a guppy.

"That's for the fucking soggy cornflakes," Isla said in her buzz saw voice before turning her attention to the stairs where her next victim appeared. The man took one look at the scene and another at her face.

"Sod this," he said and was off.

But the predator Scottish MP and the journalist now had a taste for blood. The fleeing man never reached the next landing. A lightning quick Isla ascended the flight, caught his collar and pulled him back. He slid down the stairs, landing prone at the smiling journalist's feet. "Nightie night," were the last two words the man heard.

Duncan felt he should really be helping. On noticing that a bit of the fish tank still had water in it, he picked up the writhing fish and dropped them in. With the rescue task completed, he looked to the stairs, but the journalist and MP were gone. He suddenly feared there may be more guards around, or even that one of the injured men that lay about his feet might recover, and so he legged it up after his allies. Upon arriving at the first landing, there was an open door to the dining room, and Duncan thought he heard Isla's voice emanate from within. Running through the door, here were Isla and Tom standing with their hands raised.

At the other end of the room, a man stood holding the leader of the Scottish Conservatives as a shield. He held a gun at the man's head.

"Back off or I will shoot him," the man said. David Ross, part-time football referee, MP and MSP, looked nervously out of the corner of his eye at the gun pointed at his head.

"Honestly, mate, you would be doing us a favour," Tom Hartley said.

Isla turned her head and squinted at the large reporter. "I always had you down as a Tory, Tom?"

"Who I vote for isn't the issue here, Isla. The twat gave an offside decision against us last year and we lost the game to United." Isla Wallace nodded her understanding. Football was more than a game in Tom's hometown of Dundee.

The gunman looked between the two of them as if they were idiots. Out of sight, Duncan stood beside the condiments table. With the hostage taker's attention on the comedy duo and his perspiring captive, Duncan picked up a salt cellar and launched it. Although his throw was pretty accurate, the man had time to duck. Unfortunately for him, the vicious hyenas needed only this short break in attention to land on him before he was upright. David Ross was roughly pushed aside. Tom, Isla and the gunman landed in a pile on the floor. Only two ever stood up.

"I thought these wankers were MI5," said Isla standing over the broken body at her feet. "If I knew they were hired private security, I would have done this myself days ago."

"At least it's nice here," said Tom, looking out the windows at the pristine gardens.

"Cornflakes aside, the food was pretty decent too," Isla said. The two of them completed their hotel review and then went to hunt down the remaining captors.

Duncan walked over to the Tory leader and helped him to his feet. "Are you okay there, Davie?"

"Just a bit shaken, Duncan, but nothing broken." The MP seemed more concerned by his ruffled suit.

"Good, but you better stay clear of Isla until she calms down if you want things to stay that way." Duncan picked the gun up and handed it to the MP. "Maybe keep this at hand."

* * *

With the hostilities over, the congregation of rescuers and rescued stood in the scenic hotel grounds that overlooked the river.

"My hero."

Duncan turned to see Nancy walk up to him. She looked pretty in the spring sunshine, he thought.

"Thank you, but I did very little. Isla and Tom did most of the heavy lifting," he said.

With his arm around her, the two stood, watching the who's who of Scottish politics milling about on the manicured lawns. Other than their captivity, none seemed to be the worse for wear.

Isla garnered the lion's share of the credit for the 'prison break'. Duncan had no issue with that. She and Tom dealt with the more stubborn guards. Duncan believed he was the mastermind behind the operation, but once the conflict started, it was definitely more about brawn than brains.

A young female medic fussed over Tom Hartley's forehead wound. He was relaying a blow-by-blow account of the action. Isla Wallace seemed to be giving Alex Samson a shadow boxing demonstration. Duncan smiled at her but couldn't remember her using her fists much. Several of her captors had her Doc Marten tread prints on their faces, however.

Pitlochry, Wednesday 9th April 2025

Duncan and Nancy laughed as they flicked through the wad of newspapers that sat on the police station interview table. All around, police that had congregated here from across Scotland were patting each other on the back after yesterday's successful raid.

"You haven't even been mentioned," Nancy said, disappointed by Duncan's lack of credit.

Not one picture, not one credit, but this was exactly what he'd asked Tom to organise. Tom, on the other hand, had been interviewed at great length by his own newspaper and all his competitor's publications. Likewise, Isla Wallace was spread across the news sheets. 'The Battle of Pitlochry' was maybe a bit grandiose for half a dozen punches, headbutts and more than a few kicks, but it made Duncan smile.

Alex Samson grinned broadly as he exited his interview and saw Duncan. "You can always rely on a Hearts fan to turn up," he said, shaking Duncan's hand. "You got my message then."

"I did indeed," Duncan said. "That was good thinking."

Alex patted his back. "It just shows the poor state of the secret service in Britain today, Duncan. The idiots locked me up in a hotel where the staff were at least 50% nationalists. What did they think was going to happen?" He turned to Nancy. "Thanks, Nancy, I bet they gave up when they saw you coming."

"I was just a spectator, Eck," she said, laughing.

"Sorry, folks, got to love you and leave you. We're heading down to make sure Nicola is okay. Catch you around soon." The politician headed for the door. Alex now had security, but they were uniformed police.

With their interviews over, Duncan and Nancy strolled back to their hotel. "Will we just get on down the road?" he asked.

"I suppose we should," she replied. Duncan thought she sounded a little disappointed. Was it just wishful thinking on his part?

"We could always take in the sights and maybe have dinner tonight if you would rather. I booked the hotel for two nights anyway." He tried to sound neutral about the idea.

"You're the boss, boss. Whatever you think's best."

He stopped and moved in front of her. "Nance, this is not a boss–secretary invitation. It's a Duncan–Nancy thing. What would you like to do?" He realised he was less scared standing in front of the guy with the gun yesterday.

"It would be a shame to waste all this scenery," Nancy said, smiling at him.

Westminster, Friday 11th April 2025

Prime Minister Boris Jenkins stood to talk in a nearly empty Westminster chamber. For varying reasons, most of the opposition members were elsewhere. Many were in their homes, voluntarily or not. Another tranche helped police with enquiries into a surprising number of recent criminal cases that appeared out of nowhere. In addition to the opposition absentees, some Conservatives were likewise sidelined, with those who had supported the previous PM making up most of that number.

"Madam Deputy Speaker. Today we will pass the legislation that the British people voted through this week. With more than 90% of those that voted supporting the cancellation of the Human Rights Act, and allowing the government to effectively fight terrorism, no one in this chamber or the other place should stand in the way. While speaking of that other place, it has come to my notice that many Lords have not been attending in recent weeks. Therefore, I have today appointed two hundred new peers, and they will take their place immediately." Jenkins shuffled the documents in front of him.

"I also wish to inform the House that the UK and USA are in advanced talks on a trade deal. We hope to have this signed in the next few days. Soon after the conclusion, we would welcome President Thorn for a state visit. The deal will mean cheaper food for the hard-working people of Britain. In return, the UK will be providing the USA with military technology and intelligence on their battle with the terrorists based in Albany. We look forward to a speedy resolution of this conflict so that the good peoples of America and the UK can prosper together in the years to come." He stopped long enough for a smattering of approval from the chamber.

"Finally, today I wish to announce that the UK will join the BRICS trade group as soon as our membership is cleared. I spoke with the leaders of Russia, India, Brazil and South Africa personally, and all believe the application can be fast-tracked. As a result, I have today lifted all embargoes on Russia and any other BRICS member countries."

The PM sat to calls of, "Here, here," from his back benches.

London, Friday 11th April 2025

Lady Letchford and Cassie Jenkins stood on the podium at the end of the room. It was one of the few places in the Randolf Club that Jane hadn't been in before. In the centre of the floor stood a life-size ice sculpture of a woman on a chariot. She appeared to be in the process of spear throwing. Having read her invitation to the inaugural meeting of 'The Order of Boudica', Jane assumed this to be the woman herself.

"For feck's sake," said Dana as she stood shoulder to shoulder with Jane. "Do you think they'll have us shagging a goat or something?"

Jane tried hard to keep a straight face. Out of the corner of her mouth, she mumbled, "I've done worse." Dana snorted, having to retrieve a hanky.

Jane studied the room. No men were present. Well, except the waiters that lined the walls. Most of the female Conservative MPs were present, enjoined by a sprinkling of Labour and Liberals too. Prominent women in industry and the arts were dotted through the politicians. As Jane and Dana were beckoned forward, a ripple of applause broke out across the room. As instructed, They took seats either side of Lady Letchford and Cassie Jenkins.

Lady Letchford stood.

"Welcome, ladies. This organisation is fifty years overdue. Womankind has progressed far in the last hundred years, but always at a pace no more than endured by our male colleagues. In society, the strong will always dominate the weak, so our plight has been unsurprising. Physically strong and able male leaders have deemed to grant us a freedom here, a privilege there, and we have voted them back into power, grateful for the right to vote at all. Well, change has happened, and our time has now come. The strong have left the stage. Their places have been taken by something less. Something malleable. Yes, these men will appear to hold the reins of power for a while to come. The public can only accept so much change at once, but we, ladies, now pull the strings of those that hold the reins." Applause broke out.

"Ladies, this organisation will guide the new Britain that has so recently been born. The Order of Boudica does not seek to disenfranchise the men of our country, but we will never allow ourselves to be dominated. We in this room now hold a right to choose, and a right to veto future leaders. Men or women can lead, but only with our condescension. Ladies, this new Britain is ours."

The room stood as one and applause turned to cheers. Lady Letchford stood a while, nodded a few times, and then sat down. The adulation went on.

After the hall calmed, the rest of the formal evening was filled with nominations and voting for a committee. Unsurprisingly, Lady Letchford became the first leader and Cassie Jenkins her deputy. Dana and Jane were surprised to be voted onto the Political Education Committee, along with a Conservative and Labour MP.

When future meetings and office bearers had been arranged, the official business was concluded.

Jane and Dana high-fived on learning of the remuneration that went with the new role, and Jane sat back in her chair and grinned. But then a sadness struck.

"I just wish Ed and Duncan were on board with the whole thing. I've worked hard to get here, and now they seem to resent me for succeeding." In her heart, she knew the assertion wasn't exactly true, but she did feel like the rug of success was being pulled from beneath her. That made her sad, but the deflected blame transformed that sadness to an anger that was easier to handle.

Dana took her by the shoulder. "Sod them. You can buy new friends now." Jane smiled, but the hollowness lingered. Those annoying bastards who asserted money didn't make you happy could well be right.

Edinburgh, Friday 11th April 2025

Nancy sauntered into the office and put a brown envelope on Duncan's desk. She wore the pink blouse he liked, and he knew there was now a button unfastened that hadn't been when he saw her earlier in the main office with the other girls. He smiled.

She pointed to the envelope. "These are your copies, boss." She meant his copies of the mail that she was about to deliver at the random address.

Today, their new accomplice, Tom Hartley, had arranged for the shop to be watched and the lad that collected the mail to be followed. After their help at Pitlochry, Duncan considered taking their blackmail issue to the police, but he suspected that local law enforcement was compromised. Until they knew who they could trust, they'd keep the thing in-house. Tom would keep mum for now, on the understanding that he got to run the whole story later.

"Shiela Morgan is waiting for you downstairs," said Nancy. Part of Tom's deal was that Duncan gave an interview to his paper, the Herald, about the recent Battle of Pitlochry and the current political situation. It would be run at a later date. He was a little surprised they'd sent a reporter so soon, but Duncan thought they were doing it now as the details would still be fresh in his mind.

"Cheers, Nance. Show her up on your way out, thanks."

As the reporter topped the stairs, his eye was drawn to her long and curly red locks. Dark green eyes were matched in colour by the business suit and very high heels.

"Please to meet the hero of Pitlochry," she said, looking over the top of her glasses and into his eyes. The reporter framed a nearly imperceptible smile, as if she knew everything about him in this action alone. He motioned to a seat, and she sat, crossed her legs and put her notebook on her lap. After the pleasantries were concluded and they'd chatted about traffic and weather, they quickly covered the events from earlier in the week, but Sheila knew most of the happenings already, it seemed.

"How do you view the goings-on at Westminster?" she asked.

"Well, like most people, I would think, I am utterly appalled at the restrictions on democracy. We were led to believe this Government of National Unity was an emergency action in the light of the world crisis. It appears to have been hijacked by those that would abuse the power for other reasons."

"And do you support the Scottish government in their attempt to use this situation to progress the case for independence?"

He was already sure where she sided on the issue by the question alone. "I can't see they have any option. It is without doubt that many Scots believe that the union is best for their country. However, in light of recent developments, even among those, voices are being raised against this…coup," he said.

"You would put it in as strong a term as that?" She pointed her pen at him.

"Well, Sheila, how would *you* view the suspension of democracy and the imprisonment of your opposition?" he asked.

She pulled her glasses down her nose and looked over them. "No one cares what I think."

Duncan spotted the wedding band on her finger. He wondered if this action was designed for that purpose. Either way, it didn't put him up or down. Pretty as she was, he hadn't viewed her as anything but a reporter.

"And where would you stand should they bring this to a vote?" she asked.

"Ah, Sheila, my job is to advise the Scottish government on the legal implications of the action. I would do that job to the best of my ability, whatever I believed the outcome should be."

She smiled and laid the pad and pen down on the desk. It was blank. "Have you got anywhere to be?" she asked.

His brow furrowed. "A Markies TV dinner defrosting and two bottles of beer chilling in the fridge. Rock and roll lifestyle."

"Well, as appealing as that sounds, how do you fancy going for a bar supper and we can finish this interview?" She pointed to the blank notebook.

"Okay," he said, "but I have an early start tomorrow. Hearts are playing Ross County up in Dingwall."

"That's no problem. I'll have you home in bed by nine."

Seeing her coy smile, he was no longer looking at a reporter.

With the bar supper and interview over, Sheila moved round to his side of the table, sat close, kept touching his leg and laughed at jokes even he knew weren't funny. Yet, every so often, she rolled her wedding ring. Duncan pointed to it.

"Sheila, thanks for the meal, but I better let you get back to Hubby."

She looked down at the ring, and he watched her lower lip protrude. "Yeah, I guess so," she said, he thought reluctantly, but he was an awful judge of character. "What time are you setting off tomorrow?" she asked.

"Eight," he said. "I like to stop off a few times on the way up."

She leant over, kissed his cheek and said, "Well, enjoy the game, and thanks for the info." She waved the pad as she stuck it back in her folder.

A mildly confused Duncan walked out to his car and drove home.

Tom Hartley sat in his messy midden of a Mondeo with Nancy and watched the shop on the corner of Newhaven Main Street and Craighall Road. Nancy dropped off the mail half an hour ago. They hoped the receiver wouldn't find the tracker until too late.

"Here he is." Nancy pointed up the street to where the junkie sauntered along, trying parked car doors as he went. Tom snapped a picture. They watched him collect the mail from the empty shop and then shuffle back the way he came.

Tom stared at his phone. "It's working. I have him tracked. We'll give him five minutes and then follow."

Nancy nodded and then looked out over the Forth Estuary. Although the sun shone brightly, a cold wind gusted in when she lowered the window.

"I wish I brought a warmer jacket," she said.

"Hopefully, we won't have to get out of the car," he offered, turning the heater up.

"I thought we would be doing this on foot?" She left the window open a slit and enjoyed the smell of seaweed. It always reminded her of being at Portobello Beach as a kid.

"He's heading up to Leith Walk," Tom said as he put the Mondeo into reverse and pulled out of the parking space. He drove along the High Street and took a left toward Leith.

"There he is." She pointed along Ferry Road. The journalist parked the car about a hundred yards away from the junkie.

"Stay here," he told her as he got out.

Tom slouched, put his hands in his pockets and walked toward the junkie. "You got a fag, mate?" he asked as he passed the ricket of bones in a threadbare parka.

"No, man. I'm oot. Gaggin' for een masell."

Tom stepped closer to the lad, who kept his furtive vigil along the road. He put a hand on the junkie's shoulder. "You got any dope, mate?"

"No, man." He looked down at Tom's hand and it was clear that he didn't enjoy the company.

"Okay, brother. Catch you another time." Tom patted the lad

on the back and carried on up the road. At the first junction, he doubled back to the car.

"Wasn't that a bit risky?" Nancy said, pointing to where their target still stood.

"Maybe, but we have a tracker on him as well as the mail now." He smiled at her. "I stuck it in his hood."

About twenty minutes later, the black Mercedes appeared, and the mail was collected from Deek – his payment being thrown on the pavement instead of handed to him. They watched as the junkie headed toward town and the car drove slowly toward them.

"Down," said Tom, pushing Nancy's head into his lap. She giggled. "What's funny?" He asked.

"It's been a while since I sat like this in a car," she said.

"One day, Nancy, I am going to make a fortune ghost writing your memoirs." He smiled at her, and the two sat up as the car moved away. Tom checked his phone. "Both trackers are working."

They tailed the Mercedes at a distance. Nancy held his phone as Tom drove. "I think it has stopped outside the Old Town House." She held the screen up. At the street before, he pulled in and parked.

"Yeah," he said, "the tracker is in that building. I'm not going to risk walking in. I'll do some digging on the place when I get back to the office. Let's call it a night and get you home." He started up, and they drove off.

"Good," said Nancy. "I'll give Duncan a call tomorrow and bring him up to speed."

Edinburgh, Saturday 12th April 2025

It was a fine day for a game of football. Not too warm, not too cold. No high winds and, thankfully, no rain. Of course, that didn't mean it would be the same up in Dingwall. In any event, Duncan walked from his flat to the car in anticipation. He turned into the road where he parked last night and there, sitting on the bonnet of his Mercedes, was Sheila Morgan. She wore jeans and a Hearts football shirt.

"Up the Jambos," she said as he approached.

"What are you doing here, Sheila?"

"Hopefully, getting a lift to the game." She pointed to the car.

Stopping, he regarded her closely. He just couldn't figure this woman out. "There's something different about you."

She laughed. "You men are all the same." She pulled a long lock of her hair from her shoulder and lifted it.

When the revelation sunk in, he smiled; she had died her hair maroon to suit the colour of the shirt. He slapped his hand to his forehead. "Why didn't I notice that?"

"My guess is your eyes hadn't reached my head yet," she formed a wicked smile.

He unlocked the car and pointed to the passenger seat. She jumped in. His face beamed red. He wasn't going to admit that last night's fantasy had been Sheila in a Hearts top. That was normally Nancy's role in his dreams.

After navigating relatively light city traffic, the car escaped the suburbs and was now speeding over the Queensferry crossing. Sheila lifted his phone and selected what she saw as tolerable music from his streaming playlists. He watched with dismay as his rock tracks were being deleted one by one.

"Oh, Queen. I like them," she said, and 'Hammer to Fall' began blaring out of the speakers. She started doing a passable Garth impersonation as she headbanged, her maroon hair filling the car.

"When did you get time to dye your hair?" he asked over the music.

Placing a hand on his leg, she leant over and shouted in his ear, "This morning. I put on the shirt, and it clashed with my colour."

"So, you're not a regular at Tynecastle?" He knew the answer when he had to explain to her that Hearts played their home games there. "Where did you get the shirt then?" he said.

"Borrowed it from my little brother." The music volume dipped as his phone rang. Before he could pick up the call from the car steering wheel control, Sheila pressed the screen and said, "Duncan Clark's phone…Oh, yes, Nancy, he is right here beside me…Yes, I will put him on."

He clicked the button to take the call, but there was no one on the line. He pressed another button and said, "Call Nancy." Nancy's phone rang, but it wasn't picked up. "Strange," he said. "No worries, I will give her a buzz when we stop."

Sheila suggested they stop in Pitlochry at the Finab Hotel. Maybe do a bit more background for the interview. With the hits of Freddie and the gang now playing at an acceptable level, the two chatted easily as they sped along the dual carriageway, past Perth and onto the A9. He slowed as Pitlochry approached.

"Let's do lunch," he said. They stood outside the impressive building while he gave her a walk-through of the incident. She seemed to take some notes this time. Duncan then led her up to the residents' dining room and pointed out his major contribution to the rescue. "Sorry, but you can't print any of that at the moment though. I have to keep a low profile until we get this other little problem sorted."

"What problem is that?" Sheila asked.

"This thing with the mail that Tom is working on for me," he said.

"Tom?" She lowered her eyebrows.

Duncan looked back, perplexed. "Wasn't it Tom that arranged for you to interview me?" he asked.

She didn't answer immediately, instead running her fingers through her long hair. "Oh, yes, Tom. The reporter. Sorry, my department boss gave me this task. Tom is in a different section."

Duncan nodded and then dug out his phone to try Nancy's number again. There was still no answer.

* * *

The game was dire. Nil-nil.

"How can you watch that every week?" Sheila asked as they headed back to the car among the serried ranks of away supporters.

"It's not always that bad," he said. He was dialling Nancy as he spoke. Still no answer. He'd sent several texts now and was getting worried.

"A girl could get a little hurt by the lack of attention," said Sheila, pointing to his mobile phone. Duncan looked up and then nodded, putting it away in his jacket pocket. She smiled at him. "Do you want to stop off somewhere on the way home?"

"We could do. What do you fancy?" he said.

She thought a while, "I'd love a curry if you know any good Indians?"

Not having stopped for a curry on the A9 before, he drew a blank. "Can't think of anywhere. I usually get a takeaway from the one at the end of my street."

"That sounds good," she said. Duncan was taken aback.

"Don't you have to get home?"

"He thinks I'm away for the weekend with a girlfriend. You have me until Sunday lunchtime." She said it so matter-of-factly that it sounded like the deal was already concluded. He was about to query but then thought, *Hell, let's just see where this is going*. He nodded, and she put her arm around his back.

* * *

Duncan opened the door to the flat and stood aside to let Sheila in. She ran by and headed straight for the toilet. Going into the kitchen, he hunted down plates and cutlery before setting them on the worktop and dishing up the food.

"I thought I was going to pee my pants there," Sheila said as she walked into the kitchen. Her jeans and shoes were gone. She jumped up on a stool, wearing only the football shirt and skimpy white underwear.

"Now if Hearts ladies wore that," he said, pointing at her attire, "I would never miss a match."

"You like this?" She got off the stool to give him a twirl, then paraded up and down the kitchen as if on a catwalk.

He could barely take his eyes off her. "Your husband is a very lucky man," he said, deliberately throwing a spanner in the works.

Her bottom lip stuck out again. "This would be easier if you stopped mentioning him," she said.

"What would be easier, Sheila? What's happening here?"

She stopped the little fashion show and looked at him. "Let me think. I dyed my hair, wore this hideous shirt all day, and let you drag me right across the country to watch the worst two hours of nonsense I have ever witnessed. Oh, yeah, and I have flirted outrageously with you the whole time. How long have you been single, Duncan?"

"You don't like the shirt?" He frowned.

"Oh, so that's what bothered you about my little rant?" Sheila tugged the maroon fabric.

"Well, I couldn't really take issue with the other three items," he said, smiling at her. He pushed her plate of food over the table and sat. "Eat up. I will let you try the away shirt later and see if you like it any better." Sheila laughed and set about her tikka masala.

Edinburgh, Monday 14th April 2025

Duncan whistled Queen hits as he walked up the stairs to the office. As he passed through the main area, he shouted to Nancy at the other end, "How did it go on Friday, Nance?"

She looked up at him with a scowl. "Fine."

It wasn't like Nancy to stick to one word when five hundred would do, but Duncan knew she was usually busy first thing and put it down to that. He set to head to his own office but then remembered, "Oh, Nance, you called me at the weekend. I tried to get back to you but couldn't get through."

"It was nothing." This time, she didn't even bother turning round. After considering the back of her head for a while, he shrugged, deciding to talk to her later.

Once the emails were caught up with, he dialled a number on his phone, and Tom answered.

"Hey, Tom, how did Friday go?" Duncan asked.

"Went like clockwork. Meet you at the pub across the road at lunchtime to discuss?"

"That sounds good. Hey, Tom, can I have a word with Sheila?"

"Sheila who?"

"Sheila Morgan, you numpty." Duncan scowled.

"Duncan, who the fuck is Sheila Morgan?"

Duncan scratched his head. "The lassie you sent to interview me on Friday."

"I haven't sent anyone yet. You didn't want any publicity, remember?" Duncan sat in silence. "What's going on?" Tom asked.

"Nothing. Forget it. We'll talk over lunch." He placed the handset down and looked at the phone accusingly. He exhaled. Of course, she'd said something about being in a different department of the newspaper. "Yeah, that'll be it."

Time flew as regular work took priority, and then he realised he wasn't getting coffee today. There was no issue making his own, but it had become a little ritual that Nancy brought it in once the office mayhem died down. They would drink while catching up.

Kensington, Monday 14th April 2025

Daniel pulled the BMW to a stop, and Jane got out.

"Head back to the office," she said as she closed the door.

Crossing the car park, she ran a hand over Dana's sleek and sexy Aston Martin before heading into the grand stately home that was apparently to be the headquarters of the Political Education Department. Lady Letchford had requested their attendance. Jane was hoping to find out what she was supposed to do. The two security officers at the door gave her a smile as she passed through. As ever, she was last to arrive.

"Sorry, folks. Traffic," she said, taking the remaining seat while scanning the faces around the table. Today's quorum was just the four that were voted onto the committee in the Randolph meeting, along with their illustrious leader. As usual, Lady Letchford was dressed immaculately and, Jane assumed, expensively.

"Good morning, ladies. Thank you for coming. From now on, this will be your office when on committee business, and each of you will have an apartment upstairs for your use. You can see these soon." Elizabeth smiled at each of them in turn.

Jane perused the property journal only this morning, fancying a bigger flat now that the money was rolling in. *If upstairs is as lovely as what she'd seen of the place already, living here may well save me a couple million*, she thought.

Her attention returned to Letchford. "Margaret here…" Lady Letchford pointed to the Conservative MP on her right. "…will be head of the committee. Best to keep it under democratic control," she said and smiled. "The four of you will work to raise the standard of future parliamentary candidates."

"Isn't this normally done by the parties themselves?" Dana asked.

"Of course, dear," Letchford said. "Think of this as a double-check, and from now on, any candidate failing to impress in your meetings will not be selected. We can't have the riff-raff that was permitted under the old system. It was so time-consuming. We all remember Jeremy Conway," she said, nodding toward the Labour MP, who seemed to agree.

"Such a tiresome man," the Labour MP said.

"So, we have a veto on all future MPs?" Jane asked.

Lady Letchford just smiled. "Two of you present at each meeting. I need a weekly list of naughty and nice, if you get my meaning? The nice will be allowed to stand, the naughty will find themselves deselected. Either way, you tell only me, okay?" All four of them nodded.

Jane asked, "Why are we bothering with candidates at all?"

"Well, dear, the public will expect an election at some point in the future. Your job is to ensure that whoever they choose, we win."

With the short but eye-opening meeting over, Jane and Dana stood in the bedroom of Jane's new apartment. The lavish flat boasted six high ceiling rooms, taking up half of one floor of the house. Dana's place made up the rest of the first floor.

"This is awesome," Dana said. "Do you know that this was Freddie Mercury's old house?" she added.

"Wow!" said Jane. "A lot of weird shit has gone on in here then."

"Not half as much as will do once we get settled." Dana dug her elbow into Jane's side.

Running across the room, Jane screamed as she jumped on the huge bed. "This thing could fit twelve," she spread herself out like a snow angel.

"I am so going to find out," said Dana. "Maybe the two MI5 guys on the door will be up for it," she said, licking her lips.

"I saw them first," said Jane.

"You liar!" Dana leapt on top of Jane and hugged her. "Do you know? I thought you were mad when you said that you were going to make it big," she admitted.

Jane's eyes misted over. "I just wish it didn't cost so much."

"They will come round soon," Dana said, stroking Jane's hair.

"I hope you're right. This house, this job. It's all I wanted all my life, but in getting here, I didn't want to have to trade my old one in." Jane rolled Dana off her, and the two of them lay side by side.

"You still have me," Dana said, excited eyes scanning the gold leaf cornicing that edged the ceiling in every room.

"We have each other." They solemnly shook pinkies.

Edinburgh, Monday 14th April 2025

Duncan spilled most of the beans to Tom about his weekend and the girl he believed was a *Herald* reporter.

"I made some calls round the office after we spoke. Sorry, Duncan, but no one has heard of her."

Duncan hung his head in shame. "What the hell is going on?"

"Jeez, Duncan, had I known you led such a fascinating life, I would have just sat in your office and waited for the stories to roll in. Is there any point in asking if you have any clue who she might be?"

Duncan scratched his neck. "Not one. I have replayed the weekend over and over again, but I can't figure what she had to gain by pretending."

"Have you checked to see if anything is missing?" Tom held out an open palm.

Duncan shook his head. "I will do when I get home, but there's nothing of any value in the flat. My ex-wife made sure of that already."

Tom sat rubbing his eyes. "Did she see your private phone?"

"Not that I know of," Duncan said but added, "I don't know."

"Get a new one anyway. Bin the old one. Bin Nancy's phone too. If she was MI5, she will have cloned them."

"She really didn't come across as a spook. She was quite nervous most of the time."

Tom began chuckling.

"What's funny?" Duncan asked.

"You pumped her, didn't you?" Duncan hung his head. "You dirty little bugger, Clark," Tom said, patting him on the back.

"In my defence," Duncan said, "she dyed her hair maroon and wore a Hearts top. I would have probably pumped you if you did that." The two men laughed, but the reporter stopped all of a sudden.

"Does Nancy know?"

Duncan looked at Tom. "Nancy? Why do you ask?"

"You are one lucky bugger," Tom said. "I spend all of Friday evening driving round Edinburgh shitholes with a beautiful woman that can talk about nothing but her boss, and you are away living it up with another hottie. What's your secret? I want some of that." Tom's loud laugh attracted attention from around the bar. The three men sitting watching the horse racing turned in unison to see who had found something better than the gee-gees.

Duncan hung his head. "Oh fuck."

"Anyway, Rasputin." Tom wasn't letting this go. "The druggie picking up your mail is called Derek Adams. Deek to his mates. Here is his address." Tom handed a sheet of paper over. "As you know, the car he passes the stuff to is unregistered but almost certainly government. My contact in Police Scotland told me it is on their hands-off list. We followed it to the Old Town House, Leith. My guess is that they are working out of there."

"Okay, where do we go from here?" Duncan asked.

"Not sure. I could print his picture on the front page tomorrow, but they would just replace him.

We could try looking for your mystery woman. Perhaps she is being used like Deek, instead of being an operative herself. A pro would have lost the wedding ring." Tom's phone rang, and he picked up, waving an apology. "Yeah… Okay, I can be there in fifteen." Hanging up, he stood. "Sorry, Duncan. Got to run. I will sting you for the bill this time. Text me from your new phone when you get it, and I will call you later."

Duncan nodded and headed to the bar to pay.

* * *

Tom parked his car on double yellow lines beside the zoo. He would surely get a ticket, but it would just go on expenses. He walked up a narrow lane into a small piece of waste ground, to where two policemen stood looking at something. On hearing him arrive, one turned and walked over.

"Our usual deal, Tom?" the sergeant said.

"Yeah, Hammy, £500 for first view. What've you got?"

"It looks like a murder. Maybe you could make it a grand?" The policeman put a hand on Tom's chest.

Tom looked at the hand and then up at the sergeant. "How about seven fifty?"

"Deal. Stick it through the letterbox next week, okay? And Tom, don't touch anything."

"I wasna born yesterday." Tom took out his mobile and walked over to the other PC.

After returning from lunch, Duncan leaned back in the office's tilting leather chair. "How am I going to sort this mess with Nancy?" he asked himself. Just then, his mobile beeped, and almost simultaneously, the phone on his desk rang. He let the chair swing forward and picked up the phone.

"Tell me you didn't do it?" It was Tom, but Duncan had no idea what he meant. "Check your mobile, Duncan."

He opened the message just received. It was a photo of a semi-naked body lying on waste ground. Covered in bruises from head to foot, her familiar maroon hair lay about her like spilled wine. A Hearts Away football top was over her shoulders but had been ripped open to expose her.

"She's dead, Duncan, and less than a hundred yards from your front door. Do I have to guess what forensics will find later?"

"Oh God, no," was all Duncan could say.

Duncan walked slowly down the stairs and over to Nancy's desk. She didn't want to look up at him but knew he was there. He spoke softly, "Nancy, I know you are pissed with me, and you have every right to be, but I need to tell you something. I don't care that everyone else in the world will think that I'm lying. I just need you to believe me." She looked up at him. He could feel her anger, but there was puzzlement in her eyes. "I didn't kill her, Nancy."

He could already hear heavy footsteps on the stairs.

* * *

Another heavy boot landed in Duncan's stomach. "You filthy bastard," the police officer said, spitting a huge lump of phlegm on his upturned face. The giant constable went to walk out of the cell, but he was the third visitor in an hour, and Duncan was sure he wouldn't be the last.

"I want a solicitor," Duncan said, coughing blood.

The officer turned, a hateful sneer on his face. He gave Duncan a bonus boot in the balls for his trouble. "No solicitor for the likes of you, matey. Thought you would know better, you filthy murdering freak. You are being held under the current emergency powers. We don't even have to offer you a trial. You are going to die in this cell, you pervert."

He stamped on Duncan's knee and then left.

Duncan cried out in agony as he rolled onto his back, gazing at the bright fluorescent light above. Pain wracked his entire body. He thought that death may actually be a blessing. In regular times, it would have been a hard fight to clear his name, but with things the way they were, he had no chance.

"Please kill me now," he whimpered.

There came a cruel laugh from the other side of the door. "Oh not yet, Mr Clark. We are having way too much fun for that now. Your time will come, though. Be patient."

London, Tuesday 15th April 2025

The cool stone floor was pleasing on her bare feet. Her kitchen had underfloor heating, of course, but there was something primaeval in the feel of skin on stone. Jane ran her hand over the granite worktops. She hadn't yet decided what was for breakfast, so she opened the fridge. Choosing a grapefruit, she put it on the slate and halved it. Maybe Dana would want the other half.

She skipped through to the hallway. Finding the door that connected their flats was closed puzzled her slightly. It usually stood open as they treated the two spaces as one. It wasn't locked, though, so she shrugged and went through. Dana was a lazy bitch and was probably still in bed.

"Where are you, you dozy cow?" Jane shouted. She opened the bedroom door, and there was Dana, still in bed, wedged between the two security guards.

"The greedy bitch." Jane laughed. Quietly, she closed Dana's bedroom door and headed back. "I'm going to eat your half for that." Somehow, the punishment didn't seem to fit the crime.

Once back in the kitchen, she turned on the telly to BBC News and saw her young replacement was interviewing the Home Secretary. Jane smiled; the reporter was good at her job, but God, was she plain. Dana filtered out all the lookers. She scanned around for a remote and then remembered, "Alexa, turn the TV up, please." Why she was courteous to Alexa eluded her.

The MP was speaking. "We tried to implement the ban on lefty lawyers in Scotland, too, but they have their own system up there, and the devolved administration controls it. Had they listened to us, this poor girl would be alive today." The screen split, and a picture of a pretty, red-haired woman filled the right half. "The killer was one of the insidious men that got Scotland's former first minister off sexual assault charges two years ago. In light of this, we may have to reopen those cases also."

The camera panned to the reporter, who nodded along. *They have her well trained already*, Jane thought.

"Madam Secretary, will this lead to a complete review of the Devolution Settlement?" the reporter asked an obviously scripted question.

"Almost certainly. Scotland is in a mess. Politicians and lefty lawyers run roughshod over the law. They steal, and they sexually abuse women. Their government stands back and does nothing. Well, this pervert has gone too far, and I am going to instigate an immediate emergency review to see if we can reel them in."

The picture of the girl faded from the screen, and Jane's brother appeared in her place. Jane sank to her knees.

"The murdering lawyer was also recently involved in a riot where eight government officials were badly injured. Two later died. I will be discussing our options at the COBRA meeting later today, but I am glad to say that the main culprit is already in custody. He resisted arrest and was badly beaten in the effort. It is doubtful he will live to see a courtroom but, in my opinion, that is something to celebrate."

The Home Secretary smiled gleefully at the camera.

"No," Jane said, her face in her hands.

Edinburgh, Tuesday 15th April 2025

Nancy cleaned the kitchen again. It didn't need it. It was just routine, and routine was good right now. There was no way she was going to the office today. No, her little Blackchapel Close semi was going to get another thorough going over.

"He couldn't have," she said aloud before admonishing herself for returning to the subject that the house cleaning was meant to erase. "Forget about it."

Only one pink and one yellow rubber glove could be found this morning, but she wore the mismatched pair anyway. Today was one of those where nothing was going right at all.

The music for the eight o'clock news came on the radio.

"No!" Rushing over to the windowsill, she turned the radio off before anyone talked about… that.

Absentmindedly, she stood there, running her fingers across the mini wind chimes Duncan bought her a few years back. As they tinkled softly, something moved in the distance, and her focus adjusted to see Tom Hartley standing on her lawn. Right at this moment, the press were not in her good books. Only ten minutes ago, she'd sprayed bleach on the pushy *Sun* reporter who turned up at the door seeking comment.

As if hearing her thoughts, Tom held up both palms. She stared at him a second or two more, but then her ire faded. Sighing, she went to the door.

"Nancy, I come in peace."

She stood back and ushered him in. "Second door on the right," she said softly.

The large man clumped down her wooden-floored hallway and she followed him into the living room. He walked over to the rear window and looked out into the enclosed back garden. "Nice place you have here."

"You are covering house décor now, Tom?"

He turned, walked over to her leather sofa and slumped down. His size-twelve feet bumped the coffee table out of line, and she had to slide it back into place. She realigned the placemats. "Do you want coffee or anything?" she asked, trying to make it sound like a chore.

"I'll make it." He groaned as he extricated his large, denim clad frame from the sofa. Of course, the coffee table got knocked once more, and he was already in the kitchen when Nancy sorted the fallout from his short journey. The clumsy oaf had been here a minute, and the place looked to her like a tornado had passed.

"Oh, magic, you got the good stuff. I just get instant shit at work." Tom made a pot of ground coffee while she tidied around him. He was sitting at the kitchen table, mug in hand, by the time she'd restored order. She took a seat opposite.

"You not going to work today?" he asked. She shook her head. Right at this moment, she wasn't going there again. "Nancy?"

"Yes?"

"You would be better taking the gloves off." He pointed at her latex hands. She rolled them down and threw them into the sink. The pink one missed and lay hanging over the edge like a murdered chicken. "Are you married, Nancy?"

"Why the fuck are you here, Tom?"

He held up a palm. "Sorry, it didn't feel right just to dive in."

"Dive in or get the hell out. I have a heap of cleaning to do." The two sat in silence for a minute.

"I don't believe he did it," he said, breaking the silence.

She peered over her steaming coffee mug at him with darkened, puffy eyes. "Come on out for a walk," she said, pouring his insipid effort at coffee down the sink before going to the hallway coat stand and getting her white puffer jacket. When she turned, zipping it up, he was staring at her.

"Jesus, Tom. I am not in the mood to be leched at today." She opened the front door and walked out.

He hurried to catch up. "Why are we walking?" he asked as he came alongside.

"The office was bugged. I'm being blackmailed. Makes sense they have the house monitored too. I came home about a year ago and knew damned fine somebody had been in. Stuff was moved."

"Shit, I wish you and Duncan had come to me with this earlier."

"Well, Tom, the whole point of blackmail is you can't go to the police or press."

"Of course – sorry, Nancy."

"It doesn't matter now." The small stone that she kicked bounced up and clanged on a neighbour's car. She raised her gaze to the giant by her side. "Have you any evidence he is innocent?"

"No, but the way things are, I am not sure if evidence will make any difference. I spoke to a mate that I can trust in the police. Apparently, the crowd that are holding him are taking their orders from London." He cringed as he spoke the city name.

"He told me he didn't do it." As she said the words, she realised how pathetic they sounded. Most murderers denied their crime at one time or another. However, just thinking of the word 'murderer', Nancy couldn't believe anyone would ever associate it with Duncan. He didn't have a bad bone in his body. A tear came to her eye. "This is so fucked up."

He ran a hand through his tousled hair. "You have spoken to him?"

"No, he came to me just as they arrived to arrest him." She began to cry properly. "Tom, I didn't believe him. Hated him at the time."

He tentatively put his arm around her. "He's one of the good guys. Duncan wouldn't do anything like that."

"But he obviously had sex with her. The reports say they have evidence of rape. That can only mean…" She tapered off.

Crossing fingers behind his back, he gave her a squeeze. "They might be lying. We have no idea what these folk are capable of."

Her anger filled eyes met his. "I phoned him early Saturday morning, and she answered. That bitch answered." The tirade ceased suddenly, and she turned her back. Taking a tissue from her pocket, she blew her nose. Tom put his heavy hands on her shoulders. The weight was comforting somehow.

He spoke quietly. "You loved him." It didn't sound like a question, so she didn't answer. "Nancy, I don't know if I can get him out of there, but I am going to do my damnedest to get him into the hands of the local police at the very least. They will get to the bottom of this."

Her phone rang. She looked at the screen for about ten seconds and then picked up the call. "Fuck off, Jane," she said, hanging up.

"Who was that?" Tom's brow lined.

"Duncan's bitch of a sister." After spitting the venomous answer, Nancy walked quickly back toward her house.

Kensington, Tuesday 15th April 2025

Jane looked at the phone as if she hadn't seen one before.

"She won't take your call?" Dana stood next to her, still in her robe.

"She's never liked me, but I guess Duncan told Nancy about his trip down here."

Dana asked. "Why would his secretary be bothered?"

"She's fiercely loyal to Duncan. They are like an old married couple. I think she secretly loves him, but I am unsure if it is a life partner thing or if Nancy believes she's his mother." Jane briefly smiled at the thought of Duncan and Nancy but quickly remembered her brother's situation. "I have to go see him."

"They won't let you anywhere near him. It's a very serious crime."

Jane turned angrily to Dana. "Dana, you don't know Duncan. He could never have done this."

Dana held up a hand as a sign of peace. "Sorry, Jane. Of course that's true, but they still won't let you see him. These emergency powers have suspended all human rights."

Jane nodded. Dana had reported as much on the news just recently. At the time, it did little more than raise Jane's eyebrow. It wasn't going to impinge on her life, was it? She sighed. "I have to try though."

There was a knock on the door. Dana indicated for Jane to sit down on a kitchen stool while she answered, but before Dana made it over, Lady Letchford walked in.

"Good morning, girls." Although they were all similarly aged, the woman spoke to Jane and Dana as if they were young protégés. "Jane, I came as soon as I heard about your brother. How are you coping, dear?"

"I'm not. I need to get up there to see him and to comfort my Mum."

"I could organise for your mother to be flown down here today," Letchford offered.

Jane looked at her, mouth open. "But what about Duncan?"

Elizabeth shook her head. "Even in my position, your brother is beyond help. I know you feel for him, but what he has done is surely unforgivable?"

It took all of Jane's might not to deck their visitor. Elizabeth must have detected danger in Jane's eyes as she stepped away. Shaking, with clenched fists, Jane only just contained her rage. "Duncan would never do the things they are saying."

"Okay, dear, if you say so, but you will never be allowed to see him." The words sounded like she gave credence to Jane's point of view, but her face told the real story.

Jane tried to calm herself. This woman was still her best bet. "Is there anyone you could speak to for me, Lady Letchford? Please?"

The woman stood, looking back out of the corner of her eye. With an index finger to her bottom lip, she hummed softly. They all knew she had the power to organise a visit. Jane guessed Lady Letchford was considering the price of the favour, not the process.

Elizabeth smiled. "Let me speak to a few people, dear." She patted Jane gently on the cheek, then turned and departed.

"That is going to cost me," Jane said, hearing the lift swoosh into action and carrying their devious visitor down to the ground. The Irish girl nodded. A sympathetic look written on her face.

Edinburgh, Wednesday 16th April 2025

Edinburgh Airport was home ground. True, it seldom had this many armed guards or was this quiet. Not since COVID, anyway. The lack of travellers was down to the fact that there were few flights in the air now. The UK was having another tête-à-tête with the EU, so there were no European arrivals nor departures. With the troubles in the States, North American flights were also severely curtailed.

Jane booked the first flight after Lady Letchford came good and phoned last night. She'd organised a short visit with Duncan at a police station. In passing, Elizabeth mentioned needing a favour in return. That could be worried about later.

There was a buzzing in her back pocket. Her burner phone was ringing on silent. Ducking into the toilet, she answered.

"Hi, is that Jane?"

"Yeah, who is this?"

"Jane, you don't know me." It was a man with a fairly heavy Scottish accent. She was leaning toward Dundee. "A little birdy tells me you will be seeing Duncan today. I need something from him. It might save his life."

"Go on," she said, unsure if this was a hoax.

"This is going to sound weird, but please take it at face value. I need his Amazon username and password. When you have it, call this number. Life and death, Jane." The phone went dead.

"What the fuck," she said before realising a woman was washing her hands in the next sink. Jane splashed water on her face and resumed the trip.

Sat in the outer office of the Edinburgh police station, they'd kept her waiting for over an hour, but now Jane was finally being led through a series of sparse magnolia corridors. They hadn't even bothered matching the colours of the fluorescent tubes. Some were blue-white, some warm white and some in between. This place wasn't meant to look pleasant. The man that led her had a nasty, weasel-like appearance. She could tell by his sneer that he was forced to let her be here. Pissed off as he was, he took the time to slap her arse as she walked by.

"We could maybe have a wee chat in one of the cells when you're finished with the rapist, lassie?"

She winced at the description of her brother but bit her tongue. Ignoring the man, she entered the holding cell area. The copper here was massive. He didn't say anything, just pointed at an open door. Jane walked through to find Duncan slumped on what looked like a kitchen chair. There was no other furniture in the room. As she went to close the door, the giant prison guard yelled,

"Leave it open." She nodded and walked over to Duncan and knelt beside his battered and bruised shell. Tears welled up. As she touched his shoulder, his eyes sprang open.

"No, please not again," he cried.

"It's me, Duncan. It's only me."

He looked hard at her for a long time and then tried blinking repeatedly, but he didn't seem to be able to focus. A sorry sight, Duncan's face was one big bruise. In his left eye, red entirely replaced the white and what little hair had not been ripped out was matted to his head. The cell's bloodstained walls told a story she didn't want to know.

"Oh God, Duncan, what have they done to you?"

"Jane, is that really you? Jane, I'm so sorry. I didn't mean to do it…"

A flood of tears ran down her face as she pleaded with him, "No, Duncan, you couldn't have possibly done this. Not you."

"I didn't mean to. I was angry. I just lost my head."

On her knees by his side, she locked her hands together in prayer. "No, Duncan, please say you didn't do it?"

"You know I love you. I shouldn't have done it."

"Duncan, what are you talking about?"

"I wanted to turn back. I was just so angry with you."

She wiped her eyes and let out the breath she'd held forever. "You're talking about the bridge, about London, aren't you? Tell me that you are, please!"

He made a tiny head movement that she hoped was a nod of affirmation. She kissed him gently, and although he winced, he didn't pull away.

"Five more minutes," the giant shouted from outside the door, where he stood, arms folded impatiently. Her inconvenient visit interrupted the task of handing out what the prison guards viewed as justice. Duncan, tried and convicted in the court of public opinion, now faced the brutal retribution for a crime he couldn't have committed.

Tearing her eyes away from the joyous bloodlust on the guard's face, she returned her attention to the hapless victim.

"What happened at the weekend, Duncan?"

He actually smiled, but it revealed that half his teeth were missing. The image was too much for her, and tears welled up again.

"We went to the match. The Jambos were shite, Jane. The big Swedish striker is a cart horse." Duncan scowled as if this were his main problem at the moment.

"Duncan, not the match. What happened after?" She thought they must have drugged him. His mind appeared to be fragmented. He was dotting back and forth between the game and the last time the two of them met.

"She hasn't phoned, though."

"Who hasn't?"

He laughed. "She bloody hated the game. Worst two hours of her life, she said." There was a phantom calmness in her brother that could only be present in the absence of reality.

"Who hasn't phoned, Duncan?"

"Oh, aye, Jane. I think my sister is angry with me." His addled mind flitted between issues. Time and place seemed lost to him now. She made to hug him, but even her touch caused him to wince.

"Duncan, I'm Jane. I love you, big brother. I was a bloody idiot not to run after you."

The ghost of a smile crossed his battered face. "Sheila might phone soon, hopefully. I really like her. Will you come and meet her?"

Jane knew that Sheila was the murdered girl's name, but she wasn't sure if that was who Duncan meant.

"Of course, bro. I would love to meet her. Duncan, I need you to think hard for me a second, okay?" She rubbed life back into his hand, clenched between hers.

He blinked several times. "Is that you, Jane?"

"Yes, Duncan. Look, I need to use your computer. Can you remember your Amazon login?"

As if sanity suddenly returned, he spoke softly and gave an email address she knew to be a good one.

"And your password?"

His eyes travelled right and left as if reading a book. "Where's Nance with the coffee?" He tried to look past her, expecting his secretary to walk in any second.

"Duncan, please concentrate. I need your password."

"Password." His eyes rolled.

"Yeah, Duncan. I need your password." He seemed to double down on the speed reading.

"I've done her wrong. Nancy is…password…she's angry with me."

She leaned forward and spoke in his torn ear. "Duncan, this is very important. Please remember. Is Nancy your password or is it something to do with the football? Jambos or something?"

The large guard entered and took her roughly by the arm. "Time to go, lass."

"Please, Duncan, please remember." She pleaded desperately as the guard was dragging her out.

Duncan mumbled as his head fell onto his chest. "Password."

In tears, she implored the guard, "Please, please let me have five more minutes."

"No, lass. Time to go." He hauled her arm. It felt like it may leave the socket and would surely carry bruises tomorrow if it remained attached.

"Please, sir, I will do anything." She looked up at him, wiping her eyes. "Anything," she repeated more forcibly.

He looked her up and down. "How do I know you won't change your mind after the five minutes?"

She took his hand and put it over her breast. He squeezed roughly.

"No, I canna trust you."

She needed that password. If it had any chance of saving Duncan's life, then she would do whatever it took. Grasping the man's hand, she led him to another open cell. In this one, there was a bed. She walked over to it and began to undress. When she was down to her underwear, the huge man shouted, "Weasel. Get in here now."

Heavy footsteps clattered down the stairs before the rat-faced guard who had led her down here walked in. Grinning from ear to ear at the sight of her undressed state, he closed the door.

* * *

The giant and weasel walked out of the room, high-fiving each other. Jane sobbed while dressing but did so as quickly as her shaking hands could rezip and button.

Mercifully, they'd been quick, but their brutal attentions left her sore all over. After pulling on her sweater, she ran her fingers through her static-filled hair. She walked out into the corridor, where the grinning giant stood aside, pointing toward the cell. She pushed the door open, and the room was empty. The two men burst into fits of laughter.

"Stupid bitch gave up the goods first. What did you expect,

whore? If it's any consolation, dear, you weren't half bad," the giant said.

"I preferred shagging her brother," the weasel added. "I love how he screamed."

Instantly, Jane sprang toward the rat-faced pig, but the giant put an arm out and stopped her. Seeing that she was restrained, the weasel raised a hand and beckoned her forward as if he would welcome the opportunity to fight. The larger guard pushed her back into the cell. "Behave yourself, lassie, unless you want to move in here too."

Breathing slowly, deeply, she regained an outward calm, while inside, the turmoil raged. *Don't get mad, get even*, she thought, breaking eye contact and turning to the vacant room. No matter how long she stared at the kitchen chair in the middle, it remained empty. Her brother's pain was writ large on every wall. But he was no longer here. *Was this the last time I'll see you, brother?*

She inhaled until her lungs ached. Slowly, ever so slowly, she released the breath through gritted teeth. "The world is different now. My world is different now," she whispered. She took one last look at the room where her brother's road would likely end, but Duncan's wasn't the only road that neared conclusion.

In her head, she actually heard the switch click, and in an instant, she was someone else now. Maybe someone not so nice. With a painted-on smile fixed, she turned to the two guards. "Thank you for your time, gentlemen," she said politely and walked past. *One shouldn't speak ill to the dead.*

Outside the police station, in the chilly Edinburgh wind, she pulled out the phone and redialled the number that called her.

"Jane?"

"Yes."

"Do you have the info?"

"I got his username, but he couldn't remember the password."

A grey Mondeo pulled up in front of her, and the passenger window went down. "Maybe we can figure it out," the voice said.

* * *

Duncan's flat was in disarray. Someone had been looking for something, and they hadn't bothered hiding the fact. The brown leather sofa sat shredded and upturned. Drawers and cupboards were spilled onto the floor. Bookshelves were stripped clean, and the carpets had even been lifted in places. The destruction looked more vindictive than inquisitive. Jane set about tidying up while Tom worked on reassembling the parts of the PC.

"Someone really has it in for your brother," he said, checking the screen was still intact.

There was a quiet knock at the door. Jane headed toward it, but Tom stood and put an arm out to hold her back. He opened it. A little old lady stood on the landing, her grey curly hair held in place by a silk head scarf. She wore an apron that was covered in flour and had an old and tatty pair of slippers on her feet.

"Is wee Janey in?" she asked Tom.

He stood aside to let Jane pass. "Mrs Riddell, I haven't seen you in years."

"Aye, Janey, I just wish we were meeting in better circumstances. I miss you on the telly, Janey. You're really good."

"Thanks, Mrs Riddell – what is it that we can do for you?"

"Janey, it's this horrible business with Duncan. I told the bobbies that the lassie went oot all fine and dandy. I spoke to her on the stairs myself. Duncan wouldn't hurt a flee. They didn't listen to me though. What's happening?"

"I don't really know. We are here looking for evidence to help clear him."

Mrs Riddell put her head round the door and viewed the mess. "That's a shame. Duncan aye kept the place neat and tidy. He wiz a right good neighbour."

"Well, thanks for letting us know about the girl. Tom, here, and I were sure Duncan didn't do it, but it is good to get confirmation. I will let you know if we turn anything up, okay?"

"Okay, Janey. Really nice to see you again." Mrs Riddell went to leave but stopped. "Janey, dear. Do you remember Birdy Bob?"

Jane looked at the woman. "The name is familiar, but I think I only ever heard Duncan talk about him. Wasn't he done for being a peeping Tom or something?"

"Aye, that wisnay his fault. There was some exotic bird nesting on a window ledge, but it jist happened to be a young lassie's bedroom. Bob was caught looking with his binoculars." Clouds of flour emanated from the woman as she added overexuberant hand gestures.

"So, what about him?" Jane stepped closer and stooped to meet Mrs Riddell's eyes.

"Well, yon bit of land far the lassie was found is Bob's favourite bird-watching site. He has cameras running all day and night."

"Mrs Riddell, I bloody well love you," Jane said, kissing her cheek.

"Now, now, Janey. Mind yer tongue. Hope Birdy Bob can help. Duncan does my shopping for me. I'm running oot of tatties." The old woman headed down the stairs to her flat. Jane closed the door and smiled.

"Come see this," said Tom. He had typed in Duncan's username and there was an option to have a password reminder sent to email. He flicked screens and opened Outlook.

"Brilliant, give it a go," she said. He went through the process and waited for the email.

Your password reminder is...Password.

"Bloody hell," said Jane. "That is no more help than Duncan was. Whenever I asked him about the password, he kept repeating the word."

Tom was biting his thumbnail and looking hard at the screen. Suddenly, his face broke into a gawky smile. He went back to the Amazon login, and in the password box, he typed *PASSWORD*. The account opened.

Jane stood with her mouth open. She snorted and then burst out laughing manically. He looked up at her with concern.

"You okay?"

Unable to stop, she held up a hand. Finally, she calmed down and went and sat on the upturned sofa.

"He was telling me the password all along."

"I get that, Jane, but it doesn't seem that funny," he said.

"Well, Tom, if you had any idea what I did to get another few minutes with Duncan in order to discover the password, you would be peeing yourself right now."

In spite of her mirth, there was a sadness on her face. His expression made it clear that he didn't believe he would be laughing at all.

"Do you want me to pay him a visit?" Tom didn't have to be clever to guess what had happened.

"You know, Thomas, I might just take you up on that, but let's kill one bird at a time." She laid a hand on his shoulder.

Searching through Duncan's Alexa account, they noticed that he had been playing Queen songs early on the morning of the murder. They tried a few saved recordings in the program settings and heard Duncan and Sheila chatting away. There was a lot of giggling and periods of silence, broken only by sounds of pleasure. Tom jumped the recording forward a few minutes.

"Thanks, Sheila. See you later?"

"Count on it."

There was a minute of silence. Jane guessed they were kissing.

"Thanks for a lovely day, Duncan. Football aside." The girl giggled. "See you later."

"Bye, Sheila."

The sound of the door closing and then footsteps going down the stairs faded to nothing. Duncan was whistling away and shouting up the occasional Queen song.

"I didn't think he was into them," said Jane.

"Maybe she was," Tom offered. "A pretty woman can have a strange effect on a man's music taste."

She nodded. "Skip forward to 9.35am. I read that was the time of death."

He searched for a file from just before that time. "There's one from 9.29 to 9.51 – he was in the flat the whole time." He punched the air.

She rubbed her temples. "The problem we have will be getting someone to pay any notice to this."

He copied the files onto a removable drive and emailed himself the access details. Then he changed the password. "I will go through these tonight. See if I can turn anything else up. Let's go find Pervy Bob," he said.

"Birdy Bob," Jane corrected him.

"I stand by my previous statement, Miss Clark."

Luckily for them, Birdy Bob was well-known locally and easily tracked down. Tom knocked on his flat door while Jane peered out of the landing window. Bob had a clear view over the waste ground. A portly man opened the door, wearing a faded

Heriot-Watt University sweatshirt – his belly hung out beneath it. His jeans were ripped, and not in the fashionable way. Tiny eyes peered through thick National Health style glasses.

"Mr…eh…Bob?"

"Aye," Bob said, producing a very squeaky voice for such a large man.

"Bob, I'm Tom Hartley from the Herald Newsgroup. Could we come in a second?"

"You got ID?"

"Bob, I'm a journalist, not your friggin' gasman. Now don't be a prick and let us in, eh?"

Bob looked at Tom and then at Jane. Then at Jane some more. She gave him her best seductive smile.

"Aye, okay. On ye come." With some reluctance, he ushered them in.

Jane and Tom sat on the sofa and looked round the walls. They were covered, floor to ceiling, with photographs of birds.

"You're an excellent photographer, Bob. Do you want me to put in a word at the paper? Might be a freelance job going?" Tom said.

"Oh, I canna work. Long-term sick. They'd take away my benefits."

Jane stood and walked over to a picture of a brightly coloured bird. "What's this one?"

Bob lurched up and stood close, a bit too close for her liking. He smelled like a hamster's cage. She inched away.

"That's a macaw. It may have escaped from the zoo, or maybe it was a pet. They're not indigenous."

"Thanks, Bob, but even I knew that." She looked at him indignantly.

"There are a lot of pretty local birds, though." He was trying to look down her top.

"Bob," said Tom, "we believe you may have cameras covering the waste ground out there?"

Bob reluctantly turned to Tom. "Aye, but they're no' always turned on."

"Were any on the day of the murder?" Jane asked.

Bob went over to a folder and opened it. "Yeah, I think so. For a while anyway. I haven't got round to reviewing the footage yet. I'm days behind." The birdwatcher pointed to a line of DVDs on a shelf. "I've got all that to get through first."

Tom got up off the sofa. He walked over and towered over Bob. "Can you find the disk for 9am on Sunday morning, please?"

"That sounds like a lot of work. How about making it worth my while?"

Tom first took a hold of the man's sweatshirt but quickly let go and wiped his hands. "How about I break your nose if you don't get a move on?"

Jane moved round the stunning bird pictures as the two men argued. This guy clearly had talent. There was a swallow, caught in flight with a mouthful of insects. She saw it was taken over the waste ground. To get a better look, she took the picture off the wall.

"Wow," she said, "I'm really impressed, Bob." They stopped arguing briefly.

"Please leave them on the wall, though," he said.

She nodded and went to do as he asked. The argument between the two men resumed. While rehanging it, she felt something move on the reverse of the frame. On the back was an equally graphic picture of a bird – not the avian type, but one stood in a window and in the process of undressing.

Maybe Tom was right about this guy, she thought. They needed his help, though, so she just rehung the picture. Moving along the line, one showed three crows sitting on a phone line in half dark. It looked quite atmospheric. Spooky even. In the background of the picture, was the rear view of Duncan's flat. With a little trepidation, she ran her fingers behind the frame and sure enough, there was another picture there. Moving so that Bob couldn't see what was happening, she took it off the wall and turned it over. As expected, the photo showed the same view, but now one of the windows was in close-up. Jane stood looking at herself, in Duncan's spare bedroom – she was topless. It appeared that this picture was taken last Christmas. They'd hit the town, and she'd stayed over.

"Bob," said Jane, not turning round, "how much do you want for the DVDs for all of Saturday through to Monday?"

The men stopped their discussion and Bob put a knuckle to his lips.

"A grand and they're yours."

"It's a deal," said Jane. "Coincidentally, that's exactly what I charge for topless pictures." She threw the photo onto his sofa. "So, give us the DVDs, and you can keep the pic." She smiled at him. "And, as a bonus, we don't mention any of the other stuff behind these magnificent shots. Okay?"

Bob looked at her, and Jane could see the calculator working in his head. "Be a good boy, Bob, and I'll text you next time I'm changing my clothes at Duncan's place."

As if the offer was serious, he nodded in agreement. Tom was handed a dozen disks.

Jane and Tom were in Nancy's house. Their hostess kept giving Jane black looks.

"You realise that computer is probably bugged," she said to Tom.

"It really doesn't matter now. They have everything they need. I doubt you will hear from them again."

Tom slid the first DVD into the drive while Nancy swept under his chair. Jane walked over to the disgruntled woman.

"Nancy, you have every right to be pissed off with me. However much of a shit you think I am, I feel twice as bad. We both love Duncan. I know you would never hurt him the way I did, but I can't do anything about that now. We have to work together to get him out of there. He is in a terrible mess. Please, Nancy. Let's do it for Duncan, and once he is free, I will gladly let the two of you kick the shit out of me."

Their eyes stayed locked. Jane could tell that Nancy really didn't want to communicate, but needing to know about Duncan, Nancy broke the stare and relented.

"How bad is he?" she whispered. Jane just shook her head. "Right… for Duncan though," Nancy said in hasty qualification of her agreement.

Jane didn't care if the woman hated her. The two of them always had a fractious relationship. Yeah, they had been civil, but Jane was always competing for the affection of her brother. Maybe Duncan was more than a proxy son for Nancy.

"Here we go," said Tom, pointing to the screen. The picture was clear as a bell. Birdy Bob took his work seriously. Two men in dark suits had Sheila struggling between them as they walked up the alley and onto the wasteland. She was thrown to the ground. Quickly, she made to get back up. There was no sound, but an argument was clearly in progress. Sheila kept trying to stand, but one of the men pushed her back down with his foot. Something she said seemed to stun the first man. He stepped back a little. Then he ran forward and kicked Sheila hard in the head. The girl fell back in an unnatural motion.

"Oh God, no," Jane said, guessing, maybe hoping, that Sheila was unconscious already. The man who kicked her jumped on top of her and pounded the defenceless girl with his fists. The frantic beating went on for several minutes.

Nancy sobbed. "She probably died at the kick." Mostly out of hope, Jane agreed.

The second man finally pulled his colleague off the girl, and the two stood looking down at her. They appeared to be conversing. The second man pointed back along the street toward Duncan's flat. He then bent down and ripped the girl's top open. The two of them started back down the alley before the first turned and ran back, kneeling beside Sheila's body.

"What is he doing?" Jane asked.

Tom paused the clip and zoomed in on the touchscreen with his thumb and finger. "He's doing something to her hand," he said, resuming the playback.

The assailant walked back to his colleague, and as he did, he flipped a ring in the air, caught it and put it in his pocket.

"What good is this?" asked Nancy. "These guys probably work for the people that hold Duncan."

"We're not going to take it to them," said Tom. "Leave this with me."

Nancy stared at the peaceful image on the screen. Clouds idled by while grass blew this way and that. In the middle of it all, a pale white figure lay still. A figure Nancy had wished death upon a hundred times in the last few days. She felt the shaking in her ankles first, but quickly her calves and then thighs joined in. Jane turned in time to see her collapse. She jumped over and prevented the woman's head from hitting the table, but she couldn't stop gravity from having its way, and the two of them fell. Nancy lay on the floor in a state of hysteria. All Jane could do was hold her tight until the shaking and tears subsided.

Edinburgh, Thursday 17th April 2025

In the main, Duncan's office desk was tidy. Tidy, with the exception of the thick pile of used Post-it notes, stuck to the side of his filing trays. Jane pulled the top one off.

Wear a tie on Friday and NOT a dinosaur one.

She took another. *Joan called again.*

She leafed through several more. None carried what could be considered as pearls of wisdom, nor important instructions needing to be retained. Still, she finally realised the pile constituted every note Nancy had ever written him. On the back, in Duncan's handwriting, was the date and time of each. A few carried little added notes. *Wearing pink again today.* She stuck them back in place.

"They will be here for you, Dunky," she said aloud.

With her brother still in custody, the last thing Jane wanted to do was leave, but were their newly conceived plans to work, she had to get back to London. Nancy seemed to be warming a little and had offered to drive her to the airport. *Of course, she could just want rid of me*, Jane thought. Either way, the lift was welcome.

The phone on the desk rang. Jane just left it, but someone shouted up the stairs, "Jane, Tom Hartley for you on line one."

She picked it up. Before she had a chance to speak, the reporter said, "Turn on the TV." Pressing the remote that sat on the desk, a picture appeared of a tearful man wiping his eyes.

"I can't believe she is gone. And to die in such a horrible way, to that vile man."

"It's the husband…" Tom said over the phone.

The reporter pushed the microphone nearer to catch his sobs. "I can only hope that some criminal in the prison will take vengeance on Duncan Clark for my poor, sweet wife. I miss her so much. The kids ask when their mummy is coming home."

The tearful man broke down as the camera stayed on him.

"He doesn't have kids," said Tom. "Do you recognise him?"

Standing, she walked over to the screen for a closer look, but couldn't bring the face to mind.

"No, who is he?"

"I printed some pictures out from the DVD. The not-so-grieving husband is the man who killed Sheila."

"We must go to the police with this now, Tom."

"No, stick to the plan," he said. "If we jump the gun, Duncan will probably have a mysterious accident, and the grieving husband will disappear. We go tomorrow as agreed. I am heading up to Perth soon and will let you know the moment that everything is in place."

"What if Duncan doesn't make it until tomorrow?" Jane asked agitatedly.

He didn't answer for a while. "Jane, we have no control over that. They will do what they do. Just go with what we arranged. Okay?"

"Okay," Jane said, punching the arm of the chair.

The A90, Northbound. The road to Perth, Thursday 17th April 2025

Thankfully, Tom Hartley's editor gave him a lot of scope to work on this project, but even so, he was looking for a printable story soon. "Should have something tomorrow, boss," Tom told him, but this had stopped being about a story for him a while ago. He was doing this because it was the right thing to do.

He liked to think he often did the right thing, but he knew at his core that was a lie. It was usually all about the story. No way was he a complete hack though. He had morals. A line he wouldn't normally cross. This time, someone else had crossed Tom's line, and he intended to push them back.

There was a pang of sadness when he remembered his last days in university and first weeks in his journalism career. The young and possibly naïve Tom Hartley had intended to change the world. The power of his pen would wake the good people of Dundee and, hopefully, one day, further afield to the truth of this supposed democracy.

Born to conservative-leaning parents and raised to believe in free markets, he wasn't your average left-leaning hack, railing against capitalism. No, to him, this wasn't about right or left, socialism or free markets, the state or the individual. It had become as basic as good and evil. Maybe not in the biblical sense, but he was now convinced the world could be split into those who, at least, thought they were doing good and, on the other side, those who knew how to exploit the system to their own advantage.

The hardest thing to swallow about the current situation was that the cabal intent on self-enrichment had persuaded their victims that having any sort of choice was probably just an inconvenience they could do without. The stranglehold was near total. Their insidious roots reached into everyday life and tried to crush any who opposed them. Even good people like Duncan Clark.

Tom's pen wasn't going to be the answer. This was apparent. So, although he fully intended to write the required articles, change, however unlikely, would now only ever happen through direct action. The epiphany? He would have to fight, and that could not be done alone. Needing allies, he knew the Force in Edinburgh to be compromised. Due to that inconvenient fact, he was now pulling his car into Perth Police Station.

Superintendent Bobby McKay ducked under the door lintel. "Tom, my man. How are you keeping?"

At six foot eight inches high and half as broad, the policeman made Tom look like a regular-sized guy. Tom held out his hand, and Bobby the Bobby's shovel-sized fist enclosed it. Breaking the shake, Tom checked for damage.

"I'm good, Bobby. Thanks again for the help that you and the lads gave at Pitlochry."

The bobby beamed back at him. "It was no bother at all, Tom. Anytime."

"Well, funny you should say that, Bobby." Tom smiled.

* * *

While whistling along with the radio, Tom drove back to Edinburgh. At his behest, Superintendent McKay had gathered the guys who participated in the Pitlochry incident, and Tom showed them the evidence he and Jane found. Bobby watched with interest and then asked what Tom was planning. Hearing the action was in Edinburgh, Bobby told him there was no way the Perth police could get involved.

Tom was initially crestfallen until a grinning Bobby said he hoped there wasn't any crime in Perth tomorrow, as he and the other eleven constables would be phoning in sick. Delighted they were on board, Tom ran through his plan. He did so a second time as some of the officers weren't getting it.

'Go' time was set for 7am.

London, Thursday 17th April 2025

"You have all the evidence you need here," said Dana after watching what Jane collected in Edinburgh. "Why not go to the police down here?"

"We don't know who to trust. I couldn't even take this to Dan. I believe the guys that hold Duncan are working for this new government that we work for too."

"How did Duncan look?" Jane told Dana the whole story, and she was horrified. "What do you need me to do?" she said in response.

"I need you to help me be in two places at once." Jane smiled at Dana.

Edinburgh, Friday 18th April 2025

"I don't get what you find so complicated. Two of us go looking to report a crime. Six try to get in the back door while I keep the front desk busy. Four more rush in once the others are inside," Tom said, explaining the plan for the fourth time.

With one huge hand, Bobby McKay waved away two days of planning. "That all sounds dandy, Tom, but that's no' how we work in Perth. The lot of you, follow me."

Dressed in a hoodie and jeans, looking like an oversized teenager, Bobby set off for the main entrance with his squad in tow. Only one was in uniform, and he walked in first, waving to the man behind the front desk. The careless desk sergeant buzzed him through the glass security doors. As soon as the team outside heard the buzz, they charged.

Tom shook his head and just followed. By the time he got inside, the policeman behind the front desk was lying in a pool of blood, moaning. Someone had broken his nose. In pairs, the Perth police sped through every door they found. Tom heard cries and scuffles in the side offices as he and Bobby McKay headed for the cells. One of the Perth police held a young copper by the hair and banged the lad's head off a window. Tom thought that the assailant enjoyed his task a little too much.

"What's all this noise?" Chief Superintendent Andy Crossan stepped out of his office in time to see Bobby heading his way. "Bobby, is that..." Bobby McKay headbutted the man before he could finish his sentence.

"Aye, Andy, it's me, and I have aye wanted to do that to you, you prick." Just for good measure, Bobby gave the stricken man a boot in the stomach. He let out a cry. Bobby bent over his gasping victim and took his keys and phone. Looking to the door that led to the cells, Bobby and Tom walked over the Chief Super as if he were a welcome mat. Just as they reached the door, a man bearing an uncanny resemblance to a weasel stuck his head round it.

"Oh fuck," he said as Bobby slammed into the door and trapped the weasel's neck. The huge policeman pulled the door open again, and the weasel collapsed on the floor, gasping for breath. Bobby headed along the corridor, followed by three of his officers.

"I know who you are, man." Tom bent over the still gasping victim as a look of panic came into his darting weasel eyes. He tried to speak, but his throat was too badly damaged. Tom searched the weasel's pockets, pulling out a wallet. It contained a wad of papers and fifty quid. Tom took the money and held it up. "I'll have this for my trouble, and I'll be holding on to the rest of this stuff... Simon," he said, reading the name from a driving licence. "Oh, and I have your home address now. Who's this wee lass? Jenny, is that your daughter? Well, I'll be paying wee Jenny a visit, Simon. How do you like that?"

As footsteps approached, Tom looked up to see Bobby and another officer coming back up the stairs with Duncan suspended between them. Duncan came out of his stupor as soon as he saw the weasel. He struggled to be free of the policemen.

"It's okay now. Calm down." Tom put a hand on the wreckage that was Duncan.

"Gonna kill that filthy bastard," Duncan shouted, and even Bobby and his fellow officer struggled to keep the beaten solicitor in check.

Fearful that Duncan may break free, the weasel was shaking his head furiously. Tom felt warm water lap round his feet.

"Aw for fuck's sake. My good shoes." Tom looked down as the smell of urine assailed his nostrils.

"Do you want me to arrest him?" Bobby pointed to the shaking weasel.

"No need, Bobby. You see, I've looked into him, and luckily for us, he doesn't really exist. It's a strange thing, Bobby, but there is no record of this piss-soaked piece of shit at all. So, none of us here today ever saw him, right?" Tom grinned. "Anyway, he has an appointment to make."

The Superintendent raised an eyebrow, but then just shrugged before he and his fellow officer continued their journey to the door with a partially conscious Duncan suspended between them.

London, Friday 18th April 2025

Dana filled half the screen while Birdy Bob's footage ran on the other side. Just in case someone at the BBC pulled the switch, it had all been posted on every conceivable social media site.

"There you have it. Conclusive evidence that the murderer of Sheila Morgan was her husband Philip Morgan, and not Duncan Clark. We believe that the police are releasing Duncan this morning. The search for the husband has begun. Duncan is of course the brother of our own reporter, Jane Clark. She is in our Westminster studio, and we go over there now. Jane, can you tell the viewers how you feel about this evidence coming to light?"

A smiling Jane stood, Big Ben looming over her shoulder. "Dana, it is such a relief. I always knew my brother to be incapable of such a crime. I am so relieved to hear that he is to be released. As soon as we are finished here, I'm heading up to Scotland to be with him."

"Thank you, Jane. Yes, go get your flight. We wish you and your brother well."

The image of Jane in Westminster faded, and Dana turned to other news.

Edinburgh, Friday 18th April 2025

The office was a real mess. A confetti of papers was strewn over the floor, and files lay everywhere. Tom walked around and closed the Venetian blinds.

"Jesus, does nobody ever dust this place?"

He looked at the dust matted windowsills and their dead fly graveyards. Tom turned his nose up at the vague smell of sweat. It was perhaps fortuitous that the weasel's urine was taking over.

"I see why they call these people pigs." He returned his attention to the burbling, urine-soaked officer.

"Just you and me now, Simon." Tom gave the man a boot in the stomach and then bent over to take a hold of his wiry hair. With a jerk and a loud scream, the weasel was lifted onto one of the desks. "Remember her?" Tom pointed to the TV on the far wall.

The weasel moaned, then swivelled his head to look at the screen. Jane Clark stood, apparently reporting live from Westminster. "No, no, no," the weasel tried to shout, but what came out was little more than a mumble. The fear on his face changed to abject terror when he turned back to see her now standing next to Tom. He did a quick disbelieving double take between screen and reality.

"Well, Simon, we meet again. You up for being screwed this time?" Jane had told Tom she was going to kill this man for the evil deeds he'd inflicted on Duncan. Tom went along with the plan, never actually believing she would do so, though. Now she stood next to him with the coldest look he'd ever seen in anyone's eyes. Worse still, the merest smile was set on her pretty painted lips. Tom was half aroused, half nauseated.

Calm as you like, she stuck a Taser into the man's face. Firing the clamps into his skin, he screamed, and the weasel's frame writhed as waves of pain ran through his bruised and broken body. She held it there until the charge dropped out. Unfortunately, the battery died before the weasel.

"Have we got another gun somewhere?" Jane asked calmly.

Tom grimaced at the scene and the pungent aroma of burning flesh. He put his hand on her shoulder. "Let it go. We can get Bobby to throw him in jail."

Anger clouded her features. She grabbed his collar. Standing a foot short of his height the force of her grip nearly lifted his Doc Martins off the floor. With nothing in her brown eyes but pure hate, in a scream, she roared, "You didn't see Duncan. You didn't see what this…animal did to him. If this piece of shit goes to jail, he will be out and disappeared in a few days."

After letting out a long sigh, she seemed to calm. The grip released. "Sorry, Tom, I made this piece of shit a promise that I intend to keep." Her body tensed as her voice rose to a crescendo. "NOW GET ME ANOTHER FUCKING TAZER."

Observing the vehement rage in her eyes, he quickly realised there was no point in arguing, and on looking down at the desolation that used to be the Weasel's face, he omitted a sigh of resignation. Death would most likely be a mercy. Tom went and brought back the device.

Jane's gruesome revenge spent most of the second gun's battery before the weasel stopped breathing. After removing it from the dead man's face, she put the Taser in the bag with the first. Tom twisted the bag closed and slung it over his shoulder. She seemed to wince at the odour of urine and cooked meat, then covered her mouth with her hand.

"Are you okay?" he asked. That look still resided in her eye. It left him afraid of the answer.

"I've just killed a man, Tom," she said, looking up at him.

"I'm not sure this was ever much of a man." He pointed to the smoking carcass that lay on the desk in front of them.

"That's my point. I don't feel a goddamned thing."

She put her arm around his back, and the two of them strolled out into the cool Edinburgh morning. Jane started whistling gaily. Tom started shaking.

BBC News, Friday 18th April 2025

"…and today in Parliament, two votes that you, the electorate, decided on yesterday were passed into legislation. The suspension of the devolved governments in Scotland, Wales and Northern Ireland navigated the House unopposed. An official complaint from the European Union has been received regarding the Stormont assembly, and there have already been some reports of trouble on the streets of Belfast. A government official issued a statement earlier to say that no foreign organisations would dictate policy to Britain."

The news man shuffled some papers.

"The second motion that was passed by the public was the amendment to the fixed-term Parliament act. By 95% to 5%, the public asked their MPs to enable the government of the day to fix the term of each Parliament. This again cleared the House. It had been expected that the Labour opposition would mount a rebellion against the motion, but their leader said, 'While the Labour Party will always stand for democracy, it would be hypocritical for us to oppose a motion supported by such a majority of the British public.'

"In the end, no one spoke against the motion, but it is believed that three Labour MPs have resigned the whip. In other news…"

Pitlochry, Saturday 19th April 2025

Jane stood at the hotel window and looked out. Down in the trees, Duncan walked slowly, hand in hand with Nancy. They weren't talking – nothing needed to be said.

"He'll get through this," Tom said, standing behind Jane and looking over her head at the scene outside.

"You're probably right, but I'm not sure that *I* will, though, Tom."

His large hands massaged her shoulders. "It's going to take all of us a while, I guess."

Resting her head on one of his hands. "Has there been any news of the murdering husband?" she asked.

Tom shook his head. "I doubt anyone is looking. He works for them, whoever they are. Bobby at the Perth police did some digging, but the guy has been erased. So has Sheila. It's as if they never existed. The names were probably fake."

"I wonder who she really was. It sounded like she fell for

Duncan, but maybe she was just a good liar." Jane reached out and put a hand on the glass, as if to be nearer her brother.

Tom let his hands fall back by his side. "I'll do some digging once this all dies down. My editor is pissed off with me at the moment because we broke the story online. He will come round though. I will do an in-depth background piece."

"Tom." Jane took her hand from the cold glass pane and faced the reporter. She wanted to tell him everything that happened to Duncan in prison, and to her when she visited. He would then understand why she killed the guard with relish. Tom contributed so much while gaining little personally. The rough diamond even risked his own career and, yes, had now possibly endangered his life. There had to be a better way to tell him, but struggling for the words, she sighed and then settled for, "Thanks." Mystification crossed his face. "For the weasel." She stood on her toes to give the confused man a peck on the cheek. Bumping back on her heels, she took his hand. "We still need to find the other guard. If you help me, and you are really good, I might let you kill this one." Her eyes twinkled, and she giggled at the consternation that came over his face.

Edinburgh Airport, Saturday 19th April 2025

"Last call for the 3pm flight from Edinburgh International to Barcelona."

Chief Superintendent Andy Crossan watched as his wife and kids headed for the flight to Barcelona. With the turmoil in Scotland, his newly acquired holiday home would be a safer location for a while. Now he just needed to offload the body of the stinking junkie from the boot of the car, and he, too, would be off south. The operation in Edinburgh had been a mess, but he was glad that the 'powers that be' knew it wasn't his doing. Cumbria might be a backwater, but after this shambles, he accepted the job of police chief without question.

I've been dealing with Scottish sheep shaggers long enough. I can't see English ones being too hard to manage, he thought.

"Ready to rock, Andy?"

Andy turned to see Barry 'Bez' Jones heading his way. He tried not to resent that Bez, twenty years his junior, was now his real boss. Rumours flew that Bez was ex-SAS, but this could all be pish. What was unarguably true was that Bez was ruthless. He was not only responsible for the junkie in Andy's boot, but under the false name of Philip Morgan, the man had also murdered his own wife when she fucked up the operation. Andy watched him spin a wedding ring in the air and catch it repeatedly. Each time, the balding man smiled like it was a life achievement. Andy's recently acquired bruised ribs ached as he hobbled over to Bez.

Mary Crossan had enough on her plate with the hastily packed suitcase and its sticking wheel.

"Kids, please, for God's sake, just walk to the flight as if you are not a couple of retards."

Young Andrew had challenged his sister, Jordan, to hop, all the way to the aeroplane. They turned to their mother, bottom lips protruding.

"Aw, Mum."

It scared Mary how often these two talked in unison. It was like something out of *Village of the Damned*. Had she not been there as they were cut out of her, she would swear they were adopted.

"Mrs Crossan?" A female security officer blocked their way.

"Yes?"

"Come with me, please?" The amiable woman ruffled young Andrew's hair.

"But we'll miss our flight," Mary said.

"You won't have to worry about that," the security officer said, smiling.

* * *

Bez sat in the passenger seat and ran the wedding ring through his fingers. "Just like the Romans, eh?"

"Romans?" Andy looked over but made sure they didn't make eye contact.

"Here we are, retreating south of Hadrian's Wall to lick our wounds. One day soon to return and kick Jock arse." Bez had an annoyingly whiny Nottingham accent, but Andy wasn't about to let him know any time soon. Instead, he looked out at the bleak scenery. He wasn't sure if this was still the M74 or if they had joined the M6 yet. Either way, he hated this part of the journey. Even the bloody radio wouldn't work here.

Originally from Stirling, and like most Scots, Andy had to wear a kilt at formal functions a few times, but he was all Brit. He couldn't be doing with this independence malarkey and nationalist bullshit. So why did it annoy him when the Englishman sitting next to him belittled his country? *Just one of the joys of being Scottish*, he guessed. *We can piss over our own country, but we'd gather like a hungry pack of wolves if an outsider made the same observations.* Sod it, he was obligated to rise to the defence.

"I'm not sure that it worked out well for the Romans in Scotland, Bez."

"Well, I'm sure one of the Edwards kicked your arses a few times. Anyway, William Wallace, can you pull into this next layby? I am going to piss myself if you don't."

* * *

Bez wiped the sweat from his brow and put the shovel back into the boot. He'd paid £12 for it in B&Q and was damned if he would just throw it away. With him not having a garden at the moment, he wasn't sure when it would next be needed. Shovels had uses other than digging, though. The top of Andy Crossan's skull could have verified that had it still been attached to the rest of the Jock police officer's head.

The cold hit the sweat on the back of his shirt, and Bez shivered as if someone walked over his grave. He wondered if he would indeed be lying in a shallow grave somewhere soon. He'd been asked to decapitate the Scottish government and any opposition to the new Westminster order, but now the team he was given to do the task were the ones without heads. Or complete heads, anyway.

Bez chuckled as he thought of how he had buried Andy and Deek as if they were snogging. This job had its good points. Well, if he was going to die soon, it would be a bummer, but in his line of work, it was always a strong possibility.

"Nah," said Bez to himself, "they still need me around."

He smiled and waved at the traffic camera, which almost certainly recorded most of the happenings here today. It didn't matter – only friends would ever see those images. If he could call them friends. *Let's go with acquaintances*, he decided. It was good to give those acquaintances a little demonstration of his abilities, just in case they had any ideas.

Getting in the car, he fired up the engine and headed for Carlisle. After rummaging through the compartment on the driver's door, he found his wife's Queen CD and stuck it in the machine. 'Love of My life' began to blare, but hee skipped the disk on to 'I'm in Love with My Car' and sang along at the top of his voice.

Downing Street, Monday 21st April 2025

"Go get 'em, tiger." Cassie Jenkins ruffled her husband's hair. He smiled and turned to step out into the waiting Jaguar. "Boris," she said, halting him in his tracks. "You haven't picked up your notes. These are the instructions from Lady Elizabeth. You need to clear the ten-year parliamentary term today, and she has included the subjects and results for the next six referenda. She's added a new one that replaces the London mayoral post with a government appointee. Wow! You are going to win that one 97% to 3%." She rolled her eyes and laughed. He took the papers from her. "Now be a good boy and get that done, okay?"

Boris Jenkins, nominal leader of the nation, nodded. "Yes, ma'am."

Printed in Dunstable, United Kingdom

63525916R00194